POLTIC

Michael Ikevos

ISBN 978-0-9936182-0-8

Published by Mihail Kosev

Contact info:
michaelikevos@gmail.com

First edition

Table of Contents

"The End Justifies the Means?"
Niccolo Machiavelli

M. J.

Poltic placed down the several pages on his desk and smiled again. He tried to hold back his laughter a few times while reading it. The absurdities he came across were so many that if he was interested in finding out their exact number he had to read it once again. Interestingly enough it was his very name that was signed at the top of the first page. It was hard to believe that he had written this but he instantly put his mind at rest: we all made mistakes when young. He smiled again. The light in the room was disappearing away and Poltic stood up to turn on the lamp. Then he went back on his chair and picked up the first pages of the essay he just read. He had written this figment of economics when he was a student at university. The acclaimed professor, Poltic could not think of his name, decided to break up the boredom of the lecture by persuading the class to write an essay on big economic structures. The tutor outlined his instructions beforehand to the stunned young audience in the packed university hall. He wrote down a synopsis plan comprising five points: 1. Definition, 2. Interrelations with authorities, 3. Level of productivity, 4. Relationships between companies and 5. Hierarchy.

The task to write an essay was given to the students on the first day in the second year and this caused a flurry amongst them. In their first year, they had to endure and listen to the endless lectures without really taking active part. If the teacher asked a question no one would dare answer it in case it was wrong. Moreover, almost every time the professor was the only one that could answer his questions. Very rarely one of the students would receive a moment of enlightenment and would attempt to present his answer, naturally, followed by everyone's laughter.

After Poltic had heard the topic of the essay, he remembered, the word "big" got to him most. The idea of a big company he had associated with a big building. He instantly pictured in his mind a few multi-level buildings located in the centre of town. About one of them he knew that it was owned by a world famous company. He had limited information on the others, to him – they were just office buildings. Like the rest of his colleagues, Poltic felt timorous and nervous, however, this did not hinder his ability to think. He was writing confidently and fast following the slightly vague instructions on the blackboard as if he knew what he was doing. The point of view he had presented in his written work was from the position of a person who had founded one of the world's largest companies. This was a person who had been through all the steps in his career and had reached inevitably to the top, a person with broad knowledge in areas like economics, politics, sociology, psychology and many others.

Today, nearly two decades later, after reading this essay again, Poltic realized that he had known nothing then and he could not have known anything anyway. At the time, he was just one of the many young and naïve students, however, smart enough to get a "B". To be fair there were some good points in his work but as a whole it was a fiction, rather than a scientific writing.

After he graduated from university all his student stuff that he had he packed in several boxes and gave for storage to a cousin of his. It was a bother to carry about all these unneeded textbooks, notebooks, school project, essays and other typical student creations as life led him far away. The idea to throw them away had not crossed his mind. Poltic came across the essay by accident just when he was moving in his enormous new house. His birthplace, a house in the suburb he had spent most of his life, it still stood there but it was owned by someone else.

His hometown had sprawled to such extend that Poltic felt as if he was visiting for the first time. On his arrival he had spent a few days going to different estate agencies until he decided on this particular mansion. Poltic had never lived in a large space before, on the contrary, his previous place was a small and neat two-storey house, built four decades ago. During his travels abroad he would usually rent a small flat with an area rarely larger than 50 sq. m. This time he had the opportunity to have something much more spacious and decided to take this option. The house was not his first choice.

He did see and fell in love with a gorgeous three-storey villa with a spacious garden, a swimming pool and many bedrooms that he had lost count of. It was very impressive on the outside, too, situated on a little hill. The yellow rendering absorbed the sunlight in a bizarre way and that gave a unique feel to the house. The interior and the furnishing were luxurious but this did not take Poltic aback as the sum designated for this purchase supposed only the best. His main requirement was to have a big garden as from childhood he had been used to living in a house with a yard where the kennel of his beloved dog would have been. He intended to get a dog again, even more than one, but firstly he wished to get comfortable in the house. After all he never bought it.

Poltic purchased another house, not so attractive but which had some other advantages. The reason for his change of heart was quite trivial. The first house was located in a very isolated spot. The location was still part of the city but at the same time it was out of the way, and quite so. If he had to get to the nearest supermarket, a pharmacy or the cinema, let along to the centre of town, it would take him more than an hour. In the winter, the narrow lanes leading to the motorway would require careful driving. The house Poltic bought was situated in a newly developed villa district where the architecture of the buildings was slightly old-fashioned. Observing the house from the front, it did not look very big but if seen from the air, one could notice the long extension at the back. He needed just one bedroom, however, the other six would prove quite useful if he had guests staying. The furniture was ultra modern and gave the interior a kind of sterile feel. The granite surfaces in the kitchen were especially remarkable and Poltic would stroke them unwittingly at every opportunity. The new owner liked the fact that there were only a few items of furniture in the house. He had always wondered why people would clutter their homes, even small flats, with knick-knacks and gadgets.

The most prominent feature of the house was its stone fence, which was 2.20 m high. In that way the property was only visible through the front gate made from steel posts ending with spears. Poltic did not aim to have a fortress instead of a house, however, the walls felt quite intimidating to the casual passers-by. He decided that the formidable façade of the house could only be of use considering the venture he was about to start. The main reason he chose to purchase this house was that it was situated just 5 min. drive away from one of the main roads to town. The motorway was very well designed and had a capacity for a substantial flow of vehicles, hence the rare traffic jams. As soon as Poltic transferred the money for his purchase he thought again about the incredibly gorgeous house on the small hill. Well, location proved more important than beauty qualities. This one did not have a swimming pool, either but the compromise had been already made.

On the second day in his new home, Poltic employed a housekeeper, as he believed the property needed to be maintained and cleaned regularly. The woman kept herself busy throughout the day and was always at his service. He would often ask her to make him a cup of coffee or just fetch something he needed.

Poltic stood up to put the essay away in the box he found it. There were no more than ten minutes left until dusk that he wished to spend outside. It took him a little while to walk the two hundred meters to the impressive iron gate. He imagined the spacious garden in the spring when all the trees would be in blossom and the thick foliage would prevent from curious eyes peeking into the property. When he came to the gate he turned around and looked at the façade of the house, which could be still seen quite clear despite the distance. He had a sudden brainwave to replace the metal spears and put a solid gate instead but then he thought that the property would lose its formidable ambience. One of the two security guards first noticed Poltic and nudged his mate.

"Mr. Poltic, Good evening, Sir. How are you today?"

"I am fine, thank you." Poltic replied politely without looking at the guard but his eyes wandering through the gate somewhere in the distance. "Gentlemen, I have to ask you to count every person who walks down this street from tomorrow onwards."

"Yes, Mr. Poltic, of course. We shall keep a close eye on everyone, Sir."

"I have also decided to hire two more security guards from next week. In that way, your shifts will become shorter but this will not affect your payment. You can inform your colleagues about this tonight when they come to take over."

"Thank you, Mr. Poltic. We will let them know. We are quite alright like this but I suppose it will be better if there are a few more guys, Sir."

"Just "Mr. Poltic" is fine."

It was already dark. On his way back to the house Poltic noted that the electric lighting was far too powerful that blinded him. Tomorrow he was going to call the technicians to deflect the lights so they did not dazzle any visitors who drove in right near the house.

The circumference of the property was quite extensive and the CCTV-s would have not deterred anyone. Poltic had not even bothered to activate them. The nature of his future work required security at a very high level.

The guards Poltic had hired were part of a big security company. He did not need to employ some brainless thugs but people who regarded the security business as a job that required intelligence and logic. Well, this did not prevent the three pairs of men from being as tough and strong as anything. The security company employed only people who had successfully passed a two-year training course, where the most important skill that needed to be mastered was not the ability to break your opponent's nose but the art to anticipate any physical predicament. The company reputation was very high and it was not cheap to take advantage of their services.

Poltic had an unusual requirement for a man in need of more than two guards. He did not want under any circumstances for them to carry firearms on shift. The security had to stop the possible intruders without killing them. Poltic was very pleased to see that the two guards he had a chat with this evening were only equipped with bats slightly longer than the ones, used in the police force and tear sprays, attached to the belt. Later in the evening, he picked up the phone and arranged for two more security guards to join the team on Monday as he had promised.

In his new home, Poltic appreciated its greatest advantage – the peace and tranquility, which sometimes he felt were too much. One had to strain their ears to hear something. Poltic enjoyed being surrounded by people and had the need to interact with friends as he had been used to so far. His previous workplace gave him the opportunity to communicate with minimum of twenty to thirty people he knew and at least ten others he had never met, clients. There were a few times when he reminisced about his recent employment and this made him ask himself: "What am I getting involved in now?" Then he would make a conscious effort not to think about his past but tried to concentrate only on the completion of the existing task.

In this huge house on the outskirts of town, Poltic was feeling lonely and alone, and he was alone. Soon, for all that, he would get the better of his loneliness – Charlie was coming in a few days. Until then, the quietness in and around the property would keep agitating him constantly. It was a good job that he had a lot of work to do, to let the tranquility around him get to him.

Home Again

After several years of being away, Poltic returned to his country, to his native town. There was nothing waiting for him, he did not have anything there. Maybe, that was why during his previous visit he did not make the effort to go back to his birthplace but just spent his two-week vacation in the capital. To feel a stranger in one's native country was an interesting experience but he quickly got adjusted to this new-old environment.

Poltic unpacked his luggage as soon as he moved into the fortress-house. It took him only twenty minutes to do this while taking great care of unfolding his formal suits. Then he went out and bought quite a few newspapers to check out the ads. What he was after was far from popular; nevertheless, there were surprisingly many relevant advertisements in the papers. Private detective agency he was looking for. It sounded somehow mysterious and the first mental picture that crossed Poltic's mind was Sherlock Holmes. He selected the ad that was best exposed in belief it probably represented the best in the business. He immediately discarded those comprising a sentence or two, although he jotted a couple of phone numbers down just in case.

As he had expected, some secretary answered his call. She had a pleasant voice and promptly put Poltic through to an assistant-detective. The chief detective was not available. Poltic was not quite sure that she was saying the truth. He felt that the senior detective should be at work at this time of the day. The throaty voice at the other end convinced him that he was speaking to an experienced middle-aged professional, rather than someone young and new to the job. They arranged to see each other at lunchtime the following day in a popular café in town.

A small forty something years old man dressed in grey suit who looked as if he had not had enough sleep, was striding confidently towards a table in the café. Poltic was watching him from another café on the opposite side of the street. The tiny detective was scanning the interior of the establishment in a detective kind of way. He sent the waitress away as he was still waiting for someone. Poltic crossed the street and advanced towards the half-occupied table. The men exchanged their greetings and went straight to the point of this meeting. Poltic set out in brief everything he needed to say, not forgetting to mention at the end the payment figure. It was obvious that the little man liked what he heard so he agreed to all the conditions of the job. On leaving, Poltic gave the detective ten percent from his payment and the post box number of an address. Efficiency was the key characteristic of this meeting.

On the arranged date, Poltic sent one of the security guys to the address giving him a key for the post box. An hour later the guard rang the doorbell with a large envelope in his hands. Poltic put the letter on one side in his study and decided that he would have his dinner first and then determine its mysterious contents. He finished eating very quickly and he hastened into his study. Poltic felt a little bit disappointed after he had opened the yellow envelope because he expected to find a larger quantity of pages inside. He counted them and divided into seven piles. They contained information related to the education, career, family life, hobbies, friends and habits of seven of the most prominent professionals in the country. A glance at the top page of each pile proved him that the little detective had done a good job. There was no reason for Poltic to be displeased with the quality of data because he was the one that had explicitly restricted the means of gathering the intelligence. All contact with the subjects during the surveillance was absolutely forbidden, that included tapping and close up following.

At first, Poltic thought he had to know almost everything about these people but that would have involved hiring more than one detective. Next, he would be dependent on them. Poltic was adamant about confidentiality being observed at all cost. No one but the small detective could know the persons' names. If his agents were ordered to follow several subjects, only their boss would be authorized to gather pieces of information with evident names. A leak was very possible, indeed, and probably everyone in the agency knew about who had been researched, however, Poltic hoped that the substantial amount of cash posted through the letter box by his security guard would stop the little guy's mouth and those of his agents.

While abroad, Poltic would follow closely the media in his country. He remembered that he had seen some of the people from his list on TV or in the papers. "Where could I find the best managers and how could I make them work for me?" He asked himself this question many times after he had accepted "the job". He already knew the answer.

Different professional guilds would nominate and reward their best members every year. The glittery events would be covered in the media and Poltic had caught on television the award ceremony for the best hotel manager, the best stock exchange agent and the most prosperous law office. After all, the winners were shown on TV for their professional achievements.

Many of the best professionals were employed by a few companies: they could be members of the board of directors or they were just valued management consultants, sought after for their expert opinion. The gifted specialists had already climbed to the top of the big companies. Poltic could attempt to snatch them easily but he was more inclined to look for the so-called "free electrons", professionals who were undoubtedly more flexible in their work. He would have been more than pleased to entice some large company senior managers for his project but not someone who had to climb up the ladder for twenty years. He was after independent professionals who had individualistic and unconstrained approach to work. Poltic had filtered and selected seven suitable people. Two of them were influential and much publicized in society. The other five were leading experts in their own right, too.

Poltic read twice each of the files without sticking to any order. Four of the group stood out the most. He felt they had the required skills despite the fact that he hardly knew anything about them. His choice had to be based on secondary evidence. One could favor Chinese food; the other had frequented Indian restaurants in the last year but who was more seemly for the job? Poltic was prepared to alter his decision if he had to, realizing the shortcomings of indirect information, especially if he did not agree with something in their looks or disliked their attitude when they met in person. He was prepared to encounter some impudence and arrogant behavior; nevertheless, only one could be in charge. This train of thoughts urged him to eliminate at once one of the candidates who in spite of being known as an outstanding professional did not take orders too well.

Jane's record was one of the first Poltic picked and after reading the first paragraph it became clear to him that she would receive an offer for work. He was not sentimental by any means but he was impressed by Jane's ability to manage her job and be a devoted mother of two children. The small detective had recorded every action of hers to the minute in the last two weeks. She would do the school run and was never late for work or missed to pick up her kids after classes. Jane owned a consultancy firm with an excellent record of successful deals. Her punctuality and professionalism were impressive and were probably the reasons behind her success. Jane's agency had an elite clientele in the face of top companies. Her husband owned a small restaurant located in their neighborhood. Poltic concluded that she earned a lot more than her partner. Jane's efficiency and capacity for work would suppress any man so it was quite likely that her husband felt a bit intimidated by her. Poltic was determined his future employees were in some sort of normal relationship and although in Jane's case the family roles were reversed, she seemed a suitable candidate. He did not take any notice of the update on her hobbies and interests or how she spent her weekends. His attention was drawn to Jane's transcript from university. The rest of the candidates had academic records, too, attached to their files. Jane had graduated with top marks but Poltic was fascinated with the evidence of her motherhood during her final two years at university. This was the most valuable quality of Jane. He did not need persons who in the name of their career would trample over people or neglect their families and friends. Ironically sad, this was precisely what Poltic would have become very soon.

One of the paramount criteria to make his selection of four was the potential candidates' financial status. Poltic was about to offer them a lot of money and he had to know how much is a lot for each of them. Jane had invested almost everything she had in her business and it was unlikely that she had any substantial amount of savings in the bank. On this account, however, she owned a spacious apartment, two cars and her children attended a private school. According to her record file, Jane loved shopping in expensive boutiques. And about her husband's earnings – the detective's conspicuous description of "a tiny restaurant" spoke for itself. Namely, the high standard of living was the main cause for the lack of dispensable cash in Jane's family. They followed the logic of "the more you have, the more you spend". And Poltic counted on exactly that.

Bob was the name of the second candidate who Poltic was going to offer an employment to. He was one of the highest paid stock exchange agents and was well known in financial circles. Poltic needed his own shark playing in the stock market. The predator, however, was depicted as a diffident, slightly chubby 45-years old man with spectacles. His insecurity came out when he was seen blushing over the pretty shop assistant in the food store he had visited, according to the detective's notes. Bob was a senior executive manager in a brokerage firm. His current project involved representing and dealing on behalf of a company in the mining industry on the stock market. There was not much else on the work side, mentioned in his record. Poltic again took note of Bob's university transcript. The evidence showed that the best financial broker in the country was extremely academic and an excellent scholar.

Bob was very sensible about his money. He had invested any superfluous capital in shares that brought him small but regular income. The private eye had also discovered that Bob owned a two-storey house in the suburbs of town, which was currently undergoing a major refurbishment. He lived with his wife in small apartment in the centre, which had a high value for its attractive location. Bob's partner was a housewife or in other words, she would simply spend what he had earned. Their only daughter was doing her biology degree in a prestigious college abroad and this did not come cheap. Poltic quite liked the sound of Bob and imagined him as being a quiet and chunky man.

Geri worked in a research agency. She had a degree in Sociology. The detective had pointed out that precisely Geri was responsible for conducting some of the major research campaigns held in the country and had brought success and many awards to her agency. Her professional biography could also include her attempts to be a journalist. Once a month, she provided a national newspaper with reports and articles on different researches of public opinion. At the bottom of the third page of her file, the detective had written down a curious piece of information. For seven months, Geri had been an assistant manager in the HR department of a large company. Poltic needed someone who had the key skill of working with people, albeit the HR field did not involve direct management of people. Geri's personal life, however, made him slightly alarmed. She was a divorcee and lived with her son and her mother. Being single could cause a problem in the future. If Geri found the so-called love this could have a negative effect on Poltic's plans. He felt he could risk it and decided on his third choice. That would be Geri.

Her property ownership manifested itself in a flat situated on the top floor of an eight-storey residential building. She inherited the apartment from her father after his death two years ago. She drove a small, unpractical and typical woman's car. Apparently, it was orange, with two doors and that could be parked anywhere. Poltic wondered about where all the high payments from the research agency went. It was well known fact that some corporations would commission extensive research projects and not spare resources for this. Geri either had a lot of savings or the detective had missed to discover a grand luxurious house of hers somewhere. The report gave away that she also shopped for expensive clothes like Jane did, and obviously wanted to keep pace with latest fashion trends. Once in the file record it was described that Geri had parked her car in front of the jewelers and had not left the shop for forty minutes. Poltic could not be certain about this but he thought she could be spending half of her salary on jewellery.

The volume of pages in the last pile was the largest so it stood the highest on the desk. The main character was called Harry. When looking through the seven record files at the beginning, Poltic noticed that only one candidate had legal education. Harry seemed to have an impressive career. While he was still at university, he received the opportunity to do his internship in one of the most reputable law firms, where he had stayed on as an employee for four years after graduating from university. According to the record, Harry had worked on nearly one thousand cases during his time in the attorney's office. Currently, he was a well known legal adviser to high-profile clients and judging by his time spent on the phone, as stated in the detective's notes, Harry's expert counsel was very much in demand.

Poltic knew that it was mandatory to have a first-class legal support in his forthcoming venture. He would not settle for less but the best and Harry was one of them. The lawyer also had a network of connections to other elite attorneys if needed. He often went hunting during the weekends with his good friends – all top-notch lawyers. Hunting was his hobby. The private eye had mentioned in his notes that Harry had visited a famous gun shop and his interest in expensive rifles that had engraved butt-stock. His professional CV proved to be remarkable but Poltic had to be fully informed about Harry's personal life as well. He was a divorcée after he had been in a relationship for three years. He did not have any children. Poltic preferred to work with well-balanced people who lived in a stable family environment. Harry was becoming 40 the same year and he had nothing to show in terms of his private life. Poltic thought that Harry behaved more like a teenager, based on what was noted in the record. On three separate occasions, the lawyer had taken three beautiful ladies to dinner in the space of just two weeks. "He may well be able to afford it but if he starts working for me he will not be able to go out with every woman he meets." Poltic thought, although, he was not quite sure if he was in a position to make such judgments.

With regards to money, Harry had a lot of it. Poltic decided that the barrister was the richest of the four. However, he did not own any property. Harry lived in a rented enormous maisonette. He drove a brand new big SUV and wore more expensive clothes than those of Jane and Geri. The prices in the boutiques that Harry shopped substantiated Poltic's conclusion. Based on that he realized that he would have to raise the payment offer to all of them in order to match or exceed Harry's income, which was the highest.

Poltic took a glance at the sheets of paper scattered in front of him and placed Harry's file with the rest that had been selected. He thought that the lawyer was the most volatile element in this project but truly hoped that this was not the case.

The information on the candidates was thorough and professionally compiled and Poltic was certain that he would use his little friend's services again in the future. Finally, he had to prepare the invitations and the offers to Jane, Bob, Geri and Harry. At first, Poltic intended to visit personally each one of them but then he changed his mind. He could find them too busy working and not be able to spare the time to discuss any preliminaries. He then considered making an appointment beforehand so they were prepared for an important conversation. Poltic discarded both ideas, as he did not wish to meet them on their territory. He made a decision to invite his candidates to the fortress-house. Having them as his guests, he would automatically win a point in the "hospitality chart". He also supposed that Jane, Bob, Geri and Harry would undoubtedly feel very impressed with the greatness of the property.

Poltic could distinguish four successful professionals, who had a high social status, whereas he was neither famous or had reached their level, except financially. Money was his primary weapon and he would make the most of it. He was adamant to impress them with his intelligence and brainpower, however, because if they saw him as a rich fool, who was throwing his money away, he would be manipulated and exploited every time. He was not sure how he would do that. They were all at a similar age but it should be clear from the start about who was in charge.

Poltic drew his attention back to the invites. The most appropriate day of the week for the event, he thought, was Saturday and the time – had to be eight o'clock in the evening. He believed this would be the most acceptable arrangement for them. The invitation itself should be brief, comprising no more than five sentences. He wanted his guests to feel intrigued by it all. Some questions would emerge, whose answers could not be found in the invitations. Poltic believed that key phrases like: "the biggest investor that had ever set foot in the country" and "annual salary of six hundred thousand, bonuses – not included" - would make up the essence of text. He sent the letters via courier on Tuesday. The messenger had to hand them personally even if he had to wait for the opportunity all day. The only details specified in the invites were the exact address, time and date. Any contact telephone numbers or the name of the sender were missing.

There were four days until the day of the meeting. It was good that Charlie was arriving on Thursday; otherwise the time in anticipation of the weekend would just drag on. Poltic could not wait to meet him at the airport. He was fed up of sitting around, reading people's records and different political, psychological and sociological books or literature on leaderships. He was bored to watch television and examine newspapers, and all this completely alone. Of course, the housekeeper was always there doing her job perfectly well but Poltic hardly ever saw her, so he was really alone. At times, while contemplating on each candidate's information details, he would begin talking to himself imagining his guests are present in the room and they all conversed as if for real. Feeling he was going slightly mad, Poltic believed more and more that what he had embarked on made sense, otherwise why he had accepted the job in the first place. He knew some of the four might not come; he was realistic about it. Although, he did hope the majority of them would come. He insisted on Harry's presence, as for the rest – it would be easier to replace them.

Charlie

Charlie was landing in the late afternoon and someone needed to meet him. On the way to the airport, Poltic did not think about anything but carefully followed the vehicles in front of him. The traffic was unexpectedly busy. He arrived at the South Terminal of the city airport an hour early. He left his car and headed towards the glazed waiting lounge where ordered himself a cup of coffee. Poltic was sitting alone at the table and realized that he had not been surrounded by so many people, maybe hundreds, for a very long time. Most of them were looking up at the screens; some would stumble over in rush. He could see the excitement and expectation on their faces – they were all waiting for a good friend, a loved one or someone they knew.

The airplanes approaching to land could be seen through the glass cupola. Poltic would raise his eyes after each sip of coffee and admire them. He enjoyed flying as long as it was a short haul flight because he felt plane sick on long distances. The big screen showed that the plane was expected on time, which meant it would land in 25 minutes. He had not seen Charlie for eight months but they spoke on the phone at least once a week. The main reasons for not seeing each other for so long were Charlie's busy school work-load at university just before his graduation and his willingness to have a job at the same time so he could earn his own money, although Poltic had solved the matter and had always provided.

There were 5 minutes left before the plane landed. Poltic found himself thinking about Charlie's place in the project. He was aware of the student's abilities but this somehow did not help. Passengers from an earlier flight started to appear through the gate, followed by travelers from Charlie's plane. When Poltic sighted him, he could not recognize him at first. After eight months he seemed changed and his new hairstyle did not help for that matter. Charlie saw him, too, and called out raising his arm so he could be easily noticed:

"M. J.!"

"Hello, Charlie." Poltic's words were followed by a handshake and a hearty embrace. Both of them had a wide grin on their faces. "Is this all your luggage?" Poltic asked and glanced at the big suitcase, pulled by Charlie and the rucksack on his back.

"Yes, M. J. If you knew how pleased I am to be here! You won't believe it, M. J. At university, they were on our case all the time. There was one who didn't know what he wants... My last exam-project, they kept me in for two hours, can you imagine?

"Sure, Charlie, I can imagine and by the way you described this instance in full detail two months ago when we spoke on the phone."

"Mad as a hatter, M. J.... but why me? Always happens to me. If I only meet that professor somewhere now!"

"It really shows you've just come out of university. You are here now and the college is back there, so stop thinking about it. I have an important job for you and I hope that you won't disappoint me. Young people at your age should start having considerable responsibilities."

"You can count on me, M. J. I'm now free. The endless studying has finished and I'm after a job. I'm happy I gonna work for you. What is it exactly? Am I going to have a fat salary and a secretary?"

"It all depends on you." Poltic answered in a serious manner counter to Charlie's light-hearted question. Chatting about the advantages and drawbacks of the contemporary higher education, they got to the big black limousine, whose trunk opened with a slight beep of the alarm.

"Put your stuff inside and get in the car."

"Wow! M. J., you never told me that you bought such a beauty. It's super cool! Last time you drove that ugly hatch-back, even if new it was."

"The car was functional, Charlie, not ugly. Functional!" repeated Poltic, spelling the word out.

"Eh, if you say so."

Poltic took off his jacket and put it on the back seat, waiting for the former student to finally place his luggage in the designated for that purpose compartment of the vehicle.

"I had a car, too. Well, it wasn't actually mine; I was driving it when I was doing the home deliveries. It was an old Ford that kept breaking down every two weeks. Oh, may I drive, please."

"Not now, Charlie. Get in the car."

"Where are we going? You can tell me, M. J., I'm here now, aren't I?

"Have a little patience. I want this to be a surprise."

Charlie did not intend to let Poltic say a word throughout the journey. On that note, Poltic openly did not want to speak but would allow him, as usual, to have his say and get whatever off his chest. On their way back, there were hardly any cars on the motorway and twenty minutes later, the nose of the car was facing the spears of the iron gate of the house. The security guard pressed to open the gate as soon as he noticed the limousine coming near.

"Is this yours? And you've got security. I'm really surprised, M. J., that you can afford to rent such an expensive house and guys to protect it. Or maybe, the security comes with the property? You never mentioned anything to me, neither about the house, nor the car! Any more surprises?"

"Charlie, we won't discuss any of this right now, am I clear? I'm pleased, though, that you like it."

"Sure, M. J., whatever you say."

"Come, I'll show you to your room. I wasn't quite sure which one to get ready for you and at the end I picked this one, the most south facing. If you are not happy with it, there are five more to choose from. You can change it any time." they reached the selected room, Poltic opened the door and said:

"I expect you in the dining room within half an hour for a bite to eat. You must be hungry and I didn't have much to eat at lunchtime, either."

"OK, M. J. I'll just quickly sort my clothes out and be with you shortly."

Alone in the room, Charlie was still wondering about how M. J. had come into money but then he thought that this was not that important. After all, he would probably never know if he considered that the subject was a taboo for M. J. The young man put his suitcase on the bed and began to empty its contents, mainly clothes. He managed to cover the entire double bed with his belongings and then he looked around at the rest of the room. He approved the French windows but decided that the black wardrobe was definitely not in the right place. Physically strong, Charlie moved it effortlessly twenty centimeters to the left and then it all seemed perfect. He could probably put up a poster on the big wall above his bed, well, maybe another time. Poltic was waiting for him. Charlie quickly changed his clothes and headed towards the dining room – the room with the big dining table and numerous chairs. It was a part of a large open-plan space that accommodated the modern kitchen with predominating granite everywhere, like the kitchen worktops. That was Poltic's favorite material.

"Here I am again, M. J."

"Well, Charlie, how do you like your new room?" replied Poltic while looking for a ladle.

"Yep, it's cool! Is there a way one can dislike anything in this house? What are you cooking?"

"I know you love beef, so I cooked it from a popular and very quick recipe. You can sit down now." When both of them were sitting at the table with plates full of steaming beef in front of them, Charlie asked:

"M. J., when do I start working for you? I can't wait! You see, if I get a job elsewhere the boss might be a real asshole! So whenever you say, I'm ready."

"We are going to eat now and then we'll talk about anything. Be a little more patient!"

They finished eating and cleared the table without talking. Then Poltic nodded towards the living room and Charlie followed him. They settled down on a bright orange unusual sofa. Poltic switched on the television but turned down the sound.

"Charlie, you are welcome to work for me only if you want to. If you wish to get involved in something else, I'm not going to stop you. I would support you if you decide that you'd like to try a different field or line of work, from what I can offer you, anyway. It's Thursday today. You are free to do whatever you like until Monday. I'm going to give you a car and some money so you can have a good look around town and buy anything you need. Have some fun! There's a new club opening on Saturday and I've got hold of a free pass for you. Monday – this is when the real work begins."

"Aren't you going to give me a clue about what would be expected from me, M. J.?" asked Charlie but he did not receive a reply. Poltic's eyes spoke for themselves. It would be all clear on

Monday. Charlie changed the subject back to the car he was going to get in the hope he would at least find out what model it was.

"M. J., is it OK if I have a look at the car now, if it's around? It's not some old banger, I hope?"

"This house comes with a garage that can accommodate seven vehicles! Follow me and I will show you your car, Charlie." Within a few seconds they got the designated place that could be reached from the inside of the house, too. However, Poltic chose to lead Charlie to the garage from the outside, mainly to raise the adrenalin of his impatient and excited guest even more. The automatic door went up and the young man spotted a brand new black metallic Mercedes with two doors. It was last model.

"Oh, no! Don't tell me, M. J.! Not this beauty! I can't believe it!"

"You don't see any others?" said Poltic and threw the keys to him. Charlie sat behind the wheel and turned on the engine but Poltic clearly showed him that he was not going to move out of way of the car. It was not going anywhere from the comfortable garage.

"Switch off the engine, Charlie. It's late and we need a good night sleep. You'll have all day tomorrow to indulge driving it."

"M. J., thank you so much. What a car! For me? Incredible! I don't deserve it, you know that?"

"Yes, I know." replied Poltic sincerely and they both burst into laughter. They went back in the house but this time, through the door that led to the living area directly from the inside. Poltic produced a credit card from his right pocket and gave it to Charlie.

"Here, Charlie. The card has a credit limit of 5000. You can spend it however you like but my advice to you is to buy some nice suits and they are not cheap. You'll need them in the future. Now, go to sleep and I'll see you tomorrow. I hope you'll be up by 9 o'clock. Good night."

"Good night, M.J."

Poltic remained in the company of the big orange sofa and two armchairs. He was not big on furniture. He lived alone until recently and although it was two of them now, he just did not need any clutter. The low glass coffee table in front of him suited perfectly the room, according to Poltic's ideas for a good interior design. However, there was something else on his mind. Charlie had kept his typical puerile attitude. Deep down, Poltic hoped to find him grown up and mature after his graduation but Charlie's boyishness prevailed. Poltic had an idea how to overcome this problem, namely, to turn this free child into a skilled and valued employee of the company. He would give him a task that only a professional and experienced person could manage to accomplish, a task that was obviously well out of Charlie's league. At the same time, he had to watch him because any future blunders of his would most probably cost him a lot. Charlie's loyalty compensated for his inexperience. Poltic was quite pleased that however long they had not seen each other, Charlie would not get angry with his bossy way of talking, nor he would contradict him.

It was almost midnight and it was time for bed. Poltic went to his room and lay down on the big firm bed, which was perfect for his bad back he had been having recently. He did not feel too tired as the whole day was devoted only to Charlie's arrival. Poltic recalled the beginning of their friendship, and Charlie's father, of course.

At first, his memories took him to the street he used to live a long time ago. It was a very long street with over hundred house numbers, where he spent his first happy and carefree years. Number 76 was Poltic's little house. He ignored the images with his family in his mind and continued reminiscing. School had finished and he became a student. Four years later, at the age of 23, he graduated from university. There, he had befriended an older guy, who was an assistant professor. Both of them had similar interests and thanks to Poltic's entrepreneurial qualities, they set up a successful business. Poltic's memories focused on what happened two years later. His best friend and business partner died in a car crash. Poltic carried on with his work and he was doing very well but he was alone. He could not call his few employees friends. Poltic was earning good money and he made a decision to support the wife and kid of his perished friend in the same way others would give to charities. In the following years, he visited Charlie regularly acting like a father, although it had felt more as if he was an older brother to the young boy. He believed that good education was the most important thing that he could give to the kid. Therefore, he had opened a saving account in the name of Charlie, the resources of which could cover completely all university fees. Charlie's mother never had to worry about it. Eventually Poltic went abroad and managed to go and see Charlie only a few times a year. Nevertheless, he was always welcomed like a real dad. Presents were always a must and Charlie just adored his "new" father as if he was a God. He would always do what he had been told. The last had never changed, really.

Charlie went to study overseas and left his mother alone. No one had expected her death soon after, as she appeared to be in good health. It was Poltic again, who first stood by Charlie and helped him through this difficult time. The tragedy with his mother brought the two men closer together. Poltic closely watched over Charlie's academic progress and never missed to reproach him for any second to best results at school. At the same time, Charlie felt free to confide in "the closest person in the whole world" and frankly quite often wearied him. These recollections had taken Poltic back to a time, long before he accepted his new "job" and when things still happened unexpectedly. He looked at the clock. It was 30 minutes past midnight. He turned to the right and fell asleep. On the next day he would be thinking again about what to do with his newly acquired successor.

A few minutes before the time for breakfast, set by Poltic, Charlie appeared slowly in the kitchen and still half-asleep.

"Good Morning, M. J. You are making something delicious as usual, aren't you? I can smell bacon and eggs! Is that right?" said Charlie breathed in through his nostrils.

"Good Morning, Charlie. You are just on time, breakfast is ready." Breakfast comprised eggs and sausages. Poltic also placed a glass of cold fresh milk in front of Charlie. They ate everything without a word; exactly the way the cook liked it.

"Did you sleep alright?" Poltic asked, moving his plate a little bit away from him.

"Super, M. J., but the bed is a bit on the hard side. Maybe, 'cause I am not used to it. Back in my old place, I slept on a soft mattress and although the bed was slightly short for me, I was so used to it that I was familiar with every curve."

"Have you made any plans for the day, Charlie?"

"Well, if you remember, I mentioned to you on the phone that a colleague of mine has got back in town a week before me. He is cool and a kind of friend of mine, so I'm thinking to give him a ring and meet up this afternoon. But first, I'm gonna go for a ride around town in that black beast in the garage, also get some clothes and what not…"

"Why don't you take your friend to the club on Saturday night? You won't be on your own then! Charlie, I'm sure you don't have many friends here but you'll get used to the changes in town and you'll meet, as you call them, some "cool" people!"

"I did have a lot of friends here, you know. But they've all gone away. Most of my classmates weren't from around here, anyway."

"It will all fall in the right place, Charlie!"

"You're right, M. J. It will all fall in the right place. I'm not some jobless guy, wondering the streets now, aren't I? I feel a bit strange but I'll be OK. Can I burn the breeze with my new car?" asked Charlie and grinned.

"You are not going to burn anything because soon you'll be left with no car! So drive carefully!"

"I'm just kidding, M. J., don't worry. I can drive. See ya!" Charlie ran out of the house and headed to the garage. He was definitely not ready to have what was waiting for him in there.

Poltic cleared the table and went to his study. He looked again over the record files of his potential visitors. For a second he remembered about something he should have told Charlie at breakfast but then thought it could wait.

On the next day he expected his guests – possible future employees to arrive at eight o'clock in the evening. This was a standard dinnertime across the world. He decided to order a variety of dishes from the best restaurants in town, representing different cuisines. In that way, all tastes would be satisfied. He doubted that everyone would appreciate sushi or octopus but better there was some available than not. Who could know, sushi might be the favorite dish of one of the four guests. Drinks were very important as well. Poltic believed, however, that serving alcohol would not be a wise move, taking into consideration the type of conversation that was ahead. Unwillingly, he did order a bottle of expensive red wine, thinking that it would be shared between five people; hence it would be hard for anyone to get a dizzy head. The women would possibly prefer non-alcoholic beverage so he made sure there was a selection of fruit juices and some mineral water. Poltic had to have a butler for the occasion, too, like he had seen it in movies. The presence of the housekeeper during the day was fine but for this special event he needed someone well dressed and presentable to attend to his guests' needs. The butler had to arrive at six o'clock to receive all the necessary instructions, which included a permanent smile on his face, polite greetings, aiding each visitor with their coats and handbags, etc. Poltic did not worry about the waiting staff that could be provided by any excellent restaurant in town. Four waiters would be enough – one for each guest if they all turned up, of course.

Poltic was getting slightly carried away in making speculations about people he might never actually meet. He believed that it was important to make a point of the security of the house. At the beginning of the week the guards received reinforcement in the face of two tough fellows and there were another two expected to stand in that Saturday. Poltic thought at first to let his visitors drive in right near the property but then he changed his mind. He would instruct his security guards to keep the iron gate shut and direct his guests to park their cars outside and then make their way on foot to the house. Poltic's intention was the whole atmosphere and every detail to work in his favor. And if not, at least he enjoyed the planning and preparation.

Everything seemed to be thought of and ready, while the day had slipped by. This reminded him that it was not long and Charlie would return. He probably never thought about eating all day in his excitement of driving the car and enjoying himself in town. Even as a small kid and later in high school, Charlie would get up to all sorts with his mates during the day and completely forget to get some food. Then he would come back home starving and eat quantities that bewildered anyone who watched him. Poltic stared for a bit at the television. The interesting beginning of the film was interrupted by the return of overjoyed Charlie.

"Hello, M. J." he greeted and put down a few shopping bags on the floor. "Car's great! Do you know how much it does – 170 miles? Not that I did this speed but this is what it says on the clock. Well, on the motorway, I hammered it down a bit just up to a 100. This friend of mine, I scared him to death… He told me I'm the coolest guy he's ever met, with the coolest car…"

"I'm pleased for you that you've met up with your mate and you managed to test partially the power of the car. And I see you've done some shopping, too." Charlie sat down on the sofa and continued with a slight disappointment in his voice:

"M. J., this guy, he's not my friend after all, 'cause he's kind of looking at me in a different way now and also said that the color of the car is a bit funny, too glittery, apparently!"

"Well, he is not a real friend, then, if he's been that jealous I can only advise you to stop seeing him from now on."

"Jealous! But why?" wondered Charlie. Poltic did not feel like getting into the simplicity of explaining to him such common truths and really expected that Charlie would know better about some of the faults in human character and register them in his communications with people.

"Show me now what you've bought. If you have purchased inappropriate clothes you shall return them first thing tomorrow!" the examination of the shopping was quick because Charlie had only bought a suit that was completely satisfactory and two pairs of standard and non-descript trousers in terms of their color and cut. What he needed now was some good shoes but as Charlie would say "erh, I gonna get them tomorrow".

"How do you find the town?"

"M. J., to be honest I wasn't very impressed today, although there are quite a lot of new things and a few changes. At some point I even wondered whether I've ever lived here before!"

"I felt exactly the same, Charlie."

"In your case, you haven't been here for ages, really, where I've only been away for a few years. Anyway, I noticed the odd decent new buildings in the centre but going through one residential district, don't know what is called, a real squalid place, I got lost! Some time ago, this spot was neither that big nor so dirty and we didn't even think of it as a proper neighborhood. You know where I'm talking about – by the river?"

"I know it, of course!" confirmed Poltic, although, this part of town was rarely visited by any normal citizen. It was a ghetto now.

"M. J., you know I'm used to living in a big city. The town of my university is three times bigger than this town!"

"I agree with you, Charlie. There is nothing much going for this town. It's just a peaceful little place."

"A bit boring I'd say." The topic seemed to be exhausted and Poltic decided to remind Charlie that people needed to have some food regularly.

"Have you had anything to eat today? I'm almost sure you haven't. I've had my supper, so if you are hungry I'm not going to keep you a company. It's all ready and waiting for you in the kitchen."

"OK, M. J., I am going."

"Hey, Charlie, I nearly forgot again." called out Poltic just before he lost sight of the young man, who was heading through the corridor. "I wanted you to know, that you are not going to be able to invite any guests in this house. I don't want you to talk to anyone about it or about the car you're driving. As you've probably gathered, living here and driving a car like this, it's doubtful that you'd ever have friends who have nothing. In other words – keep your mouth closed! I understand the importance of you being friends with people of your age and have fun but pick each of them carefully! If you think it's a good idea, you can always say that you are only visiting this place, which is true anyway and the car is temporarily given to you to use, which is correct, too. It's your call."

"This sounds a bit lousy." sulked Charlie, showing a little resentment towards the veto Poltic's just placed upon him. He made a few steps back and just when Poltic expected to be showered with his pleas, Charlie said:

"I suppose you're right, M. J. I am not gonna speak to no one about the car or the house, and I got no problem with that but folks gonna ask, M. J., and will be imagining who knows what scenarios in their heads…"

"What's important, Charlie is the scenario in your head, not theirs."

"OK, then, what about if I get a good-looking bird? Where can we go?"

"Well, when you get in a situation like this, you'll have to deal with it and find a solution yourself. The security has been warned and instructed so don't try anything stupid. Now, go have your dinner and leave me watch television!"

"Whatever you say, M. J."

Charlie did not feel very good about all this but he knew Poltic was right. If he brought friends and had a party in this house, there was always something that could go wrong. They would also disturb Poltic's work.

After dinner, Charlie found his stern host in his study. There, Poltic was looking again through the following day's schedule. Charlie knocked and entered the room in a slow manner.

"Dinner was delicious, M. J., but this time the food seemed to be from a restaurant?"

"I didn't have time so I ordered from a restaurant. I'm glad you enjoyed it. It means we'll be ordering again from there."

"M. J., you mentioned something about a club tomorrow but I see you're busy now and I was going to bed in a minute but if…"

"Come here! I'll give you the free pass. The club is located on one of the biggest streets in town; you know the place very well. It's new and according to the owner, the club will be a smash-hit. The official opening is at six o'clock but I suggest you be there half an hour earlier." Charlie was right next the desk and eagerly stretched out his arm to take the pass. "Have fun and if you like it I'll arrange for you to have a reserved table every time you want to go there."

"Thanks, M. J., I've had a long day today and I feel quite tired. Good night!"

"Good night, Charlie."

The Team

It was a very pleasant morning on that Saturday. Poltic got up earlier than usual and decided to go for a walk in the spacious garden. Apart of the main drive, the garden had many alleys and paths, ideal for cycling or walking. Poltic went for a stroll onto one of those narrow lanes. He reached the end where a bench was placed under an old oak tree. He did not particularly feel like sitting down. He wandered about for nearly an hour. Back in the house, Poltic realized that he did not think about anything while he was out, most probably because his mind was still in bed. He needed a cup of coffee otherwise he would not last until the evening. He set the coffee-machine to produce a double strong beverage to which he liked adding a little bit of milk. He went in his study to check everything once again, not that he worried about anything but just wanted to keep himself busy. Poltic drank his coffee in a couple of swigs and started to mumble to himself: "Firstly, the butler comes at six, then, the security arrives as well. The catering staff from the restaurant appears a bit later so the food is still warm... And I'll have time to instruct everyone else. Should I phone the restaurant to remind them about tonight? Or maybe not, they've taken my order, after all!" Looking at his schedule for the evening, Poltic realized that he had forgotten to ask the housekeeper to go home before five o'clock. This was not a serious oversight because at weekends, she rarely stayed on until the end of her working day – by six o'clock.

It was nearly lunchtime and Poltic was still sitting in his study. There were two knocks at the door and Charlie showed up after just rising from bed.

"Good Morning!" uttered the young man rubbing his eyes.

"It was a good one, really. You must have been very tired yesterday!"

"Aha!" replied Charlie and yawned. "Oh, M. J., you are busy again! I won't take up your time. I think I'll take the car again for a drive. Yesterday, I spotted a cool shop but I ran out of time, so I'll go today."

"There are some croissants left from the morning. Delicious they are. So do have a bite to eat before you go out. Are you coming back before you head for the club?"

"I haven't decided, yet. You mentioned I should be there at about 17:30. I'll have time to come by and change my clothes. Don't know, yet. I'll see."

"Alright. If I don't see you before then, have a great time and enjoy yourself all night!"

"Cheers, M. J., can't wait! You really recommended quite well the place to me. OK, then, I better shoot 'cause my baby's waiting for me in the garage!"

"Bye, Charlie!"

It was 17:20 and an hour had gone since the housekeeper left for home. Time was flying and it inexorably shortened the distance between then and the forthcoming key evening event. Poltic felt slightly as if he was going on a date with a bird that he did not know how it would end. He strongly hoped for a favorable finale. Charlie did not come back, which meant that he had gone directly to the club.

The hands of the clock showed that it was quarter past seven. The last two hours just flew. Everyone employed for the evening was on time and had received their instructions. The butler was in position, waiting by the door, ready to let in the first guest. The restaurants had fulfilled the orders accurately and the hired waiting staff had familiarized themselves with the workings of the modern kitchen. That evening, Poltic could rely on some extra security guards. The reinforcement of two strong fellows was placed at the entry of the house. They were also dressed in smart uniforms.

The intercom announced the arrival of a vehicle. The security directed the driver to park along the solid wall surrounding the property.

"Good Evening, Sir. Please, welcome!" The guard addressed a smartly dressed man in a suit, who had just come out of the car. The heavy gate was opened for him. "Through here, Sir. Mr. Poltic is expecting you."

The newcomer spotted the house in the distance, although, not very clearly because of the trees, which were in the way. Bob walked slowly towards the target in front of him.

"Good Evening, Sir." The guards at the entry greeted him both at once.

"Good Evening!" Bob answered. He climbed up the three decorative steps to the door and looked around for a bell. There was not one. In that moment, the door opened and in the frame stood a presentable man who also greeted him with "good evening". Poltic was waiting in the hallway, two meters behind the butler. He stepped forward and shaking the visitor's hand said:

"Good Evening, Bob. I am truly delighted that you managed to respond to my invitation. My name is M. J. Poltic and we'll be your host this evening." Poltic tried to conceal his pleasure that at least one of the guests had replied to his interesting invite, organized with so much effort.

"It is very nice to meet you, too, Mr. Poltic. Your invitation seemed very attractive and there was no way I could turn it down."

"I'm glad you appreciate my offer."

"Appreciate, ha-ha! Curious definition, Mr. Poltic!" According to his record file, Bob should have been a bit more self-controlled and demure but possibly, the unusual way he was summoned that evening, made him behave more impulsively. "My wife liked it so much, the way the invitation card was contrived... She wants to know how! You will tell me, won't you? Or she won't be very happy, otherwise."

"Sure, Bob. It's not a hard task as long as you know where to go. You see, it's a bit off the wall and there aren't many craftsmen out there, who can do the job. And now, I'll have to ask if you would follow this person to the dining room!" M. J. pointed towards one of the waiters. The guest nodded and quietly went after the attendant. Poltic, on the other hand, felt he was gaining back his confidence and prepared himself for his next visitor. He undoubtedly believed that there would be another one.

Only a few minutes had passed and Jane was already trying to park her car in front of the house. The exchanged civilities with the security and the butler were repeated. The final greeting for a good evening she heard from Poltic himself just when she was taking her coat off.

"Good Evening, Mr. Poltic. I am pleased to meet you. You have a gorgeous house!"

"Thank you, Jane, you look stunning in this dress." uttered Poltic and looked at her elegant black dress. She smiled, thrilled by the compliment and said:

"I hope, this evening I learn more about you and the purpose of this meeting. Your invitation card was more or less ambiguous and I didn't gather much, I'm afraid."

"Are you hungry, Jane?" Poltic wished to send Jane off to join Bob as quick as he could so they did not go into great detail about the invitation cards. At that moment, the intercom announced about the arrival of the next guest.

"Please, follow on the waiter and I promise to let you and the rest of my guests know about all the details."

The lengthy consecution of exchanged civilities reiterated again at the arrivals of Geri and Harry. Poltic was beginning to get fed up with saying the trivial "Good evening!" over and over again. He wondered whether the phrase had a substitute but could not think of one.

Harry appeared ten minutes after eight o'clock and was last. The rest of the guests were in the hands of experienced waiters, who were eager to find out what everyone's wishes were in terms of drinks and starters. Poltic and Harry entered the dining room together. The host invited the final visitor to sit down and settled himself in his seat at the far end of the big rectangular table. "Everyone was here", Poltic thought, "It was 100% success result in this first serious enterprise!"

"I'd like to thank you all again for responding to my invitation. It is a great honor for me to be in the company of such distinguished professionals like you! I imagine you all wish to know the purpose of all this?" saying that, Poltic raised his arms a little as if to embrace the whole room. "As I've already informed Jane, everything in good time! I shall explain after dinner."

Poltic's idea was straightforward. He believed that giving them time to get adjusted to their surroundings would facilitate the task. They would be much more well-disposed towards his offer and the essential part of this meeting. In addition, mentally tormenting them to wait a little for the outcome would not hurt, either! Well, the guests had minds of their own.

"Mr. Poltic, we haven't come here to eat, at least not me, therefore I would like you to explicate to us the point of this gathering." uttered Harry in contrast to the courtesy up to that moment. "If you were that serious about your offer reflected in the invitation card I received, in that case, I demand to know all the details. Now, Mr. Poltic!

"It's serious, Harry. I can assure you!"

"Don't assure me, Mr. Poltic but speak to the point!" pushed forward once more the insolent lawyer.

"Harry, I do understand your impatience! However, you arrived last and our three guests have already ordered their dinner and I am famished myself! I hoped for you to show some consideration for our natural needs for food."

"Fine. It's your call! I shall take a bite as well."

"Mr. Poltic, forgive us our general eagerness but I doubt that any of us has ever received a job offer like this before! We all want to know the purpose of this meeting, why we are summoned here this evening." spoke Geri on behalf of everyone without really being authorized. No one said anything as they all agreed with her. She continued in the same spirit:

"I don't get an offer like this every day. That's the reason I've come here and not to... as this gentleman has just pointed out..."

"Harry! My name is Harry."

"Yes. Harry. Not to have dinner."

"Everything in its good time." responded Poltic and began to cut restively his stake in the hope that the rest would stop hassle him and follow his example – get back to their food.

Dinner did not start well as Poltic had imagined it. He felt if the conversation continued on these lines, he would lose the lead of the host, which manifested itself in the fact that Poltic should determine the what, the how and the when of the meeting. He had to do something immediately. The problem was that he did not know what. Things took their own course. To Poltic's relief, Harry and Geri had resorted to the idea that all the talking would take place after everyone had finished eating. Bob was the only one who did not feel like taking part in the argument. He completely indulged in eating his dinner. Jane also ventured to taste her salad in a couple of bites; however, her facial expression was clearly in agreement with the opinion of the more assertive people around the table. The next few minutes passed in silence apart of the occasional polite remark about the excellence of the food. Poltic realized that the four had not met each other before from the way they looked at each other and talked. He thought that it was better this way because their future relationship would not depend on past events. Or it might be not so good but there was no way for him to know this in advance.

His guests' personalities had partially lived up to Poltic's expectations. Harry's loftiness was far too obvious. Geri was not outfaced by him either – she behaved as if she was a queen. Bob and Jane had a bit more reasonable and moderate demeanor.

After all, they all turned up. Why? At the beginning of the evening, this might have been a relevant question. However, Poltic realized the answer straight after Bob and Geri pointed out about the uniqueness of the invitation card. They had thrown themselves in this meeting like vultures to a carcass. It did not sound very nice but Poltic felt it was true. They all had their own expectations derived from the offer presented to them. The three key points that promised a huge salary, a company car and free accommodation for each of them could have lacked substantiation as they were made by a stranger they had never met. However, gold was gold! The text of the invitation card was engraved on a framed golden plate, which was half a centimeter thick, and ten by thirteen centimeters in size. Poltic decided that this was a very impressive way to invite someone.

The dinner was coming to an end and the host took matters into his hands.

"Ladies and Gentlemen, please, follow me! It's time to get to the essence of this meeting." everybody quietly followed Poltic. Harry whispered to himself: "About time!" but no one heard him. They left the dining room and headed through the corridor towards a hall that Poltic had chosen to become their future meeting room for their possible gatherings. The room they entered had some specific features. In the centre, there was an ordinary table and six chairs. One had to get down three steps that surrounded the floor, to reach the table. If people were sitting on the steps and there was a ring instead of a table, then the fight Poltic expected this evening would have satisfied completely the bloody imagination of the audience. There was no fight after all.

The wall opposite the door was in effect a large glass partition between the room and the garden outside. The heavy curtains were drawn in. The wainscoting, covering the bare walls, was made from the same wood as the table and chairs. Poltic went straight towards the imaginary ring and directed each person to their seat. He also sat down in the place any head of the family would sit.

"I am M. J. Poltic and I represent the interests of a foreign business organization." Poltic broached in the manner of a college boy who intended to share his future career plans with the rest of the class. "The influential members of this organization have entrusted me with the task to do everything in my power in order to carry through their business interests. You are here tonight because I need to work with the best professionals in the country. There will be a strikingly high volume of investments that would require the best management…"

"How much?" interpolated Harry. "And where is this money going to be invested?"

"Even I don't know the exact figures but the initial sum is about 100 million. And with regards to the area of economic interests on our part, I was just coming to that point. The money is in store for buying factories and manufacturers of meat produce. The target would be large and medium-size enterprises of this type. In the next couple of years, we have to take the lead in the meat production market. The plan and the sequence of our actions will vary according to the fluctuations in the market, of course. You understand that a company of this size requires numerous and qualified personnel. The four of you have a substantial experience in your own field. Each of you has achieved no less than the highest recognition in your professional life." Poltic did not exaggerate here in the slightest and the well-deserved praises provoked some unctuous grins on his listeners' faces. They were delighted to hear how great they were by someone who sincerely believed in their greatness. "Some of you are responsible for the management of your own employees, where others follow the orders of their bosses and people like Harry, correct me if I'm wrong, is self-employed."

"That's right, Mr. Poltic. It appears you have vetted us very well."

"Very well, indeed, Harry. After all, I couldn't possibly entrust people I don't know with the management of hundreds maybe thousands of employees who work for a company worth millions. Well, not that I really know you. Not as persons, anyway, but I am familiar with your professional biographies. And they speak for themselves, that you are the best in what you are doing! Here you go, the answer to your question that has caused the most of anxieties this evening: What is your role in all this?" asked Poltic and began his answer before Harry managed to interfere with some unnecessary "What?"

"Your job will be to manage this company. You'll be involved in absolutely everything. For instance, you'll be managing all assets of the company, you'll be responsible for drawing up all contracts and agreements on behalf of the company and last but not least, you will do all the negotiations for the company. Basically, anything you could think of is going to be your responsibility! On the other hand, I will be the mediator between you and those above me. My patrons will be defining the company policy and progress with my help because I'll be monitoring all your activities in relation to the smooth operation of the business. Well, that's all in brief. I present everything to you in a clear and straightforward way, exactly how I was asked to explain all the details."

Actually, Poltic had rehearsed a much longer speech but decided on a succinct version of his presentation. He felt that it worked better and also some of his enthusiasm had evaporated after Harry's arrogant interjection. Everyone in the room was staring at him intently. He guessed they were all trying to take in every word. The first person who spoke out was the best stockbroker in the last two years:

"Mr. Poltic, considering you are acquainted with our work, could you explain to me what am I doing here? The last thing I wish is to be rude but I don't really see my role in this, my responsibilities, etc. It's true that quite a few people are working for me but I have nothing to do with the meat market or companies that manufacture meat produce. I'm just not sure if I could be of any help to you!" Bob instinctively gulped when he mentioned the word meat, which caused for a spontaneous smile to appear on Poltic's face.

"You are a stockbroker Bob, right?"

"Yes, I am."

"Some of the companies, we have marked down, have put shares on the stock market that would be of future interest to our company. I can assure you that if you accept our offer, Bob, your job will be very important. It doesn't really matter that you are not so clued up about that sector of the economy. The personnel who are going to work for you will have the necessary knowledge about the meat industry. Everyone will be in their right position according to their qualifications and experience."

"Yes, I imagine so." mumbled Bob, pleased with Poltic's answer but still wondering about his exact place in the whole project. The attractive woman next to him joined in the conversation:

"It sounds great to become a boss in a big company, Mr. Poltic, but I can't just leave my own job. I imagine, all of us here have some professional commitments at present. Also, from what I gather, nothing has been done, yet!"

Poltic did not answer straight away in attempt to understand the contradictory statement he just heard. Jane emphasized on her professional obligations, however, she did not come this evening for the sake of pure curiosity. "Women!" Poltic thought to himself and replied in a serious manner:

"The most important thing for me is to build up a team, which will invest the money that's been provided in the best possible way. The team will manage and direct the company. So, yes, we are at the very beginning. Jane, I do understand completely your anxiety. You feel uncomfortable to desert the business you've built up over the years. Nonetheless, the contract you are about to receive at the end of this meeting excludes any possibility for you to work elsewhere! The good news is that you'll be able to commission your own company to provide for you consultancy services. Bob, you can still work with your old colleagues by assigning jobs to them on behalf of our company, for which they'll get paid. Geri, you know how important opinion polls for the business are! So even if you don't work for your research agency anymore, you could still commission it for our own research."

"Hang on! So in that case they'll be redirecting company money to their close firms even so there might be other companies that can do a better deal for the same services? It doesn't sound very pragmatic! You'll be draining improperly financial resources!

"You are right, Harry, but no one is going to appropriate money on the sly! I will monitor all the contracts with your companies. My patrons will have to approve them first before any decision is made. If you present us with a damaging contract, say, with your consultancy firm, Jane, that causes a big financial loss to us, you will get simply fired. Nothing personal here, Jane, it's just an example."

"Yes, of course, Mr. Poltic." replied she, not offended in the slightest about being made an example of for a shady business.

"So if I assign a project to my colleagues from my research agency I'll be still able to work with them until the assignment is completed?"

"It is actually recommended, Geri as you best know workings of the whole process. I'd like to sum up: you accept my conditions by leaving the positions at your own work. However, every contact with your companies is not only valuable to us but we hope that any collaboration with your ex-colleagues would facilitate your future work. If we imagined that you were forbidden to communicate with your companies, then you had to find similar firms to do the same job. Geri, would you commission a rival company to carry out a research poll?"

"If I didn't have a choice, then – yes. But you said it could be mine, so I don't have a problem, do I? We are the best, anyway, everyone knows that!" Poltic was very pleased with the affirmative answer and hoped that the rest of his guests would understand his example.

"You don't say a word about me, Mr. Poltic. You know I work for myself, I have no boss, nor employees!"

"Well, it's of a primary importance that our company is run and operated by abiding the law! You, Harry, are a lawyer, one of the best in the country. Now you are working alone. Not long ago, however, you were a part of a law office, so you could always rely on your fellow-solicitors from those times, I would imagine."

"Rightly so, Mr. Poltic. In my old office work not only the best lawyers but they are all good friends of mine." uttered Harry with a huge contentedness in his voice.

"Superb, Harry! If you accept my offer you'll be free to hire them. And, of course, they will receive a first-class payment for their first-class services."

"They deserve their money, Mr. Poltic, I can assure you!" Geri happily redirected the conversation towards the money, namely – the amount of it:

"So how much are we getting, then? On the invitation card, it was written 600 000, also there was a car, a house and bonuses mentioned – is this all true or it's some sort of a bait so we all come here tonight?" asked Geri and smiled. Poltic answered the smile with a question:

"And what do you think?"

"I believe that you are not joking, judging by the house we are in right now!"

"Hmm, it could be rented, and the security, as well as everything else… It's not so expensive. I could afford all this but I don't have 100 million to invest, do I?" said Harry, hinting at the fact that whatever was happening that evening could be just one big lie, a very possible lie. "Me, personally, until I see my bank account in a new light, I shall remain a Doubting Thomas, I'm afraid. Nothing personal, Mr. Poltic!"

"You are right, Harry. Presently, there's no change in your account balance. You are right to doubt every word I say. The absolute trust is a privilege for people who can be simply called naïve."

"No, seriously, Mr. Poltic! Tell us!" asked Geri worried. She was obviously taken in by the provocation.

"It's all very serious, Geri. You'll see when you read the contract I'm going to give you all a little later. Besides the financial parameters, there are material considerations, drawn up in the contract as well. The salary of 600 000 is annual. It's paid at the end of every month. I can show you bank references that state we have the capital that would cover your salaries for the next ten years. The bonus scheme will be determined by those above me and it will be exclusively result-orientated. No bonus for a job not done! The other material perks include a luxury car with your personal chauffeur who will be at your disposal throughout the day, as well as a house to live while you are employees of the company."

"Wow, it sounds pretty good!" exclaimed Geri and made a quick estimation that her monthly wage would equal 50 grand. She had never earned that much in such a short period.

No one was particularly impressed by the idea of being driven in company cars. They were aware that it was the norm for a company to provide its high-rank personnel with means of transport. Poltic's guests, however, could not work out why they should move in new houses. They all had a place to live. Poltic had a plan. He did not view the properties only as accommodation where one just lived and went about their business. He rated their significance much higher to the level of being his most loyal "associates".

"Mr. Poltic, what do I need a house for? I have my own apartment and I have no intention of moving anywhere. So you can count me out if I accept your offer, anyway!"

"I'm afraid, I have to disappoint you, Jane. It's explicitly stated in the contract that by taking up the offer you agree to move in the houses, granted to you or we withdraw our proposition."

"I don't want to change my accommodation, all my mates live in the neighborhood and my kids' school is quite near by. It's just pointless!" said Jane, annoyed that she might miss the chance to get the attractive work proposal for such a silly and superfluous technicality.

"I agree with you but let me explain it better. I hope you will change your mind. The houses are situated in the same villa district as this house. They are two-storey buildings without gardens. Your workplace is located on the first floor. You will have your own study and if you need to employ a secretary – there is a room for her, too. You will not have a fixed working time or the bother to travel every day to your office. When you receive a task you will have a deadline to complete it. You will have the flexibility to decide how many hours a day and when to devote your time to finish the assignment. Meetings connected to work can take place in your study or wherever in town, to where you will be driven in the company vehicle. The four of you are going to be neighbors, hence, any job-related problems you can discuss in whichever house you feel comfortable at the time. I think that this proximity will be only in your favor. Your children, Jane will be taken to school and back every day by another company car. And to add for your reassurance, our chauffeurs are very confident because they have passed a six-month driving course for skillful driving."

"What you want from us is to move in these houses and work from home. But my husband runs a restaurant where we live. Are you going to drive him to work?"

"I am sorry, Jane. The company can't take care of him, too." Jane was not pleased with the answer. She turned her head away to avoid Poltic's eyes and replied grumpily:

"Don't feel like moving anywhere."

"You will really like the houses when you see their interior. They are magnificent!"

Poltic knew that Jane did not have such a big problem with it all as she had been trying to present it. He doubted that her work-schedule so far had allowed her to meet up with her friends regularly. She did not seem to be the type of woman who would waste her time in girls' gossip, either. She deceived about her kids. Their school was not close to where they lived. According to Poltic's calculations, it would take about 20-25 minutes to drive to it or about the same if they lived in the new house. It was interesting that she tried to justify hesitation with her husband's work. Poltic, however, was aware of how insignificant was his restaurant. Whether from solidarity or not, but Geri, too, decided to question the moving houses part. Up to that moment she had not shown any qualms about the idea:

"Mr. Poltic, I live with my son and my mother. She is very attached to our apartment. She and my dad, before he died, they've spent almost their entire life there and I doubt she would follow me to live in a new place."

"Geri, who says that your mother has to go with you? I can assure you that every time she wants to visit you or you'd like to go and see her, there will be a car at your disposal. Don't worry about your son, either! I guarantee that he would be always on time for school even if he didn't like it. There will be always a car waiting for him after classes." Poltic was not taken in by the over exaggerated fondness of the apartment. He was aware from the little detective's files that her place was far from special and that was also located in one of the oldest districts in town. Therefore, Poltic did not think that Geri would want to live there all her life with her son and the fact that her mother had spent so much time in it, did not make the apartment any better. Sentimentality was a weakness that could not overthrow a beautiful new two-storey villa.

"All right. I'll see what I can do. My mother will be quite disappointed but I may go for it!"

"Bob, do you have any problems with the forthcoming translocation?"

"I'm not sure. I have to discuss it with my wife but I'm quite positive that she would like the idea."

If the wife said 'yes' then he would say 'yes'. If she said 'no', this would be the perfect example for mixing personal stuff with work, which would lead to making the wrong decision in the name of some emotions. She would probably tell him that if he loved her he would not make her move. And that would be it. Poltic imagined this scenario and felt if he could only tease the under the thumb stockbroker and ask him: "Are you out of your mind?"

"What about you, Harry?

"For me, it's not a problem to move, Mr. Poltic. I live in a very noisy place, anyway."

"Brilliant, Harry. Anyhow, nothing has been signed, yet and nothing is certain. The list I've obtained includes other names, too. So if all of you rejected my offer, I would definitely find the people I need. You have one chance and that is now. You won't get a second one! You have one week to sign the contract and bring it here. If not, I can only wish you in advance successful career in the future." Poltic concluded and passed a folder to each of them that contained the contract for working in the future company. Harry glanced at the first couple of pages and then placed the folder in front of him:

"Mr. Poltic, I'm a bit confused."

"What about exactly, Harry? I won't be surprised if you argue against some of the clauses, being a lawyer after all, but you haven't become acquainted with it in more detail!"

"It's not about the contract. If we accept, we'll be getting a salary that is at least three times as much for such a type of position. No one deserves that much money, Mr. Poltic. You told us that we were the best but that's not good enough. Not only that but you are eager to give us a house in a VIP neighborhood and a company limo."

"That's right, Harry."

"What's the catch, Mr. Poltic? You are very well aware of the fact that no one could refuse such a lucrative offer, not any sane person, anyway! I'm not trying to offend anyone present here." said Harry and looked around at everyone at the table.

"Oh, I do hope you are right and in a week's time I hold these folders again with your signatures on the last page. There's no catch. The offer is impressive and unmatchable for the standard of living in this country. However, great objectives require a great sacrifice. You all need to be well provided for in every way, in order to work effectively. What we are looking for is results and efficiency. As you can see on page 16 in the contract, failure to perform your duties would result in losing everything the company has given to you. The damages you will have to pay back if you make a muddle of everything and things go wrong, will lead to your bankruptcy. All of you! We can give a lot but we can take it all back with the interest included. Don't get me wrong, please! It's a company policy to always offer you much more for what it will receive back from you. I draw your attention to this section of the contract only to remind you that nothing is ever for free but one has to put a lot of effort!"

"I have never come across that sort of company management policy before. Efficiency is sought after through cutting down the costs and trying to increase profitability."

"Yes, Harry, but it's not you who determine company policy! Accept the offer or don't. The subject is exhausted!" snapped Poltic. Harry did not say anything.

"Yes, Geri?" he looked at her, who was sitting to his right.

"Mr. Poltic, if we accept your proposition, we get everything that you've talked about... But I think you missed to mention the name of the organization you're a representative of! Who are your generous patrons?"

"As I said at the very beginning, I am a mediator, an agent for this organization. I have a full authority and everything will be my responsibility. I will act on the company's behalf. The members of the organization seek anonymity in view of possible wheels within wheels in the works that could hinder our activities. When it all boils down to a lot of money, it is best if things are kept a low profile."

"So you are not going to tell us, Mr. Poltic?"

"I'm positive, Geri. You do not need this piece of information."

"Mr. Poltic is right. It's the same in our field. All big deals are carried out by agents. We never learn who the buyer is when it's a question of purchasing shares worth several millions. The company and its owner are known but they are always figureheads. Always!"

"Thank you, Bob. This only validates my patrons' view about anonymity."

"You're welcome, Mr. Poltic. I pointed out the facts because I'm very experienced in matters as such."

"I believe that's all I had to say to you. Get acquainted with the contracts and get back to me by the end of the week with your decision. Don't rush! I imagine you'd like to confer with your loved ones. If you feel unsettled about parts in the contract, I may be able to offer a compromise but not for the important stuff."

They chatted on for a minute more after which Poltic put official end of the meeting. He left the room heading the main exit of the house followed by his four interesting guests. Now they appeared a lot more cheerful and there was no trace of their stern look on their faces from the beginning.

"Thank you for coming, Jane!" Poltic turned to the pretty financial consultant, who was getting ready for leaving.

"Thank you, Mr. Poltic. Dinner was fantastic and the meeting – more interesting than I expected. I'm certain I'll see you again and that will be very soon. Have a nice evening!"

"The same to you, Jane."

Bob got ready very quickly but let Jane first to say good-bye to the host. He made a step forward and put out his hand:

"Mr. Poltic, I can tell you right off that you can count me in. My wife will be very pleased, too. I'll just look through what's in the folder and that will be it!"

"I'm delighted to hear it, Bob."

"I'll see you soon, Mr. Poltic."

"Good bye, Bob, and drive carefully."

Geri was also very enthusiastic on leaving the house. So far she did not show that sort of emotions. Poltic was certain that she would sign. Harry was last. Poltic addressed him in a friendly voice in the hope that the end of the evening was going to be more amicable than the trenchant start:

"Harry, you were the most skeptical of all this evening! Have I managed to convince you in the genuineness of my offer?"

"Mr. Poltic, I believe you. Just this company of yours has picked a bizarre way to select its high-rank employees and has a strange management approach. Now that you've confirmed the wage I'll be getting, I have no other problems."

"I can see your point, Harry. I would not have allocated such massive salaries if it was down to me. But I do what I'm told and that way, I stay out of trouble."

"Good bye, Mr. Poltic. And just to let you know, I'm gonna read the contract word by word at least three times." Harry uttered jokingly.

"Good bye, Harry."

Poltic closed the door and went in the kitchen. He was quite nervous at dinner and hardly ate. He made himself a big sandwich and leaned on the granite kitchen top. The waiters had cleaned everything and the table in front of his was clear. He was chewing on noisily but he was alone in the house, after all. The butler had gone, too.

"That Harry is going to be a problem." Poltic said to himself. He continued to reason in his own mind: "I don't need someone like that who allows himself to speak to me in that way in my own house. The other three are alright", Poltic did not want to make rushed conclusions but he felt he wanted to remove Harry from the project that very moment. "How would he work as a team player as he showed no tolerance towards the opinion of others?"

Poltic went to bed, as he felt very exhausted. His tired brain could not handle any guesswork and analysis of the event that evening. He briefly thought about Charlie who had not come home, yet. It was only ten o'clock. "The party at his end had probably just started", this was Poltic's last thought before he fell asleep.

Charlie at Work

Poltic was woken by the door bell at half eight. He did not intend to get up but wondered who could this might be if the security had allowed them through! When he opened the door he realized that it could be no one else but the guards themselves. The shorter guy of the two on shift was standing on the doorstep slightly nervous:

"Mr. Poltic, I'm sorry to disturb you but you've told us that you get up at about this time in the morning, so… well, I have to tell you something…that maybe…aaa…"

"Spell it out!" said Poltic in order to cut short the guard's incoherent rambling.

"Charlie was quite tipsy last night. And you said to report straight away when there was something…"

"That's right. Thanks for letting me know and don't worry! Whenever it's related to Charlie, you can come and see me at any time. Was he very drunk?"

"Quite so, 'cause I even had to support him to stay upright so he could get to the house."

Poltic remembered something and froze.

"And the car? Where is his car? How had he managed to drive so drunk? I'll kill him!"

"Mr. Poltic, he came home by taxi. I even paid for it. Charlie was unable to get money out of his pocket, let along to drive!"

"You've done a great job." Poltic calmed down. "You'll get a bonus at the end of month."

The security guard felt happy, although, it seemed that he had some objections:

"Mr. Poltic, I don't want to sound too pushy but I think my colleague should get something for this, too. While I was taking Charlie to the house, my mate was kind of covering for me down at the gate. I left my position, you see! And as far as I remember, you've told us that for something like this we can get the sack, right?"

"Hmm, I never thought about this. You are right. I imagine your colleague deserves a bonus, as well. Now you can go back to your work." The guard followed the order and door got closed behind him. Poltic needed a cup of coffee and immediately so. On his way to the kitchen, he met the housekeeper, who was mopping the shoes-prints on the floor in the corridor. They were probably left by the drunken Charlie, who must have forgotten to take them off.

He was at the age of sixteen or there about when Poltic had a serious conversation with him on the subject of drinking. Since that day, the youngster became a total abstainer. However, he had started to drink while at university. Poltic remembered the parties during his student years. He would drink alcohol but never to any excess. In this instance, Charlie probably left the car behind and came home by taxi only for his fear of Poltic. Well, he hoped that was the case. At noon, Charlie came in Poltic's study, still unsteady on his legs. The older man was pondering on the future duties of his visitors from last night.

"Good Morning, M. J." quietly greeted Charlie and making every effort not to look so hung-over.

"Have you got a head-ache? Come here, I have some pills that will help."

"Oh, M. J., I really don't know how it all happened! The club was cool, and the music... I'm sorry, I feel so queasy now...."

"Where's the car? Thank God you didn't drive home because if you did that, you would have walked on foot in the rest of your life." Poltic scolded him not trying to hide his desire to reach out over his desk and slap Charlie across the face.

"M. J., I wouldn't ever drink and drive! I know you will kill me after!"

"Charlie, I want you to understand what all this is about. As you can see, the consequences are at your expense, not mine! Anyway, it's good that at least you didn't sit behind the wheel. Next time, have two beers less, alright? So you had a good time?"

"Yes, M. J., it was awesome! And it seems that you are quite good pals with the manager, 'cause he met me personally at the door and I had the best seat in the club. And I never paid a thing, he said that I was from the guests that should not worry about paying!"

"So everything went exactly how I had arranged it. You are going to receive the same treatment there in the future, every time you go to the club! Be polite and don't overdo it! The fact that you are not paying there doesn't give you a green light to misbehave towards the other visitors. Is that clear?"

"I'm not like this, M. J., but yesterday, I felt as if I owned the place."

"Get this idea out of your head because you don't! Today, it's your last day that you can do whatever you like. It's best if you have a good rest now after the heavy night you've had. I have business to attend in town and will be out all day."

"OK, M. J. I'll have to go and collect the car and then I may watch some television quietly at home, 'cause I can still hear a band playing in my head."

"Don't worry about the car! Someone from the security will fetch it. Give them the keys later. You've still got them, haven't you? You haven't lost them?"

"They've been in my trousers since last night, M. J. I don't lose my things anymore. I'm not a kid!"

"I know you are not, Charlie, although, sometimes you make me doubt that. Now, I'm going out. If I don't see you later this evening, be aware that tomorrow is a very important day for you. I'll be waiting you in my study at nine o'clock."

"I'll be there, M. J."

After sending off M. J., Charlie went to lie down on the sofa in the living room and switched on the enormous television set. He was not sure about what he wanted to watch and just kept changing the channels. There was a basketball game on one and he left it on. In the evening he went to bed early, while Poltic was still out. Charlie did not have any idea about what was awaiting him on his first working day or what he was going to do from then on.

On the next day, absolutely sober and with a clear head, Charlie was waiting in front of Poltic's office. He looked at his watch. There were seven minutes until nine. The watch was a present from Poltic for his birthday three years ago. It was quite expensive brand.

"Hi, M. J. I'm a bit early. It's not a problem…?"

"You are just on time, Charlie. Have a seat." replied Poltic and pointed at the chair in front of his desk. "I'd like you to listen very carefully and if you have something that's not clear to you, just ask! It's important that you understand everything."

"OK, M. J."

"The house we live in and the vehicles we drive, including yours, are very expensive. I can afford them thanks to the company I work for. To enjoy the privilege of owning all of this, I have been entrusted with a very responsible job, which is too much for me a lot of the times. I make significant compromises sometimes that I shouldn't, if I had a loyal assistant who helped me. That's exactly what I'm going to ask you – I want you to become my assistant. Charlie, you haven't been dealt with such a responsibility before, that's why you need to show a professional approach. It'll be hard for you at the beginning because you don't have much of an experience. Don't worry, though! I'll be always here for you, to give you guidance and advice. I'm telling you everything as it is, so you don't think that because I'm going to be your boss, you won't be expected to work hard! I'll give you a hard time and if you fail, you will be out at once."

Charlie raised his hand as if he was a schoolboy at his desk and said:

"M. J., I'm not experienced, and understandably so – at my age! It can't just happen overnight. You haven't had any experience, either, when you were young."

"That's right, Charlie. Everybody has to start from somewhere! I'm giving you exactly that – a chance. The company has many activities, which different people are in charge of. I am a director of several subsidiary companies in the food processing industry. Besides manufacturing foods, namely meat produce, we have decided to build up our own supermarket chain. My work on other projects for the company does not allow me physically to concentrate on this particular venture. That's why I would like you to focus and manage the entire process of developing this chain of supermarkets. You will have a small team working alongside on this." Charlie's eyes nearly popped out and his bottom jaw inadvertently moved an inch down:

"M. J., you want me to build shops, those big ones that we've seen a few further down on the motorway? But I'm not an engineer or an architect; I don't know anything about that sort of job! I can't, I just…" the denial was a normal human reaction, when one came across the unknown only to equate it to the impossible. Poltic had expected such an answer and calmly continued with his instructions:

"Don't be afraid, Charlie. You are not going to build anything, well not personally. There is some time before the actual building works start. Firstly, we need a site, then – building plans and much later we set up the foundations. Your presence is not even needed during the building process. Every building project has a site-manager. Your job is simple and at the same time not so easy!" Poltic was beginning to contradict himself and sensed that Charlie did not understand the sentence. "In other words, Charlie, you will manage the development process without taking part in any of the building works."

"I see, M. J. I guess…"

"Above all, you have to find the people who are going to do it all under your supervision. Two of the best universities of Economics in the whole country are located in this town. You need to pay them a visit and collect some data on the recent graduates. These people are like you. They have just got their degrees and are probably looking for a job, if not already employed elsewhere."

"What do you mean by data, M. J.? I know what it means but what kind of information exactly do you need?"

"What we need is those students' grade records. I'll help you by telling you that every university provides this information on request. You only have to say that you'd like to employ some students but you want to select them on the basis of their score. You may be charged a small fee for that. Do you understand?"

"I do, M. J., I need to get their grades." nodded Charlie.

"When you get hold of the list rolls, you'll need then to choose four people – two girls and two guys. The subjects that you should be interested in are accountancy, marketing and management. I don't need to see the lists with names. It's all down to you who you select but you can't pick students that have full marks at every subject. I'm sure you would have gone for them first!"

"But why not, M. J.? Obviously they would be the best."

"Were there any prize students in your course, Charlie?"

"Yes, just two or three, maybe…"

"How were they treated by the rest of the students?"

"E-r-h, no one really liked them that much. They are bookworm-nerds, only read, absolute geeks!"

"How would you like to work with people like these?" Poltic asked rhetorically.

"Oh, no, M. J. It won't be work but punishment."

"Now you can see why we don't need such employees. Top achievements do not always speak for someone's abilities. The development of a supermarket chain requires some good organizational skills and loners like those from your course would not be able to cope with the job."

"So who should I go for?"

"The most suitable candidates are those that have achieved well above average results in their studies. You may come across quite a few students with that sort of marks. In that case you should filter them down to the number you need by looking into their attendance record."

"M. J., I got it, but what if I like more than four persons. You know that there are about 50 students in one course."

"Yes, Charlie, I am aware of that. Say, you've got them down to ten in the list after sifting them through. Then I'll check out their financial situation, because we don't need some rich kids. The student fees in these universities don't come cheap and some of the young scholars are put in there because of their ambitious parents. We require people whose main motivation to work is money."

"There is logic in this, M. J., but if someone has good grades but is in debt to the neck to pay back his fees, we gonna take him?"

"Well, probably not. Still, avoid the extreme cases! Such employee may well just try to steal from us. While you get on with this task, my job would be to arrange a place for them to work."

"And for me." corrected him Charlie.

"No, Charlie, you are not going to be there while they are working. The office place I'm going to rent will be fully equipped for four people."

"But I'm gonna be the boss? You said that you are leaving this job for me."

"You are going to be the boss but this doesn't mean that you'll sit around their office. What are you going to do there? You will give out orders and reprimand them when they look at you the wrong way?"

"No, M. J., I just…"

"Listen now carefully. You will report to me weekly about the work progress of new team. You will go there every morning at about ten o'clock to check on them or ask them questions after they have received their assignment. You shouldn't impose yourself on them. You spend some time in the office and go out. You go back later just before the end of the working day. It will be best if you go there at different times."

"But in that case, they will be free to do whatever they feel like. M. J., I really don't understand..."

"What is the purpose of all this, Charlie? Come on, think about it!" Poltic urged him.

"So they feel at ease while at work, maybe, but I've never heard about anywhere, where people worked in such a strange way!"

"Right so, Charlie, but do you know what the boss is for?"

"To apply control so his staff does their job and don't just fill the time." replied Charlie with a great deal of confidence.

"Correct, Charlie. We'll supervise them but in a different way and you are not going to play the baddy every time you visit them in the office."

"How do you mean, M. J.? I can't think of anything…"

"We will give them everything that people at their age can only dream of, i.e. money. Their salary will be 5 000 a month."

"Wow, M. J., that's far too much money…"

"Yes, it's a lot and they'll also have brand new company cars at their disposal. Their office will be furnished with the best innovation technologies. That's the only way to make them work conscientiously. Notice the look on their faces when they hear about that part of the offer. They have to put the hours to deserve their fat salary and the rest of it. Charlie, still, if one of them mucks things up and just enjoys the privileged lifestyle but doesn't work fast enough, you will have to play the baddy, then and just sack them. All given to them by the company belongs to the company."

"Aha, M. J. I got it! You will pay them a good wage and give them other perks so they work harder, 'cause they won't do anything for a little money?"

"I wouldn't use those words exactly, but yes, Charlie! You will have to learn the other side of the work process and the way you express yourself – no one will take you seriously! They have to know their place. Even if they are seeing you just for 5 minutes a day, they need to know that you are the boss and they are the workers. Don't forget that you all are at similar age and you will have to carry yourself with a certain authority in front of them! That's why you have to wear suits and try to be a bit better-spoken."

"Like you, M. J.? 'Cause I think I can do it like you."

"Be yourself, Charlie! Just use the words appropriately and don't use their short version. You cannot say: "cause"."

"OK, M. J. I will try."

"I'm not keen on this "OK", either!" correcting Charlie's speech was quite a difficult task. However, Poltic knew that if he put the effort, the results would follow. Although, not today.

"OK. Oops, sorry, M. J. I didn't think…"

"Besides all this, Charlie you will be regularly taking them out to dinner or what not. In other words, you will have team-building events out of the workplace. You could take them to the newly opened club. You will invite them to expensive restaurants or go to the movies. Use your imagination! Take them to the zoo if you have to."

"As if!" said Charlie, taking Poltic's words as a joke but the latter was totally serious.

"Choose these people very carefully, Charlie, as if you are choosing friends for life. The nature of our work requires a strong team bond out of the workplace, as well. If they just interact between themselves only as colleagues, our task may prove to be quite difficult for them. However, if the team spirit is strong, you will find it easier to cope. Trust me it's better to work with four friends than four strangers!"

"But why should I cringe to them, M. J.? They can be friends if they like but why me to play it all mates with them? It doesn't sound good to me. What about if I don't like one of them?"

"It will mean that you've picked the wrong person. You sack him and employ another one! Charlie, when you actually meet the four, then we'll discuss again the subject about your behavior towards them."

"M. J., how am I going to find these people? They've graduated from university and they could be anywhere now! As far as I know, the university staff won't give out their addresses and where they live, will they?"

"That's my problem, Charlie. You just give me names and I'll provide you with the necessary information. Even if they live abroad, we are going to know which country, city, everything. Do you get it, Charlie?"

"Yes, M. J. I only didn't get the bit about that I'm their boss and their friend at the same time…"

"Do you think you'll manage? You can still change your mind. Think about it."

"I will do everything in my power, M. J. I won't let you down!"

"In that case, here is the location of the two universities. You know where one of them is. The other one is a little bit outside of town." after these words Poltic passed him a piece of paper with the addresses. "I want four names on my desk by the end of the week."

"You will get them, M. J."

"I'm pleased that you've accepted the job." Poltic replied with a genuine delight in his voice. Not that he expected a negative response. Knowing Charlie so well, that possibility did not exist. "Now, go! You have a job to do."

"OK, M. J. I am going." Charlie said the last three words while already running towards the exit.

Poltic remained alone in his study and the only thought that he had in his mind was: "Charlie will fail!" He hoped he was wrong. Otherwise, he had to find someone else, a person he did not know and that, Poltic did not want to do.

Charlie stopped the car at the STOP sign, which was placed at the junction, directing towards the motorway. He felt his mind was going to explode after the super interesting meeting with Poltic. He was going to be a boss and was on his way to choose his employees. The feeling he was experiencing at this thought was beyond words. It almost made him feel uncomfortable in the leather seat of his car. While driving towards one of the marked university, Charlie relived again the whole conversation he had with Poltic. M. J. had really put his trust upon him and he had to prove that he deserved it. The young man had never tried to avoid taking up responsibilities, however, the tasks he had to deal with in the past did not involve anything more than going to do the shopping and get everything that he had been asked to. He experienced a certain anxiety that made the car seem smaller. Poltic was going to help him in any situation but this time he had to manage on his own.

The university building in front of him had four floors and it was painted white. Actually, this was one of the three buildings designated for the students. Charlie was coming here for the first time and when he parked the car at the front, he did not know which direction to choose. He should definitely go for the main big entrance, where students were coming and going at all times. He wondered if they would let him in. What about if entry was prohibited for non-students? Charlie panicked and got out his phone to ask M. J. A second later, he put it back in his pocket. "To phone him just because I don't know how to get in a pile of bricks and concrete! I'm an idiot!" he said to himself and boldly headed towards the main entrance, believing as if he was Poltic. He straightened his posture a bit as if to look fearless, although his legs were shaking. The security did not stop him and he found himself in the enormous entry hall on the first floor. There were many students around him, walking in a hurry in all directions. Charlie decided he would ask one of them but he could not formulate his question. He went nearer towards one of the walls, where he noticed a large information chart. He quickly looked across the lines and his eyes stopped at 'room 18; floor 1' – the administration department. He followed the pointed arrow and turned right along the corridor. Charlie felt a bit calmer and gained back his composure and some of his self-confidence – he had found the room, after all. He reached room 18 and without thinking too much, knocked twice and pressed the door-handle downwards. He entered a very large room and realized that this was a department indeed. There were six desks in a row along each of the two walls and a wide pathway in the middle. A woman behind the front desk on the right side first noticed Charlie and kindly asked:

"How can I help you, Sir? Please, have a seat!" she pointed at the chair in front of her desk.

"Good Morning!" said Charlie and took advantage of her invitation to sit down. "I think I'm in the right place… I need some information on the students who graduated last year. I'm interested in the following subjects: accountancy, marketing and management."

"That is the right place, Sir. What type of information do you need? I suppose, you are after their score-records or something. I receive a lot of enquiries about that."

"Actually, yes. This is exactly what I need and also, their attendance record for the whole period of education. I am a representative of a big company and I'm looking for staff. Your university is famous for producing outstanding professionals."

"That is correct, Sir. Our institution of higher education is one of the best in the country." replied politely the employee in the administrative department, while typing on the keyboard of her computer. Staring at the monitor, she continued:

"164 graduates have obtained their degrees in the three subjects you are interested in. Give me a minute, please, until I print it out for you. And while waiting, please, fill this form, it's a policy for everyone."

"Sure. Thanks."

"There you go, Sir." she said around thirty two seconds later and gave him the print out comprising a few pages. "The data-records on our graduates' attendance are stored in my colleague's computer, on the next desk."

Charlie thanked her again and went to see the next member of staff. Five minutes later, he left the campus with everything he needed in his hands.

He sat in the car but did not turn the engine straight away. The young man placed a few sheets of paper on the passenger seat, took a deep breath and slowly breathed out. He did it. He got the information without a hitch. To be honest, it was all down to M. J. Charlie behaved exactly like him inside the university building. He acted self-assured and informed and hence the two clerks in the administrative department took him seriously. If he behaved like the old Charlie, he would have burst into laughter at the sound of "Sir" first time. Maybe, he should not have said that he represented a big company. It kind of sounded silly from the mouth of such a young person like him. Well, the woman did not notice anything and besides, he had to fill in the form about who had required the information. He had to give details about his employer. Charlie accelerated and drove off in a mad speed towards home to bring the good news to M. J. He sensed he should slow down a little bit if he wanted to arrive in one piece. At the gate he stopped and put down his window as the security guard insisted.

"Hey, Charlie, I have a message from Mr. Poltic for you. He said he was going abroad for a week. He would have told you this in person but had to leave immediately."

"Did M. J. say where he was going?"

"No. He didn't say anything else."

Charlie felt a bit disappointed. There was no one to boast to the good news.

In the same time, Poltic was just 500 meters away, if on a straight line, in one of the houses, which were designated for each of his Saturday guests and almost surely they would decide to move in. The properties were much smaller than his but designed in a far more modern manner. Poltic had bought one for Charlie, too. This was where he was – in Charlie's new house. The houses were absolutely the same. They only differed on the inside in some tiny detail to compensate for the unevenness of the terrain they had been built on. Poltic undertook this move for a week, leaving Charlie to indulge in the spacious fortress-house, because he believed that this was the right thing to do. He wanted to give the young guy a lesson and make him realize that he would not be always there for him, although the fact, that this was exactly what he had promised to him. If Poltic was there with him the following week, he would have to listen to Charlie's stories every day, where he had been or what he had achieved that day. Sometimes Charlie would come disappointed to him and Poltic would have to console him. Other times, the boy would be happy and M. J. would have to listen about his feats of the day. This had to change. If he managed on his own this week, he would be able to cope by himself in the future. If Charlie failed, it would mean that the child in him had won. Poltic had no intentions of giving him a second chance. He would just employ another young man, who was a well-educated and qualified worker, although, he would never be that loyal to him like Charlie.

Poltic went up on the second floor to find out where he would sleep for the following week. The bedroom he chose was smaller than his in the big house but this was not a problem. The second bedroom on that floor was facing the street and he did not like this at all. He came down to the first floor and went straight to the table in the living room. It was going to be his workplace, where he would think of the tasks for Bob, Jane, Geri and Harry, if they signed the contract. No one turned up in the first day of the week. There were six days left to go.

Charlie got up at about 9 o'clock on Tuesday morning. He was feeling great, in full state, as if he was the proprietor of the house, purchased with his winnings from successful deals worth millions. Yesterday's victory had an adverse influence upon his self-confidence. To go somewhere and utter a couple of sentences in order to obtain what one wanted, was not really an achievement, but not according to Charlie! The target for him that day was another university, which was located outside of town. He had a vague idea where it was, but not exactly. On the table in the living room, he spotted a map of the city amongst some newspapers and magazines. Poltic had possibly bought it because he was still not very familiar with the town, especially the newly developed parts. Just because he had spent more than half of his life in this town, did not mean that he should know well some of the residential districts, built surprisingly fast in the last four-five years, on the outskirts of the city.

Charlie decided he did not need the map and headed towards the ambiguous location of the university. Driving much faster than he should, he arrived at the turning he believed he should take. He made a right turn and spent the next forty minutes driving in circles in a residential area, which comprised of numerous high-rise blocks, all looking alike, numbered in a way that it did not make any sense. The buildings were situated in close proximity to the industrial part of town and 90% of the residents were in effect employees of different factories and industrial plants in the vicinity. Charlie stopped to ask someone, whether the educational institution was located near-by. He realized he had got lost when his question was met by a sneering remark, produced by a guy in overalls. Charlie managed to get out of the labyrinth and followed another pedestrian's directions. He continued to be in high spirits and the small road confusion did not override his enthusiasm that easy.

In twenty minutes he was already in front of the university feeling exulted. He had found it! On his entry, Charlie considered the possibility of being confronted with difficulties that time, or just a few. He was greatly mistaken! He had to waste almost the entire day, going from one room to another. Although, he had put the full on appearance, as if he was Poltic again and spoke correctly, asking the right questions, he kept being sent away to "room number such and such". At some point, he had to wait through the staff's lunch break and when he was finally seen, the plump woman kindly sent him off to a different room in the other wing of the building, where he would find exactly what he was looking for. This was where the computers with the required information were located. Charlie was climbing up the stairs to the third floor, where he had been directed and was repeating to himself: "Don't get angry, keep it cool, like M. J., like M. J..." This means of calming himself down worked and a second before he entered the next room, he would appear unruffled and composed. The gentleman, who was sitting behind the machine with the data, whether on purpose or that was just his way, questioned him for half an hour. The employee wanted to know why a young person like him would need information on the students' attendance records and grades. Finally, Charlie managed to overcome the curiosity of the man only to be told that there was a fee to pay in order to acquire the details. Not only was that, but the room, where the fees were collected, was situated in the far end of the building. Charlie felt mentally defeated by all this. He had wasted his time all day and his self-confidence, he had experienced the previous day, had suffered tremendously. "How am I going to be a boss of four young and intelligent professionals if I've just been sent on a goose chase all day in this university? How am I going to give out orders to these people? They'll make me go off my head!" Charlie was thinking and had a point. He managed to get all the necessary information and finally was able to go home. Again, he was driving well over the limit.

In the late afternoon, Charlie was already settled on the sofa in the living room. He did not turn the television on but was looking through the name lists from that day and the previous day. He thought that it would have been great if he had pictures of the students but knew that there was no way anyone would give them to him. He started to cross most of the names out from the top of the list. The people he left uncrossed were those, whose grades were just under excellent. Both universities were very prestigious and expensive. Any students, who had enrolled to study there, had the ambition to excel themselves. In the first name list, Charlie ended up with 23 persons from 164, who fulfilled the criteria. He was surprised to see that more than 100 students had graduated with top marks. The second list gave him another 17 people to choose from. All together 40. To filter them further down, he acknowledged that some of the students had a poor attendance record. "They must be some snotty rich kids who feel privileged with the protection of daddy!" He had witnessed the attitude of some of his fellow students at his university, who somehow received special treatment. Charlie continued to process the data and managed to sift down the candidates to 7 people by employing the second criterion. Their attendance record was the best and their final marks proved to be good enough, with lower grades in just the odd subject. He decided that the task had been completed, as there were no other criteria to apply. So by Tuesday evening, he had fulfilled his job and just had to wait for M. J.'s return at the end of the week. Charlie also decided that he should buy at least one more suit on the next day, as well as some other formal clothes. He realized the benefit of being dressed smart – one got to be called "Sir!"

While planning about what he was going to do in the next few days, alone in the house, Charlie thought of something that had never crossed his mind before. He was not from the people who were usually able to look at a situation from every angle, irrelevant whether he took part in it directly or indirectly. Moreover, the high emotions and the excitement about the newly assigned job were kind of in the way, for him to ask himself a very simple question. "Why had M. J. entrusted him with the management of a team, who was supposed to develop a supermarket chain? Why would Poltic delegate to him such a responsibility, when he knew that Charlie was not that competent and had hardly any experience? He was given a chance for employment?" He doubted that. Charlie knew M. J. very well and was convinced that the latter never rushed into ill-considered decisions. "Stacking shelves in one of these supermarkets would have been more suitable job for me."

Charlie recalled his last job when he was a student – doing deliveries. Quite often he would deliver to the wrong address. The consequences were never that serious for him and the only reason he had stayed in the job for so long was that his workmates would make even bigger errors than him.

During the days until M. J. returned home, Charlie could not get that question: "Why me?" out of his mind. This would be the first thing that he would want to know from his employer. An answer about M. J. needing a trusted person, an assistant or whatever he would call it was just not very compelling. Charlie believed that there was something else and he wanted to know exactly what.

On Sunday morning, Poltic was walking towards his fortress-house. He was stopped by one of the guards at the iron gate to be told that Charlie had gone out on Friday night but had returned home absolutely sober this time. Poltic showed his appreciation about that piece of information and carried on walking. The pleasant morning made him jog the 200-metres stretch to the house. He went straight into his study, and was slightly short of breath. Everything was how he had left it with the only difference that there was the list with seven names on his desk.

It was nearly lunchtime when Charlie got up. He expected Poltic's return later in the day but when he noticed that someone had moved the newspaper, left on the sofa the previous night, to the table, Charlie hurried towards the right room in house. The young man entered without knocking and M. J.'s first words addressed precisely that small slip of Charlie's:

"Knock before you come in, Charlie! Well, Good Morning, now!"

"I'm sorry, M. J., but I just rushed in as soon as I realized you were back. Next time, I'll knock, I promise! When did you get back?"

"This morning! You were still asleep and I know how much you like to have a Sunday lie-in. I see you've prepared the list with seven names! We only need four."

"I know M. J. but all of them cover the criteria and besides, you told me that in this instance, you'd step in to check them out and reduce them to four!"

"That's right, Charlie. I'll gather some more information and three of them will be eliminated. Did you encounter any difficulties on your rounds at the universities? Did you find any part of the job hard?"

"No, I didn't, M. J." there was a hint of impatience in the young man's voice. He felt like skipping over this subject and just wanted to ask the question that bothered him in the last few days. Poltic sensed Charlie's strange behavior and asked him:

"Is there any problem? I was preparing myself for a detailed report on everything you did in my absence but as I see you have no such intentions!"

"Why me, M. J.? I'm not good for this job and you know it! Before I even set foot in the first university, I panicked to the extent of almost ringing you. And on the next day, it was a real nightmare! They nearly drove me crazy – from one room to the next one! I wasted four hours running up and down the stairs until I found the exact place. And before that, I got lost, driving around for almost an hour among the ugly high-rise blocks of a residential area..." Charlie was beginning to break down and Poltic decided to stop this at the start, otherwise the whining would continue incessantly:

"Be quiet!" Poltic raised his voice and Charlie slightly jumped. "Who told you that it will all be easy and pleasant? You had a job to do and judging by the name-list on my desk, you've achieved it. I left you on your own, only to find out how seriously you would take your assignment! From now on, I'm going to be there for you, in every moment. You can count on me every time you come across some difficulties. We are a team, Charlie, a team, where your role is going to increase by the day. Why you? Because you are the only person I trust. Just because you are much younger, it does not mean that I can't think of you as a friend of mine. After your father's death, you've been like a little brother to me. Who can I entrust with investment projects worth millions, my closest person or an employee? Possibly, the latter would perform much better than you but I could never trust him 100%. In big business, when there is big money involved, there is no place for friendship. I am certain that you and I are always going to be friends and yet we could manage billions. Am I right?"

"Yes, you are, M. J." just about able to say the benumbed Charlie. Poltic was right; they would be always friends, no matter what. He could never imagine that there would be a situation where they fell out. Ever!

"Charlie, don't underestimate your abilities! When you feel you cannot manage to do something, just make a bit more effort! And if you don't succeed again, then come to me. If we both fail, at least we'll know that we've tried our best! Do you get me now? And don't get your head inhibited with nonsense because this results in my time being wasted afterwards! I hope, now, you realize the way I see you and you're going to stop asking yourself dim questions."

"Sure, M. J. I just never thought you had such trust in me and besides, you know that I've never been big on any serious stuff so far..."

"I know. Now leave me alone as I've got work to do. Tomorrow, I'm going to give you the four students' addresses, from your list. That will be your next week's task – to visit each of them and present our job offer to them. You'll be provided with instructions about the way you need to conduct the actual meetings at a later time." said M. J. and leaned over some documents on his desk.

Charlie left the room without saying a word. He was feeling strange, unlike his usual self. M. J.'s open confession encouraged him to sense the ambition, running through his veins. Knowing Poltic's real motive behind his nomination for the job, Charlie was prepared to do anything to achieve peak results. After all, who would want to disappoint their best friend?

Poltic was looking at the already signed contracts of Bob, Jane, Geri and Harry. To be precise, Harry's was the one that had drawn Poltic's attention because in his capacity of being a renowned lawyer, he had made a few amendments to the document. They were not that important. One of his wishes included using his own car, as it was more spacious, being a SUV. Harry was in his right to want this, however, if he was driving his own car, Poltic would not be aware of the places his employee went to, where the driver would report everything if Harry used the company car. Well, the lawyer had signed, so Poltic decided to satisfy his insignificant requests for amendments. The other three contracts had been accepted and signed without objections. The only thing that everyone had found displeasing was Poltic's absence when the four arrived to hand their agreements in. On the guards' account, the four were dressed as smartly as they could, which meant that they had undoubtedly imagined to get invited in the house, rather than being left stood outside. The most affected by this had been Geri, where Bob and Jane resigned without complaint to the fact that Poltic was not there. He was not surprised in the slightest that Harry came on Saturday. Although, he had the freedom to decide when to work, he had given his signed contract last, as usual. Poltic was beginning to get used to this characteristic of his and when he actually thought about it, he realized that Harry could only win from that sort of attitude.

People who go to the theatre, for instance, half an hour earlier, would wait in frustration in their seats, whereas Harry arrived just before the start but was never late. For the meeting he attended at Poltic's house last week, he arrived around 10 minutes later. Well, this could be put down to some sort of tradition that most people resorted to. Even Poltic followed this unwritten law of avoiding on purpose the exact arranged time by a few minutes.

During the days Poltic spent in Charlie's future den, he managed to conjure up the working task for each of the professionals working now for him. By putting their signature and date, the contract came into effect and the four had become his employees. As a result, Bob was the first who got hired as he brought the signed document even as early on Tuesday. The next step was to conduct as soon as possible another meeting in the house.

Every beginning is hard. The four needed some time to move and settle in the new houses, to get used to the idea that they would be their new homes, to leave their current jobs and say "good bye" to the colleagues they loved and those they hated. And then, after all this, they had to start working on their new duties. The time they needed to adapt to everything new had to be as short as possible. Poltic believed that taking time to acclimatize to the new environment and to get acquainted with each other was a waste of valuable time. He thought that it was better to speed up things at the beginning so it was easier later. Not always, however, rushing led to good results. Knowing this, Poltic was prepared to give them time to synchronize their actions if the job halted at any moment due to the lack of sufficient familiarity between Bob, Geri, Jane and Harry.

The information about the financial well being of the seven young candidates would have been available by noon of the following day, after which Poltic would bring the number down to four. He would give the selected names and addresses to Charlie, as well as the keys to his house. It was very near but Poltic was certain that it would take at least five-six hours for the slovenly and untidy Charlie, to move all his stuff to the new house. That was the reason why he had set the meeting with the Team the day after tomorrow. M. J. had named them "the Team" from the moment he had the four-signed contracts in his hand. He did not intend to part in any way with Charlie. The real problem was that the people from the Team would be frequent guests in the house and their possible introduction to Charlie would be intolerable. According to Poltic's plan the two teams, the one under his management and the other that Charlie had to gather and supervise, would be working in totally opposite directions. It was nothing personal, just business.

Tuesday

The four professionals arrived precisely at eight o'clock in the evening. It was quite noticeable that everyone had made a real effort about their appearance. The women looked prettier with new hair-dos, especially done for the occasion. Bob was wearing a slightly different suit than last time and Harry had replaced his jeans with black trousers, which made him look much more elegant. Poltic led the mini-fashion parade to the room with the three steps. They entered the hall and instinctively sat down in the same places that Poltic had earmarked for them last time. There was a glass of water on the table in front of each of them. The host unbuttoned his jacket and sat down last, without showing any signs of nervousness or uneasiness about anything at all. He started speaking in calm and even voice that it did not express any emotions.

"Firstly, I would like to thank you all for accepting this work offer. I'm honored to work with professionals of this rank. As you can see, we don't have a bottle of champagne to celebrate, not because we don't have an occasion for it but because the purpose of our meeting today is to note the beginning of our work together. Let's not waste our time with idle talk and start with the commentary on your relocation to your new homes. Each of you will speak up in a strict order, beginning with Bob, then Jane, Geri and lastly – Harry." Poltic looked at each of them straight into their eyes and continued: "The sequence of speaking derives from the order you've handed in your contracts. The second topic of our agenda will be me presenting you with a summary of the specific task that each of you is going to receive. I would appreciate if you do not interrupt me at any point. You can ask questions when I'm finished or if I ask you to. I repeat again," Poltic stressed "do not interject until I have stopped talking about a certain topic." The puzzling authoritarian prohibition to open their mouth required an explanation for the present four.

"Why do I insist on that procedure? To most people, free discussions on specific questions, related to our work, are considered most effective as we all try to find the best solution. Other people, including me, believe that the above is a waste of time. I think the following would fit best our purposes: After I have introduced to you the main points of your obligations and I finish clarifying everything that is important, then we can talk a bit more freely. Until then it will be only me who speaks!"

Poltic felt slightly surprised that no one had interrupted him so far. He expected Harry to be the one who butted in but he, like the rest, was listening carefully, in attempt to comprehend the dictatorial way of speaking of their host.

"Let's start! You, Bob, can begin first with your comments on your forthcoming relocation to the new house!" Bob came out of the daze he had been in until that moment, raised himself a bit from his chair to attain a better position and said:

"Thank you, Mr. Poltic, for letting me speak first. I'll be brief. My wife and I discussed the plan of moving and as you can gather from my signature on the contract, we accept the idea with no objection whatsoever. My wife wanted to know whether she'd be allowed to make some changes to the interior of the house! For instance, could she change some furniture around or even replace some with different furnishings? Well, she likes that sort of stuff." Bob tried to excuse his wife and added. "You mentioned that there is everything necessary in the properties but my wife would like to apply her own style. It's important to her, while for me, it doesn't bother me, to be honest."

"Don't worry, Bob. You can do anything you want to the house you are in charge of. So your wife has the complete freedom to transform the house to her own taste." "Poor Bob!" thought Poltic. "Such a capable person and yet, he is under the control of a woman!"

"This applies to you all", continued Poltic and looked consecutively at Jane, Geri and Harry. "Please, do whatever changes to your new homes, as long as you feel comfortable in them. Is there anything else, Bob, on the subject of the relocation?"

"No, Mr. Poltic, there isn't. That is all. Now, my wife will be more than happy."

"Jane, now it's your turn. Have you discussed the idea with your family? At our first meeting, you shared your concerns with us about a certain dependency on your family's opinion on the subject! What has your husband made of the idea?"

"It's all fine, Mr. Poltic. I've signed, too, haven't I? My husband was not that happy but he'd get used to it!" Poltic felt like finishing her sentence and nearly asked: "Does he have any say in the matter?"

"Surprisingly enough for me, the kids embraced the idea straight away. They find every change exciting and I hope that this one will be as such. About the house, I imagine I'll make some alterations as well and I'm glad that there's permission for that. Well, I've got nothing else to add, maybe, when I see it, then..."

"You're going to see it, Jane, very soon. I've got some information of interest to you, considering your circumstances. Your husband could get a job very near-by. There is an exquisite restaurant located just ten minutes away in the next-door residential area. They are looking for an assistant manager. Your husband has the required experience, so you can mention this opportunity to him!"

"I don't think he'd like that deep down! He loves his restaurant very much, purely because he owns it. He has invested a lot of his time and efforts and I doubt that he would work for someone else but himself. Thank you for the information, Mr. Poltic! I'll mention to him to go and check out the place."

Poltic noticed that Jane was talking about her husband's restaurant as if it was only part of his life and she had nothing to do with it. His observation was not far from the truth. Jane had helped out financially a few times when the struggling eatery was on the rocks. She had done this only because she was married to the owner but never would she go and eat there or visit the place for any other reason! She considered the whole venture, which brought such a small profit, as being futile or to say the least – just a hobby for her partner. Jane thought of the restaurant in the same way she thought of her husband. She did not think much of her partner; hardly respected him and sometimes, she even despised him for the life he had chosen to have, where his only success was his wife.

"It's your call, Jane, but the place is really worth considering. I also have to point out something else for your benefit! It concerns Geri, too. The company has already provided us with a vehicle that will take your children to school and back. What I need from you is the time-schedule of their lessons. If they finish classes at different times, I'll have to supply another car. All three children go to the same school. It's private as far as I am aware, isn't it? What I mean is if, say, your son Geri, goes to an after school club and Jane's kids don't, one car could not physically accommodate everyone's needs. No one wants their children to be waiting for hours, do we?" Poltic drew a close to the subject about school and kids and the two mothers agreed to all with a slight nod. M. J. turned to Geri with the question:

"Have you spoken to your mother about the move, Geri? I recall that you were slightly apprehensive about how she would take the news!"

"Yes, Mr. Poltic, she wouldn't move under any circumstances, as I've expected! It will be just me and my son! At first, my mother was against the idea altogether. You know, she is quite used to living with us two. But then she slowly resigned to my decision, once she realized that she'd be able to come and visit us whenever she wanted and I would go and see her quite regularly. Mr. Poltic, I would not have signed the contract without having my mother's permission first! She means much more than the job offer to me." Geri was overreacting as usual, but this time the word "permission" had topped it all.

"That is quite understandable, Geri! Our family is the most precious thing we've got and one needs to put a lot of effort to keep it together! Please, reassure your mother that she would have a car at her disposal any time around the clock, whenever she feels like seeing you. For me, that's a priority!"

"She'll be over the moon when she hears about you taking our case so seriously! Thank you, Mr. Poltic! I also intended to ask you about possible changes to the interior of our new houses but you've already made it clear to us. So I don't really have anything else to add." Geri said this and had a sip of water. Then she leaned back in her seat, contended with herself. She somehow believed that her little theatrical performance, revealing her fondness of her mother, had just gained her another privilege over the others. It was hardly a coincidence that Jane's credo in life was "More is better than less!"

Finally, it was Harry's turn to speak. Poltic glanced at him as if to invite him to start.

"Mr. Poltic, I have nothing to comment about my new home. Moving is not a problem for me. I have another question, though!"

"I'm listening, Harry. Although, it's not connected to the topic, do share with us what's on your mind!" Poltic allowed Harry to ask his unrelated question, outside their agenda, only to compensate him for his waiting.

"Will our meetings follow the same scenario and order every time so I speak last? I am very unhappy to always wait until I can say my say! Why don't we apply some sort of rotational standard, where we take turns? I was fourth today but next time I start first, then second, etc."

"Harry, at the very start I've made it clear and explained the strict order of speaking that everyone has to follow. You may not like it but these are the interior regulations. Exceptions are possible only in the case of something very important needed saying or if I allow you. This question is no longer under debate! Get used to it, Harry, you have no say in this!" Poltic detected the open hostility in the lawyer's eyes but he took no notice of it and carried on:

"Now, we move on to the next point on our agenda, which involves my detailed account of your tasks. My patrons have sent me some orders related to your first assignments and to be honest, I still remain a little bit surprised about how very few jobs, than I have expected, will be required from you to do within two weeks! The reason for this is that your relocation coincides with your first work engagements. I hope, it won't take you too much time to move in your new places and than by the end of this week, you have completed with your new domestic arrangements. Now, we start with Bob again according to the already established order. Oh, I nearly forgot, before we continue…" Poltic put his hand in his pocket and got four keys out which he passed to each of them.

"The houses are identical so you'll know which is yours by the number on the key. It matches the one visible from the street. You all know where your new homes are, don't you?" A general "yes" from everyone received M. J. to his question. The houses were situated on the same road that led to Poltic's property. In that respect the four had passed them a few times, even so if in the dark. Charlie was already waiting for his new neighbors without having a clue that they, too, were working for Poltic.

"You, Bob, you have a specific knowledge in the share trading field. A number of people have worked for you and you are experienced in all sorts of transactions on the stock market! As I've mentioned to you at our previous meeting, the company's main objective will be looking at the large and medium-sized meat manufacturers. The two largest businesses on the market, with the largest production volume, have put some of their shares on the stock exchange. The first company is trading around 37% of its shares and the controlling stake is in the hands of about ten people, whereas for the second one, the percentage is reaching almost 40 and just eight people control the majority of shares. We want to become the largest company in the meat market within five years and this automatically turns the two already mentioned manufacturers in becoming our main rivals. Through the medium of your expertise, Bob, we plan to purchase all shares available on the stock market. All of them! By the way, I've been explicitly told not to disclose any names, so I'll use numbers and call these companies "the first" and "the second". We are aware that by acquiring the shares for sale, we won't gain that much of an influence over those companies. It will be just an initial move on our side. With a job well done at hand, in the forthcoming years, our biggest competition is going to be under our control. As things stand, we need to obtain a full analysis of the financial state of the two companies and most importantly – of the price movement of the shares we are interested in. Well, Bob, that will be your task. The research analysis has to cover the previous year, starting from the beginning of this month. Please, do not hesitate to employ staff to help you. Actually, that is quite necessary. I do apologize for the way I describe your future job but I do not have much knowledge about shares and so on. At the end of our meeting, you will receive everything you require and need, organized by an employee of the company, who has more expertise in this field than me. Now, Bob, I am ready to listen to your questions if you have any."

In reality, the expert-employee was Poltic himself. He struggled quite a bit until he had managed to draw up the task in written form. He was determined to present the paper work without leaving any doubt that it was written by someone, who had no understanding, whatsoever, about the stock market trade. Poltic had coped with his own ignorance on the subject by adeptly referring to volumes of academic literature and in some places; he even openly cribbed from the texts. He applied exactly the same approach when formulating the tasks for Jane, Geri and Harry.

"Mr. Poltic, my assignment sounds very interesting. From what I gather, it involves making a research analysis. I have made hundreds of these, Mr. Poltic. I have no queries about the assignment itself but I feel uncertain about the fixed time limit. Two weeks is not enough to analyze such great volume of data. We need to examine not only the average value of the shares of these companies for a period of one year but we also have to look into their major contractors that trade with them. I'm afraid to say this but they are probably more than hundred. That is quite a lot and not out of the norm when we talk about big businesses. They will always attract an interest." Poltic noticed how Bob had turned very confident when he mentioned that he had done hundred such analyses. That meant he did not lie. He did not look like someone who could lie easily and plausibly. Poltic replied in the following manner:

"The time limit is quite short, that's true! However, our objectives require fast actions. You, Bob, are going to prepare a very detailed and professional analysis! I have no doubts about this! Efficiency is of prime importance to us. Therefore, we require less information. In order to complete the task by the deadline, my advice is to glean only information that has a direct influence to our future work. In other words and figuratively speaking, we need data, related to our main characters and really so much the bigger picture! Do you understand, Bob?"

"Yes, Mr. Poltic. I do. At first, I had a slightly different understanding but now I see what you mean. I'll only need 4-5 people to process the data faster and that's it!"

"It's up to you how many people you need. Think carefully about it and if you require more assistants, do not hesitate to hire them. Well, that will be all, Bob! And before we continue and discuss your job, Jane, I'd like to enquire about your previous occupational engagements. Have you all managed to discontinue your working contracts? Legally, you can take up as many employments as you can physically manage, however, on the basis of the conditions in our working agreement, that you are all very familiar with by now, you need to leave your old jobs as soon as possible!" the person, whose turn from then on was always first, uttered:

"Mr. Poltic, I handed my resignation in, which was approved straight away on Friday. So now, I am totally committed to working for you!"

The second person to speak said:

"In my case, it's all clear, too! I'm the sole owner of my consultancy company and the only thing I need to do is to appoint one of the assistant managers to take charge of the business. My intention is to sort this out tomorrow but I can arrange it over the phone this evening, if you like!"

"No, Jane, there's no need for that. Follow your plans about it. It's your decision exactly when to part with your occupational duties if there are no difficulties to do it. It's your turn, Geri!"

"Well, today is Tuesday, Mr. Poltic, and I reckon I could draw my contractual obligations at the research agency to a close by Friday. Presently, we are doing an extensive research poll, to which, of course, I'm head of and I couldn't really leave my colleagues to their own devices."

"Oh, Geri, do finish your project, please. It's not professional to desert your workmates in time they need your help! I gather you are under a bit of pressure with this assignment. Do you think you will find the time to move with your son to your new house by the end of this week?"

"Don't worry about this, Mr. Poltic! On Saturday and Sunday, there'll be enough time to move our stuff. My mother will pack all our belongings, ready to move. We'll hire a truck and a few strong guys to help with the removal and everything will be done very quickly."

"Perfect, Geri! You've thought about everything! And you Harry, when do you intend to move in your home?"

"Any time, Mr. Poltic, it's not a problem for me. I can move straight away. I don't have that much stuff to take, so it won't take long." replied Harry, who showed no real desire to talk at a length. He was obviously feeling still a bit hurt that his democratic proposal was rejected undemocratically by Poltic.

"Alright, then, let's move on and talk about Jane's duties. Your consultancy firm has been involved in giving out financial advice. It recommends financial solutions to companies and provides professional services like asset management. In other words, you help businesses to become more efficient in their dealings, to decrease expenditure and improve their profitability. Is that so, Jane? Please, correct me if I'm wrong!"

"In broad outlines, Mr. Poltic, that's correct! I'd only like to add, that we specialize in working for clients, who experience substantial financial lost. Our assistance is hardly ever sought after, when companies are doing well."

"Well, logically!" Poltic thought to himself. "Jane, your job is going to be slightly different than the job you've been doing so far! The reason is that the company that requires your advice on how to achieve financial stability has not been set up, yet. This, in any case, does not mean that your efforts right now are unwarranted! Our company will expand in good time and then you are going to be a valuable asset to us, giving us some priceless piece of advice. I firmly believe that thanks to you, we are going to prosper! We are far from that moment in future so your present assignment involves drawing up an exemplary model for a good asset management of the future company. You can start from the basic rules, applicable for, say, small businesses and then move on to much bigger economic structures." Poltic remembered his essay but he knew it was not the right time for recollections. "When we meet again in two weeks and everyone presents the result of their assigned task, Jane, you will have to deliver a lecture to us about how to avoid wasting resources for the newly born company. You understand what's required from you, Jane, don't you?"

"Indeed, I do, Mr. Poltic, despite the descriptive way you used to explain it to me. It seems, my job is going to be the easiest because the basic methods of managing capitals have been known for centuries. I don't want to sound as if I boast but the volumes of literature on the subject that I have read… It will be my pleasure to introduce you to some of the most important economic principles, which we'll have to follow closely."

"Please, Jane, prepare a copy of your written presentation for each of us, in the instance we need to refer to some facts during your speech."

"No problem, Mr. Poltic! I could even illustrate my work with some diagrams and tables and visualize my examples in that way."

"It's a very good idea. I can see that your project invokes some pleasant emotions. Before I continue with Geri, have you got any questions?" Jane delayed her reply by 5 seconds and uttered:

"Oh, I'm sorry! I've already fond myself, in my mind, in some of the books I'm going to need! I can't think of anything else, Mr. Poltic. Maybe, you could advise me on the volume of my work! How extensive would you like it to be?"

"What I've told Bob, the same applies for you! We expect only the most important stuff and we are not interested in the insignificant details. I don't even question your abilities and I'm certain that you could prepare a detailed report for our next meeting. However, it will be great if your lecture does not last more than 20 minutes. Well, I don't want to be the killjoy of your enthusiasm, so your written presentation can be more informative."

"I shall summarize only the points of importance, Mr. Poltic. I won't find it hard to do this. I'll have to resort to some of my ex-employees' services but you've already clarified this matter."

"Good! Next, I need to introduce our sociologist Geri to her task." Poltic stopped for a moment and looked around at the four people round the table. Interestingly, Bob and Jane had changed their lukewarm and concentrated look on their face, they had at first. They appeared absolutely elated after they heard what their jobs would involve. The only logical reason for this transformation could be that the goose that laid the golden eggs, in other words – Poltic had given them some very easy tasks and in return they would receive a huge salary, a car and a personal chauffeur, a new house in a VIP residential district. Their professional skills were much greater than the efforts they needed to apply in order to achieve what was required from them. Poltic did not doubt that he would receive the same reaction from Geri and Harry. Neither of the four, however, knew that their contractual relationship with him was based on a kind of "agreement for life". He believed that their entire life was in his hands and what they considered easy then, would become later on so hard that they had never imagined. Of course, these theoretical speculations only existed in Poltic's imagination.

"Geri, you are going to be a key factor in our company!" the sociologist ceased to look at the enormous curtains that were blocking the view to the garden, and turn her eyes towards the man, who addressed her.

"The market is unpredictable, no matter what product we are talking about! But there is a way to find out some information about the future of the market and get a full picture. The opinion poll is a good means to obtain this information. The research poll you need to conduct has one peculiarity and that is to find out about the influence the largest six companies on the meat production market have in their respective areas. You really need to look into just these six companies and not bother with the rest, which are too small for us to incite our interest. We want a reliable data about the consumers' preferences with regards to the products they like to buy and the popularity of the manufacturers by location. You will require quite a few people to fulfill the task. They will have to carry out the research poll in each region. You are completely aware of this, of course!" Geri was listening very carefully. She regarded Poltic's words as if he was talking to a child:

"Mr. Poltic, what you require from me is to conduct a standard research poll but I think that you don't really need it. I believe, what you need to know is which meat products are most sold and have made their name on the market, as well as which companies are behind those products, etc.! This sort of information you could easily obtain from the official documentation of the respective companies, published every six months. We could also make our inquiries with the advertising agencies, which provide services to the businesses in question. In that way, we can find out about the state of the market in any region without having to go out on the streets and ask people about what they eat and who has made their food! A research poll will only confirm what we can get without actually going on the streets."

"You have a point, Geri! The way you've put it, an opinion poll seems unnecessary. I need to ask you, though... To what extent do you think "the official", as you called it, data is trustworthy?"

"Well, the information might be slightly distorted but that's not out of the norm. On the whole, we can rely on it."

"Look, Geri, if you like you could prepare some official information from the sources you've mentioned. Nevertheless, your job is to discover what people like! We are not interested in the fact that they change their preferences every day and one moment they purchase one product and in the next it's something else. In the future, when our company becomes a major player on the market, we are going to resort to your expertise in carrying out some research polls again. We won't really trust any public information data. I'm certain that when our company establishes itself, our rivals would intensify their efforts in releasing, even more so, officially misrepresented information. Do you get me, Geri? Please, keep in mind that I am purely a mediator to my patrons' idea of the priority of conducting a research about the consumers' dispositions."

"Alright, Mr. Poltic! There's no problem for me to do it. I'll need three people in each area to conduct the study. I shall gather some official data and bring it next time if you don't mind, Mr. Poltic, just in case!"

"We could have a look at it, too, but apply your efforts mainly to performing the research well. Do you have questions before we move on to Harry's assignment?"

"Just one. How representative should the study be? Have you got any specific requirements, because if you don't, I'm thinking to apply the standard method of questioning 0.5% of the population in each region?"

"Geri, I don't have any explicit orders on the matter, so I leave it up to you. Anything else?"

"No, Mr. Poltic. I can't think of anything else!"

"It's Harry's turn now." Poltic said and tried to meet the eyes of the only jurist in the room. He was silent and still this evening and the reason was blatantly written on his face. Harry was very tired. Poltic did not really intend to rush when explaining his duties but decided that there was no point to be too detailed, considering the lawyer's state of mind.

"Harry, you are last to hear about your job. You'll take care of the legality of every action of our company. Firstly, you will be responsible for all the commercial agreements between us and our business partners. These contracts have to be flawless to the tiniest detail. I hope, our company will sign sound agreements, based on your good knowledge of the Law and with the help of your formal colleagues." Almost without taking a breath Poltic continued. "Secondly, you will direct the law departments of the companies we're going to buy. All these are your future obligations! In relation to our meeting in two weeks, I'm going to ask you to draw up a draft agreement for a purchase of a company, worth 40 million and which has a staff of 3300. These figures nearly match those in the financial report of a real company we may be interested in the future. Do your research; find the information you need in order to prepare the model purchase agreement. How you're going to do this is entirely up to you. The main thing we'd like to know is what this kind of contract looks like: how it is structured, its clauses and particulars, etc. So later on, when we reach the point of the real purchase, we know exactly what alterations and improvements to suggest. Any questions, Harry?"

"There is a small problem, Mr. Poltic, but judging by your words to my three colleagues before me, I believe you won't find it disconcerting. I've made many of these agreements in the past, even though; they were for much smaller companies. Their structure is nearly always strictly confined by certain legal requirements. We take into consideration the company business activity, of course. I'm looking at minimum of 500 pages if I take your data facts as a starting point and that's the problem. But as you've said already that you need only the important stuff, so I could bring it down to 100."

"I'm glad you've understood correctly my requisite for concision when completing your assignments. Harry, will you need some assistance? Do you intend to hire more people?"

"Mr. Poltic, this sort of contract could never be drawn up by just one lawyer. It's usually done by a team so I'm thinking of employing at least three colleagues."

"Excuse my ignorance, I really didn't know that! It'll be three of them, then. Right, now we can move on to a free discussion about everything that's been mentioned this evening." A moment of democracy has taken place at the meeting. Harry slightly raised his left hand and began:

"Mr. Poltic, I suggest we draw an end to our meeting and go home! My colleagues and I have been introduced to our assignments and it's better to just get our hands on with the real work! Colleagues, what do you think?" At this moment, Poltic felt that someone else had just taken his role to direct the meeting and ask questions. To retain his leadership, he immediately spoke:

"It's a very good idea, Harry! If you all have nothing important to ask, we better end our meeting. You need to sleep on it and process the information. Then more questions may occur that you can't think of them right now. What would you say about it, Bob? You're first to speak, as usual." Bob and the rest took their turn only to agree with the proposal, so the meeting was drawn to a close. Just before everyone left the fortress-house, Poltic brought the written versions of everyone's work-project.

He sent his guests out to the exit door as any polite host was expected to do and then he returned to the meeting room. "They are all really good professionals!" Poltic said to himself, while slowly going around the rectangular table. He was not in a state to sit in one place. "Hmm, they've all worked out what's in their interest and have behaved themselves this evening. They've been much calmer than at the first meeting, when Geri and especially Harry showed their real character. Well, what can you do? Money is money!" He had noticed something quite interesting this evening. It was the same like last time; no one tried to get to know each other on a personal level. They hardly looked at each other, as if they were too shy. Poltic considered this kind of coldness between people as quite normal when a new team was formed. He expected, however, that in time, they would get closer to each other and through their vigorous commitment to working for the company, they would become the Team, he had pictured in his mind. He also hoped that them being neighbors as well, it would help them befriend each other, which in itself was in the interest of their work and this would make them more efficient. The only drawback he could see was that none of them had anything in common, with regards to their professional qualifications and skills. Each of them was an expert in a field that the rest had no knowledge whatsoever. Poltic decided that this sort of thoughts in his head were absolute nonsense. Only time would show whether a friendship between the members of the Team was possible and how it would affect their efficiency.

Poltic stopped his circular motion around the table and sat down to have a little rest from the numerous ideas and speculations about the Team that were overtaking his mind and as much as from going physically in circles. This activity, he knew, was typical for people who had some kind of mental problems and it was not appropriate to be practiced by someone, destined to become a great person in the future. He was normal, sane and mentally sound human being. Poltic just remembered that it was Tuesday, the day that another one of his most significant employees had met up with the first former student from the name-list. It was almost 9 o'clock in the evening, which meant, by that time; Charlie must have completed his task successfully and had gained the young specialist over to work for him.

The Young Ones

Charlie was driving his Mercedes towards the location, where the first student lived. He managed to find the address without getting lost like last time. This time, he made sure he found the right place and the route to it on the map beforehand. Charlie parked the car in front of a big nine-storey block of flats. It had seven entrances. He sat for a few minutes in the car so he could mull over once again the instructions, given to him by M. J. The main points included: "Be brief and precise, present them with our offer and emphasize on the huge salary, and no idle talk! If they accept your conditions, make them an appointment for the end of the week, when they'll learn about their strict obligations and sign a contract. Don't answer any additional questions! Make sure every meeting does not take longer than 15 minutes." he remembered Poltic's words almost by heart.

Charlie came out of the car and headed towards the third floor of entrance "B", where Tony, who graduated a month ago, lived together with his parents and sister. He climbed up the stairs instead of taking the lift in the hope that he would calm down a bit. His heart speeded up from the physical exertion. On reaching his target, he took a deep breath and breathed out loudly. He repeated the divers' exercise three times and rang the bell.

A woman in her 50-ies, wearing a dressing gown, opened the door. Charlie stood there with a straight back and a serious look on his face. His smart suit was the final touch of his whole appearance. The jacket cleverly concealed the heart muscle, which was eager to escape from the prison of Charlie's chest.

"Good morning, madam! I am looking for Tony. Is he in?" Charlie said softly and smiled. Poltic specifically told him to be as polite as possible and to always think before he said anything when it was his turn to speak. He did not want him to say something stupid and fail everything just because he rushed to open his mouth before thinking about it.

"Yes, he is here. And you are? I know all his friends but I don't know you!" the mother asked harshly. Charlie felt nervous because he did not expect such unfriendly welcome. Still with a wide grin on his face he answered:

"Madam, I don't know your son and I'm here precisely to meet him. I have a good business proposal for him. He's recently graduated and because he is a young specialist with a lot of potential in the field of management, I'm here to offer him a job."

"What job?" the mother asked again as if she was the one sought after for the employment opportunity. Charlie felt he had to put a stop to the pointless rigmarole with the far too nosy woman and left the good manners aside, despite M. J.'s orders not to do this:

"I can't tell you that! This is only of your son's concern. If you don't call him now, I'm leaving and he is going to miss on the attractive proposition that I've come here for." Charlie turned around and pressed the button to call the elevator, totally aware that the start was not a success.

"Sir, wait a second! I'm just going to get him. I don't want him to miss on some good job, do I?"

Tony was a fine-looking young fellow, despite the fact that he was quite short. He was well mannered, too, in contrast to his tetchy mother. Tony invited the stranger to his room where Charlie went straight to the point, according to the scenario.

"Thank you for agreeing to see me, Tony. My name is Charlie and I represent a large company that has different business activities. The firm is interested in developing a chain of supermarkets in the near future. I've been entrusted with this project and I have to find four young specialists, who will manage the process. I want you to be one of them!" Charlie fired away those few sentences with such a speed that made it difficult for anyone to decipher his words. He continued in the same spirit. "You will have a company car, a modern office will be your work-place and you'll get a salary of 5000. If you are interested and accept my offer, I shall be waiting for you at this address." Charlie gave him a piece of paper. "At 12 o'clock on Saturday." The man opposite him had been gaping at him with a mouth wide open from the moment Charlie mentioned the salary figure until the final word of his monologue.

"Is this some kind of joke?"

"No, it's not a joke! You have time to think until Saturday and now, I have to go, I'm afraid…"

"Is that all? You come in to my home, offer me a job and lots of money and then just leave! You can't just do this!" Tony raised his voice and stood in his way. To leave, Charlie had to resort to his physical strength and apply it towards the short man. Instead, he decided to warm up the situation and avert a fight with the clear winner:

"You are right, Tony. It sounds incredible but my bosses instructed me to tell you only this. To be honest, what I know is that they are looking for four people to manage the building process of several big stores and everything in connection with it. I can't tell you more. Can I go now?"

"Yes, sure. I'm sorry but it all came to me like a bolt from the blue! I'll think about Saturday."

Charlie left the building and stopped the timer on his wristwatch. Tony and his mother took up exactly 13 minutes of his time. It was all done within the time limit. Charlie was certain that Tony was coming on Saturday, especially after he had just seen the poor conditions he was living in. He felt a bit guilty that he has a car and his own place, and someone, who was his own age and who probably had more and better skills than him, was living in such a hovel. "That's life!" Charlie said to himself, not that he had any idea about what life was…

Next was Lorrie. After she had graduated from university, she started to look for a job straight away. Her not excellent grades had sent her to this neighboring little town, where the competition at the labor market was significantly less. She found employment as an assistant-accountant. Apart of being good with figures, Lorrie loved some other subjects, that she had studied, and very much so "Management Fundamentals". She seriously knew her stuff on the subject, that she liked to imagine she was a director of a big company, where she successfully applied the methods she had learned from the textbook.

Charlie had his name list at hand that comprised of four names and addresses. He looked at the piece of paper a few times to double-check that the number matched the one on the sign. He was 100%

sure about the name of the street. Then he thought that Poltic had made a mistake but cast this thought away as wicked. He got off the car and entered the building. There was a very big sign above the entry door that said "Accountancy Services". In effect, this was a two-storey house, turned into an office building so it had lost its residential function for a long time. Charlie was met by a woman, a secretary, he thought, judging by her age and short skirt. "Didn't all secretaries wear these?" he asked himself, knowing the correct answer.

"Good morning, Sir! How can help you?"

"Good morning! I am looking for Lorrie. Just work…"

"Lorrie is in room number 3, through here, Sir!" Charlie followed the directions and noticed that there was a corridor, leading from the secretary's office to several numbered rooms, situated on both sides. Before he attempted to knock and meet candidate number 2 from the list, he remembered Poltic's words about being as brief as possible. The timer had counted out three minutes already and the young man felt he had to hurry up. He knocked twice and entered. Lorrie was typing on the computer keyboard but the stranger made her stop.

"What are you looking for, Sir? You seem you have come to the wrong room. Tell me who do you need to see so I can show you the right way?" Lorrie decided that this young man, who was her age, had got lost because she personally did not work with clients but just processed data and paper work all day.

"I don't think I've got it wrong. That's number 3, isn't it?"

"That's right, it is number 3, but it's only me, who works here."

"Right then, so you must be Lorrie. I am looking for you. I can see you're busy so I'll try to be quick. Let me introduce myself and explain why I'm here. My name is Charlie and I represent a big company that has different interests. The company wants to invest in developing a chain of supermarkets. I'm here to offer you a job to become a part of a team of four people, who are going to coordinate and manage the whole process of building these shops." Charlie took a breath and continued. "You will receive a car, a modern office and a salary of 5000. If you are interested, please, come to this address on Saturday at 12 o'clock." the unexpected guest came closer and gave Lorrie a small piece of paper. He felt that the moment for numerous questions on her part, that he had to avoid, was coming.

"Good bye, Lorrie and don't be late!" These were his last words before he left the room.

The effect of the words, so perfectly declaimed, was spectacular. His speech made small Tony to turn on against big Charlie and now, it made one person completely lose the ability to speak. Charlie sat in his car and true to himself he did not drive off straight away. "Maybe, Lorrie won't come? Maybe I scared her off? If Poltic did not surprise me with giving me her work address and I visited her at home instead, maybe things would have gone more smoothly. No, maybe not. M. J. is always right." Charlie ended the dialogue with himself and drove off to his new house. He thought to call by and see Poltic, so he could report of how the two meetings went that day, but then he gave up on the idea, knowing that Poltic would not be very happy about how he conducted them.

Charlie could not understand Poltic's way of thinking and probably he would never manage to understand it. The idea, to just go to a stranger and make him such an attractive offer and then, to just turn around and leave, was something beyond his imagination. Moreover, he offered Lorrie a job, while she was at her workplace. Charlie could see the absurdity in all this and he felt that what had happened today only proved that he was right. But he was wrong! About everything! Well, at least he followed the instructions and his different opinion did not affect him doing his job. Loyalty surpassed straightforward logic. Poltic was aware of Charlie's occasional incapability to comprehend some of the situations he would find himself in but with time passing, he would learn. It was still early days!

On Wednesday morning, Charlie left the house with the intention to fulfill his task there and then, and the days left until Saturday, he would spend watching television. He did not know then, that his time off would be cut short by one day.

The address he had to find, where a girl called Kate was supposed to be, was located on the Main Street in town. This did not surprise Charlie in the slightest and he confidently headed towards the restaurant that matched the required address. A few minutes later, he came out of the place, looking gloomy and mumbling something to himself. He had to come back on the next day, at 7 o'clock in the evening, when Kate, the waitress was beginning her shift. The restaurant manager had refused to give him her home address, which added to his mood being spoiled even further. Yet, the day was not a complete failure because there was the fourth student left to visit.

Charlie found himself in one of the poorest and unwelcoming residential areas in town. A slight fear took hold of him for a moment, when a group of some youths stared out at his car for longer than usual. Despite this, he went into the block of flats he was looking for, which resembled very much the one Tony lived in. He rang the bell twice as he always did and waited. A woman, who was clearly in her 70s, slightly bent down with age, opened the door.

"Good afternoon, Madam! Is Michael here?" When he was just getting ready to receive another rude response, the old woman replied in a manner, more polite than his:

"Michael is out at work. Can I take a message, Sir?"

"It's very kind of you but I need to speak to him in person. Could you, please, tell me when he's finishing work, so I can call by again? I don't want to disturb you gratuitously!" the dialogue was beginning to look a lot like something from a Latin soap series and those, Charlie – the sworn television addict, did not watch.

"You can find him usually at about 7 o'clock in the evening. I'm almost certain that he is home by this time. He finishes work at 6 but until he makes his way to our remote neighborhood…, you know? Wait! I almost forgot. Tonight he works double shift and he won't be at home before midnight, I am really sorry…" the woman appeared truly uncomfortable about the fact that she could not please the mysterious visitor.

"Thank you very much, Madam. I will come tomorrow then. Have a good day!" She wished him back the same and closed the door.

Charlie's mood remained positive, despite the fact that the entire day had been wasted. The old woman had made him feel an important and valued person, someone who could be trusted. It is a good job that M. J. made sure and required of him to dress smartly, as well as to watch the way he spoke, otherwise he would have probably witnessed some doors being slammed in front of him at the first clumsy sentence that came out of his mouth.

Charlie had discovered two factors that helped towards his new image and contributed to the different attitude towards him, he received from people he met. Poltic would add a third contributory aspect in the image-making process for turning the carefree youth into a valuable professional. That was the flash car he was awarded first. It acted as a main tool in the formation of a positive public opinion about Charlie for one simple reason: it was the first thing everyone saw, when he went out on the street. Naturally, speculations would follow: "Who is this rich, educated and good young man driving the car?" Poltic knew that even if a poor beggar sat behind the wheel, people would be thinking in the same way. Charlie started the engine of the unsuspected image-making instrument and drove on to the motorway towards home. He got there just before 2 o'clock in the afternoon and gave himself up to a nice nap in front of his favorite television set. It was only a few inches smaller than the one in Poltic's house.

The phone had been ringing for the tenth time and it was then when Charlie went to pick it up. He thought he was dreaming but the persistent ring refuted that idea. He lifted the receiver and said "hello", not knowing who was at the other end. There was only one possible person that could be phoning him – Poltic.

"What are you up to, Charlie? I didn't expect to find you at home."

"Oh, M. J., is that you? E-eh, I was just having a little nap and by the time I got to the phone…"

"You're sleeping at 4 in the afternoon? Don't you have things to do? How's the job going?" Poltic decided that if Charlie allowed himself to sleep in the middle of the day, something had gone pear-shape!

"E-erh…cool, M. J., if you wanna I'll come over to tell you all about."

"If everything is fine, I'm glad. I'm busy tonight and I can't see you and give you any attention, Charlie. When you find the four, come over so I give you new instructions. You are aware you must complete the task until the end of the week?"

"I know, M. J. I haven't forgotten."

"Have you decided what day and where you're going to meet them, if they come, of course?"

"I've met up with the first two in the list so far and I've told them to come over to my house on Saturday. Does this sound good, M. J.?" Poltic did not say anything for a few seconds before he replied. He was not very happy with the idea about the meeting, taking place in Charlie's house, while the people from the Team were moving their stuff next door. He had to suggest something else:

"Listen, Charlie, I thought of a better place to hold the meeting and that is the office they are going to work in from now on. It is completely ready now. Have you got anything to write on at hand so I can give you the address?"

"Just a moment, M. J.! Yes, go on!" he jotted down the address and with that, the first ever phone call in this house had come to an end. Charlie went back to the sofa but remembered that Tony and Lorrie had not been told about the new meeting place on Saturday. This would create extra work for him the next day. At least he knew now how to find them and he had a whole day before seeing to Kate and Michael in the evening.

The fourth day of this week was cold and wet. Charlie did not like the rain and was not keen on umbrellas, either. He had just passed the message about the changed location of the meeting to Tony's mother, who did not miss to ask him, this second time round, whether he was not from some sect, trying to win her son over. Charlie did not reply, leaving her in doubt about the truthfulness of his intentions. After he left the vehicle for a second time to inform Lorrie as well, on his return he became even wetter.

Charlie made a wish like a small kid for the rain to stop by this evening and even better if it did before 7 p. m. At half past six, there was not a trace of the rain. He stopped about 5 meters away from the entrance of the restaurant and began to wait for Kate's arrival. He had never seen her, neither had he had a picture of her, but the manager, who refused to give him her home address on the previous day, had inadvertently helped him. He could not answer Charlie's question, at first, whether a Kate worked in the restaurant because the girl's full name was Kathleen. Then her boss remembered: "Oh, yes, there is this small girl with curly hair, she is one of the new waitresses." Charlie noticed a young woman, who fitted the description, walking on his side towards the restaurant. Her head was bowed down so if he wanted to speak to her, he had to step in her way. Instead, he called out her name when she came near him. Kate raised her eyes and looked at the polished tall young man. Having drawn her attention, Charlie greeted her with "Good afternoon", although it was already getting dark outside and it had been raining all day. He introduced himself and recited his say even faster this time. Kate listened carefully but did not show any sign of emotion when she heard the amazing offer from the stranger.

"O. K. I'll come. On Saturday, I work evening shifts, anyway. I'm free during the day."

Charlie stood there startled and speechless. Something was not right! What did just happen here a minute ago? There was no explanation. She said just "OK" and sneaked in the restaurant. Again, Charlie had presented himself as a very polite young gentleman, who had a remarkable offer. "What did happen and why?" He was asking himself without being able to answer. It was simple but not for Charlie.

All people are different and they react to the same thing in their own different way. In this case, Tony's and Lorrie's different responses were followed by a third type of behavior, that of Kate. And the reason? The reason was her different personality or another way of thinking. The possibilities of how one could react were endless but Charlie believed that Tony's and Lorrie's ways to react to instances like this were typical and that also exhausted all other alternatives. He expected a surprise, temporary lost of the ability to speak, mild aggression or in other words – the emotions, exhibited by Tony and Lorrie. That is why he was so astonished by Kate's open indifference.

Charlie collected himself after the strange encounter with Kate and then, he was on his way to meet the last person from the list. Approaching the remote district, he felt really anxious to remember the youth gang that had examined his car the previous day. Today was even worse because it was already dark outside. "What about if the street lights don't work and someone nicks my car, or I get mugged?" He was getting a little paranoid but managed to calm down. For safety reasons, he parked the vehicle as close as possible to the entrance, although, in this way it blocked the street. He was feeling reassured by the knowledge that he had to spend no more than 15 minutes with Michael. Charlie believed he would make sure it was even just 10.

A man at his age opened the door. He was dressed in a blue long-sleeved T-shirt with no writing on it and tracksuit bottoms. Charlie introduced himself and for the fourth time, like an actor, he spelled out his lines he had learnt by heart. Michael was keeping the door ajar, showing clearly that he was not in the mood for having guests at 8 p. m.

"Well, I'll come on one condition." Charlie did not have to answer any additional questions, according to the instructions he had, but he felt he could not afford to miss the last from the list, just because of one inquiry.

"I'm listening, Michael."

"I've been working all day like a dog, come home and you just appear from somewhere to offer me a job. Why me?"

"We want to employ young and perspective specialists and…"

"Oh, come on! Think of something better to say!" Charlie had to put an end to this conversation as things were getting out of control. An idea suddenly came to his mind and put a wide smile on his face. He remembered Poltic's explanation about why they did not need the top students but those with average grades. It took Charlie just a couple of sentences to convince Michael why he had been selected; in the same way Poltic had done it to him.

The car was still waiting for him intact in front of the block and Charlie, feeling happy with his own quick-wittedness, set off for M. J.'s house. It was already quite late but he had to follow the instructions and go straight to Poltic, after he met up with all four. The two-door black Mercedes approached the property and the security guards rushed to open the iron gate. Charlie found M. J. eating his supper alone in the enormous dining room. On the table, which could accommodate for at least 14 people, there was a dish served for one more person. Charlie greeted M. J. with "Good evening" and sat down to keep him company. He was not surprised to see a second plate on the table. The reason: there was plenty of time, from the gate being open for him to his arrival to the house itself, for Poltic to fill the bowl with some of the still warm potato soup. They finished eating in silence, as usual.

"Right, Charlie, you must have managed to complete your job so far, if you are here now." M. J. spoke out at last. Charlie had finished his dinner a couple of minutes earlier than Poltic and was waiting for him to start a conversation.

"Yes, M. J. I've actually come back straight from Michael's house and a little while before that I've met up with Kate, too. Everything's cool! The three of them were very surprised when I offered them the job. Only Kate reacted in a strange way, I even think that she did not understand me at all."

"Charlie, she has understood everything, quite well. They all have comprehended everything. Don't worry about it. How many of them will come to the meeting on Saturday, do you reckon?" Poltic knew the right answer but just felt like testing Charlie, if he had realized the effect the given offer had had on these people.

"U-uh, what can I tell ya? They all agreed, I think. But I don't know... I haven't seen so startled people. Who knows, they might just change their minds..."

"The surprise, Charlie, is our chief means to attract qualified personnel to work for us."

"I don't get it, M. J. I think I even scared off Lorrie, we nearly had a fight with Tony and Kate, she didn't care at all. She was not surprised in the slightest. How come?" Poltic owed an explanation to Charlie; otherwise instances like this could torture his mind for a long time ahead. He leaned over, put his hands on the table, clasped his fingers and asked:

"Charlie, what would you do if someone came to you and offered you exactly the same thing like you did to these four young people? Please, don't answer me!" Poltic raised his hand as if to stop him from speaking. "I'll tell you. You'll be surprised, you'll want to ask questions, and you'll shout and think it's a joke or that you're the luckiest guy. But when the emotions fade away and you are left alone with your thoughts, you'll be pondering over what you've heard. Am I right?"

"I haven't put myself in their shoes but you're probably right M. J."

"What does a car, an office and a salary of 5000 mean to each of them?" Poltic carried on with the questions. He did not want to simply spell it out for him by saying: "They'll come, because we give them everything they've wanted!" he hoped that Charlie would come to this conclusion by himself.

"M. J., I'm pretty tired, don't grill me here! I've done everything you asked me to but how many of them would come and why, I just haven't got a clue! I know we are giving them a great deal of money and all should show up on Saturday. But I don't know for sure, I can't control people. If they come, they come." Poltic realized that Charlie had no problem to understand everything but in his own way. That's why he stopped tormenting him with questions.

"I can only agree with you, Charlie. Now come with me to give you the materials you need for the meeting. I've written down everything in a way for you to only read it out."

Charlie picked the few pages and left the house. Back home he went straight to bed and fell asleep. He had enough time to have a good rest until the day of the meeting and to familiarize himself in detail with the new instructions.

It was 11:30 a. m. on Saturday and Charlie was on his way to the new meeting location. He personally did not know exactly where the place was situated and together with the four expected guests, he was going to visit it for the first time. The building was located in the purposefully developed business-centre in town, where thousands of offices, different in their size, were there to meet the needs of any type of company. Most of the business properties were still waiting for the right lessee to come along, because the rent-prices were on a very "business" level. Charlie stopped the car in front of a super-modern five-storey building with a façade, made entirely from glass. He wanted to have a look at the meeting place first and then to go down and meet the former students at the entrance. There was an information desk on the ground floor, where the visitors could be helped to find the office they needed to go to. Charlie was standing precisely in front of it, not because he could not find the right office but because the door was locked.

"Excuse me!" he said and knocked on the window to draw the man's attention. "I have a very important meeting today in the office on the third floor, rented by Mr. Poltic. It's locked. May I get the key to it?"

"I'm sorry, Sir, but Mr. Poltic have explicitly stressed not to give the key before 12 o'clock sharp! You'll have to wait another 8 minutes, I'm afraid." the clerk uttered this after he looked at the clock on the wall. Charlie submitted to the condition and went out on the steps to wait for Tony, Lorrie, Kate and Michael to appear.

They all arrived one after another. Lorrie was last and she explained that public transport was delayed by a few minutes because of the heavy traffic. Charlie got the key and led everyone to the right place on the third floor of the building. When they got there four chairs in a row could be seen placed on a platform in the middle of the room. There were four identical desks with computers on them, arranged along the two walls. They all sat down on their chairs in expectation to hear the reason they had been invited here. Only Charlie remained standing. He looked around for a chair but could not find one. Well, M. J. had pointed out that he would not hang out with them all day, so there! It was time for a serious conversation.

"Thank you all for coming and responding to my invitation!" he read out ceremoniously the first sentence. Actually, he tried to learn the text by heart as he did with its short version but he would always forget parts of it. Further on in the text, it was noted what it was expected from them, what their specific tasks were and how they would get rewarded. All emphases were explained in detail. The last few sentences comprised several notes, addressed to him: "After you read it out, you hand a copy of the contract to each of them and ask firmly (will you sign it?), if the answer is negative, you reply (have a good day) – the phrases in brackets to be read out by the letter, without a change! Those, who sign, need to come in the office first thing, at 8 a. m. on Monday morning." Charlie had no doubts about the identity of the author, who wrote these instructions. He fulfilled the orders even to the last comma. Everyone was given a contract to sign, which was placed on each desk with the correct name on it. Charlie asked the question of the day and that was it. The four had nothing important to ask, as the highly sophisticated details in the document had not left any possibility for ambiguities. They signed, then congratulated each other on their new employment and left. All done!

Charlie remained in the empty office and finally took a seat on one of the chairs. He was wondering why everything went so smoothly and without a hitch! He remembered the huge efforts he had to apply, when he visited the second university, where it took him several hours to collect just one piece of documentation. The only rational answer that came to his mind was that Poltic stood behind the planning of today's meeting, where before, he had to deal with everything on his own.

The first working day began at 8 o'clock but Lorrie had arrived to the office 20 minutes earlier. She was eager to start her new job and to receive her first paycheck. It was going to be five and a half times bigger than the salary she was on in the small accountancy firm until then. Lorrie hated her previous job. Firstly, she had to travel every day. Then, her older colleagues treated her in a disparaging kind of way and above all, she worked completely alone in a room with no one to talk to. The loneliness had somehow grabbed hold of her personal life, too. Lorrie could count the few friends she had on one of her hands. She lived in a small apartment, together with her parents, which was uncomfortable for three people. One of her dreams was to have her own place and move out but she could not afford to do it on her old salary. Lorrie was no different to any other normal person and she knew that to live well it all came down to money or to be precise – to its amount!

Happy and with open enthusiasm, she stood in front of the office, where according to the contract, she would be working there from that day on. Being well brought up, she knocked on the door a few times. No one answered. There was no sound coming from the inside. Just when Lorrie thought that her boss, Charlie, had not arrived yet, she spotted the key, left in the door. She hesitated for a moment and then she turned the key like some criminal. She looked around and slowly sneaked in. There was no one there. Now she was in, Lorrie decided to wait for her boss and colleagues to appear. When Charlie turned up, she would innocently explain about the key that was left in the keyhole. While waiting, Lorrie intended to have a look around in the office and mainly, to check out her own working place. It was identical to the other desks. The chairs, the computers, the equipment, even the pens were exactly the same. Lorrie smiled at the idea if one morning she felt a bit sleepy and sat down at the wrong desk. Let's hope she would, at least, notice the person, sitting in the chair behind it!

Her attention was drawn to the documents, which were officially placed in the centre of the grey desk. She picked them up and began to examine them. A part of them represented a statute book with interior regulations about working in the office and it consisted of 23 clauses. Charlie never mentioned anything about this because he did not know himself of its existence. The first rule said: "Smoking on the premises is absolutely prohibited. The offenders will be fined with the full amount of their monthly wage." The following pages comprised an exact copy of the contract she signed two days ago. And on the last page, there were instructions about their tasks on their first working day: "to find a site for the company's first supermarket. The four options for a building site are stored in your computers." Lorrie had not yet switched anything on but the lights. She felt curious to see the alternatives for the building location that she could find in her computer. She was born and bred in this town and was familiar with it like the back of her hand. Hence, she believed that she knew all the best places, suitable for such a large building project. She was scanning over the contract again and reading it through selectively, when someone knocked at the door. This startled Lorrie slightly and she raised her eyes to see Tony and

Kate, who entered the room. They bumped into each other at the entrance of the building a minute ago.

"Good morning!"

"Good morning!" Kate replied first. "You are Lorrie, right? I'm sorry but I'm not very good with names."

"Oh, no problem! We'll be working together from now on so I'm sure we're going to get to know a lot more than our names!" Tony also rendered a greeting but did not get involved in this small chat because he had managed to remember everyone's name on Saturday. He asked a more meaningful question:

"Where's Charlie?"

"I don't know. I only came in because I saw the key in the door. I imagine he'll be here any moment."

Kate approached the desk, designated to her. She gave it a little stroke. Tony was standing in the centre of the office, looking at Lorrie, while she was reading her contract. It was almost 8 a. m. Michael, yet last, also joined his new colleagues. He sat down behind his desk and began to read the documents after he noticed that this was what Lorrie was doing. The four of them were trying to make themselves busy, in silence. They were waiting for their boss to turn up so he could set some tasks for the day. Half an hour after the working day had commenced Charlie had still not arrived. Michael decided to break the silence:

"Hey, guys, I think we have to start work alone. At least this is what it says here at the last page of the documents?"

"Hmm, it seems that way, doesn't it? Although, isn't it a little bit strange that today is our first working day, after all and...?"

"I don't find it strange at all, Lorrie, especially when I think of the day how Charlie turned up on my door-step and offered me the job! And as far as I remember, he never mentioned on Saturday that he's coming here on Monday. Correct me if I'm wrong!" Tony replied.

"I didn't hear him saying this, either!" Kate joined in.

"Well, if that's the case, we just have to select or more precisely, to approve one of the building sites options, stored in our computers." Michael said this and he was first to turn his computer on.

A strange ambience could be felt in the office. Having had very little working experience and irrelevant to the type of jobs they had had, the four employees had been used to following orders from someone superior before they did anything at the workplace. In this instance, such person was missing. It was a good job that Michael had a slightly arrogant personality and managed to assert the beginning of what was called a working process. The other person in the room, who could initiate the working activity, was Tony. If all of them were hesitant like Lorrie and Kate, they would have probably started work at 10:45AM when the boss suddenly appeared.

"You've started without me, I see!" Charlie said jokingly to his employees, who had piled up around Michael's computer.

"Oh, no, we're just looking at the building sites and discussing which one to choose!" worried that she was not at her desk, Lorrie answered. She loved complying with the rules or else, she did not feel complete somehow.

"Don't worry! Just continue with your job as if I'm not here. I only came to give you half of your salary in advance, as well as the keys to the company cars that you are entitled to. I am aware that according to your contract, you have to receive your wages in your bank accounts but as you haven't given your account numbers to me yet, today, the money is in cash." the big boss handed out an envelope to each of them. One could feel the bulge, as expected, because inside, there was a key for each car. "The vehicles are parked on the big car-park at the entrance of the business centre. You can see them in your lunch break in about an hour or when you finish work. It's up to you."

"What brand are they?" impatiently asked Michael. He loved driving and at that moment he did not own a car. He really felt the need of having his own means of transport, when he was doing his last job. He had to rely on the public buses, which were always late and in a bad state, and spent an hour travelling in each direction every single day.

"That's a surprise. You will find out when you get to the car-park."

"And how am I going to know about which one is mine, boss?" Lorrie, who was very shy, asked. Charlie's heart nearly melted with delight, when he heard being called "boss". The feeling was the same or even better than the time he became "Sir" when he visited the university. He answered as gently as possible the ever so dull question and decided to extenuate her stupidity after he noticed that Michael could hardly hold his sneer.

"Lorrie, you've got every right to ask because all cars are totally identical. However, as it is with all cars, one key opens just one vehicle!"

"Who knows? She may well open ours, too!" Lorrie blushed with shame and was about to start crying like a little girl. She had no experience with cocky, arrogant and over-confident people like Michael. Charlie recalled some of the advice M. J. had given him. Poltic had described to him in detail the potential situation of the equality violation amongst the four that could occur and the measures Charlie should take in order to restore it.

"Michael, these types of jokes are inappropriate at the workplace. I have to ask you to abstain from making them in the future! Is that clear?"

"No problem, boss." Michael replied shortly but his face showed no remorse about the joke, neither did he agreed whatsoever. Charlie acknowledged his expression but he was not sure how to answer to that. He simply did not have instructions. Changing the subject, he directed the conversation to the other two in the room.

"Kate, have you had a look at the given options where to build the first shop?"

"Well, boss, just before you arrived, we decided on one, though, I reckon we kind of rushed into making our choice. Also, Tony is not very keen on it…"

"Not very keen? I'm against it, Kate! The second option is my choice!" Tony was right; his choice was most appropriate. She was talking about the one, suggested by Michael, who the two girls had silently agreed with. Naturally, Charlie could not possibly know about these details.

"Listen, don't rush things! You've got plenty of time. Coordinate your opinions and then make your decision. You'll come to some sort of a conclusion more or less until the end of the week? I'll be coming here a few times a day, every day, to oversee how the job's going. Unfortunately, I'm unable to be with you all the time, as I have other important business engagements to attend." this was an absolute lie; he was going to watch television. "Well, I'll be going now… any questions?"

"What are we doing next, after we've pick a building ground?"

"Then, Kate, you point it out to me, the company buys it and you carry on with your work as described in your employment agreement. You all have a copy of it on your desk, in case you don't remember your job description."

"We've read it, but what exactly are we gonna do? In the order it's all written there, is it so?"

"I understand that things are explained in a complicated way but my boss ordered that the duties, described in the contract should be followed closely step by step. Lorrie, can I have a look at it again, please!"

"...to organize and monitor all activities concomitant to the building development... Ah, here it is! "...need to hire a building project design firm that will draw up the architectural plans for the building project, to employ a building company and entrust it with the development of the project." As you've probably seen already all shop characteristic data is here, so I doubt any questions would arise on this matter. I think this at the end is very important, too: "a priority for every employee of the company is to seek a maximum efficiency in the process of selecting contractors and subcontractors." Charlie read out a couple more sentences that covered almost everything that it would be required from them.

"So when we choose the building ground, we have to find some architects and engineers to draw the plans for the building project for the shop?" asked Michael.

"And later we select a building company to actually do the construction." Tony added.

"That's right. That's your job, described in detail right here!"

Poltic had told him not to hang about too much with them and he realized why. He noticed that ever since he arrived in the office, everyone had stopped doing any work, but they were just wasting their time chatting. Everything was in the contract. He had read the important points to them, so for the day he had no business there anymore.

"I'll leave you now to work. Just follow carefully what's written in the contract. As you've noticed there are no restrictions, regarding the companies you are going to hire. Well, you will need my approval before you sign an agreement with any contractor so do chose only the best of them."

Two minutes later, back in his car Charlie, started to self-analyze his performance in the office. He was not very pleased with it; he could have done better! He wondered if he was convincing enough when he was explaining to them what they had to do. He liked the way he scolded Michael for the joke he made, however, on his way out, Charlie felt he was leaving four people, who had no idea what their job was. Yes, it was all clearly written, yes, he read it out to them and still, it looked that there was an urgent need of a leader, someone to guide them. Charlie had to speak to Poltic about that, otherwise he believed that employing the young professionals would appear to be a total waste of time.

Left alone, Lorrie, Tony and Kate surrounded again Michael, who clicked on the second image for a building plot. Each variant had a few general photos, attached, which represented and gave some idea of the land area. The photos were made from the air, as Tony had rightly guessed. In addition to the pictures, there was also some information on the size of the plots and their exact location. The first and the fourth had been unanimously rejected for their unsuitable location in two remote residential districts. One was also three times larger than required. The debate was about the second and the third building ground.

"I think," Tony began. "The second is just perfect and we have to choose it! You only need to look at its location – right on the motorway junction, if you are coming in town from the North. People, who are returning from the countryside or from a business trip, they would definitely want to stop and do some shopping! And voila! Here is our shop, right there. Exactly there, where it's needed, moreover, there aren't any big supermarkets in the area. Ours will be the only one, with no competition whatsoever!"

"The way you explain it, it sounds good, but for the people from the inner centre of town or those from the opposite side, this supermarket would be their last choice to do their shopping." Michael opposed to Tony's idea. He did not take into an account that the supermarket was not going to serve all citizens' needs. It was doubtful that someone from the other side of town would rush to that particular shop just to fill his fridge up. The four inexperienced professionals continued the debate:

"If I've been somewhere out of town, I doubt that I'd stop there on the way back. And why no one has already built one there? That means there shouldn't be one!" Michael said.

"I think almost in the same way! If there was a shop where Tony has just suggested, I imagine I'd never go there. The place is not worth it."

"Right, Kate supports the third option, so we pick that one!"

"I think we should select the second one, like Tony does." Lorrie announced slightly offended. She wanted to settle the scores with Michael and that was the best way. "The accountancy firm I worked for was located 20km away out of town and if there was a nice big shop there, I would have stopped every time." She hid the fact that she did not have a car and she could not possibly fulfill her intent.

"The situation has evened out!" said Tony elated by Lorrie's support.

"In fact, I don't have an opinion, because I think that both of them are no good." Kate clarified her position.

Michael was obviously losing. He got up from his chair and headed towards the door to leave the room. His three colleagues looked at him puzzled.

"Hey, Michael, where are you going? We haven't decided yet." Tony quickly asked him. For a second, he thought that his colleague had got offended by Lorrie's revenge.

"To have my lunch. We have one hour lunch-break from 12 till 1."

Tony got ready first and patiently waited for his female colleagues. The three went out like a real work-team. "Where do you want to go?" was the question. Tony left for the girls to choose. Both of them expressed an opinion that they would like some hot cooked food and not take-away like pizza or a hamburger. That's why they headed towards a restaurant that had a sign "Traditional cuisine". On their way, they were looking around to see if they could spot Michael anywhere but there was not a trace of him.

Michael had decided to have his lunch as quick as possible and then to get to the car park, where his new car was waiting for him. He was walking down the street, surrounded by many ultra modern office buildings, passing by different people in suits, employees of other companies. He recalled how on Friday, that was exactly three days ago, he finished his last 12-hour shift as a general warehouse worker. He had preferred this physical job instead of the internship, related to his specialty, after graduation, simply for one reason – the money. Well, the heavy loading-unloading job had come to an end. There was an enticing new beginning! From the very first day, there was money in cash and a brand new car and not to forget – three easy to manipulate work mates – real soft touches. Maybe, not including Tony, but he would not have any problems with Lorrie and Kate. The boss had no idea about their job. He was this dapper with no brains that had got the chance to supervise and manage much smarter people than him.

Michael was deep in similar thoughts all the way to his personal new vehicle. When he saw the hundreds of neatly parked cars before him, he realized that Lorrie's worry about how they would spot the right one made some sense. He had to be no more than 30m away from the car if he wanted to be able to activate the central locking-system with the keyless remote control locking device. Michael started walking along one of the sides of the car park and began to strenuously press the button. After a few minutes of wandering amidst the long rows of parked cars, he heard the specific beep of one car, being unlocked, and accompanied by a quick flash of the indicators. Just when he got nearer, he realized that he could have discovered it in another much easier way. There were no other four identical cars, parked next to each other, to be seen anywhere else in the whole car park. The cars were medium to high-class sedan and for him it was the best thing he had ever driven. He got in the car, just to have a peek but he spotted the clock showing 1:00. So he had to drive if he did not want to be late for work.

He found the rest sitting in the office behind their computer screens, still pondering over the dilemma between the second and third option for a building plot. Michael had decided to play it friendly. He felt he should turn around the three against one correlation within the group that had occurred so far and make the effort for all of them to feel like one loving family. He did not believe sincerely in this but he thought if had a better relationship with Lorrie and Kate, and possibly Tony, it would be easier for him to use them. Well, at least, this was how he thought.

"Hi, guys! I'm sorry I couldn't join you for lunch but I wanted to see what type of car we all got."

"It's not some small old banger, is it?"

"Just have a look, Tony! I parked mine just outside, in front of the building." The four went to the big window behind Kate's workplace and saw for the first time what their company cars look like.

"Wow, it's incredible!" Kate exclaimed. "I've never driven one like this." The faces of the other two young people showed a great satisfaction of the fact that Michael had demonstrated the cars to them. It was time to make the second move towards him becoming the "good guy" and everyone's favorite.

"Guys, I had a little think in my lunch break about our work-task. It's our first day at work today and we haven't really got to know each other... So I suppose in the name of a compromise we should suggest to Charlie the second building ground." Michael used the word "compromise" by no accident. He wanted to make them feel as if they owe him something. And he succeeded.

"I'm glad that you've changed your mind about this." Lorrie showed a real empathy for his sacrifice, forgetting too soon about what happened a little while ago. The other two welcomed Michael's new position, although, they still considered him as being the insensitive person from the morning.

The first working day finished successfully for the four, according their idea of success. On Tuesday, the procedure of finding the best architects was initiated. They would be assigned with making the plans of the building project for the first supermarket. Neither of the four had ever heard who the best in this field was. The architectural and building sector was "terra incognita" for the students, who had their education in Economics. Well, life in its rich variety, sometimes presents us with unexpected challenges, which we take into our stride and overcome with ease. At the very beginning of the working day, Michael decided to take the leadership as usual. He suggested to his colleagues that they should have a briefing before they start work. This would involve everyone to express their opinion about the day-targets and in this instance, about who had any knowledge about architects, projects and plans and to what extend! It appeared that no one had come across or had to deal with plans, drafts, engineers, architects, etc. in their young life.

Everyone felt a bit embarrassed to initiate the discussion, simply because no one had any idea what to say. Probably, they would have managed much better if they had to talk about Space, relying on the information from the educational programs on TV that everyone had watched at some point. Lorrie spoke first, not because she knew anything on the subject but to draw everyone's attention to the infinity of the Internet. She pointed out that this was where they could find the required specialists. She also added there would be some useful information in the traditional media like the newspapers and magazines. Michael felt jealous that he did not think of this simple, at first glance, but genius idea first! Tony and Kate also gave her a well-deserved appraisal and sincerely admitted that this was the best way to acquire a substantial and all-rounded knowledge on architecture.

In the next three days, Charlie would always find his employees peering into the computer screens, looking through numerous websites of design companies or reading the press and publications, related to building. Even he got into it, after scanning a couple of editions of the magazine "Architecture". To be fair, until that moment, the boss did not know the first thing about architecture.

In the late afternoon on Friday, Charlie went to see M. J. to tell him all about the good job, accomplished by the workers he was in charge of. He was proud that the people who he had personally selected and discovered were working like clockwork. Not only that, but they were performing their duties with great enthusiasm. The thought he had on the first working day of the week that they would not manage to cope without their boss had been forgotten.

Charlie did not even expect what M. J. had prepared for him. It would destroy his idea about Lorrie, Tony, Kate and Michael or their skills, in particular.

"Hi, M. J., how was your trip?"

"Hello, Charlie. You know I don't enjoy long-halt flights! I am still feeling a little bit dizzy."

"I really can't get you, M. J. So many people just love flying, whereas you find it unpleasant. Anyway, you just don't know how much I've got to tell you! My people are grafting real hard and I'm very pleased with them!"

"You are going to tell me while we are taking a walk in the garden. I want to get some fresh air."

Charlie began his account on his first week of being a boss before they had managed to go outside. Poltic decided not to interrupt because he knew him well and his need to tell everything, even sharing some silly details like when the elevator had stopped him on the wrong floor once. Charlie was just about to finish his outburst, when Poltic made a sign with his hand to stop. The alley they were walking on was ending with a bench, and placed under a big tree. Poltic was not very good with plants but thought it might be a beech-tree or an oak, although, he could not remember what any of them looked like. He sat down on the bench, crossed his legs and put his hands on his lap. Charlie was standing in front of him, blocking the view to the white solid wall surrounding the house.

"M. J., do you feel better now? You seem very quiet!"

"Sit down, Charlie. I have something very important to tell you. Your employees, our new members of staff, are not doing their job as they should, if not at all, to say the least!"

"But how come, after I've just told you all about it?"

"That's right, you've told me all about it in great detail: everything they did in the last five days, how they behaved towards each other, while you were there. They've picked and approved a building plot and then they've started to look for a company, which could design the project, etc., etc. Charlie, think about it! Do you realize that you have just described to me the volume of work that four people have achieved in one week, which would take one averagely intelligent person only a few hours, maybe, a day the most!

"What? That's nonsense, M. J. You don't know how hard they worked, looking all day for a designing company in the Internet, in newspapers and magazines..." Charlie had never raised his voice like this to Poltic before. The way Poltic looked at him made him realize that he had gone too far. He quickly tried to put things right: "I'm sorry for my..., you know, but I don't get it, M. J.!"

"Calm down, Charlie. It's not your fault! I take full responsibility because I've put you in this situation. I shall explain everything to you and you'll see how on Monday, your four lazybones are going to feel sorry for accepting this job in the first place!" a spiteful smile appeared across Poltic's face.

"I'm sorry, M. J. I'm listening. I won't interrupt you."

"Every beginning is difficult." Poltic started and Charlie sat down on the bench next to him. "There is always an adjusting period for everyone, when a person needs to get used to the new things in his life, no matter what they are: a new job, a car, a new home or new colleagues at the workplace. I actually didn't really expect our young workers to be that efficient in their first five days in the job! That was their period of adapting to each other's company, as well as to their new office, the cars and you, Charlie. From now on, every new task they receive will be bound by a fixed time period for its execution. The deadlines will force the four to really work for every banknote of their salary, even if they have to stay on after the regular working hours. Their life will be just work! As you said yourself, at the moment, they are looking for a company, which they would entrust with designing the building project for our supermarket. On Monday, you will inform them that they have to hand in the completed plans for the project within four weeks. I do understand that you don't have the vaguest idea about these things, so I'll give you a clue: it usually takes about three months for even the best architects in the country to complete a design project of such size." Charlie was listening very carefully but felt the need to ask something so he raised his right arm a little.

"What is it, Charlie?"

"I'm sorry, M. J., but if we give them such a short period, they will never manage. Isn't this pointless?"

"This would be the case if the same task was assigned to four ordinary specialists who receive regular wages in a non-descript company! Charlie, we give much, which gives us the right to expect that much in return. The time period is totally feasible only because we have vast financial resources. If it takes three months to complete a project of that size at the standard cost, our company can pay as much as it's necessary so this period is reduced to one month. Do you understand, Charlie?"

"Yes, I do, M. J. But in that way, we'll be spending so much company's money, won't we? Why do we have to waste so much money? What's the rush?" Charlie's question had its grounds and probably, anyone in his shoes would have asked the same thing.

"Charlie, have you heard the expression: "The ends justify the means.""

"Of course, I have. That's a very popular saying. Everyone's heard it."

"Well, then, this expression applies absolutely to our company's credo. There are some unspoken rules in the big business and one of them says: "If you want to be on the top, you have to work harder than your competition!" In other words, all our staff needs to work harder and in return, we'll reward them with more than they deserve. Now, Charlie, I'd like to point out to you some of the actions of your workers, which will not be tolerated from next week." Poltic changed his sitting position by stretching his arms along the back of the bench as if in accordance with the new topic of the conversation. Charlie decided not to interject anymore but just listen. He was still feeling awful for shouting at Poltic. "He is like a father to me!" He thought, while looking in expectation at his closest person to speak.

"Did you know, Charlie, that the four were late for work this week by about three hours between them? This is intolerable and from now on, there will be a penalty for the offenders, in agreement with par. 14 of the internal regulation code. The fine is calculated in the following manner: the minutes of being late will equal a percentage, deducted from one's wage. You know how much I hate someone being late?" Poltic became a little angry at the very thought of that.

"The other important thing you need to know is related to your duties. From Monday onwards, you'll be going to the office at least twice a day and you are going to supervise their work for at least four hours altogether. Any disagreement with a certain task, including the time-schedule, attached to it, will not be open for a debate! If you notice any arrogant behavior between them, you act on it in the same manner like when you defended Lorrie, with the only difference, that this time you'll be sterner! It's time for you to play the boss! Also, maybe, you remember that I've suggested to you that you should make the effort to go out with them once a week in the evening. In that way, Charlie, we achieve a balance in our relationships. You need to make them feel that you are their friend, too. This Friday, you can take them to the club you liked. Be very careful, Charlie. If you are too harsh with them, they are going to hate you and if you are very lenient, they'll just take advantage of you. The most important thing, Charlie, is: 'Think!' I can only guide you along the way but, inevitably, you are going to find yourself in situations, where you have to rely on your judgment alone. Let's go inside, Charlie. I feel better now."

Both of them were walking slowly and in silence along the narrow alleyway, covered with stone slabs. Having finished talking to Charlie, Poltic could allow himself to look around and note that the trees nearest to the house gate had very thin trunks and were of the same kind. He also looked at the tarmac in front of the house, a designated area, where the visitors, who were permitted to drive in right next to the property, could park their cars. Well, only Charlie's black Mercedes had been allowed to park there so far and that would be the case in future.

Charlie remained completely silent until the end of the day, although he stayed in the house until dusk. He was not interested in what the trees in the garden looked like or anything. He was deep in thought about the things Poltic had just told him, namely, about his four workers coming late for work. He believed that Poltic did not trust him and that he must have hired someone to watch Charlie's work and that of the four new recruits. If that was the case, then

Charlie's presence in the entire scheme was becoming meaningless, if his actions were checked at all times. Hadn't he proved that he could manage things by himself, that he always followed Poltic's instructions and he clearly made a real effort in his work?

Charlie came to a decision to take different routes to the business centre from next week. In that way he would find out if someone, hired by Poltic, was following him. He was 100% certain that the four in the office were watched. Otherwise, how Poltic would know the exact minutes they were late in their first working week? Charlie did not give out any signs that he had discovered Poltic's "plot", and decided to carry on with his work, following all instructions he had heard under the big tree, to the tiniest detail. He continued thinking about the spy plot when he was back in his house and his certainty that he was right only grew bigger.

Poor Charlie! He was prepared to do everything Poltic had told him to but one very important thing: to think! Common sense – and that Charlie did have – could explain that no one had been following him or anyone else from his team. There was a simple way how Poltic had got the information about when they all arrived at work!

The business centre was built in about six years to meet the needs of more and more companies, which were mainly foreign. The centre was a separate unit from the city and at the entry; there was security surveillance and a barrier. Naturally, there were CCTVs everywhere, which recorded the exact time of everyone, entering on the premises or when they made their exit. The pedestrians also had to go through the system, so no one could be left unnoticed. Poltic had demanded official information about Charlie's work members of staff and this was how he found out that their delays for work had accumulated to almost three hours, not including the late arrivals after the lunch break. The records showed that Lorrie was always on time; Kate and Tony arrived, on average, about 10-15 minutes late every day, which was down to them being stuck constantly in very bad, at times, traffic. Michael, who lived nearest to his new workplace, arrived late deliberately. Knowing there would not be any repercussions, he purely indulged in this.

Poltic had noticed the change in Charlie's behavior but he could not guess that it was due to some conspiracy, existing only in the young manager's mind. There was something much more important to think about – the forthcoming meeting, at which Bob, Jane, Geri and Harry had to present the fruits of their two-week work. He could not wait to also hear from them their opinion about their new houses. This time, the meeting was set to commence at 4 o'clock in the afternoon.

The four arrived on foot to the fortress-house. It was pointless really to drive there – no one of them was such a snob, either. Bob, Jane and Geri walked together on the way, as they had arranged this beforehand. This was Jane's initiative and she did invite Harry, as well. However, he kindly declined the offer with the excuse that he was still busy and he did not want three people to wait for him, until he had finished his job. So there were four people, walking towards the house, but one of them was a child – Geri's son had finished school earlier and she decided to take him with her. She had the option to ask the chauffeur to drive him to his grandmother but the elderly woman could still not accept the moving of her dearest people. The woman just needed more time. Poltic liked children and he did not have anything against the idea Geri's kid to wait for mom until the meeting finished. The big boy was almost ten years old but the housekeeper of the property had been asked to mind him, just in case, while he was watching cartoon films on the big television.

Harry appeared last and late by two minutes, as usual. He found the rest of the key participants to be looking through their presentations in a flurry. Each of the four had brought five copies of their report. Before the official part of the meeting started, everyone had a few folders, placed in front of them, as Poltic had suggested. Only Harry's two-week work had resulted meekly in just four pages. Harry noticed the surprise in everyone's eyes, especially those of the two women, when he gave out his copies to his colleagues.

The participants were ready and the host announced the start of their most significant meeting to that moment:

"Thank you all for your presence here today! I can see you have managed successfully with completing your assignment." Poltic said, glancing at the pile of documentation in front of him. He was sitting again at shorter side of the table and behind him, one could see a section of the garden through the high French window, which served as the fourth wall of the room. In the previous two meetings, heavy curtains blocked the pleasant view from the guests. This was not intentional whatsoever – it was just dark outside at the time.

"I don't doubt you've succeeded working on your projects but we still have to check this, don't we?" Last time, Poltic played the strict boss, who could only talk about serious stuff. For that reason, he considered changing his style a little today. Moreover, it would be the others, who had to speak more than him at that meeting. "As you all already know by our regulations, we start with you, Bob. There will be a small change this time. Each of you will make their presentation from the seat that is opposite me. That's the best spot for us, the audience. And now, Bob, please, make your way to the designated place."

Bob became more tensed and it was not hard for everyone present in the room to notice this. He made quite a bit of noise while getting up off his chair and as clumsily collected the few scattered pages before him. After putting a lot of effort, he finally dragged himself to the chair that gave the right for one to speak. Poltic noticed that no one from the people at the table had even thought of laughing at Bob's ridiculous act of shifting. They all behaved in a professional and respectful manner towards their colleague.

"Mr. Poltic, colleagues." Bob started officially and looked around at everyone present. "My assignment consisted of preparing an analysis for a period of one year going back, on the state of the shares of two large companies, or in other words, the trading with them and the change in their price values. I shall start with a brief introduction to the fundamental principles, which are applicable to all stock markets around the globe." Bob uttered those words with an extrinsic self-confidence that made an impression on everyone and left no place for anyone to doubt him. "I've divided my report into several sections. The first part I devote to the players in the stock market trade – who can take part and who cannot! You all know that shares are traded on the stock market, but there are also other financial instruments, which are exclusively under governmental and state control. Here, we are not interested in the latter so I'll only speak about the shares. Let's all imagine that we have a company that has been transformed into a joint-stock company or it's been one since its founding and that company is not trading its shares on the stock market. These shares are held by different persons, who we call 'share-holders'. The number of shares they have, determines how much of the value of the company, in percentage, they own. For example, I have 10 000 shares that are the equivalent of 10% of the value of the company, which means that the total amount of shares is 100 000." Poltic looked around to check whether the rest were listening as careful as he was but his action was wrongly perceived by Bob.

"Is there anything you don't understand, Mr. Poltic? Do not hesitate to ask, please, so I can clarify if there is a need to!"

"No, there's no need, Bob. You can continue, please."

"Right, then, where was I? Joint-stock companies trading shares on the stock market and those, which don't... The other example I'd like to give you is that of a company, which has shares on the market. The board of directors decides on their number for sale. Only as a reference, it's a worldwide practice, this number to equal no more than 30-40% of the value of the company. I'm not going to explain now how the initial price of one share is formed because it's quite complex subject and I'll jump straight to the main reasons for that price to change. Firstly, the financial stability of the company is a great factor, about which one can learn from the quarterly reports. Secondly, major fluctuations in the economic sector that the company is positioned in, can play a key role. Thirdly, there are government policies like tax regulations in particular, also bills that are of the company's concern, etc. There are many others, which I'm going to miss here, so I can emphasize only on what's important." It was very obvious that Bob was finding it hard to be succinct in his presentation. He could probably talk on the subject for days. Every sentence that he felt he should include the word 'etc.', Bob pronounced feeling as if obliged to his audience. Poltic noticed that detail and changed his mind about interrupting Bob.

"As you all know, I am a stockbroker!" Bob proudly reminded everyone what his profession was. Then, what followed was about ten minutes of detailed account on how important and responsible the job of the people, trading shares on the stock market is. Slightly over the top, his next words sounded: "We don't sleep because we have to always think of how best we could bring more profits to our trusted clients!" On the other hand, what this meant was – the more profits for his clients, the more money for Bob and people like him. Well, not that any of them would admit to this. Bob was idealizing his job. Who didn't?

Poltic was not interested in how people perceived their ways of making money, mainly because for him – money was money! Money could not speak, it had no feelings, what mattered was only its amount!

If Bob's general talk continued a minute or two more, Poltic had firmly made his decision to really prompt him, so he began with the analysis that everyone was eager to hear.

"I hope I haven't tired you with my inaugural explanation I've made but I believe I could not avoid that, with a view to the information on the two companies I'm about to present to you!"

"It was quite interesting, Bob, for me and for everyone else, but please, share your analysis with us in brief! Don't forget that your colleagues are also waiting to demonstrate how they have accomplished their assignments!"

"Alright, Mr. Poltic, I'll be quick, I promise." he felt nervous again and an indicator for that was the pen he was fidgeting in his hands with. Before, his uneasiness was showing through adjusting the few sheets of paper he had, at regular intervals of about 20 seconds.

"Firstly, I'd like to stress that I only managed to complete my task, thanks to a few former colleagues of mine, who worked around the clock to process all the data. There is a black folder in front of you, which contains the full analysis, including diagrams that illustrate the figures. My colleagues and I have come to a conclusion that it would be almost impossible for us to purchase all the shares of the two companies, which have been made available for trade on the stock market. Now, I'll tell you why not!" Bob left his pen and picked up the glass of water in front of him, then, he carried on from where he had stopped.

"The available shares for sale that are part of different every day's transactions on the stock market, are not going to be a problem for us. We can buy them out within less than a month if we really press on. The main shareholders of the two companies are not selling right now. I know that you know but just to remind you that the two Boards of Directors of the two companies, these are the people that possess more than 51% altogether and run the business are not the shareholders I am talking about. The members of each Board of Directors would never sell their shares for as much as hell.

"I think we got the difference, Bob. Please continue."

"Right, Mr. Poltic. It's a little bit disappointing that around 400 shareholders are not selling, at present. They probably believe that the price will be going up and this will bring good profit. They are not too far from the truth, as the price has really gone up in the last 12 months. These people hold 35-38% of all shares but what we could purchase now is maybe only about 4-5%. Mr. Poltic, I suggest we wait at least for one year when I expect the price will go down and the market conditions are a bit more favorable. Although, we could be never certain fully about our prognosis and we may see how the majority of shareholders still refrain from selling in expectation of the price going up, I believe, the moment to buy then will be better. Presently, every offer is going to be at unacceptably high cost for us."

"I don't make the decisions, Bob. Those above me do. There is logic in everything you told us but to be honest with you, we don't have the time waiting for so long."

"I'm certain we'll have to!" Bob firmly stressed. "In my long experience, I've never seen anyone selling such a great number of their shares, especially when they are so profitable."

"As I've already said – it's not me who decides! Nevertheless, there's always a first time for everything. Knowing my patrons so well, I doubt we'll leave things as they are. Do you have anything else to add, Bob?"

The stoke broker explained the monthly price movement of one share for each of the two companies. He concluded again with his professional opinion that it was best if they waited and did not go ahead with trying to make a purchase. Then, he stood up and went to his seat. He found it hard again to collect his documents from the table but this time because he felt exasperated rather than nervous. His irritation was due to Poltic's rejection to accept his professional advice as a face value.

It was Jane's turn to present her ideas on how the company could achieve financial stability. She did not start until Geri returned in the room after seeing to her son.

"Dear colleagues! Mr. Poltic! I'd like to ask you if you could look at page 2 of my report." Jane sounded like some school teacher, as if Poltic had asked to.

"As you can see, the contents of the report have been divided to a few sections. Everything is described in great detail, hence the volume of 93 pages. I'm going to be concise and say a few words on each section."

"Let' hope so! Otherwise the meeting would take as twice as long as planned and Harry would really get vexed, being last and so on!" Poltic thought to himself before she started with chapter one on "Staff Policy".

"People are those who make and manage a company. A large company requires a large number of staff. But these days that's not always the case! Today what's more important is quality rather than quantity. That's it on section one."

"Number 2 – "Innovations". It is inevitably related to the first point. As you all can guess, new technologies replace the need of employing too many workers. If we want to be the best, as Mr. Poltic told us last time, we need to be more technologically advanced than our competition. Of course, the problem of cost-effectiveness, that I have come across numerous times in my experience, is not to be underestimated! Many companies would rely on cheap labor by employing many workers, rather than invest in expensive technologies. My personal opinion is that a balance between people and machines is the key factor for the success of a company." Jane did not waste any time and went on to chapter 3: "High Management Body"

"Mr. Poltic, here, I've allowed myself to write down some piece of advice to you with regards to the fact that you'd like us four to manage the entire company! My suggestion is we form a team of 4-5 people, who would coordinate the work between the different departments of the company. Bob, Geri, Harry and I are narrow specialists and we would find our communications with those working for us quite complex. I don't doubt that we would manage but I believe that it would be much better if we had some assistants, who could duplicate our roles if needed. One person each would be sufficient. Anymore of that would cause internal competition."

"Something like a PA, is it so, Jane?"

"Yes, that's right."

"I'll give my answer to your proposal, Jane, after I read your report in full and present it to my bosses. Me personally, I think you have a point here and a PA for each of you would be of use. What do you all think about this? Do you think it's a good idea?" Poltic asked to check the rest of the Team's predispositions. Bob and Geri answered with "I do", as if they were at their own wedding and Harry disagreed as usual:

"With all due respect, Jane, I can manage by myself. I can also rely on my colleagues at the Law Office, so I don't need a secretary. If you have any queries connected to my work, you'll just have to speak directly to me!"

"Please, Jane, continue with your report."

"Thank you, Mr. Poltic. Section 4 contains the method how the workers' pay is formulated." Jane explained very briefly that the level of pay is directly related to the employer's liability, as well as, to the state of the company – higher profits would mean more leeway for bonuses for the staff and vice versa. Night labor, different shift work, etc. are factors that also play part in deciding how much the worker deserves to get.

Poltic was very pleased with Jane's efficiency in explaining her ideas. She was so much faster than Bob and also had a perfect elocution. The rest were also very impressed with the way she presented the information. They saw her in this light for the first time. She professionally worked with her voice and intonation, very well aware that even important words could lose their effect and diminish their significance if mumbled. Listening to such a fine orator, Poltic thought about Charlie's teenage way of expressing himself and quickly felt uncomfortable that at this moment, he could think about someone, who hardly ever pronounced a sentence without eating his words. Well, M. J. could not know that before his workers, Charlie managed to produce a speech delivery almost to the level of Jane.

She, on the other hand, was discussing the 18th and last section of her report. When Jane finished she vacated the orator's spot for Geri. She had to present the research poll results on people's preferences, regarding six leading meat manufacturers. Well, the nature of her actual work was slightly different because Geri had hired 23 people to do the whole job, where she, as the big boss, just relied on others and did nothing. Poltic knew this very well. That was why he did not feel surprised when he saw the large volume of her paper work in comparison to that of the rest. So from the comfort of her sofa in her new house and without moving her little finger, Geri knew how to complete her task. She sat down in the "hot" seat and got ready to begin without even looking at her papers. She looked exactly in the same arrogant and smug way like when she came to the dinner that nearly became a disaster. Poltic considered this as her "working" attitude, which differed tremendously from her image of a caring single mother and obedient daughter. There was a similar analogy with Jane, too. She would always change her voice in an obvious manner, when speaking about her family and when speaking about business. Bob, who was shy and unconfident in his personal life, would appear self-assured and very assertive when talking about shares and the stock market. Poltic could not wait to see Harry's "working" face in a little while, which, at that moment, expressed boredom with his colleagues' tongue wagging as he was last to speak, as usual.

"Mr. Poltic, firstly, I want to print out that you were partially correct about the reliability of the official information, we discussed last time. Why partially? Because three of the companies in our research are openly misleading the public about the popularity of their products, whereas the other three, are almost 100% truthful to their customers."

"Some tell the truth, some don't – that's always been the case! I'm interested in the poll's results, Geri!" he wanted to direct her to go straight to the point and to suppress her intent for lengthy introduction. We had all been taught at school how to structure an essay in three parts – introduction, main part and conclusion. Poltic really wanted to hear only the end of the main part and a concise conclusion from Geri.

"As you wish, Mr. Poltic, but I have included some official data in my report, just in case. If you like you can have a quick look."

"I'm definitely going to read it but now I'd like to concentrate on the research poll." despite that Geri's ego was hurt, she accepted Poltic's promise and continued:

"My team and I have done an awful lot of work in the last two weeks in order to complete this research in the most professional manner possible. The results of the public poll showed us that 84% of the consumers approve and buy the products of the first two of the six companies nationally. This is the total figure, however, there is data by regions in our report, as well." Geri talked separately about each of the companies, saying exact figures without needing to look. Everyone in the audience found this quite impressive but Poltic. He could see that she had learnt only the most important information by heart like some diligent schoolgirl and only seemed as if she was some genius who could memorize hundreds of pages. After she finished her babbling on about percentages and figures, Geri summarized the result of her research in a couple sentences:

"According to our data, Mr. Poltic, there is a deep-rooted trust in the first two companies on the market. The reason for their popularity is due to their powerful advertising. Their rich history and tradition also contribute to attracting clients but mainly it's the advertising! In our survey, there was a question about where people had heard about the company from and 92% of them, as far as I remember, answered: "from the media". The two have basically taken over completely the advertising market in meat products in the country. Just to compare, the rest of the companies altogether are popular twice as less amongst the consumers than the first two producers. Although that they are little known, they still have devoted clients and play an important role for creating a rich variety and choice in the meat market. The small companies, outside the six, have influence only in a regional sense and almost do not affect the national market. I cannot say for sure but I think that these companies represent even less than 5% of the whole market. However, in the process of our work we distinguished some of them as being prosperous and potentially growing fast in the future. This was my personal initiative, Mr. Poltic, and despite the fact that I only looked into this on a superficial level and I couldn't give you the full picture about them, I thought that in this way, my research would be complete!"

"We are very grateful to you, Geri, for providing us with this additional and valuable information."

"Mr. Poltic, even if we manage to buy out the four smaller companies we would still not be able to achieve a leadership in the market. The name-labels of the largest two are their greatest asset and they have been known in the market for a long time. If we have to start pouring money in medium-sized businesses in order to popularize the brand and increase production, I doubt that this would lead to success. It is quite hard to make people trust something new and different from what they are used to buying. It will probably take us about ten years to get even closer to their level, let along reach it. The conclusion, Mr. Poltic, is that your patrons should redefine their unfeasible idea and set themselves objectives that are in line with realities."

"I can only join you, Geri, in this!" Bob butted in even from the "wrong" chair. "The initial budget at our disposal that you've told us about, Mr. Poltic, is 100 million. This is only enough to buy one of the companies that our colleague Geri has just mentioned to us as being a contributor to the market's diversity. I have some friends, who told me that the market value of Sevko Corporation is... Oh, I'm sorry, Mr. Poltic, I shouldn't mention names – my mistake, sorry. I am saying that the market value of one of the companies is about 70-75 million. So we'll need at least 300 million if we want to buy the four companies, I mean these immediately after the two largest ones, and that is without the investment modernization schemes. I imagine this would be required by their current owners."

Poltic patiently and without showing any disconcertedness, listened to the suggestions made by two of the members of the Team. He only frowned when Bob mentioned accidentally the name of one of the companies. This was not allowed and the companies were supposed to be referred to only as numbers and their order was determined according to their size. The one Bob was talking about corresponded to number four. On top of everything, Harry decided to support his colleagues and joined in ignoring Poltic's rule about speaker's chair:

"By the way, I was going to ask the same as Bob and Geri but couldn't, always being last to speak... So how are we going to become leaders on the market if we can't get companies 1 and 2 and we can't make the consumers to change their preferences? Please, explain this to me, well, to us, Mr. Poltic!" Harry was not the most diplomatic person but this attitude was somehow approved by the rest. Even Jane, who had not taken a stance to this moment, showed her contentedness.

"Firstly," Poltic began in the same manner as his Team. "We'll become number one on the market by putting a lot of effort, mainly by the four of you! As soon as my bosses receive your reports, they'll map out the strategy for our invasion in the economic sector of our interest. You will be following this strategy very closely and the means to its success is not 100 million but much more. Perhaps, you remember that I mentioned this figure only as being the start capital. This is not our limited budget!" Poltic was getting into it and no one dared to interrupt him. "Secondly, Geri, we don't really want people to stop buying the products of companies 1 and 2. Let's hope they buy more and more if we are going to own both of them. I may still not know when and how this will become a fact but I'm certain that there are plenty of ways to react to the market changes and we shall apply these methods to our general strategy. Of course, our plan will be flexible in correspondence to the fluctuations of the market. However, the end result will be favorable if we all do our job properly! And finally, before I give the floor to Harry, I'd like to know whether there is anyone amongst you, who wants to end their part in achieving this unfeasible goal! I won't ask this again. If there is anyone in doubt, I shall remind you the relevant clauses in your work agreement, in the event of termination on your part!" Poltic enjoyed playing this game with them. He was very much aware that they would not dare resign after having a little taste of life in a new house, a personal chauffeur for the company car and a huge salary. Well, there was nothing wrong to test them! The most audacious of them kept quiet, so Bob spoke out:

"You're right, Mr. Poltic. I actually do think we've got a chance to reach our target if we work hard, as you said, and if have the money allocated to our disposal. After all, the market is unpredictable and it may take less time for us to obtain the controlling stake of the capital of the two major companies somehow. Nothing is ever certain and that is probably the most exciting part of my job!" Bob partially contradicted his own statement from before. It was not about that he had changed his opinion but he realized that it was a bit extreme. Geri also agreed that everything was possible if they had more than 100 million to play with. Harry withheld comment and Jane simply confirmed that she thought in the same way as the rest.

Poltic could not believe that a couple of words on his part made these outstanding professionals change their view even if to an extent. He could be easily convincing to people like young Charlie but he had never imagined that he could influence to such a degree the members of the Team. Actually, it was not him, who did it. It was the money.

"Harry, it's your turn to speak now. By looking at your report, I imagine you're going to be very quick. You were talking about some hundred pages but I can see only four."

"There are eight pages, both sides of the paper are used. I'll be brief, indeed because you've asked me to draw up a contract for buying a non-existing business. Jurisprudence relies on the letter of the law. I don't have the imagination to do what you've requested from me. I could have done it, of course..." Harry confidently uttered. He wanted to be certain that no one would have any reservations about his professional abilities. "Instead, I just followed the advice of my colleagues at the Law office and selected a few purchase agreements used for buying real companies. Their business activity is various but I've adhered to your condition – the top asking price is about 40 million. Take your pick, Mr. Poltic, and I shall bring and give you the full contracts any time. Just to warn you, though, some of them consist of more than 1000 pages. You will find out that this type of agreements follow a strict set of principles. I can explain everything in detail after you familiarize yourself with these. Finally, I'd like to point out, that these sorts of documents are strictly confidential. Well, that's it."

"Alright, Harry. I accept you have completed your assignment. However, I expect you to show me the contracts I pick by tomorrow."

"Whenever you say, Mr. Poltic, my colleagues have been informed by me in advance, so I can go to the office at any point and fetch them."

Bob felt hard done by the fact that he had put so much effort in his work, whereas it took Harry so little to present his report and got away with it. Poltic managed to read this on the broker's face because he would make a similar expression when thinking of his wife.

The meeting ended without further discussions.

Poltic was going to fetch the reports and take them to his study, where in the coming few weeks, he had to conjure up the future strategy of the company completely by himself. The Team had no assignments to do during this lengthy period so Bob, Jane, Geri and Harry would receive their huge salaries for doing practically nothing. They all headed back home feeling contented. Geri's son was happy, too. Ha had watched some cartoon films about four characters with supernatural powers on television for two hours, while waiting for his mom. The child was admiring his heroes in a very innocent and unbiased way, whereas if Poltic had found himself in front of the TV, he would have immediately associated the characters with the members of the Team, as absurd as it sounded.

Poltic sat in the speaker's chair. He was wondering about the purpose of this strange room. When he saw it for the first time, the room was furnished with two law-rise filing cabinets with numerous drawers and compartments, situated along both of the parallel walls, which somehow did not suit well. The ring with the table and six chairs, which was formed by the descending steps, did not fit the picture, either. Even when Poltic 'boned' the room by removing the cabinets and a small coffee table with a few chairs and leaving the room barely furnished for its size, something still did not look right. The area in the middle resembled a crater, formed as if by some explosion of a bomb and then someone had just carved the steps. This odd feature irked him every time he opened the door and saw the big hole in the centre. No one from the Team had allowed themselves to comment the interior or exterior of the house. There were some general remarks made out of courtesy but this did not count. Poltic was curious to know what they thought of the meeting room. As they were not there to ask them, he continued with his own speculations about the function of the place.

If there was a formal dinner for six at the house, it could be held in the room. It was possible but it would be very stupid for many reasons. Firstly, the kitchen was connected to the dining room, where a lovely solid table, perfect to accommodate the needs of twice as many guests, stood in the middle. There were not the high steps, as well, which would make any attempt to serve a bowl of hot soup a dangerous one. Not to mention the relatively slippery floor where there was not a rug or carpet. Poltic could think of a dozen of different reasons why the room was unsuitable for dinner parties but still could not figure out its original purpose. He decided not to fixate his mind on this anymore and headed towards his study, which he knew what it was for very well.

I Know Everything

Bob completed his report in six out of the fourteen days. He had worked really hard. This was clearly visible from the meetings he had with his formal colleagues from the stock exchange and the numerous phone calls he had made. In the rest of the time, however, his wife had dragged him around different shops to pick new things for the house. She needed his opinion but whenever it differed from hers, she would make a terrible scene, ready to cry and always get it her way. Poltic was aware of these details of their personal life and would often feel sorry for the outstanding professional. In addition, Bob was relatively honest. This characteristic of his shone through when he had to determine his assistants' salaries. He could have easily bumped up their fees but at the end of the day, they got exactly what they were worth.

Jane did worry that she would have to cover a large volume of literature in order to fulfill her task but at the end she was ready with her report quite quickly. It took only four days. She read one of the fundamental books on the subject and assigned the reading of the rest of the important written works to a few employees of her consultancy agency. She had to visit the office just once and the report was put together. She personally wrote only three of the eighteen subheadings in the document. The free time she had, she dedicated to shopping and in the evenings, she would hassle her husband to take her out to the movies or a restaurant, not his, of course, where she would always foot the bill. He, on the other hand, would always try to please her. This only proved that he was one of the many week men out there, who was being outshined by his own wife. Jane also spent a lot of time with her children. She never missed to check if they had done their homework and she would always make sure they ate healthy and regularly. Poltic realized he was thinking about his staff in the order they took turns to speak at the meeting today.

The third person was Geri. Poltic guessed straight away how she had prepared her survey. He imagined an army of pollsters, roaming the streets in different parts of the country and her – settled on the sofa in front of the TV. This was an absolute epitome of sloth. She went to see her mother almost every day and stayed quite often there until the evening. Her child finished school at six and she would wait for the company car to deliver him back in their new house, where they would sit and watch television. Geri did not do anything with regards to her assignment for two weeks. Picking the heavy phone receiver to instruct her former colleagues could hardly count as some work done. And after all this, she made the biggest impression at the meeting.

With Harry – Poltic had been fooled by the lawyer. Poltic regarded the ten visits to the Law Office that he had made, as being part of his job. But when M. J. saw the fruits of Harry's huge amount of work, consisting of four sheets of paper, he realized that the lawyer had visited his friends just to socialize. He had not made many phone calls, either, and only one was related to the agreement he was supposed to make.

The four assignments had been completed no matter how. Contacts and experience seemed to have played an important role. Poltic made this conclusion and decided that he should stop this train of thoughts but see to his own needs.

He went to the kitchen and made himself an enormous sandwich, not the best choice health wise, but his natural love for food and getting a pleasure out of it, won. Chewing on in a bit of a bad manner that was inappropriate for a man of his position, Poltic thought of a very interesting idea. If the young specialists, assigned to Charlie were matched up with the old dogs from the Team, this would result in the perfect work combination. He even thought for a second that Lorrie, Tony, Kate and Michael could take the positions of personal assistants, taking up on the idea proposed by Jane. The members of the Team would just pick up the phone and ask favors from their influential friends and the young inexperienced former students would play the errand boys and girls. Then, Poltic quickly rejected the idea. He did not want to risk an eventual clash of two different generations.

How did he know about everything they did?

Poltic was exceptionally forethoughtful person and not only in this instance because of the importance of his venture, but also in general. He just had to know absolutely everything about what Bob, Jane, Geri and Harry did! He felt he could not rely merely on their good will and honesty, or on their professional attitude towards their work. When big money, a house and a car are involved, people could change and almost every time for the worse. The likelihood some of his staff to agree to act against him was not to be ignored. They could misappropriate big sums of company money. They could tell him anything they wanted in connection to work – he would not know any different. After all, he was not as qualified as them and was well below their level. Every word of theirs could be a possible lie. Today, it was their third meeting only but their confidence would grow inevitably as time went by, especially when they made their first important business deals. Poltic knew that at the moment they sensed that the company could not progress without them, the demands would flood in.

They had everything, even more than enough, but who knows, in a few months, their new houses might suddenly feel a bit small and cramped, or the company cars became too old and they felt the need of urgent pay-increase. Harry proved that he was the most arrogant of them all so Poltic expected him to lead a possible future revolution. Geri also showed herself as being quite an impertinent person at the meetings. Bob, on the other hand, was dangerous because one could never know which side he would choose. Probably, it would be that of his workmates. Jane would also certainly join her colleagues, well, to be precise – she would follow Geri.

Surprisingly, the two women had become very good friends for the short time of living next door to each other. They had similar interests, taste in clothes and the subject about the children was also something in common to talk about. In the last week, they visited each other at home – sometimes in the mornings for a cup of coffee or in the evenings, when the children were home.

Poltic had thought a lot about the eventual problems with his staff he might have in the future. This was well before he introduced himself to the Team on their first meeting. At the time, his head was full of extreme but feasible ideas and options. That was one of the reasons Poltic regarded their work agreement as being a contract for life. He intended to be in control literally of their entire life.

Provisionally, for Poltic, a person's life could be divided into his personal and professional one. In order to be in control of both, he gave the Team a house and a car each and made them work from home, rather than from some office. The houses and cars were company property and they were totally bugged, cram-full of secret cameras and tapping devices. And the chauffeurs were obliged to report on a daily basis about where and when they had driven their prominent passengers on the back seat. The vehicles were armored by applying the highest of technological standards and it was hard to be detected by a non-specialist. The cars also had 12-cylinder gasoline engines. So the chance for any member of the Team to get seriously hurt in a road accident or some kind of attack, which would stop them from working, was brought down to a minimum with these measures. They included the professional driving skills of the chauffeurs, of course. The situation with the houses was similar but it was all on a bigger scale.

There were 27 cameras in each house, even in the bathroom. Some of them had infrared sensors and recorded when the lights were switched off. In that way, nothing could be left a secret. The telephones in the properties were tapped around the clock. The mobile phones were no exception. Poltic gave his staff special SIM cards. They kept their old numbers but could speak for free to any network. He could not take the risk to allow his personnel to use their own private mobile phones, although, Harry had already got one.

The most interesting innovation of the spy-ware was installed in the frame of front door. It was a weapon detector. Poltic wanted to know when an armed person visited anyone from the Team because he knew that they would be getting more and more enemies by the day. When a person, who had a gun, entered the property, the system was activated and it sent a message to Poltic, wherever he was, via a satellite connection. He could send one of his security guards to check out the problem or leave things as they were – after all, not every armed man was a killer. Poltic was aware that some of the closest friends of the Team staff had a license to carry a weapon. So if Harry invited a mate, who had a legal gun, and system was activated, Poltic would know not react to this.

Where did Poltic get hold of these technological wonders?

He wanted to have the best innovations on the market that one could buy. It was not hard to find the best manufacturers of these specialized gadgets as they all advertised their spy-products very well. He picked a foreign company for this purpose. The producer had invested a lot in research and more than a half of their devices were patented because they had been invented by their own designers. Poltic made himself acquainted with all the available information about the company before he actually went to its headquarters. This happened only a few days after he became a proud owner of the five two-storey villas. Poltic had a two-hour conversation with the executive director himself, who personally took on the case when he realized that the special client had intended to install audio and video surveillance system in four large properties. It was a big order and he should not miss out on such an opportunity. Poltic's requirements were straightforward – he needed top range of everything, multiplied by four.

To obtain the SIM cards, Poltic had to pay double as it was illegal one to sell them privately. They were designed for military purposes only. The manufacturer had warned him that if anything leaked out about the deal, they would announce that the cards had been stolen. And when the person, who had them, got caught, he would end up being prosecuted by the government as well as by the company itself.

There was an important human factor to the whole surveillance venture – a number of people had to watch the video recordings and the taped conversations around the clock. The company had provided this service so Poltic did not pay their wages. The owner of the company was elated by the lucrative order Poltic had made that he offered the cost for this. Much later he realized that a client like him would not be bothered to pay some five or six thousand per month for salaries when he was buying equipment worth more than a million.

The hired force behind the monitors and the tapping devices had to prepare three reports per week on everything they had seen or heard, noting the exact time and place of precisely what had happened. Poltic had pointed out to them, however, that he did not want to appear as some voyeur, nor did he intend to interfere with the personal lives of his Team. Therefore, if any of them had a personal conversation with a friend, that was unrelated to work, the report should reflect this by saying: "talked about fishing with such and such, not connected to work". When the conversation involved the company, Poltic wanted the full print out of the recordings.

The requirements regarding the video surveillance were simple. He wanted a brief account about what the residents did while at home, as well as what they were talking about, when and with whom. He was interested in the relationships between the members of the families. Poltic gave an example to the owner of the company: "...she was in her study all afternoon, then she went to cook a meal and then watched TV in the evening" or "...today, at about 6 o'clock, there was a light argument over..." Poltic was not interested in any detail but only in the general picture, when things were not related to work. He was the one, who was going to read everything at the end, so the last thing he needed was hundreds of pages, taking up his time.

His main objective was to be informed about their natural behavior and if sudden changes occurred in how they conducted themselves at home, he could be able to take measures. Poltic believed that if one did something wrong at work, a blunder or even a crime, then this would reflect their attitude at home. Ungrounded arguments, unprovoked anxiety, problems sleeping or unusual distance between partners, etc. would follow in such instances.

The high rank in the "spy" company listened very carefully and approved every demand in the manner of "The customer is always right!" In this case, the customer was also very rich. Poltic was very pleased with the manager's promise for an expeditious job because soon the houses would have to accommodate their new occupants and there was not much time left. The technicians, who were coming to install the equipment, arrived two days later. There was a lot of work to do but for the special customer, it was all completed for less than a week.

At the time, Poltic had some well-founded concerns. Despite the fact that this sort of businesses had to have their policy of strict confidentiality as a high priority, he felt he could not trust them. There was a possibility for the nice and friendly manager of the company to blackmail him once his business became a leader in the market of meat products due to his Team's hard work. The scandal with the non-stop surveillance of his staff would turn disastrous for the business and the four specialists would sue him for decades. Modern society was very sensitive about its rights to personal freedom, etc. and Poltic's wish to avoid being lied to and to always know the truth about his workers could not be an excuse to violate their rights.

So to be on the safe side, he decided to meet the director of the company once again. He was not going to order anything but offer him something. Poltic spent almost a whole week abroad doing some serious negotiating. He was very much aware that he could not buy the foreign company out because its market value was well too high for it was having rare and unusual business activity. Therefore, he decided to pledge his loyalty by the means of making it dependant on him. He proposed to be part of the scientific research side to business and to sponsor two of its future projects, which were frozen for the time being due to lack of funding. The director was elated. He believed that Poltic was doing this for one reason – his interest in new technologies and innovations. He never thought that the rich foreign client was afraid of being tied down. The second visit made Poltic much calmer. He was in total control of the Team, who had no knowledge about it and now that he had paid the director to keep it quiet, they would probably never come to know. However, there was always a possible "but"!

RA

On Wednesday morning, Poltic got up an hour earlier than his usual. He made the first few steps that took him to the kitchen with his eyes closed, leaning against both walls. He made himself a double strength coffee, which did not manage to quench his enormous need for caffeine but intensified it. He decided to have another one at about 10 o'clock.

It was a regular day outside for the season; there was a moderate wind but nothing out of common. Poltic considered this Wednesday as being more than just an ordinary day. It was a turning point for his business venture because he had to go through the final part of finding his key employees for the company.

Poltic made a construed analysis of the staff he had at his disposal. There were the four biggest specialists in the country, each of them – a professional in their particular field of work. They had demonstrated some excellent results in their work and good future prospects that they would keep up the quality work. They appeared to be the mainstay of the company and had proved that they could take responsibilities, indeed. Moreover, the Team had everything that takes to achieve a maximum effectiveness to reach the objectives of the company i. e., a leadership in the market of meat products. Almost nothing could go pear-shape with the Team due to the surveillance devices installed, which would give Poltic a timely warning in the eventuality of undermining activities on their part. Described as it was, it all looked perfect and it really was but perhaps, not enough for the end successful result.

Charlie's four were of secondary importance but the significance of their role would become more and more substantial with time, especially in the first year. They were young, highly paid, inexperienced but ambitious specialists, who, according to Poltic, would become even more valuable than the Team if good methods of education and training were applied. Poltic was very aware of these facts, however, he was aware of the company's need for a third group of four people. He could have managed just with the two groups he had already had and Charlie but it would cost him more and it would take longer.

The final four important employees of the company Poltic had to personally find and convince them to work for him. They would have to employ, on the other hand, slightly illegal methods, in order to speed up the progress of the company.

Poltic believed that the laws in force are useful and should exist but they set limits to people, who are into breaking them and subsequently get punished for it. The new personnel should not actually break the law but only guide fate in a certain direction by using unlawful means. Even Bob and Geri had pointed out at the yesterday's meeting: "This just can't happen – heaps of cash and straight to the top!" Yes, the market itself did not present such opportunities.

The three groups of four were supposed to work independently from each other. The Team and the Young ones, as Poltic referred to them, eventually would meet up and begin to work together. The last four would never learn about the existence of the others, about the company's activities, nor should they ever discover Poltic's actual dealings. He did not have any qualms about his ability to gain control over these people. Life was not so kind to them, which made them straight away less demanding and quite harmless when compared to the members of the Team or the Young ones. The actions against the law were going to be perpetrated by people, who only had secondary education and had obtained their academic degree on the streets. At least, this was what Poltic wanted and he was already guessing of the way to achieve this. Generally, less educated people had to resign to the idea of getting a lower paid job than those with a degree, as well as to be prepared of becoming the laughing stock of everyone smarter than them. For his purposes, Poltic did not need some genius guys but ordinary people, who experienced chronic financial problems.

It was curious why the number 'four' was predominantly in his mind and the members of the groups had to be four, not three or five but four. This number had no sacred meaning for Poltic and really, he was not superstitious whatsoever. He could not think why he had decided everything to be around the number 'four', although, later, he would find some good excuses for it.

Three people were not enough and it was likely that two of them would gang up against the third, which would hinder their work. Two people would just not be able to cope with the numerous duties around the company. Five members of the Team, for instance, sounded good but Poltic considered it as being too many. Moreover, he was taking part to a degree as the fifth member. The principle of four did not have to apply to the lower tiers of the company. As seen, Geri employed 23 persons to conduct the survey. Charlie's people could also subcontract as many architects and engineers to design the building project of the first store. There were no restrictions. Some petty-minded person could argue about the prevailing number 'four' because Poltic and the Team equaled five, as well as Charlie and the Young ones came to the same number. In addition, Poltic and Charlie could be regarded as separate entities, working for the company in their respective positions. What Poltic considered important was him being at the top of the pyramid.

◆ ◆ ◆

Daniel was promoted to a deputy chief inspector only a month ago. He had much more responsibilities than before. This did not scare off Daniel in the slightest. During his service, he had always followed and believed in the maxim: "Straight to the top!" He could not think otherwise and could not understand others, who were happy to stay where they were and not strive to succeed. He regarded their lack of ambition as being due to fear. Well, no one from his colleagues could accuse the new deputy chief inspector of being a coward. The evidence could be found in the numerous awards he had received, from which the most precious one was 'a policeman of the year', even if rewarded to him on a regional level only.

Besides the good service, time was a factor, too, for climbing up the hierarchical ladder. That was why those above him believed that within ten years, Daniel could easily take their place after they got retired. And those, who were really close to him, could even see him as becoming a chief director of one of the departments of the Interior Ministry. His loyalty was one of his most valued characteristics, which had allowed for his 20-year steady and upward progress. When Poltic phoned to arrange to meet him, Daniel had decided to respond at once, although, he had lost track of how many years he had not seen his best childhood friend. They had gone their different ways since one went to university and the other enlisted himself in the Police Academy.

It's said when one is young, they have many friends but the older one gets, the less real friends they can count on. Daniel believed in this saying. He had found the truth in it in his own experience, hence he felt delighted about the prospect of meeting up with an old dear friend. Poltic also felt a bit strange when he heard Daniel's voice on the phone. It seemed as if he was some stranger at first. The conversation was very brief and they both demonstrated some level of nervousness, mainly because both of them were not sure where to start.

Poltic invited Daniel to one of the most expensive restaurants in town. Daniel was too busy at work so they had to meet no earlier than 8 o'clock in the evening. This suited Poltic perfectly. He would spend the light part of the day, reading the Team's reports. Actually, it did not quite work out as planned. His anxiety before the tonight's event grew more and more, so he could not really concentrate on the reports for more than two hours. He went out for a brisk walk in the garden.

When one knew they were going to meet a friend they had not seen for so long, the feeling they experienced could be described as excitement. In Poltic's instance, it was more like apprehension because what he was going to ask from his old friend was more than a small favor. Poltic had great memories from when they were kids – a time they broke a window or a fight with other boys, or how both swore to be friends forever and now he had to ask high rank policeman to find some criminals, who were going to commit crimes for him. Poltic was feeling remorse but there was no other way – the ends justify the means!

The black Mercedes stop right outside the entrance of the posh restaurant. Poltic flung the car keys to the young guy, responsible for parking his car and then slowly went indoors. He was guided to the table he had booked and went up the three steps that led to the platform it was on. Daniel arrived at 8 o'clock sharp as if he was coming to work. He had never set foot in this place before. A regular policeman had no business in such an expensive restaurant even if he could afford to pay for something on the menu. On arrival, his attention was drawn to an amazing black Mercedes that he had seen one like it just once before. Daniel was a little bit taken aback by the elegance of the restaurant settings but he managed to spot Poltic. The two old friends had a hug after a strong handshake and this led to the first joke of the evening:

"Hey, you've toughened up, at last!"

"I've always been stronger than you and you know it! Why did you bring me here M. J.? This restaurant is not for us." Daniel shared his concern as soon as he got in the chair and tried to settle. Apparently it was too soft. Poltic realized it was not such a great idea to pick this place for their meeting. Daniel was dressed in a way more suitable for going to a pizza place or some fast food eatery. His dark blue denims, combined with a black top and a brown jacket – every inspector's trademark, however, it clashed with Poltic's perfectly elegant black suit, which cost about Daniel's three monthly salaries.

"I invited you, so I picked the place!"

"Fine, but you have to know that the police force is not greatly paid. Judging by your smart look – you're minted, whereas I'm still the same modest boy." Both of them burst into laughter, which some of the customers found a bit too much. Poltic's position, however, did not allow for them to tell him off. It was not that he was some kind of celebrity or a regular customer, who deserved a special treatment. He just knew the owner. The man worked for Poltic a long time ago when he first started out with his business ventures.

"I've put on my best clothes. I've got a meeting with you, don't I?" Poltic uttered in a very serious voice but only two seconds later he burst into laughter. Everything was fine in the first few minutes but when they had to order their food, Poltic felt a bit uncomfortable again. Daniel was pulling some strange faces. The menu was not bad. In fact, it was a work of art. The prices were bad; actually, they were very bad. If measured up in police terms, they all deserved a life sentence and the evidence stood in the face of far too many figures opposite each meal.

"Pick anything you want, Danny! I'm paying!"

"No, no, M. J., you are not my mother. I don't come here every day, so I can afford to pay for a meal. You can worry if I don't like the food as you brought me here."

Poltic forced a smile and decided that he should not bring up the subject again. Daniel's ego was always big, even as a kid. The food came and interrupted the heated debate about who had had a better-looking girlfriend in High school. They continued arguing while eating but no one expected a winner very soon. Poltic recalled how as children, they always chatted during meal times, when visiting each other. They concluded their dinner and talked about all sorts of things, in the manner of starting a topic and never finish it. Poltic thought it was time to ask the question, which was the reason he wanted to meet his friend about.

"Do you trust me, Daniel? Do you trust me like before?"

"Of course, what's up, M. J.? The policeman felt sincerely worried because the question was in a sharp contrast with the light-heartedness of the evening. "Are you into trouble or something? I am a deputy chief inspector now and I have to watch it because I'm one step away from getting into boss's chair! If it's not something too serious I can press a few buttons here and there and get it sorted."

"Oh, please, I haven't done anything. I don't even break the speed limit when I'm driving."

"OK, than, what do you want?"

"I need some information about a few people and I think you can find it for me!"

"What kind of information?" Daniel asked in relief that his best friend had not broken the law. Indeed, he did not have any closer friends than Poltic. "Go on, spit it out, or the restaurant will close and they'll chuck us out."

"I want to know about all the criminals caught in town for the last four years, who have committed crimes but have only received a suspended sentence. I don't need any of those who are into guns, drug dealers or have been caught for assault. Maybe, car thieves or someone that have defended his property and overdone it a bit – those would be fine, I imagine. You know, Daniel, I can't think of better examples. I'm not such an expert on crime."

"M. J., the people you need information on, we call petty criminals. There are so many of them, just wasting police time and we end up with piles of paperwork afterwards."

"So you can do the job, then?"

"That's easy, M. J. I'll make one of the new boys to prepare a list tomorrow and job's done! I'm the boss, so I'm not going to do it myself."

"I'll pay you."

"How much?" with a huge smile on the face asked Daniel.

"Look, I can't just ask you to do this for the sake of good old times. We are not kids anymore. That's why I'm giving you 5 000 and I want the list by Friday. You know very well that we all need money to live. Ah, and another thing, the people in the list should be between 25 and 30 years old.

"Five grand? You crazy? I'm not taking this sort of money, not from you, anyway! Never!"

"You're going to take it exactly because it's from me, you fool!" Poltic insulted him deliberately to show that he would not change his mind. Knowing him well, the policeman replied:

"OK, if you insist. But it's far too much for so little work. I'll owe you."

"You're not going to owe me anything. Just be discreet about our conversation and discuss what I've asked from you with no one! You can only mention that my girlfriend in High school was hotter than yours. You've got my permission about this." It took Daniel some time to get the joke but this did not stop him from chuckling for quite some time. The clients on the next table left demonstratively in protest of the constant cackle, coming from next-door table.

The meeting came to an end at about ten o'clock. Daniel and Poltic left the establishment and each of them headed towards their vehicles. While they were still indoors, chatting away and remembering interesting stories from their past together, Poltic offered to drive his friend home. He suggested that, perhaps, Daniel was over the limit. Trying to scare the deputy chief inspector with a traffic cop was ridiculous. Also Daniel insisted that two beers were far too little to make him drunk. Well, his sparkling eyes spoke for themselves.

Poltic waited for his car to be brought to him and at that time, Daniel was already sitting in his, ready to start the engine. He had parked about hundred meters away from the designated area for cars that belonged to the customers of the restaurant. Daniel just did not want anyone else to drive his car. Every year, he was growing more and more attached to it, instead of feeling that he should get a new one. The daily use of it for ten years had led to a number of irritating noises one could hear, as well as for the mileage to go round twice. Just before driving away in his old banger, Daniel remembered the black Mercedes that grabbed his attention on arrival at the restaurant. "It probably belongs to one of those snobs that left before us. Hmm, we can't have a bit of a laugh… It's not a church, is it? What is it with these empty-headed well-offs?" he carried on talking to himself on the subject and ended it cursing how unfair life was. He did not know that his best childhood friend was sitting in what caused his bitter thoughts.

Poltic was heading home, to his fortress-house, at a speed that was almost identical to the one, represented on the road signs. He was a conscientious driver. He never speeded not because he did not have the skills to drive faster but because he was always determined to get to where he was going. He called this a cautious, not cowardly, driving. Good job he did not know about Charlie's habit to 'fill up' the odometer, otherwise he would have swapped his Mercedes with a bicycle.

"How interesting! Daniel hasn't changed in the slightest! I probably look the same to him. I doubt I've changed more than him!" With a broad smile on his face Poltic continued thinking: "The personality of a man forms by the age of 20 and any small changes that follow, do not have any major effect. One cannot alter their way of walking or their voce, for instance. People have the same type of walk all their life, unless they had an accident or something. A man's voice breaks in puberty and remains more or less the same throughout until the end." Poltic reprimanded himself for thinking about such nonsense, which was all due to his tiredness. His headache grew and forced him to abandon the speculations on "what did and what did not change in a person's life over the years." Finally at home he went straight to bed.

The sound of the alarm could raise even the dead, so Poltic quickly reached for the button that said 'stop'. He was feeling very sleepy and decided to set the alarm again for one hour later. He managed to avoid hearing the irritating sound for a second time by waking up and pressing the button two minutes before 9 o'clock. The day started with his usual cup of coffee, two pieces of toast and a glass of milk. He liked milky coffee but he always had a separate glass of milk, too. He was used to this from when he was a child. After the effect of the first two sips of his coffee, Poltic felt totally ready for work and able to face the hard challenge, awaiting him in his study. He also had to confront the contracts Harry had brought to him. How many pages they had he could not say but in weight – they were about two-three kilos.

Poltic rolled up his sleeves and started. Firstly, he had Bob's report in his hands that contained data about the two largest companies and their share trading for one year back. Without even stopping for a minute's break or distraction, he concluded with Bob's report by lunchtime. The conclusion that was beginning to crystallize in his mind was going to spoil not only his day but also the next 12 to 18 months of his life. Well, this was what it said in the document. Bob had pointed this time frame as the minimum period of waiting before they could purchase any shares of the two companies. If they did decide to buy there and then, the amount of money they needed to spend was… Poltic looked at the figure a few times and even put the page closer to his eyes, not that he had problems with his vision but just to be certain. Bob was right, absolutely right. They needed to wait. Actually, Poltic hardly understood the contents of the report, which was full of diagrams and many words that required checking in the dictionary.

Poltic had to get on with Jane's eighteen sections on how the company could ensure its financial stability. He wanted to have some lunch first and to have a little walk in the garden in the hope to counteract his rising pessimism. Two hours later, he was already sitting in his study, feeling charged up with some positive energy. While walking in the garden, he allowed himself to distract his mind away from work. He decided that he wanted to get a dog, the sooner the better. Poltic had this idea at the very beginning of his life in the new house. He had already adapted to his new environment and it was time for the new inhabitant to be selected and brought here to live. The dog had to be large and of character so it could protect his owner. Poltic vaguely remembered his pet he had when he was a kid but he was sure he loved it a lot.

Jane's report was much easier to understand than Bob's. It was still written in a high-level manner but the principles were broadly known and were presented in a logical way. "The more the work is, the more money there is!" or "Less people – less problems" and vice versa. Poltic made things so simple that even a fool could grasp the gist. While reading Jane's written work, he referred a few times back to Bob's data. The truth was that Poltic did not need Jane's report whatsoever, in order to be able to develop his strategy for his company to become a leader on the market of meat products. Harry's fat contracts were of no use as well, for all it mattered. Only the documents of Bob and Geri contributed to clarifying the real picture about the current market conditions. Poltic picked up again Bob's report. He felt he should read it at least three more times in order to understand everything, until he reached a point as if he had written it.

The day was coming to its end slowly but surely. Friday was going to prove whether a long-term friendship could still mean anything. Poltic was also going to try to find out where to get a dog from. He already knew who he was going to ask. And Charlie? He had not phoned for four days; neither did he call by to see his boss. Poltic never found a spare moment to think about why his most trusted friend had withdrawn in such a strange way.

◆ ◆ ◆

The sealed envelope was quite thin as it contained just a page printed for each person. The age limit that Poltic had attached as a condition had also contributed to the small number of what came out as a result. Basically, most petty criminals were much younger and fell into the age bracket of 16 to 23 years old. The information had been found, printed out and packed since Thursday, ready to be collected.

The young servant of the Law was wondering why his boss had required such information. After all, someone with his rank investigated more serious crimes like armed robberies, murders, etc. There was unspoken rule at the police force: "the old dogs" were always right even if they were not. That was why the young policeman ignored his curiosity and did not ask any questions but took part in the conversation with the deputy chief inspector by only uttering words like "Yes, Sir, right away, Sir!"

Another day came and started in the usual manner for Poltic, since he had occupied the big house – with a cup of coffee. That day's agenda consisted of three points: a dog, Daniel and Bob. The morning was unusually cold and this urged Poltic to go back inside, after he made a couple of steps outside, and put a jacket on. It was a leather jacket that did not go with his black trousers or dark blue top but well, he was not attending a fashion show. He went to the two security guards and called one of them to get closer. Poltic told him where to go and what to do, making sure his work mate did not hear anything. There was a small problem. The guard's car was at the garage, his colleagues had driven him to work that day, and so he did not have a vehicle to use. Poltic handed to him the keys for the black Mercedes. He had no desire to ever give them to anyone else but the work was more important. Moreover, he had arranged an appointment and if the guard did not leave straight away he would be late. Envy sparkled in the other security guard's eyes, who would have also loved to drive such a car – a dream never to be fulfilled.

And now someone of the same position as him would be driving this wonder of technology. When Poltic approached him, however, the dark thoughts with regards to his colleague's lucky day quickly vanished.

"Do you know where I could get a good guard dog from? I really need some well trained dogs, perhaps a German Sheppard?"

"Yes, Sir, German Sheppard dogs are very smart and if well trained, they remain loyal for life."

"The firm you work for can provide these dogs I think?"

"Yes, Sir, we only have a few, though. And I'm not sure where my boss has got them from. I believe there are some dog-breeders out there, where they breed and train the dogs. You can ask him."

Poltic agreed with the advice given to him and went back in the house.

Someone rang twice at the door just before the two hands of the clock appeared one above the other. Poltic had no doubt who that was. He opened up and took the envelope and the keys that were handed to him. If he was not so impatient to see what was the important contents of the envelope, he would have told his guard off for driving so fast – the guy had come back far too soon than he should have. Poltic put the contents on the coffee table and sat down on the comfortable sofa. He counted the pages in front of him to check the number of the listed names, from which he was going to meet four people in person.

There were 78 of them and this was not far too many, he thought. The police record on each of them included information like a name and address, their family status, convictions and the number of arrests. It filled ¾ of a page for each person. The first few pages presented males as the main characters, responsible for petty robberies, involving small sums of money. There was one car thief and two who had been into a fight. Poltic wanted to separate those of any females. He definitely needed at least one member of the third group to be a woman.

His choice was quite limited as he ended up only with six female criminals from the entire list. One of them provoked a smile, when Poltic found out that she had hit her husband with a frying pan, who had got a suspended sentence for premeditated attack, causing an average bodily harm. The face that looked at him from the photo in the top left corner of the page did not show any signs that she was capable of doing something like this. However, on further examination, Poltic discovered the possible cause for her aggression – her cheek was swollen and he doubted the reason was toothache. Obviously, the husband had not treated her right. Poltic felt ashamed about finding this woman's case funny at first. He did not need a victim of some domestic violence so he put her record aside. He read through all the records involving women and selected the right candidate.

She was called Emma, who was 26 years old. The black-white photo showed the evidence of her outstanding beauty. Opposite her occupation, it was written a 'night watch'. This stunned Poltic tremendously. "A beautiful blond young woman, working as a security and more so – she was doing nights! Couldn't she find something better than that like a waitress or shop-assistant?" A few lines down in the document he found the likely reason for that. The girl had never finished even high school and most job positions required at least completed secondary education. So the lack of any qualifications had forced Emma to take the low-paid job of a night watch and it seemed that she had reached the peak of her professional realization. Perhaps, she was very well aware of her beauty but did not want to make her way taking advantage of her good looks. This was apparent from the offences she had committed. She had been convicted of assault twice. The first time, she had beaten up her boss because, in her words, he tried to touch her. The second time, someone had attempted to take a golden necklace off her and she badly hammered her attacker, who later sued her for causing him a grave bodily harm. The court had given her probation of eight months for the conviction of average bodily harm. According to the date of her court decision issued, Emma had been enjoying a clean court record for a few weeks already. By law, one could obtain a clean certificate of conviction, once the suspended sentence was over and this was something like a second chance.

This was exactly the kind of girl Poltic needed. She was a woman of a character, who was not afraid to defend her dignity or as in the second instance – her property. He wondered how such a fragile creature could stand up to two huge guys. The answer to that he would soon find out, when he visited her at her address. Opposite the block she lived in, there was her second home, where she would spend most of her time. Poltic could not wait to meet this gorgeous and dangerous woman. He did not give it a second thought, which was quite unusual for him, and decided that he would go there first thing on the following day.

To make his selection of three other criminals from the male contingent, Poltic left for a later time. He was certain that he would not find someone as half as interesting as Emma amongst them. He was going to leave the strategy development on his waiting list, too, but the reason for that was different. Poltic wanted to acquaint himself with Geri's sociological research, first. In reality, he was ready to go ahead as soon as he read thoroughly Bob's analysis for the third time. However, the data provided by Geri would only reinstate the methods he was going to use approaching the market situation. He believed that any actions on their part towards the two largest companies would be put on hold for the time being, anyhow. Most probably, the Team members would not appear indifferent to the fact that they would have to focus on some of the smaller businesses. Poltic was hardly concerned about what his staff would think of his strategy. It was not going to be a subject for discussion nor was it going to have an alternative! From that moment, Poltic was determined to act as uncompromising and austere leader. He was going to abandon any word games and lengthy talks and change them for a real decision making action.

The mission began on Saturday morning, when Poltic parked outside a huge panel block. This was where Emma had lived all her 26 years of her life. His attention was drawn to the building on the opposite side. It was as high as a three-storey house; about 50m long and had huge glass windows facing the street. Poltic entered the block of flats where Emma lived on the fourth floor, at number 21. The stifling air urged him to leave the door open, ignoring the note asking not to. He called the lift and a minute later, he found himself outside the front door, behind which was supposed to live the beautiful feisty young woman, who would hopefully become his employee very soon. He reached for the ring bell but stopped just before he pressed the plastic button. Surely, a night watch was asleep at 10 in the morning. She had probably gone to bed just a couple of hours ago. Poltic was not that sort of person, who stopped just before he reached the finish line. He risked to get a beating and pressed the button. There was no answer. He rang again, a melodic sound followed. Emma was either not in or she was fast asleep. He was just about to turn and leave when the elevator opened and an old woman appeared. She was holding a small child by the hand – her grandson.

"What are you doing here? Emma is getting paid soon and she'll settle her bills. Are you from the phone company?" The old woman did not try to hide her hostility. Poltic felt slightly offended that he could be taken as some ordinary company clerk, dressed in his expensive suit and replied politely:

"No, Madam, I don't represent any other company but my own and I don't want anything from Emma! I'm here to offer her a job. Could you tell me where she is or where I could find her? I rang the bell a few times but no answer…"

"You don't lie to me, boy, do you? Because our Emma gave her last boss such a beating…"

"I can assure, Madam, I am totally honest with you."

"You seem harmless enough but dressed like this you are more like a crook! I won't tell you anything." She pulled the child and started looking in her bag for the keys for the opposite door where she obviously lived. Poltic had no more than 20 seconds before she and the cute small boy entered their flat. He had money he could offer but felt it won't be the best thing to do with someone of the older generation like this granny.

"Madam, I really need to find Emma. It's very important, mostly for her sake. If you want to ruin an amazing opportunity for her that she undoubtedly deserves, then, don't say a word to me. But if you wish this young woman to be able to always pay her bills from now on, please, tell me where I could find her." The emotional plead made no difference and the woman slammed the door in respond. The grandson muttered something about Emma and mentioned the word 'boxing'. At first, Poltic could not make any sense out of those words. They were somewhat in conflict. But while moving down in the lift, he realized what it was all about and how come that Emma was capable of fighting much stronger people than her. She was a boxer!

He left the block and the first thing he saw in front of him was the building that drew his attention at first, the sport hall. There was faded sign above the big windows that only two letters could be read out due to the long time exposure to weather conditions – 'o' and 'x'. Poltic hurried up crossing the street, towards what surely seemed to be a boxing club. He hoped to find the woman he was looking for or at least, to get some information about where and when he could find her.

After a long and boring night shift, Emma was doing her training session. As soon as she finished work, she would call by her flat to fetch her boxing kit and straight to the club she went. While people felt exhausted after an eight-hour working day, this was when Emma felt at her best to do her training.

At the entry of the sport establishment, there was a man in his sixties, who was smoking a cigarette. Judging by his outfit, one could guess that he was most probably a boxing coach of young hopefuls. Poltic was dashing on so concentrated towards the door that he noticed the old man in the last moment before he nearly bumped into him.

"Good morning, Sir. Can I just pass?"

"Oh, Mister, you've come the wrong way. Common, turn around and off you go before I get to show you the right direction!" The 62-year old former boxer replied and took a position as if to apply a right straight one. Poltic made a step back to get out of his range.

"Fine, I won't come in as I don't want to enter in any conflict with you. But please, could you tell me if a girl, who lives opposite here, comes and trains in this club? Her name's Emma." Poltic pointed at the building and in this moment of distraction, his opponent managed to come nearer and sway as if to hit him. Poltic moved his head back in the last second. He realized more of this might follow, judging by the skillful movements of the old man – and surely one of his attempts would succeed. Poltic raised his hands to show he did not want to fight and dashed back to his car. He sat in and felt his racing pulse. He felt weird about getting scared from someone at an age that could be his father. He could have hit back and get inside. Well, who would hit his father? Definitely not Poltic! Instead he decided to patiently wait for Emma to show up, hoping she would not behave like this.

From the recent events, Poltic came to the conclusion that everyone in the neighborhood was prepared to defend Emma. What so precious could they see in her? He had no answer to that and he could not really know any details of Emma's life.

Her parents' arguing forced her to drop out of school at 13 and get a job. A year later, she returned to school only to leave at 16 and never to get to college. She was young girl earning a living and as little as it was she decided she would rather work than continue with her education. Her love for boxing she discovered when she turned 14. Through this typically male and aggressive sport, she got the chance to relieve herself from all the negative emotions, caused by her parents. All her neighbors felt sorry for her and loved her as if she was their own. When Emma lost her parents in a car crash and became an orphan at the age of 20, everyone saw this as a positive outcome in her life.

She had won people's hearts. And it did not matter that she was not very well educated and was constantly stranded for cash that she could never pay her bills on time. With time, people have stopped feeling sorry for her but realized they had a great respect and love for her. Her sound personality and strength of character had helped her take her life into her own hands, earn her living, doing an honest job and overcome the psychological pressure she had experienced most of her life. This was why she deserved everyone's respect and proved wrong all those people who predicted for her a life of a drug addict or a prostitute.

Why did everyone love her? No one knew why they liked the bullied child, woman with no family, the boxer-girl! They just did, naturally, as soon as they saw her beautiful smile, which was able to make everything negative and bad in this world somehow disappear!

When Poltic was 26 years old, he was very prejudiced towards ill-educated and poverty-stricken people on low income because he was earning at least twice as much as his peers and could also proudly point at his university degree, hanging on the wall. To his deepest regret now, he alienated some of his closest friends because of these advantages he had. When young, he believed that the poor and uneducated were ridiculed and despised but they should serve their right because it was purely their own fault for the position they were in. They had to fight and overcome the challenges if they wanted a better life. Musing on his totally wrong perspective in his younger years, Poltic felt sudden guilt towards Emma – the poor and ignorant stranger.

A woman with a ponytail appeared out of the sport club. She carried a black sport sack across her shoulder. Even from a distance, Poltic recognized her straight away. He came out of his car to meet her. He remembered that his smart clothes might provoke a similar aggressive reaction like that of her advocates but it was too late to think about changing them. He stood at the entrance of her block in a way that she could not pass him and asked nervously:

"Good day, Miss. Before you think I'm after money or something else, I want to assure you that it's not the case!"

"If I got nothing to give you, then what do you want from me?" Emma asked quite calm, in contrast of her reputation of a woman, who often end up beating up men.

"I'm here to give you something, if you want it, of course!"

"Give me what?"

"I'd like to offer you a highly paid job. You are totally qualified for it and you won't find any difficulties to do it."

"What's that job, then?" Emma was sincerely eager to learn more. She felt she could not doubt the words said by someone of such appearance.

Her first conviction came about precisely because of her being so gullible and naïve when it came to rich looking folks. When she was employed as a secretary, despite the fact that she had never worked before as one, Emma took the job without being able to see the sexual element in the offer. Her rich boss got a beating, whereas she got a suspended sentence.

"Here is my invitation to meet me in two days, when you'll understand everything. I can't tell you more right now. You'll be working as part of a team and I'd like to inform everyone about the job at the same time." Poltic gave her a small piece of paper with the address of his fortress-house and the time and date, written on it. She picked it and said:

"I sleep at this time so I can't come. And you're not telling me what it's all about!"

"You'll find out when you come. Believe me, one rarely gets this sort of opportunity. Don't miss it!"

"I'll mess up my daily routine if I come and can't box. No sleep and I can't fight and all goes to hell! So I'm out! Now get off my way!" her last words sounded like an order. Poltic felt he was losing and if he stayed there any longer, he might lose a tooth, too. He resorted to his usual weapon. It worked with the Team, it worked with the Young ones, and it would work with anyone, who stood up against him.

"Emma, I can only reveal that your monthly salary will be five thousand. If you accept, of course! You don't get an offer of five thousand every day, do you?"

"This much money is no to miss. I might just manage if I spend less than my usual in training but I can promise nothing."

"I'll be waiting for you. Have a nice day!"

Her pupils became wider, as if she had a strong coffee, when she heard the figure. Poltic noticed that and he was certain that Emma would come but still he never forgot that nothing was ever sure.

She was so gorgeous that Poltic found it difficult to stop himself from staring at her so he was just looking in her brown eyes throughout the whole time. They were nice, too. Boxing had sculptured her perfect female body – every man's dream. Being less than a meter away from her, while talking, Poltic felt a very strong energy coming from her, some kind of charisma. He could not put a finger on it but it was captivating. How was it possible for someone you had never met before to have such a spell on you! Poltic had never experienced anything like this before, especially with a woman of Emma's age. "She is perfect for Charlie, not me!"

Her image was very familiar but Poltic could not think where from exactly. Of course, it was from television. He had seen a film very long time ago, where the main character was a female boxer. The story went how she overcame many difficulties in her life to win at the end against her biggest rival on the boxing ring. She, then, put a gilded belt around her waist and her coach victoriously lifted her on his shoulders. A trivial fictional story but how amazingly reminded Poltic of the real Emma he had met that day. She even looked like the film actress; only the color of her hair was different. Her height, her weight, the tight stomach with a well-formed six-pack, the beautiful nicely shaped shoulders, and her thighs – everything was identical. Well, not everything. One could not miss to see that the actress had a look on her face, which spoke for an opulent life due to the money she earned for every film she played in. She tried to play a broken woman at the start and a triumphant one at the end but what one had not lived through for real, they could not re-enact it even if they were the greatest actress of all times. Poltic had a solution for this problem. Emma should have played in the first part of the film, when the young woman was on the verge of suicide, after she realized that she was unwanted product of her divorced parents' relationship. Actually, Poltic had no idea about Emma's family tragedy neither did he suspect about it but he could see that she had not grown up with a silver spoon in her mouth. Also, her leaving school so soon plausibly hinted at her was having unpleasant childhood.

The woman in the film got a job as a waitress so she could afford to leave her alcoholic mother and rent a place of her own. Her life changed when she went to the local boxing hall to find her neighbor and borrow some money from him. She fell in love with the sport and from that moment in the film, the actress should have continued with the role. The way for her was only upwards full of fake sweat and fake boxing skills.

Poltic managed to get rid of the film storyline, along with all the characters in it and he tried to go for an afternoon nap. It took him some time to fall asleep because Emma did not want to go out of his mind.

◆ ◆ ◆

Charlie had a heavy night that had turned into a heavy morning. The party he had with his employees was great but the subsequences – quite bad! That time, his headache was not down to too much alcohol but due to the horrendously loud music in the club. They stayed until six o'clock in the morning, when the place closed and, the result was that Charlie's brain was hitting about inside his skull when the young man was not even moving. He needed a good sleep.

The working week passed exactly in the way M. J. had predicted. Tony, Kate, Lorrie and even Michael were staying after working hours to finish the off whatever job needed to be done. When they heard that their new task was bound by a time frame, they nearly gave up. At that point, Charlie really showed his leadership skills that he never knew he had and lifted up the spirits of the young people in despair. The work picked up again, as soon as he personally tried to persuade one of the architects over the phone. He promised they would pay as much as they had to as long as the project was done by the deadline. Charlie wasted two hours with the phone in his hand because the man refused after all, but this was good example, which had a positive effect over everyone in the office. Until Friday, the phones never stopped ringing, the computers never stopped working and no one stopped doing stuff even for a minute. They all made a decision to use only a quarter of an hour for their lunch and ordered food to have at the office so they did not waste time to go out to. What really did it was the warning they got, which was if they did not complete the task within the time frame, they would lose their job. Charlie was not certain whether M. J. would really fire them if they failed to keep to the deadline, but he felt that he should remind his workers of his power over them, from time to time. Basically, Charlie was living the part.

Charlie discarded his suspicion that someone was watching them. He realized that Poltic had not sent anyone after them when on the third day he picked a different route to work. There was not such person, hired to watch his people, either. He had found out that it was the porter in the building, who was probably paid to inform Poltic about everyone's arrival time and that of leaving the premises at the end of work. He did not regard this as a lack of trust on Poltic's part, anymore, but as a necessity – someone had to do the supervision when he was not around!

Charlie woke up in the late afternoon and the first thing he thought of was that he should phone M. J. After he managed to free himself from the headache with the help of a few painkillers, he dialed Poltic's house number. He felt tired and lazy to go and see him in person.

The nap had turned into a four-hour sound sleep and it would have continued for even longer if it was not for the insistent ringing noise that was coming from somewhere in the house. Poltic picked up the phone and lied back on the sofa, speaking to Charlie. The conversation did not last very long due to the responder's wish to learn only about the most important stuff that had happened. He invited Charlie for dinner on the following day and hanged the phone down. The five-minute of non-stop talking had made Charlie's unbearable headache to resume.

Fully awake, Poltic began the process of selecting the other three offenders. He picked the records, which were still on his coffee table and skimmed through them. He did not have the time to read the files in detail. Poltic had to find at least two of them on the following day and one on Monday – a day before the invitation date to meet them in the house. What was left, as Geri would point out, was finding 75% of the required four in the following two days.

Poltic opted for two tough guys, who obviously worked as a team, judging by the circumstances, in which they were caught the three times. Their records were identical in terms of their education, occupation and sentences. They had been both trained to become car mechanics, they co-owned the garage they were working in and they had been to court for stealing cars. Their address, Poltic was going to visit them at, differed only by its number. If he picked them, this could cause problems in the future – they would make up half of the last group of four and in this way – they would outnumber Emma and the last person. Poltic, however, needed people, who knew about cars so he did not hesitate to put their records on one side. He wanted to kill two birds with one stone. He decided that the best time to visit them would be 8 o'clock in the morning on Sunday, when everyone was still in bed.

His thinking to surprise them in their pyjamas did not quite work out because the moment Poltic turned his car onto the street, where Johnny and Ted lived he passed a small red car, in which there they were. There was no mistake. Right behind the wheel, there was Johnny driving and next to him was sitting Ted. Poltic was certain it was them because he could never forget Johnny's easy to recognize egg-shaped head, which looked much bigger on the photo in his police record. He probably weighed about 120 kg. The enormous black Mercedes required much more space to make a U-turn and there was not such along the entire street. The randomly parked vehicles on both sides of the road made this maneuver practically impossible. Poltic put his foot down on the accelerator for the first time since he had had this car and within 20 seconds, he reached the first cross-street, where he could turn. The car he was following, had an advance of two minutes, enough to get to one of the main boulevards in town, as the two car mechanics lived in the heart of it. Poltic joined the traffic on the wide road but he could not spot the small red car. For a second, he wondered how two monsters of men could fit in this small old banger. The traffic lights made the cars stop, letting the traffic parallel to them to go and this was, when he noticed Johnny and Ted's vehicle. He waited to see what direction they would take and carried on following them. His progress was about to reverse when he spotted the right indicator on their car, pointing that they were heading to the car park of a huge supermarket. If he did not see where they parked it would be almost impossible for him to find them. Sunday was busy day when everyone was shopping to stock up until the following Sunday. Poltic had no chance of finding them on foot amongst hundreds of parked vehicles and haphazardly placed trolleys.

Well, it was his lucky day because he spotted the car after making just a few steps out of his vehicle. Poltic thought that this was not a car but some error of technology and design. He leaned onto the non-car and began waiting for its owner and companion to return. The store was very busy. A vast number of shoppers would spend 4-5 minutes at the checkouts and if one wished to return a purchase or their credit card was declined or whatever, this period doubled. After 40 minutes of waiting, Poltic saw Johnny and Ted approaching with a shopping bag in each hand. Both of them were enormous. One was more of a big guy and the other – more kind of fat. Just a few meters away from them, Poltic straightened up and made a step forward. No, he was not trying to help them with their load but wanted to introduce himself:

"Hi, guys? I'm Poltic."

"Hey, you, sleek midget! You're leaning on my car!" Johnny shouted maliciously to the shorter than him man in a suit. Poltic thought to himself "not the clothes again" and tried to correct the form of address he had just heard:

"Poltic, my name is Poltic. It is not 'sleek midget."

"We don't care what you're called. Common, f**k off!" Ted joined in, who also disliked short men, without a doubt. They were only at an arm distance from him and in a second, possibly not one but a few arms would remove him by force. Poltic was not aware that he was standing outside the driver's door. The car did not have a central locking system and Johnny and Ted could not get in. Being nice, obviously would not get him anywhere with these mean guys so Poltic turned mean, too:

"I'm not wasting my time here with illiterate thieves like you two. I got a job for you. Five thousand a month and you'll get a real car, not like this piece of garbage." Poltic kicked the right front door and the metal dented. "Here's the address, the date and time where to meet." He left the piece of paper on the top of the red non-car and paced towards his in a hurry, expecting the two gorillas to attack him from behind.

Johnny and Ted did not make a move for some time. They had a long history together and they could not remember someone of that size and appearance to have spoken to them like this. They felt scared by the tone used when the job was offered. The sleek midget must have been someone important.

The driver picked the piece of paper and without saying a word he gave it to Ted. They loaded themselves and the shopping in the car and just before they were pulling out of their parking spot, a black Mercedes cut their way off. The right window screen went down and the small man, they spoke to a minute ago called out: "Don't be late, guys!" Then, he pressed on the accelerator, which made the 12-cylinder engine to produce a sound that was beyond the two car mechanics' imagination.

When Poltic got home he had almost stopped shaking. He could still not figure out why the two bouncers did not give the cocky short man a good hiding. They might have not been that well educated but they were not so stupid. Books could not teach one about everything! Poltic was aware of that and he felt glad they had something going in their heads and did not always go physical. Emma, on the other hand, seemed to have nothing going on. Poltic felt guilty he was thinking of her as being stupid but really, after meeting her, he did not get the impression that she had much of an intellect. He hoped he was wrong and when they all came in the house, to see a speck of rationality and logic in her head.

Poltic was wondering whether Johnny and Ted would turn up, maybe not. He was too much in rush to leave the car park in one piece for him to notice their reaction to his offer of a huge salary and a new car. He had an advantage over them. Their garage was in the red. The small old banger probably cost as much as the wheel of his Mercedes. It looked that they lived at their parents still – there was a newspaper on the back seat, called "The middle-aged" – probably bought for one of them. The men needed money. Poltic also thought that he should definitely apologize for his rudeness. It was never too late to get a beating for it.

Charlie was coming to dinner tonight and Poltic ordered Indian food aware of his love for spicy food. It was not delivered until 8 o'clock so he had plenty of time to pick the final criminal to form the last group of four, which he would call RA in short. Scanning through the rest of the candidates, Poltic felt the same when he was trying to pick the members of the Team. The small detective, then, had done a superb job when it all started. But lately, Poltic was beginning to get tired of it all. He was fed up with doing preparations and just wanted to get on directly with the market, to get the better of it and finish up with "the job" assigned to him. Mentally sane, Poltic was beginning to feel exhausted by all this checking such and such and the meetings with Charlie and the Team. And now he had to meet Emma, Johnny and Ted, and the last person, who was probably going to be some Guillen. It could not continue like this! He should have the last four put together, introduce the Team to the strategy and start with the buying, and all this – by the end of the next week. His inner voice was telling him that if ten days went by when he did not manage to conclude a deal by buying of at least one company, he would just give up. Well, not completely but he would give himself a break, until he could carry on again stronger. These thoughts made Poltic to cancel his dinner with Charlie. He needed to concentrate on choosing the last person and did not feel like listening to Charlie's nonsense. They spoke on the phone, did they not? Everything was fine so there was no need to see him.

Poltic's ambitious plan included finding Guillen on Monday and inviting him to a meeting for the same day. He would find the phone numbers of the others in the Yellow pages and tell them about the change of date. He was certain that as soon as they set foot in his house, they would immediately start working for him. He would not allow for anyone to refuse his generous offer. If one of them did, then he would not bother with looking for a replacement but go ahead with whoever he got. Just he did not want to waste another couple of days. To save time, his plan envisaged a second meeting in the house on the next day, when he would enlighten his Team about the strategy or how the company was going to become 'number one'. In the last three working days of the week, the Team or he personally, would spend in serious negotiations to purchase one of the medium-sized companies in the sector, where at the end of it all, the owner of which, would be ready to sell up. Poltic was not convinced that this was possible but he ought to try. In his experience, plans were made to fail so new ones followed to only end up in the same way.

Early Monday morning seemed to be the most appropriate time to visit Guillen at home. He was a builder, who had been to court eight times for assault, though, never too heavy. Poltic chose that bully amongst so many, because the guy had a family, although there was no marriage. It was not hard to manipulate someone, who had something to lose. Not that Poltic was going to put the wife and kid in any danger! No, he was going to help them have a better life in exchange for Guillen's loyal service.

Poltic rang the bell twice, as usual, and waited. It was 7 o'clock in the morning, an hour before the man he was looking for, was leaving for work. A young woman in her twenties, dressed in black tracksuit bottoms and a non-descript long-sleeved grey top, opened the door. Poltic swallowed his criticism with regards to her clothes and asked:

"Good morning, is Guillen home?"

"Sure, I'll go and get him, just a second!" The inappropriately dressed builder's wife replied and went in. She left the door ajar by

10 cm, enough for Poltic to feel the smell of bacon and eggs. He breathed in the aroma of someone else's breakfast to give the honor to the rising sounds of hunger, coming out of his stomach. As badly dressed as his woman, a man of Poltic's height, (a midget, as Johnny would call him), appeared at the door. Despite the early hour, in which he was disturbed, the man's approach towards the stranger was more than civilized:

"Hi. I'm Guillen, Sir."

"I'm Poltic, nice to meet you. I'm here to offer you to work for me. The salary is 5000. You're going to find out more today, when you come to this address at this time." he gave the notorious piece of paper to the builder. He looked at the written address and said:

"There are many building sites in this area but I've never heard anyone paying so much…"

"Dear, Guillen, you won't be building anything. This is where I live and where my meeting with you and a few others will take place. When you come I'll tell you what work I'll need from you to do, if you accept it, of course!"

"But I've only worked in construction, can't do anything else..."

"Look, everything that will be required from you is going to be within your abilities skills. Don't worry, Guillen, just come along tonight! Five grand is five grand, isn't it?" Desperate, Poltic resorted to the payment figure again that everyone from the future RA was going to receive every month. Guillen calmed down, realizing how much was on offer and confidently uttered:

"I'll come. But can you tell me who's recommended me so I say 'thanks' to him if I get the job? The guy deserves a drink on me!"

"Nobody has. I personally selected you. See you later and don't be late, please!" Guillen resorted to a plain "Good bye!" and closed the door. He sat down at the table to finish up his breakfast in the company of his loved ones. He smiled. Guillen's tired face rarely lit into a jolly expression and this was noticed by his wife, who was feeding their cute little daughter at that moment.

"What happened? Who was this rich guy?"

"He offered me a job that pays 5000 a month!" He said elated and stressed on the sum. In reply, his wife started to scream, to shriek hysterically how much she loved him, what they were going to buy, where they would go on holiday, she was kissing the child and the whole day passed in making plans how they could spend so much money they had not earned yet. Like a true mother, she was beginning to see a bright future for their infant child if daddy kept up his new job. She gave herself up to dreams about it. What Guillen had to do for the money was the least of her worries! She even repeated the ultimatum a few times: "Whatever they ask you to do, you'll do it!"

Guillen did not turn up for work that day, knowing he would get the sack for his waywardness. Well, there were many construction sites out there so he could always get back to his old job if things did not work out with the rich visitor from this morning.

The rich visitor in question returned to his fortress-house and went back to bed because he had got up at 5.30 am so he could catch Guillen while still at home. He had succeeded in this and maybe that's why he enjoyed his sleep so much that he did not want to wake up. In the early afternoon naturally he did. He immediately resorted to the use of the coffee maker and found himself thinking about the events from six hours ago.

The young couple lived in what everyone would call a ghetto. Poltic saw for himself that the place was not suitable to live for any normal person but the lack of money had made people to do the impossible and subject themselves to those squalid conditions. All the residential blocks in the area were identical six-storey buildings with three flats on each floor. Each apartment had a 50sq.m living space on average, which was just about enough for two people. The outside area, including the streets, the small gardens between the blocks, everything was like from a film scene, representing as if a storyline about 'life after war'. Poverty, in this case, would guarantee that Guillen was going to show up that evening. Something, though, did not fit with the bully-image from Guillen's police record. Poltic did not notice any aggression – not in his demeanor or in the eyes of the laborer. If he had turned into a harmless sheep that can hurt no one, then he would be useless. The record showed that his last fight was two years ago, which corresponded to the noise of a crying child of a similar age, Poltic heard from inside their flat. It looked that becoming a father had made Guillen part with some of his old ways. Of course, the reasons might lay elsewhere but nevertheless, Poltic knew how to bring his aggression back and direct it in the way he wanted. Since money came to exist, people always fought over them and now it was Guillen, who had to do the same to provide a future for his family.

The arrangements, organized for the meeting with Emma, Johnny, Ted and Guillen had to be nothing but perfect. Overlooking even the tiniest detail would change the impression that Poltic wanted to make. And this had to be fear and veneration. Money alone was just simply not enough to make these people work well and become loyal. Poltic was aware that he was probably physically stronger only than Emma, although, he was not so sure in that, either. He was not a big person, had short arms and this was not going to do much for showing off power. That's why he bought some. A special surprise for his guests would be the four heavily armed security guards along with a couple of well trained guard dogs. Poltic broke his rule about anyone from the security guys to never have a gun on them. However, was there anything more effective than a machine gun pointing at you if one wanted to evoke fear? He would resort to this drastic measure just this time as the RA members would never set foot in the house again. After this event, the extra hired security was going. Only the dogs were staying for good. The butler, of course, would not be staying, either. His job, apart of opening doors for his boss, was different and not in the slightest to scare them. It would be to demonstrate the high class of the person, who could afford to employ him. Poltic did not doubt that at least one of the four would appreciate his effort to achieve that effect. If not, then the armed men would do the job.

Guillen, who was the most in need, came first where Emma – the hesitant one, turned up last. They all were already waiting for Poltic in his study. He entered leisurely as he was feeling at home and sat down in his chair. In this meeting, he did not envisage a conversation, as it would just waste his time. It did not seem very democratic but these people did not have much to say of interest to him. The monopoly of the speaker was applied with the Team in the past and the benefits of it were clear – one said important stuff and the rest just listened without resorting to unnecessary commentary. This kept meetings short and assured that only significant stuff was emphasized on.

"Welcome, everyone. Please, listen to me carefully, without interrupting me. I shall explain everything you need to know regarding my offer to you. When I finish, I'm going to give you a contract for confidentiality to sign. You agree to it with 'yes' and sign it or say 'no' and leave. I'm not interested in your personal motives about your decision. The work involves doing criminal actions when I order. For instance, you may have to give someone a light beating that in legal terms does not go further than an average bodily harm. It will all depend on the situation, in terms what I'm going to ask you to do. Your actions against the law should not go to any extremes." Poltic raised his index finger, stressing on the words. "Any extremes, lead to a long-term prison sentence and once convicted, there's nothing to stop you from grassing me up. I'm not keen on this, neither are you? " Johnny and Guillen nodded instinctively.

"Now, let me introduce you to some essential rules you need to follow when you carry out the jobs I give you. A compulsory condition is wearing gloves, when needed. Never carry a gun on you, no matter if you legally own one. Even if you don't kill but someone gets hurt by a gunshot – that carries a minimum of 10-year sentence. Knives are a NO, too! One could die from a blood loss should you get an artery or something. Get this, please! We don't want to kill anyone. It should always look like a standard beating, resulting in no more than the odd bruise or the most – a broken arm, finger or a rib." Poltic listed those parts of the human body that could be snapped. "In return, you get 5000 a month. Often, you may have to follow and watch someone, so you get a car, as well. If you get caught, you remain silent until the best possible lawyers, I've hired, come to see you. If they can't do much for you and it comes to getting an effective sentence, you will be still getting your salary in a bank account in your name or in the name of a member of your family, while in prison. To friends and family, you are working in the security sector. That's the official line. If you excel yourselves, fat bonuses will follow. And finally, before I get your decision – you should never come to this house again. Don't ever come looking for me, I'll be getting in touch with you via the phones I give you. You must be at my disposal 24 hours. Excuses like: "I didn't hear it ringing or I left it in my jacket" are not on! For those, who sign, the phone becomes their most important piece of item. Those, who do not accept my offer – watch it! If anything leaks, I'll know it is you and you'll be gravely sorry! This is not a threat but my company's principles." They all seemed fazed by Poltic's words. The fear was a good sign – it meant they needed to use their heads and try to overcome it.

Their decision lay in the contracts they had to sign. Guillen did not think twice and put his signature. He had been in prison, even for less than a month, and it was the last thing he wanted to happen again. However, even if things came to the worse, at least his wife and daughter would be provided for. That was the most important! Johnny also signed after making sure that Ted, who was sitting next to him, was working with the pen. Emma did not move. Again, she looked exceptionally beautiful this evening but this did not make her put her signature down. Poltic was about to ask her why. Well, he did not have to because eventually she signed, too. Poltic, very pleased, carried on talking but this time, he was much mellower:

"Excellent! Congratulations on your new employment and I hope we're going to work together for a long time in the future! As a sign of my good will, you are going to receive half of your wages now and the two motor fans could give the car outside a good test drive." Poltic gave out the envelopes with the money and the car key and was about to send them off but remembered that he had missed to mention a very significant detail of their future collaboration. "You are all paid equal so there's no place for competition. Work like brothers and sisters. And if someone tries to assert themselves and disturbs the equality in the group, they'll lose their job and a lot more. You are free to go now."

The host did not bother to get up and send them off. He left this to the butler, who initially led them in his study on their arrival. Left on his own, Poltic picked Bob's and Geri's reports ready to read them again. On the following day, in less than 20 hours, the Team was coming to learn about the strategy, thanks to which the impossible would become possible.

The Strategy

M. J. woke up with a head, buried in dozens of scattered sheets of paper, only two hours before Bob, Jane, Geri and Harry were going to turn up. The guests today, who were much more refined than the riffraff from the evening before, could not wait to hear what clever stuff the patrons of their boss had come up with. That was the reason why everyone arrived a bit earlier, even Harry. The lack of sleep had made Poltic's movements slow and his eyes quite red. He skillfully tried to conceal his not so great physical state but even if he felt perfect, that would not made the outcome tonight any different. Poltic ignored the fact that four pairs of eyes were staring at him, as well as he tried to forget that he needed a good sleep, some food, water and so on. He focused and began to tell the long tale, which could only contest a sci-fi novel. The main idea in the storyline was for them to make an offer to the companies from number three to six. This was the strategy, which even if it worked, it would not make theirs a leader. Poltic hoped to think of a way how to acquire the first two main players, while the negotiations with the other four companies were taking place.

"Firstly, I'd like to thank you on behalf of my patrons for the great work you've done. The reports have impressed with the information, which has been professionally processed and presented." he uttered a few more meaningless sentences before he got to the point.

In the past, he never bothered to look at their appearance, the women's jewelry or what color were Bob's and Harry's ties. This time, however, their keen looks made him notice exactly these tiny details. He felt awkward when he caught himself staring at Jane's cleavage for longer than he should and said as if scalded:

"The contract – that will be the most important part of our job." this sentence, in itself, did not make any sense but it somehow inspired the members of the Team, who were patiently waiting. "We shall offer the four companies, which are lagging behind the first two large ones in popularity, contracts of purchase. My bosses believe that's the best way we start out our progress."

"What if they don't want to sell?

"Good question, Harry, but according to the instructions I've got, the contracts that you and your colleagues are going to draw up, will have conditions, which will be hard for anyone to refuse."

"Mr. Poltic, that's impossible. We can't just force people if they decline the offer."

"We are not going to force anyone. They will sign on their own, freely and willfully."

"Hmm..., as if! Things like this don't happen in the real world, Mr. Poltic! Or do you have a magic wand?"

"Harry, just listen to me and you'll understand. How did you all start working for the company? I'll tell you. It's very simple – you got everything you wanted! The result: all of you are here today and you are working for me. So the present owners of the companies we're interested in will get what they want." Poltic really believed what he said. Bob hesitantly raised his hand to say something. He spoke after getting an affirmative nod:

"It's not quite like this, Mr. Poltic. Some companies have become a brand and they won't sell under any circumstances, unless a huge sum is involved."

"That's right, Bob, but can you see such company in the meat sector, amongst the four we've marked? I don't. Ah, another thing that's quite important – they've trebled our budget and we've now got 300 million to play with, and there'll be more coming! Again, that's not the final figure!"

"Wow, that really changes the picture, Mr. Poltic." exclaimed Jane.

"We'll be working alongside starting with numbers 4 and 5. You will make an offer to the fourth company, which Bob named nonchalantly last time and I'll do the same with the next up in the list." The stockbroker felt embarrassed when he got reminded of his mistake and looked down in guilt. Poltic's confidence, on the other hand, grew and managed to conceal the tiredness of his face to some extent. If his staff saw him looking weak, they would feel the same, so he should not succumb to his weariness. He kept this wisdom to himself and went on explaining why no one would refuse their offer by giving an example:

"Right, we've got a company with an annual net profit of 5 million, which general market value is around 70 million. What price are we going to offer so we don't get a rejection? I'm going to tell you." Poltic stopped Geri's attempt to speak by raising his hand. "Here's the formula we'll use to calculate our offering price. We double the value plus the total, made from the profits for ten years ahead. And that's not all. We are going to pay the former owner 4% of our annual revenue, again, for ten years. To top this up, we're going to develop an investment strategy. What exactly will that be – it all depends on the specific characteristics of the company. My estimate points at 190 million, which you will offer to company number 4 by going to their headquarters as early as you have the contract in your hands. The time frame will be one month and all other particulars will be down mostly to you, Harry."

The bomb was dropped and the effect – breathtaking. To offer such price for something of much lesser value could not be seen in any textbooks in Economics.

"Harry, how long do you need to prepare a contract, containing these conditions?"

"At least a week but I could get it over and done within just a couple of days, if I pick a ready made contract and simply replace some figures. It will be three days."

"Fine! Let's make them five. I expect two non-declinable contracts on Monday. Please, apply the same formula for the fifth company."

"What base value should I use?" Poltic had no idea what that company had been estimated for but he knew it was cheaper. So he made a guess:

"I believe 40 million is the right value for number 5, so you could use this as a starting point."

"So the total is…, 40 multiplied by two, plus the annual profits and this makes… how much?"

"Two and a half million…" Poltic revealed the unknown quantity.

"105 million, excluding the investment program, is the final sum. What do we put it as in the contract, Mr. Poltic? What is the value, the time period?"

"We'll negotiate the conditions for this individually, with each company. It is best if write that future investments are our priority and that we have budgeted funds for that."

"I got it, Mr. Poltic!"

Geri, being quite overconfident, was the first to butt in amongst the three listeners at the table.

"Don't you think we can reduce these sums? This is a lot of money, Mr. Poltic!"

"These are the instructions, Geri, and we are going to abide by them. Any new orders we have, you're going to learn about straight away!"

"Mr. Poltic, the rule, when negotiating, is to start lower and increase the price gradually until the seller's expectations are met."

"Of course, Jane, that's possible but we're not taking this route. I've told you everything I needed to say. Do follow all the instructions without improvising. There'll be sanctions for any willfulness on your part."

The unexpectedly short meeting drew to an end with Geri's final query. She wanted to know whether the companies they were going to approach, had any idea about it. "Not at all" was Poltic's answer.

Harry walked the way to his house along with his three colleagues. He did not join in their debate about whether it was right or wrong so much money to be spent. Bob would not change his opinion that Poltic's strategy was totally wrong, where the two women, would argue that the easiest way to get into any market was by having a lot of money. The women never asked themselves where the money came from, neither did Bob.

Harry was alone in his beautiful house, which did not belong to him, and the numerous questions just kept coming. When he was a student, he was much more desperate to always be a leader than his fellow students. He wanted to prove to everyone that he knew everything and could do anything. He did manage to achieve leadership by always winning in verbal battles rather than physical. It was very hard for him to be around people, who were more knowledgeable than him, unless they were renowned authorities on whatever subject. In this case, Harry could never regard Poltic as being one. The lawyer knew that he was much more competent than his boss and he could be a much better manager than him. What they all just listened to a few minutes ago could not be considered as an economic strategy whatsoever. It was pure nonsense. That was why,

Harry slowly got to the idea that if he could find the people, who were above Poltic, he could take his place. He would present them his irreproachable professional CV, which they had probably seen, but it would not hurt if he reminded them about it. Harry would also tell them that Poltic looked like a zombie in one of their meetings, probably under the influence of alcohol or even drugs.

The thought of dethroning Poltic settled firmly in Harry's mind and he could already see himself as the new master of the fortress-house and not living in this small villa. He believed that he should draw Bob, Jane and Geri on his side if he wanted to succeed. Four against one was much better than one against one. And if he failed, he would drag them down with him. He did not like them for many reasons and one of the main was that they did not have the innate ambition to win. Perhaps, only Geri had displayed she had the seed of victory in her and probably it would be easier for her to support his candidature. He was certain about this. Bob and Jane were some of the many people, who lacked individuality, submitted to what they had learned in university. They never made the effort to give something extra and original of themselves as if simply relying on their knowledge was good enough. Harry hated that sort of intellectual go-getters but he knew how to cope with them and eliminated them from his path all the way to the top. Who was up there, though? It did not matter if there were ten or eight rich guys, 'sitting' on the top. As soon as Harry got hold of the address and contact details of just one of them, then, that would be the end for Poltic. Until then, Harry decided to do his job conscientiously and prepare the two contracts as he had been asked.

Jane was genuinely crossed with Poltic. Twice she asked him a question this evening and he pretended as if he had not heard her, unless he did not. She was bewildered by his inadequate behavior at the meeting, which had managed to change her opinion about the highly respected Mr. Poltic until recently. "He's forced us to be quiet, just to listen as if we are in some prison. Good job that Harry and Geri are a bit more assertive and sharp-tongued, otherwise no one will dare speak. And Bob was so funny with his infantile raising of his hand when he wanted to speak." Jane felt hating herself for thinking so spitefully of her colleague and tried to look for the positive sides of the meeting. She was pleased that Poltic had told them that from next week they would start the buying process and their real job would begin. However, being someone, who had founded her own consultancy firm that advises companies on financial matters so they became more cost-effective, Jane knew that something was not right. She would have never advised on offering such price because it was obvious that the invested resources could be never recovered. It would probably take a century for the purchased company to pay off. Maybe, Mr. Poltic had something else in mind but what? Despite everything, she brought herself to accept the huge sum of money approach because it was clear that Poltic's patrons had enough funds to pay her the huge salary and the other extras for the next at least ten years.

Since Jane started her new job, she began to have problems with her husband. The restaurant was not doing well and it would be best if it was closed down, however, her expert opinion meant nothing at home. Her husband wanted to prove that he could support his family and not depends on his wife. His low self-esteem grew into anger and he would just flip over nothing that would lead to their everyday arguments. Jane was beginning to see her future more and more as being a single mother with two children. That was why, it was crucially important to her to be sure of her work prospects with Mr. Poltic.

Jane visited her best friend Geri on the following day and both of them had a good gossip about their boss.

"He looked like he had flu. Did you see his eyes? He probably had temperature!"

"Yes, Jane it's very possible!"

"You know what? Yesterday, I just didn't get anything. I mean, I have my own business and almost 20 years of working experience but last night was like I didn't understand a thing!"

"It was the same with me. I couldn't sleep. Where's Mr. Poltic going to get this sort of money from, so he can just throw it all away? I wanted to ask him but when he didn't answer you, I thought: "what's the point?" He is an odd ball – comes across as polite and rich but makes us just sit quietly and listen to him."

"Ah, and did you see Harry? His eyes popped out when he heard about the millions? He is such a greedy guy!"

"He's a nasty piece but a terrific lawyer! He's got such a reputation that's why he's so aloof! You've noticed that the three of us have kind of become friends but he won't. He thinks we are below him. That's the truth!"

"Stuck-up bastard! Good job that Poltic brings him down a bit, otherwise he'll just do our heads in. Geri, have you thought what about you're going to do on Monday because I don't know…?"

"We'll go to SEVKO Corporation's central office and get to the members of the board of directors. We give them the contract and we sit and wait for a month. It's easy-peasy!" Geri naturally looked around as if to check whether Poltic was in the room to tell her off for mentioning the name of the company.

"Yea, but it seems the three of us will be only going there to accompany Harry and I just don't like this. He won't forget to rub it in, either!"

"Well, he should do some real work, too, and acquit himself well for the mere four pages he handed in last time."

The women burst into a loud laughter and carried on talking about the kids, clothes and cooking. They decided to go shopping together at the weekend and get some nice clothes they could wear at the important meeting. The girlie chat was occasionally colored with the odd malicious remark about Harry.

Poltic was already informed about all this when on Friday he received the report from the spying foreign partner. Everything happened as he had expected – a wave of negative emotions had taken over the Team. The 'all against one' principle ruled at the time. Poltic should put a stop to this, although, it would be hard because Harry, the cause of it all, had the future of the company in his hands, then.

There were a couple of things that troubled him, apart from Jane's and Geri's hatred for Harry. Bob had constant quarrels with his wife, who made him sleep on the sofa a few times. Bob's well-being was more important to Poltic than how the others felt. The reason was that the stockbroker was going to negotiate the purchase deal of one of the companies alone. He would have the honor to do this after the contracts with 4 and 5 had been signed. At first, Poltic thought to make Charlie to do the job but then he quickly talked himself out of it, remembering how inexperienced he was. Bob had the experience but he was quite shy and this made him look unnoticeable when he was amongst people. Well, with a bit of guidance he would manage to do it, Poltic was convinced.

◆ ◆ ◆

The important day arrived. Poltic went up the stairs to the director's office of company 5, with the 200-page contract in his hands. He did not have an appointment and like most people, who had a lot of money, he just burst into the room. He completely ignored the secretary, who insisted that her boss was busy. A conversation did not really take place. Poltic introduced himself; he explained what he had come for and left the contract on the table by kind of letting it go demonstratively from 10cm distance, so it fell on the glass surface. He left the building and went home. He thought he was quite rude a minute ago and took this on board.

At the same time four limousines parked outside the 9-storey building – the headquarters of company 4. Bob and Harry opened their doors, while Jane and Geri waited for the drivers to open theirs. The board of directors of the company consisted of 12 people, one of whom happened to be an acquaintance of Harry. The spacious hall reminded the members of the Team of Poltic's dining room. There was a similar big table that could accommodate for at least 14 people. They settled comfortably with the three already present members of the board. The people were some of the actual owners of the company.

Harry had prepared a little surprise for them. When he announced the price of 120 million, the audience jumped from astonishment. Bob, Jane and Geri did the same. Harry had missed to confer with them about that he had changed the figure. They were shocked not because they had anything against the amendment he had made but because it was counter to Poltic's orders. Jane felt terrible thinking that she could get fired just because of this idiot. She nicely asked the startled hosts if they could be excused for a moment and discussed something.

Harry's grin was stuck on his face and it had no intention to disappear from it, even when his colleagues erupted against the revision he had applied without their consent first. No one from the Team could really understand why Harry was so pleased with himself, when he actually had disobeyed the orders. The reason was simple: his price was almost accepted by a quarter of the company's board of directors which meant that even if they argue about some extra 10-20 million, he would still manage to save 50 million of the initial sum. This automatically was going to put him in a better light in front of Poltic's bosses and who knows, they just might let him take over his place.

Harry phoned Poltic from his car to tell him the good news. The conversation was short as usual and he was immediately invited to his boss's house. The impudent lawyer imagined how he was welcomed with a glass of Champagne and relaxed back in the car seat. Within half an hour, the car was parked outside the house on the tarmac. The high personage got out of the car bursting with pride. Poltic personally met him at the door and nicely asked him to follow him to his study. Harry had never been in this room before and he liked it straight away because it lacked those annoying three steps. He sat down on the chair that was offered to him and awaited the well-deserved praises, owed to him the job good done. Not Bob, not Jane, not even Geri – but only he was chosen. Poltic, by the way, had received a printed record statement of some phone calls between Harry and another lawyer, who had been discussing the price reduction and whether it was possible to redirect part of the saved money into their bank accounts. It would have been impossible, they realized, due to how large the amount was. Poltic could not believe that Harry was capable of going ahead with it. It was in correspondence with his character but still he was working in a team. So what Harry had done meant only that Poltic was in charge of three obedient employees and one rebel.

"Harry, you've done a good job and you've saved us a lot of money."

"Well, Mr. Poltic, I'm a professional and I always strive for reaching perfect results. In this case, it worked but it's not always so easy." Harry was nearly going to burst with pride for being praised by his incompetent boss and he really did not expect the next words, which were totally free of any logic:

"But you've messed up by contravened my order, which I've received from my bosses so it's very possible they want to fire you. Discipline is an imperative and you've breached the principle of teamwork. You did not share with your colleagues your decision."

"Are you crazy? Listen to yourself! We're talking about at least 50 million that you would have thrown away if it was not for me! I want to see someone higher than you, Mr. Poltic! I prefer to explain about my huge success to the people who give the money, in person! I'm sure they will appreciate what I've achieved." Harry's knuckles turned white when he clutched the sides of the chair and threateningly stood up.

"Calm down, Harry! No one's knocking down what you've achieved. However, breaching an order is perhaps, the gravest offence one could commit in our company. I shall present your accomplishment in the best of light before my patrons and let's hope you won't get fired. Hopefully, you'll get away just with a fine!"

"A fine? I want to speak to someone else, not you, now! Call your boss and hand me the phone. Common, do it! What are you staring at me for?" The good tone had disappeared and Poltic responded to Harry's disgraceful behavior by treading on this toes:

"I can't fulfill your request but what I can do for you is to fire you single-handedly if you continue speaking to me like this! Both of us will lose out from this. So I'll compromise by suggesting you never breach an order of mine in the future and I'll turn a blind eye to your waywardness just this time! You agree to this and you will stay at work for a long time, otherwise you can look for another job from tomorrow! Am I clear?"

"Yes, Mr. Poltic, it is all clear. I apologize for my outburst. This won't happen again."

"Good, and now, as far as I am aware, you will be quite busy dealing with the legal departments of companies 4 and 5. You'll have to find some common ground and reach an agreement, regarding our offer to them and specify the future investment programs. So you can go now and carry on with your work." getting the marching orders, Harry wanted to throw Poltic out of his director's comfortable chair more than anything! That was why he did not take the option to get fired – it was all getting too personal! The mission to find the people above Poltic and discredit him, so he could remove his enemy out of the way and take his place had to be concluded.

Thirty days passed, during which Poltic managed to regain his mental stability. He spent a few hours a day working on what came next but he could still not see a light in the tunnel, at which end stood companies One and Two. The dogs had a positive effect on Poltic, who really enjoyed spending time around them. They would never get bored of 'fetch the stick'-game, they never complained about anything and they always happily welcomed their master with their tongue hanging out. If he found people as loyal as his dogs, Poltic would have employed them straight away.

Every day M. J. wondered about what he could do with Harry. His work on the contracts would be completed very soon and Poltic would become the owner of companies 4 and 5. After, he could hire other lawyers to carry on with the preparation of the future agreements. Well, Poltic's good heart made him believe that everyone deserved a second chance, whereas his common sense reminded him that the conflict he had with Harry, was deepening. Poltic's rational thinking prevailed and he decided to demote Harry to a supporting role in the future and to override his initial promise to him of making Harry a head of the legal departments of the newly acquired businesses.

RA in Action

Poltic assigned the first task to the newly formed RA on the tenth day of hiring them. It was connected to company 3, which was slightly different from the rest. The company was the oldest amongst the meat products manufacturers in the country. It was founded 150 years ago. It had been through many crises, governments, natural disasters and wars but there was something intransient about it – a heritage. Ownership was passed down from generation to generation. Every son replaced his father and this tradition had been preserved for a century and a half. Poltic knew that money alone would not be enough to break this cycle. He decided to provoke fate in the face of RA, who were about to act ruthlessly. There was no other way. On a second thought, money could have done the job alright because company 3 experienced hardship due to their unwillingness to invest in new technologies. However, Poltic did not feel like taking the risk. He wanted to insure himself before he loosened the bag with the millions. He contacted Johnny, Ted, Guillen and Emma separately and told them about the address they had to go to.

They were standing outside the modern business building, unaware that a floor below the place they were going, there were four persons, who also worked for Mr. Poltic, well, five if one included Charlie. Emma, Guillen, Johnny and Ted had no qualms about their scruffy appearance, which was in contrast with the dozens of smartly dressed young professionals, pacing about determinedly. The members of RA just knew that they were cut from a different cloth! The porter at the entrance gave them a key and they all went to find room 41. Guillen guessed that the first number meant which floor it was and the second determined which office.

They found the room and the boxer-girl turned the key to open the door. There was absolutely nothing inside. Only the light was hanging from the ceiling, broke the grayness and flatness that was characteristic of the walls around them. Emma suggested they left this place as they must have come to the wrong room but then Guillen saw something. In the corner to the left, along the wall, where the door was, he spotted a small rectangular safe. Johnny went near it and squatted down to have a good look. His large back prevented from the rest to see what was happening. Ted suggested they move and put the safe in the centre of the room. It was a typical cash-box with a dial.

"I think I know how to open it!"

"I think I know too, Guillen." Emma uttered.

"Do we all think about the same thing? About what Mr. Poltic told us to remember without telling anyone?"

"What about, Johnny? Tell me, I want to know, too!" Ted asked like a spoilt child, as he could not figure it for himself. "Ah, the numbers... Oh, yes!"

"Who's first?" Guillen, standing out as the smartest of them, asked.

"Ah, Emma is a woman, so maybe, she has to be first." Gorgeous Emma did not like Johnny's attempt to define what she was but agreed with his proposal, as it matched with the instructions of their boss. She leaned in a way no one saw what direction her right hand turned the dial to and after a second she stood up:

"I'm done, who is next? Actually, did Mr. Poltic mention about what's inside because what I gathered – it's the task we have to do!"

"I was told the same, Emma. We'll just open it in a minute and we'll see. Now, it's one of you guys, but who?"

"Hmm, how did you figure out this, Guillen? I think it's you!" Ted snapped without thinking, not that he was ever good at this activity – 'the thinking'.

"Mr. Poltic told me over the phone that I'm going to be last. At the time, I didn't get what he meant but it must've been about this thing here, down by our feet. So just turn the dial according to the numbers you've been told."

"He's right, Ted. I kind of remember now, a part of the two numbers, also something about being second. He speaks funny, our boss!" Johnny leaned over the object, followed by Ted and Guillen. A gentle click accompanied the small door's opening. Inside, Guillen found a small piece of paper. He stood up and read it out loud. His work-fellows listened impatiently. They were all feeling as if they were taking part in a TV game show and had just come to the big question for the jackpot.

"Emma, Johnny, Ted and Guillen that is your first assignment as employees of my company. You have the total freedom of choice how exactly to fulfill the given task below. Every expense, you need to resort to that will help you achieving success, is justified, no matter how big it is. The time frame is not subject to change, so you need to act fast and efficiently. 1/ Name: John, Address: 10 Lake Shore Drive, Age: 24, Car: Mercedes SL 55, Registration plate: 4444. You need to cause that person a medium bodily harm within three days. A broken leg or an arm is a must! 2/ on the following day, after the assault, you have to block road C492 for more than twelve hours. I recommend you use cars, trucks, wood load or anything of large size for that purpose. You can improvise as long as you achieve the result! It is absolutely prohibited to hurt any innocent citizens. Now put the piece of paper back in the safe and leave the building. Good luck! M. J. P.

P. S. I'm going to send a man to Johnny and Ted's garage this afternoon. He will give you the sum of two hundred thousand, which should cover your expenses for your first task. The money is for everyone and you can only use it after you have agreed on what your roles are in all this. If you need more, you can call me on the number, recorded in the phones I gave you. Do not dial this number under any other circumstances. Never!"

Guillen followed exactly what it said in the letter but Johnny angrily shouted at him:

"Why did you put it back inside? You've remembered it all, have you?"

"Oh, I just didn't think. Just did it 'cause it said so in the letter!"

"Let's open it again!" said Emma and dialed her combination of numbers. The guys took their turn faster than the first time. They did open the safe again, however, the important information had gone – the paper was blackened by very high temperature and the text could not be read anymore. The curious gadget had been invented by the foreign company that Poltic was a sponsor of. They opened it alright the first time because on entry, they had triggered a sensor device, which allowed them to do so, as it sent a signal to the box. The second time, they only had to open the office door and close it again.

In this way, they would have avoided the bad result by activating the device again. They were simply not aware about the interdependence of the two mechanisms and the fact that they knew the right numbers did not prevent the contents to be subjected to the destructive effect of the heat.

The four went back to the car that so far, had been used only by the two car mechanics. Inside the vehicle, Guillen made every effort to restore his mates' memories about the content of the paper by asking them questions. They managed to reconstruct the text just about and only Johnny and Ted had a heated debate over the model of the Mercedes, whether it was SL55 or 500. They all knew where the address was as they were born and bred in this town. They also found out that the road they had to block for twelve hours was actually a street in the industrial estate, where Johnny worked in a car-breakers scrap-yard about eight years ago. His old job could actually come handy for doing the job. "After all, a dozen of scrapped old bangers could block nicely a two-lane road, no problem!"

Guillen wanted all of them to discuss together, in peace, what they were going to do in detail and thought that his newly rented apartment was the perfect place for this. It was double in size if compared to the hovel, he used to live, and it gave plenty of space for them to have a good talk about "How we could best make Mr. Poltic happy!" The four settled in the spacious living room and Guillen's girlfriend made sure they got something to drink from the now well-stocked fridge. The young woman was over the moon she had money that she just bought so much stuff she had never tried before. She had no idea whether some things tasted nice or they were bitter, if some of the food was hot or sour. It just did not matter because she fulfilled her long-time dream by doing her irrational shopping. For any affluent person, this sort of attitude remained inexplicable but it made every sense to her and the numerous people in the country, who were in a similar financial position or even worse.

Within a few hours, the RA team concocted a plan how to go about their tasks. Emma gave the idea how to beat up the guy, without him seeing their faces. They all also agreed that they should not wear masks, as this would draw unwanted attention to them. Emma's short skirt would have to do the job, giving Ted, Johnny and Guillen enough time to get ready and attack from behind and give the target a good beating. Guillen's personal experience made him to explain that the best way of doing it was applying a single blow with a metal pipe, which had to be in a jerky manner and be medium in strength. Any blow that was too strong could shatter the bone and do irreparable damage. He sounded like someone who broke bones all his life or as if he was an orthopedist. Ted, who initially disliked Guillen, was impressed by this the most.

On the next day, they were going to pin down the whereabouts of their victim and pick a suitable spot where Emma would draw John's attention and distract him. They conjured up an interesting plan that would help them achieve their second goal, too. The idea to stage a car crash with four vehicles involved, one for each of them, was discarded immediately. The emergency road services could clear the mess within an hour or two, as well as, lots of questions would follow. A truckload of wood sounded perfect but neither Johnny nor Ted wanted to be the driver. It was too risky and life threatening. Explosion sprang to mind but how could they do this and at the same time manage to get the entire police force off their back? Johnny resolved the problem accidentally. An old car that drove on natural gas rather than petrol carried a 'time-bomb' if driven recklessly. It had to be at least fifteen years old as the newer models had more safety features. They were going to cause the car to explode from a distance so nobody got hurt. They would leave the valve open to fill the trunk with gas and then throw a lighter from 5-6 meters away. Job done! Guillen, however, pointed out that the damage on the tarmac would be superficial, as well as, only one of the lanes would be really affected. This meant – less work for the emergency road services. Johnny had thought about this problem, too. He suggested that they should go the previous evening and drill lots of small holes about 10cm from each other. The subsequent explosion would cause far worse damage to the road surface by littering it with deep pits. Genius if it worked! An academic with two university degrees could envy the way these "simpletons'" brain worked at this moment.

No one of them thought about why their rich boss was asking them to do such things. The young guy might have deserved a beating due to some bad vibe in a common business venture they had together. So much, they could think of! But the 12-hour blockade of the road remained a mystery.

The owner of company number 3 had something very precious. That was his son John, who was going to get a beating. The road blockade was the key element for Poltic to get hold of the business through a successful purchase deal. The road was the only way, which led to the motorway and the trucks could distribute and deliver the company's meat produce throughout the country. A blow to his family's safety was supposed to distract the businessman from his work, when very worried, he would run to the hospital to see his son. Then, the delayed by one day product deliveries, would force him to run to the spot of the incident. The explosion would bring only insignificant financial loss to his company. Nevertheless, the game that would affect his personal and professional life should make him more inclined to sell two weeks later, when Poltic intended to approach him with a contract in his hands. Of course, things could turn pear-shape, RA's efforts could fail and the company – not purchased by Poltic, after all. However, he wanted to believe in the success of his intricate and complex planning rather than rely on some mere chance.

On the following day, Emma went shopping in some of the most expensive boutiques. She needed to get a 'uniform' for the next day's mission. Being poor all her life, she had never been to any of these glittery shops so at first, she felt very shy. She had to buy some provocative clothes because her wardrobe contained just sports gear like many tracksuit bottoms and some tops. She also had a couple of pairs of jeans, as her best, for special occasions like going to a birthday party of one of boxing coaches or on a first date with the latest sucker, who was inevitably also a boxer. A second date almost never followed.

Emma very quickly got used to the attention she received just by living the difference between 'having money' and 'not having money'. The girls in the shops treated her like a princess and fulfilled every whim of hers and no one saw in her the illiterate boxer girl. It would take time, however, for her to get rid of some her old habits – a tell-sign that she had been poor in the past. She was still checking the price label on every piece of clothing she liked. She needed time to learn to be rich. Emma finished with her shopping after a couple of hours, which in itself was a record for a woman. Her strong arms were finding now the bags quite heavy.

In the mean time, her colleagues were waiting with a cup of coffee in their hands for John to come out of his flat. They were not sure exactly which apartment he was living in but this was not important to them, anyway. They did not go there in the car, Poltic gave them but in Johnny's ugly one. The driver thought that in that way they would draw less attention to themselves. No one argued against his pointless decision. The SL was nowhere to be seen but who would leave that type of car all night parked on the street? In both cases, if stolen or just crashed in by some drunk, the car insurance would cover the damage. However, in the second instance, the poor owner would witness a sight that was not very pretty. It would just wound his heart!

Generally, people start work at eight. They would wake up at seven o'clock and half an hour later, they should get to the car so they arrived on time. For a young man, who worked in his father's factory and got there in a super-expensive vehicle, these common worldwide rules did not apply to him. That was the reason why John, ear-marked to get a beating, showed up as late as 11 o'clock. He appeared from the underground garage in the building, looking very comfortable in his SL and speeded towards daddy's factory. "This swine was in for such a thumping!" The three of them agreed on this. So, the plan was: Emma had to break down in her car at about 10-11 o'clock on the next day. The rich young man would kindly offer his help to the most beautiful girl he had seen lately. Actually they could not just block the road and wait for their victim to appear. It was best if they parked in such a way that their vehicle did not obstruct the traffic on the small street and in the same time, John was not able to pass them. It was quite hard but very possible. Then, they just attack him from behind and job done!

Until that moment, the members of RA had to spend some time preparing the road they were going to block for around twelve hours. In the nighttime they would drill some holes, where they picked a 30cm attachment bit. Johnny warned them about being careful not to damage the top surface of the tarmac. Otherwise, some prudent driver would notice and contact the road services, which were going to arrive and fix things straight away.

To turn the car into a kind of bomb, Johnny and Ted needed no more than two hours. They were skilled enough to make any old car that drove on natural gas, explode. Who was going to be the 'driver' of this car, the person, who was going to wait for the Police to turn up and give them an account on what happened and how he nearly died in this tragedy? Their rich boss had explicitly told them that they were free to use any methods to complete the task. Johnny had an old friend, whom he trusted well enough. He was slightly worried about Mr. Poltic's unawareness about the new member of the group but no one wanted to go and tell him at his house. It was strictly forbidden to disturb him there.

The second day, since they had received their instructions, went very well. They managed to beat up the young man accordingly without any witnesses and leave fast away from the scene. There was a bit of a commotion at some point, when Johnny and Ted found themselves mesmerized, just staring at Emma. So Guillen, completely by himself, ended up pushing John on the ground and breaking his arm with a metal pipe in one blow. When they brought themselves to their senses and stopped admiring their female workmate's beauty, the two mechanics rendered a couple of kicks to the guy on the floor, who was already bent in double from pain.

They all but Johnny had a beer at lunchtime in honor of the hospitalized John. Emma got quite unusually chatty from the light alcoholic drink. That was not surprising at 12 and on an empty stomach. Despite having a great time, none of them forgot that there was the second part of the task still waiting to be fulfilled. Johnny and Ted headed towards the garage to set up the bomb, which was supposed to explode tomorrow around six in the morning. They both were going to be at safe distance behind the vehicle when the big boom would destroy the road, seeing with their own eyes that the mission has been completed.

Emma and Guillen were not going to be present. It was unnecessary. Both of them could not sleep all night. They were up since five o'clock, waiting for their colleagues' phone call, as arranged beforehand. An hour had gone, since the car's supposed explosion and still, no one had called, yet. Guillen turned the TV on to see the news and jumped from joy. The top news was the explosion on road C492. Fortunately, no one was hurt. He called Emma to tell her the good news and went back to bed to catch up on his sleep. The overexcitement from their successfully completed jobs in the last two days prevented him from falling asleep. For a few hours, he just enjoyed watching his little daughter, sleeping in her new cot. Guillen was beginning to feel emotionally unstable. Until recently, his life was hell; he lived like an animal, depriving himself from food, so there was enough for his closest people. Then, money came, bringing him all that stuff and for the first time, he felt like human again. Guillen could not stop a few tears running down his face, thinking about the path that took him from hard bottom right to the top, in less than a month.

Poltic heard about the good results RA had achieved, in the same way Guillen did – from the news. The comments pointed out at some good two days of repair work that was going to take place, as the crater on the road was nearly a feet deep. He was very pleased and became even more so, when he read the following title in the newspaper: "The son of a meat tycoon ends up in hospital". The article below informed that the young man was a victim of mugging, where his wallet and expensive wristwatch were missing. Poltic called the four of RA and congratulated them for the good job, and then he reminded them that they should throw their trophies at once. They complied with the order, although Ted was unwilling to get rid of the gold watch that he had liked so much.

The Next Step

They say time flies when one is busy doing stuff.

This was exactly how Poltic felt, when he was on his way to the factory, owned by the person, who experienced a heavy blow to his both, personal and professional life, only two weeks ago. The road was already fixed, where the crater, caused by the car-'bomb', was filled leaving a visible spot of new tarmac. Poltic parked outside the office part of the factory, where he had to find the owner with a contract in his hand. He did not have to wait and was invited straight away in the luxurious office-room. The first impression he had was that the interior was too cluttered. The walls were over laden with portrays of the owner's ancestors, below which one could see their dates of birth and death. The entire wall to the right was filled with awards and honorary diplomas, placed in a glass cabinet, especially made for that purpose, so it looked like a wall of fame. The director's working desk was even more overburdened than that of Poltic. There were even some sheets of paper, fallen on the floor.

The visitor sat down after being invited to do so and immediately stopped noticing about his surroundings, as he always did when he had an important conversation ahead.

"I am glad you have come, Mr. Poltic. You've mentioned some very interesting details on the phone. I cannot wait to hear more!" The 50-year old man, who was as smartly dressed as his guest but had a slight beer-belly, 'passed the buck' to Poltic. However, he seemed totally distracted by the fact that on entry, the man, he was coming to see, looked very cheerful if not even happy. His face did not give out any sign of the problems he had experienced recently like his son ending up in hospital after a beating or the road events that caused the man some losses due to the delayed delivery of his produce. "Hmm, maybe, this is just his 'working face'!" Poltic thought and continued with the purpose of his visit.

"I've come here with the intent to introduce you to my employers' business plans, in the hope that I could tell them some good news they expect to hear from me, when this meeting concludes".

"And what is that, Mr. Poltic? You've mentioned you'd like to have some mutual business with me and my company!"

"Mutual business... I'm afraid, I wouldn't put it this way. I'm here to present you with an offer for buying your business!"

"What do you mean? You want to buy it? But it is not for sale, Mr. Poltic, definitely not!" 'Number 3', looked at his ancestors' portrays, as if seeking some support for his decision.

"Look, I've brought this contract for you. I'm going to leave it here and I hope, you examine it in detail because the conditions we offer you are unprecedented, for this sort of business. In other words, we'll pay you a price that is very hard to imagine."

"It's not for sale. End of story! I don't care what it says here, though, I'm a little curious. Mr. Poltic, my grandfathers, my father, one of my uncles, then, me, and my son have directed this company and will continue to do so from this very chair that I'm sitting on right now! This business is more than just work for our family, it's our life!"

"I couldn't agree more with you and I'm very aware of the tradition that runs through your company. That is why, we would like you and your son to remain and manage the company. You will be in charge of the business even at the event of a possible purchase on our part. That is a very special clause in the contract, along with all the exceptional financial characteristics, you will find." Poltic had added this at the last minute, knowing that he might get a negative answer, precisely for that sort of sentimental reasons.

"Hmm, you have really intrigued me! And now, I'm going to have to read it!"

"We also have prepared a long-term investment program, which is going to strengthen the business altogether and bring about greater profitability to the company."

"What percentage are we talking about here, Mr. Poltic?

"We want it all but we will accept what will give us the power to direct the business if it comes to that. Of course, you will be a manager for life, as I've already said, but you will have to follow our economic policy."

"I understand that, Mr. Poltic. Every company has different views about the market and I hope that mine correspond to yours. That is if I accept your offer, of course." He replied, expressing far greater interest in the idea.

"I am certain we could achieve unanimity with regards to future objectives of the company. I'd like to assure you that the end results would be very satisfying to you, and to us." The secretary came in to bring a glass of juice to the visitor. Poltic, however, remained faithful to his principles that one should not waste valuable time and only talk about what was important. He considered that this part was over and prepared to leave. 'Number 3', who also stood up to send his interesting guest off, repeated a few times his promise that he would read the contract very carefully. Poltic's time frame, this time, was just two weeks, when he would return to learn the answer of the company director. M. J. also gave him Harry's business card, in the instance of some questions occurred, regarding the conditions of the agreement.

Poltic knew that the deal would happen only for the special clause he had attached additionally. When he mentioned about it, his host's eyes clearly expressed his determination to rescue his sinking ship. He was prepared to stay on board even if he failed. Poltic realized that what RA did was not necessary at all and that the end result would have only depended on the special clause. Anyhow, he still considered them as still quite valuable.

◆ ◆ ◆

The problems amongst the people that Charlie was in charge of, deepened by the day. According to him, Michael did a lot of work but he ignored his colleagues and they felt much better when he was not around. Poltic hoped to find out what kind of person was that rat Michael after working hours, and whether he had a reason for his bad attitude. Poltic might be able to help him if he found out what was behind his behavior instead of losing a valuable worker. If there was nothing that caused it, then he would be out at once! This was RA's next job – to follow Michael.

Poltic was faced with a serious problem, regarding company 'number 6'. With companies 4 and 5, he did not expect a refusal of his offer. As it looked, in two weeks, company 3 was going to be also owned by him, however, 'number 6' had some specific characteristics, which made it almost impossible for him to get hold of it.

The company was the most innovative, most effectively run and modern business in the sector, despite its relatively short history. 'Number 6' had a bright future ahead and the prognosis was – more and more profits. Paying up the 20-years bank loan was not a problem, as the investment in modern technologies had been almost paid off through the factory's constant operation, around the clock. The number of workers, employed was 'criminally' small. After all this, how was it possible for the owner to decide to sell up? The company was worth about 50 million and the predictions were more than optimistic: it would be worth no less than 300 million within just five years, taking it up to a third position in this market sector. Poltic knew all this and the owner did, too.

At first sight, it seemed that there was no solution to this but Poltic, believed that he should at least try. He did not have any particular expectations that 'number 6' would respond to his generous offer but no one would get hurt if he made his attempt. His initial idea was to acquire the last four main players on the market, before making an effort towards companies 1 and 2. Nevertheless, reality turned out differently – so far, he was given the chance to own three of them, well, actually it was two. The third one was still 'cooking'. So he had achieved 75% of his target but Poltic considered this a step backwards in his grand plan of swallowing up the entire market. He hoped that he would win over the odds and buy the last company after just a short phone call.

18 days later and just one day before the most awaited by Poltic event took place, he invited Bob, the loyal and kind-hearted of them all, to the fortress-house. Lately, the reports on him had showed that his personal life had improved, probably after he suggested to his wife to take her on holiday.

"Hi, Bob, please, welcome! Have a seat. How are you, Bob? How are things with the management of the new companies? Any problems?"

"No, Mr. Poltic, there are no problems! We are still finding it a bit hard as we have so much to do. Also we are kind of still getting acquainted with this type of business." Bob was slightly nervous. He had not done anything wrong, worked as hard as he could – almost 16 hours a day, and still he had been called to a personal meeting with the boss. Like most people, he associated this unexpected invitation with some kind of castigation; he was about to be subjected to. Yes, this was exactly what he prepared himself to get from Poltic – some criticism.

"I totally understand, Bob. You will all get used to it. As far as I'm aware, Jane has informed me, only one of the three companies has shown poor financial indications, the rest are working at a profit."

"Yes, that's right, Mr. Poltic. The most recent one you've acquired the one that's been passed from generations, it is about 15 million in debt, I mean, it was, after you've managed to pay them. To be honest, it's not in good shape at all in a technological way or looking at its location. Transportation costs make the end prices too high." Poltic decided to leave Bob speaking a bit more about work and make him relaxed in that way. Like most specialists, Bob felt best talking about his work. He inadvertently hit the nail on the head by mentioning the precise reason, for which Poltic had called him that day.

"Number 6…, that's why I've asked you to come over, Bob!"

"Are we going to buy it, Mr. Poltic, because if we are, then, we're going to be in quite good competition with the first two companies? When the four become one, then we could…"

"Listen to me carefully, please!" Bob realized that he would not be allowed to say more than one or two words from that moment on. The same as his colleagues, he did not agree with Poltic's bossy approach, although, in the past he had stated that he approved of any free discussions, taking place after.

"What I want from you is to pick up the phone, dial the number I tell you and say clearly what I ask you to say. Do you understand, Bob?"

"Yes, Mr. Poltic. Absolutely."

"The person on the other side of the line is the owner of 'number 6'. He's received a contract in the post. He's probably not had the time to look at it, yet." Poltic had not informed Harry about all this. He used a ready sample, where he just modified some of the information, he also added some new stuff and there you go – the contract was completed. If it came to going through actual negotiations, then, Harry would be informed straight away so he could take over. "You will tell him that you want to buy his business and you want the contract signed within two weeks. No matter what he answers you, just put the phone down. That's it. Do you think you can do it, Bob?"

"Yes, boss, I can do it." Bob picked up the phone and did what he was asked. There was a lot of shouting on the opposite side of the line but this did not make him hesitant, maybe, just for a few seconds.

"It was perfect, Bob! Well done! You will phone this gentleman again in a few weeks and you're going to offer him the same thing! What I asked you to do today remains between you and me. I don't want anyone to know about it, right?"

"Yes, Mr. Poltic. I'll keep it quiet!" Bob said, ready to swear on his life if asked.

"Is everything ready for tomorrow?"

"What should have been ready, Mr. Poltic?"

"Oh, yes, sorry, you don't know about this… Well, Bob, you'll be the first to know about our next move that will take us right to the top. The management of the advertising departments and that of production have been informed personally by me. No one else knows. What day is it tomorrow, Bob?"

"It's the 16th, Mr. Poltic. It's Wednesday."

"That's right, Bob. Tomorrow, one of the most influential health organizations in the world is releasing a report study on healthy eating, according to which the population in our country consumes 60% less meat than it should, in order to get the right amount of proteins."

"How is this study important to us, Mr. Poltic?"

"It means that people should eat more meat and we're going to provide it for them by decreasing our prices by 60%. The campaign, of making the study and our good intentions as popular as possible, starts from tomorrow, and it will affect the whole country. That's the big news, Bob. You are free to go now."

Bob was not sure what to think or say. Putting the prices down to that level was crazy. It would be a tremendous financial loss to the company. He just stood up and left the room. Poltic needed him no sooner than in 14 days, when he was supposed to make another phone call. Until then, the speculation on the market should bring some good results. Poltic hoped that the correlation of forces would swing in his favor.

All had happened in just one day. The entire population would learn of the noble initiative of several companies, which had radically put their prices down for a whole month, so people could afford consuming more meat. The government and the competition companies would not dare stop this populist measure because they would bring people's anger upon themselves. Especially, the poor and the old, who had nothing to lose, they could easily revolt out on the streets. Advertising would make these manufacturers popular and the products of the first two companies would just sit on the shelves, as they would remain too expensive. Actually, they could decide to follow and decrease their prices, too, knowing that they would be working at a loss. Their losses would not be that great, of course, because the increased volume of production, due to the higher demand, was going to compensate for that.

The advertising campaign was going to be persistent for the entire 30 days and this had to result in 'company 6's inability to keep up with the installments of the loan and companies' 1 and 2 loss of popularity amongst the consumers. In that way, Bob's offer would be very realistic, when he phoned second time and the price of shares of 1 and 2 would just plummet along with the drop of their popularity. Poltic firmly believed in these suppositions purely because he had no other alternative.

His companies would also work at a loss in the next month. The money, which was going to be literarily given away to the people, would be equal to what company 3 was worth, for example. Weighing the alternatives up, Poltic decided that he could sacrifice 220 million if this would mean that the total price for 1, 2 and 6 was going to fall from 2.3 billion to just around 1.6 billion. It was not the case whether Poltic had that much but he was quite satisfied with the initial calculations as a rough guide.

Now, he was the driving force behind major changes that were going to affect the entire country. The report study and the subsequent promotion of low prices were both reflected in the 8 o'clock morning news of all influential media. Trucks, loaded with low-priced products, had managed to stock up major supermarkets one day before the new prices were announced. Thousands of people were rushing in to stock up with meat that was given away almost free. People were pushing each other, arguing and queuing. By lunchtime, all stock, produced by one of Poltic's companies had sold out. Poltic had calmed his staff down that the situation would not cause them any inconvenience like cuts in wages or redundancies. Only some increase of the production capacities had to be expected.

When Geri, Jane and Harry heard the news, they immediately phoned their boss to find out what was happening. Poltic told them that his bosses had instructed him and that he was only following orders. He also told them to continue their work as before.

Interviews and commentaries by all sorts of people involved or not in that business, followed in the coming days. Representatives of the competition announced their support for the initiative, hiding their anger behind fake smiles. On television, sworn vegetarians and meat lovers got into a debate: "pro or con eating meat". Different NGOs and Animal Right groups condemned the idea because the increased consumption of meat led to more animals being killed. The ministry of Economics and the one of Social affairs both took a stance and expressed an opinion. Whatever that took place in the first few days in terms of broadcasts and statements resulted in the same thing – the names of Poltic's companies were most mentioned in the media. The first two biggest companies in the business made an attempt to steal away some of the credits, however, their products legged well behind because Poltic had invested much more in the advertising of his produce.

Company 6 had no choice, either. They kept quiet for a few days, hoping that everything that was happening was just a bad dream. At the end, they also announced that they were cutting down their prices. Despite operating their production by using the best of technologies, which made their products cheaper to manufacture, 60% decrease was far too much. Most of their substantial profits went directly into the lender-bank. There was nothing to cover the installments due to the new situation. The interests just piled up and the load became overdue by the day.

On the eighth day, the counter-reactions occurred: the former owner of 'number 3', who was now just the managing director of the company, complained to Poltic that he had been receiving death-threats. If he did not put up the prices he would get killed he thought. He feared for his son's life, too, as he could be attacked again. Poltic advised the worried father to hire some bodyguards and gave him the contact details of the security firm, responsible for his own safety. The high-ranked managers in 4 and 5 were also provided with security guards.

As the Team was not being in the public eye, a real threat to them did not exist. Although, Poltic had made sure this had been reflected as a clause in their employment contract 'for life', he still hired a bodyguard each, just in case. The security would accompany them everywhere they went in their cars.

Poltic met up a few times with Charlie during this period. The youngster had no idea that behind all this media attention stood no one else but M. J. The basic structure of the supermarket had been built, Charlie would explain to his boss excitingly. His people were managing perfectly, only things with Michael remained unchanged. Poltic let himself be absorbed in Charlie's world every time they had a meeting. By getting into his young friend's thinking or problems, M. J. managed to get a rest and withdraw from his own world, which appeared to be much more complicated than he first thought.

The second week went by. The market had calmed a little bit down, after the initial madness. People were not stocking up with products as much as but still it seemed the production capacity was far from sufficient to respond to the consumers' needs. Bob turned up to make the second phone call.

"4863…"

"What do I say, now Mr. Poltic?" waiting to get connected, Bob anxiously asked.

"The same as last time." There was no change in the response of owner 'number 6'. He refused to sell and even threatened to call the Police as he considered this harassment. "Hmm, the bastard's not giving in!" Poltic thought. "It's understandable, of course. Working for two weeks at a loss, the loan installments have been in arrears but he could easily borrow more and consolidate his debt. Many businesses operated on credit, relying not only on the banks but also on varied international funds, which often offered better conditions of repayment."

"Tomorrow, Bob, the prices are going down by another 15% for five days, after which we'll restore the back to the 60% decrease. This would devaluate the shares of the first two companies further, wouldn't it?

"Yes, it would, definitely, Mr. Poltic."

"According to you, when is best for us to start buying? I want you to corner the 400 shareholders or however many are important to us, and get hold of their shares, available for sale. You will have unlimited budget at your disposal. Nevertheless, don't splash out but bargain as much as possible, considering the new development in the market. Do you think it will work, Bob?"

"I think so, Mr. Poltic. I believe that minimum 300 of them will be happy to sell, possibly more, if there's another decrease in prices. Initially, the shares were traded at 62 points for the first one and 48 points – for the second company. At the time, no one would sell under 70-80 and respectively – under 60-67. At present, the values are as follows: 34 and 22. I could offer the standard price plus 20%. If they don't back down, I'll just go up until they do. In this way, even if we reach the impossible high of 50% dearer, we'll still end up getting them quite cheap, namely, at 51 and 33." Bob was dropping about numbers and percentages for a good ten minutes and the more he got into the subject, the more he could not stop talking. He mentioned a couple of times how genius he thought the whole idea was and that Poltic should really congratulate the people above him for coming up with this incredible plan to hit the market. Poltic managed to grasp Bob's way of thinking but he had to interrupt him because he had realized that now getting hold of the shares had been sorted out, there was another important matter that needed solving. Who on earth was going to be the person behind the purchase? It would be too suspicious if one person or a company went ahead with this venture! It would not have been a problem if more than 50% of the shares were available for sale. Then, whoever was buying them had no reason to hide. In their instance, however, Bob could only attempt to obtain just 37% from the first and about 40% from the second company. The shareholders of the controlling stake would never agree to sell for less than heaps of money. They actually did not even have to put theirs for sale.

"Bob, all this remains strictly confidential. Nobody should know that the shares are bought out by the same company. Can you do this?"

"Of course, Mr. Poltic, I can! That's the oldest trick in the stock market game, which I've resorted to a thousand times. It all depends on how many clients one has. The more – the easier it is! Let's say that hundred people have entrusted me with a few thousands to invest in shares of my choice that will be potentially profitable to the clients in question. If the money is lost, I lose the customer. If I succeed – the client's happy and I'm happy. We are going to get the shares through many different agents, my former colleagues, who will be buying them on behalf of their own clients. Then, my friends will just sell them to me and I'll reimburse all these people with the resources you've allocated to me. In that way, the shares will be stored in one place." Bob really appeared to know his business.

"What about if someone reveals that you are behind all this? Is the plan going to fail, then, Bob?"

"It's not going to fail because it won't be me but my company, which will do the trading. No one will doubt my course of actions because there is nothing more plausible for a good agent to do but sit and wait for the prices to go up."

The problem with company 6 remained. It was not a joint-stock company. It was owned by only one person. Poltic even thought to entrust RA with the task of applying their ways and influence over the stubborn businessman but he did not really believe that a beating would make any difference. Before Bob was dismissed Poltic asked him if he could make another phone call on the following day, after the prices had been cut even further. If he failed again, Poltic would cease making any more attempts but focus on getting hold of companies 1 and 2.

This time, Poltic did not leave the Team to learn the news from the media but warned them in advance. The reports from the 'partner'-foreign company stated that Harry and Geri were the ones that most enthusiastically took an interest in everything that was happening. The lawyer was far too busy with the three companies but somehow; he found the time to speak regularly on the phone to his former colleagues in the Law office. He would elaborate on how everyone, who worked in the companies' law departments, was a waste of time. Harry would slag Poltic off about his ludicrous decision on cutting the prices down and how his nasty and brainless boss had forced him to draw up contracts that had stupidly generous conditions. Despite the fact that Poltic worked for other individuals, who most probably had issued these orders, Harry continued obstinately to accuse just him.

Geri had no bad feelings towards her boss and just carried on as usual with the research polls, which had illustrated so far a positive shift in the larger part of the population, with regards to Poltic's companies. She was only slightly disconcerted about not knowing the real reasons behind the aggressive advertising, as well as why the prices had been so radically decreased. Her education in sociology could not prevent her from rational thinking. She could only come to one conclusion and that was: huge sums of money had been thrown away with no chance of ever recovering it.

Jane had no queries and just went to work without giving it too much thought. She would often think about her personal problems back home. She had finally come to a decision to file up for divorce. Poltic believed that this was the last thing the company needed – an employee, who was inadequate at the workplace due to serious problems in their private life! It was well clear that Jane's husband was a level below her in nearly every aspect. He was quite plain, not very well educated, and not very successful at his restaurant running. Poltic thought he could wait for a few days before he went and visited her if the situation did not change. He was not sure how he could really help her but he would at least tell her that she could rely on him. Anyone in similar circumstances would feel more confident if they were promised support by someone, who had the power of Poltic. Well, it did not come to all this because the next report showed that Jane was feeling happier after her husband left the family home. She actually worked better, spending almost 16 hours a day to complete the given tasks.

The third attempt Poltic to make a deal with company 6 failed like all previous times. He sent Bob away to get back to his shares and sat down alone in his study. He was beginning to get more and more irritated by the stubbornness of the owner of 'number 6'. The only way he could succeed was if he offered not twice, not three times but at least five times more money than the real value of the business. He had not planned for such expenditure so Poltic decided to forget about it for the time being, until he achieved acquiring the two largest in the industry. As soon as he purchased them, he would, then, destroy the modern factory and its pigheaded director. Brought down to a complete isolation, he would not stand a chance.

On the second day of the new campaign of even lower prices, problems started to arise. The authorities sent auditors to Poltic's factories in suspicion he was laundering money. The Ministry of Finances accused him of tax evasion – by selling his products cheaper, less VAT went back to the treasury. The Ministry of Social Affairs suspected him of overexploiting his factory workers. Inspectors were sent to examine the working conditions and so forth. The competition had stopped playing the game and refrained from further cuts in the prices. The rival companies simply condemned this as being against the law of the country. The consumers, on the other hand, had already stocked up on meat products and trade had slowed down. The commercials were beginning to have the opposite effect and openly annoyed people.

The five days were tense and went slowly. The only positive result was that Bob and his friends managed to do their job very professionally. No one realized that almost 40% of the two largest companies in the meat products business had changed hands and became Poltic's property. Major shareholders were more than happy to part with their losing shares. They did not bother to negotiate that much over the price, they were selling at. Pleased with his secret success, Poltic put up the prices back so they were only 20% cheaper in the remaining part of that month. The authorities had backed down and left Poltic alone. The competition could relax a bit now, before another attack on Poltic's part.

Michael

A bove all, Poltic had some other problems to solve. Actually, at first there was one problem that was known by the pretty name of Michael. RA reported on a few very bad habits they had discovered about the person they kept under observation. This time, Poltic had instructed them on their new assignment over the phone, instead of sending them to struggle with same cash-box like on their first job. He did not miss to tell them that Michael worked in the same building they had already been to. The boss also stressed on the importance of keeping as far as they could from the target. They had only one vehicle at their disposal and this was a drawback. Anyone could get suspicious if they saw the same car every day in their rear-view mirror. None of them had raised the subject about having another car, so Johnny promised he was going to ask on their next job. They worked in shifts in pairs, which had formed naturally. Johnny worked with Ted, where Emma paired with Guillen.

So far, none of them seemed to argue or had any dissensions amongst themselves. Strangely enough, there was not anyone in RA, who was injurious to the group like Harry and Michael were to their respective – the Team and the Young ones. Ill-educated but not in any case stupid, the members of RA managed to get on fine and understand each other without too much unnecessary talking. The early hostility between Ted and Guillen had long gone. Now that they were working apart, they actually got on better. Emma's beauty had ceased to invoke jokes at her expense, anymore. Whether it was because Poltic had instructed them to treat her like a sister, or her good looks were slightly daunting, but she had just fitted perfectly in the group. Guillen, who was becoming more like the leader of their team, was always asking her about her opinion. Johnny and Ted, on the other hand, would never interrupt her, when she expressing her position on things. In the spirit of union and supreme harmony, the members of RA embarked on their next job – following Michael, who was only a few years younger than them.

The first shift was taken by the two mechanics. They were sitting in the car at 7 o'clock in the morning, waiting for the guy to leave the building, so they could trail behind him and check where he would go. They were responsible to watch him until 6 o'clock, when Emma and Guillen had to step in and take over. The first day did not bring any pleasant emotions to Johnny and Ted due to excruciatingly long waiting – a bad reminder of when they hanged around for five hours and gave John a good hiding.

Guillen took his place behind the wheel, along with the stunning Emma by his side. As early as the 15th minute since their shift had begun, they already had to start working. Michael had come back home from work and went out at 6:15pm. It was getting already dark, which made any conscientious driver to switch on the headlights. They joined in one of the main boulevards in town and kept driving behind the target with about six cars between them. Emma was quiet and tried to keep a close eye on Michael's car, in case she lost it. The young guy stopped, came out and hastened into a casino. He stayed in until 10 o'clock, which made Guillen very fidgety. He felt the car was too crammed and tiny and had to open the door a few times to ease his sense of claustrophobia. There in the dark car, parked in a dark spot, Guillen did not have any improper thoughts about Emma. On the contrary, he started a sincere and warm chat about kids, about his own little daughter and how this had changed his life. He mentioned his girlfriend a few times, too. Emma was listening with a great interest about the feelings a father had towards his child. She was overwhelmed by his words and the hard boxer-girl felt slightly weepy. Emma wanted to have children one day but two persons were needed for that. She had never experienced love, the way it could be seen in films. She often thought that there was something wrong with her. She had asked herself over and over again why other people had a chance in this but not her. She could not comprehend that the reasons lay well back in her difficult past and her parents. People, who knew her well, could see why she behaved out of the ordinary and her incapability to have a relationship. Not her, however, which was really sad!

Guillen sensed the rising tension, coming from his right side and tactfully shut his mouth. At last, Michael showed up. His noticeable wobble and three-minute attempt to unlock his car clearly pointed at him not only indulging in some good gambling, but also in a solid quantity of alcohol, too. The next stop of the drunken gambler was the most popular nightclub in town, the one that Charlie took the Young Ones one Friday. Emma did not even think of asking for permission or approval but just announced that she was going in, after him. She told Guillen that he should not wait for her if Michael came out from the club, but just follow him at once. The former builder did not have time to object his workmate's spontaneous decision and was left on his own in the darkness of the vehicle. He put on the radio and just waited as told.

Emma wanted to prove a point that she was doing something as well. So far, her contribution was only that story with the provocative short skirt, a while ago and she did not think of it as being much of an input. She had learnt from doing sport that one had to deserve their victory and that no one achieved anything by just sitting around. At the club entrance, she experienced the same awkwardness she encountered in the flash boutiques. She paid the entry fee and went in the bar feeling unconfident and with low self-esteem. The noise from the powerful speakers just hit her and she felt bewildered. She had gone out to nightclubs merely a few times and had never really been in a place of this class before. She lost her target immediately amongst the tipsy and happy visitors, who were dancing away. Emma wondered how so many people let themselves go out and have fun in the middle of the week and then, managed to get up for work on the next morning. "What will happen if they need to do their training tomorrow? They'll be in bad form and their opponent, who's had a good night sleep, will just defeat them!" Only a boxer's mind could have thoughts like this.

Emma checked both floors in the place, looking for Michael but to no avail. She went to the exit and rested her back, standing on the right side. She thought that Michael would show up sooner or later. She hoped it would be soon as the loud music was beginning to have an adverse effect on her. Her heart was beating irregularly and she felt she could faint. This would be too bad – it was the wrong time for accidents and emergency services to be called out.

Michael left the noisy establishment one hour after midnight. Walking a couple of steps in front of the girl, she did not worry about keeping such a short distance from him because his zigzagging was even more apparent. Emma went in the car and they drove off after Michael's vehicle, which meandered ahead of them. The intoxicated young man parked his car outside his block of flats and really took his time to unlock the entrance door. Emma and Guillen were free to go home and get a good sleep before their next shift. In six hours only, Michael was going to be under the vigilant eyes of both car mechanics.

The second day was very different but the night was exactly the same – the same casino and the same club. It was unknown how much effort it had cost Michael to get to work, followed closely by Johnny and Ted. They, on the other hand, had stocked up on plenty of coffee, expecting that the young guy would not be leaving the office before 5 o'clock. For all this waiting, they were beginning to hate the man, without even knowing him well. This time they were wrong. Michael left the building in a rush and drove off in a speed well above the limit in unknown direction. This happened as early as 8:20 am.

Ted got excited by the sudden change of the situation and although he was still feeling quite sleepy, he managed a wide grin, rubbing cheerfully his hands and uttered his order to the driver: "After him!" Johnny followed the instructions not because Ted could tell him what to do but because this was what needed to be done. He was so excited that their car nearly touched the back of the vehicle they were chasing. Johnny got back his composure and kept a better distance. There was hardly any traffic on the road as people were already at their workplace.

The mechanics' shift that entire day involved driving around after Michael, who managed to visit four companies trading in exterior wall covering, two – selling lights and just before he got back to the office at 4:30 pm., he stopped at a huge warehouse, full of diggers and other large machinery. The flask with hot refreshing drink was long forgotten on the back seat. The pair was just happy that the target was so active. Although, Guillen had told them about their busy night with Emma, Johnny and Ted strongly believed that they had to do more work that day than the others. This idea just made them feel good. Finally, they handed in the car to Emma and Guillen at 6:10 pm outside Michael's apartment. Johnny and Ted went to celebrate their successful day, which they had modestly presented to their workmates as nothing special.

Even as children, Johnny had always been the brighter of the two. He had always been interested in different things, asked a lot more about staff, had more friends. And amongst them – there was Ted, who loved to be alone, with not that many people around him. Maybe that's why many questions arose in Johnny's mind, whereas Ted had none. They went to their local pub, where everyone knew each other, and ordered a beer. Johnny only allowed himself to drink when he was without a car.

"Who's that guy we're following?" Johnny asked kind of himself rather than his friend. Actually, they had not discussed their job so far in terms of "What's the boss gaining from all that?" They just did their best for which they got rewarded with a big wage pack.

"Don't know." Ted replied staring unnecessarily at the sweaty beer bottle.

"I think that guy probably works in a rival company and Mr. Poltic wants to know where he goes and what he does. The boy must be someone important but..." Johnny stopped for a second his detective analysis. "...but he seems too young to be a boss. He looks about our age, doesn't he, Ted?"

"Yea, there about!"

"The guy we gave a beating was rich and I can see why Mr. Poltic asked us to do it. But this guy is driving in a company car and he's maybe, just an employee like us. You noticed, Ted, he works in the same building where the small cash-box was... This is not accidentally, I bet!" Johnny carried on with thinking up more conspiracy theories, which he could not see that they were just absurd and could be easily refuted. He concluded that the guy was possibly Mr. Poltic's son. Ted butted in with his genius conclusion:

"I don't care as long as I get paid... I'm not interested about who we follow and what they are!" Johnny agreed with colleague's wise decision and both of them left the pub after their second bottle of beer.

In the forthcoming days, they continued watching closely their target. The day shift had come to the conclusion that Michael must be some building entrepreneur, going to all these building material shops, where the night shift pair had decided that the guy loves playing roulette and alcohol is a fixed part of his life. Poltic called them a couple of times to check whether they needed something to help them with their job. Finally, he put a close to their activity and required a report from them. Four people gave him four different stories, however, they had all come to the same conclusion: Michael worked hard but had some really bad habits.

At the end of their mission, the four had become quite close friends. Now they could not wait for the moment when their boss entrusted them with another bizarre job. Emma and Guillen had become much closer, due to the many hours they spent together, often, in a confined space. She had started to confide personal things in someone for the first time. Life had never given her the chance to have somebody she could call a best friend so she saw in Guillen a person, who never judged or criticized her, never wanted anything from her, nor did he mocked her for being a bit silly. He just did his job in a responsible way. Guillen was not aware of her past and this urged her to share with him things suppressed for a long time that she simply had no one to tell. As soon as she heard Guillen was interested in martial arts and sports, including boxing, she immediately began to trust him even more. For her, anyone, who likes boxing, was a reliable person and a very good friend.

Johnny and Ted knew each other all their lives and they could not surprise each other with anything. Both of them, however, were astonished by how easy was to work with Emma and Guillen, without any arguments and fallings out. Johnny fancied Emma a little but never made any attempts to show it because he did not want to lose his job – it was awfully good money. He had some plans for the future. He wanted to buy some machines and equipment for his garage and extend the grounds where he was doing the car repairs. And all this was coming out of his wages. He intended to employ a few mechanics and skip the past when it was just him and Ted doing long hours for almost no money. His opinion about Guillen was quite high after he heard him explaining how to break one's bones. Johnny believed that a person, who knew about these things, deserved his respect; in the same way he deserved respect for his skills as a mechanic.

Their work in pairs united the foursome so at the end of the job Guillen invited them for dinner at his place. His girlfriend who loved cooking, especially now when she could get anything, was going to make a meal for his workmates. Emma agreed to come to her best friend's dinner party as long as she could watch a boxing match on one of the TV sports channels. Johnny and Ted suggested they all went to a pub at the end of town that had live music. They all could afford it now. Laughing away they had come to a compromise – first they visited Guillen's place and two days later they went out to the pub.

Michael never realized that he had been watched for a while. He never even imagined that someone would bother to watch him. He made sure he did his job, which was always way too much, giving the time frame Charlie would set for him. He was a very capable person, who always aimed at achieving his objectives without any help. That was one of the reasons he got a job in a warehouse after his graduation. He had no contacts or connections. He believed that the change in his life was pure luck, which, however, had to come his way sooner or later. When Charlie turned up at the doorstep of his old dingy flat, he knew that the moment had come. Michael had no problems with his new job down to his intrinsic communication skills and good appearance. The only setback of the job he saw in the face of his colleagues: Lorrie, Kate and Tony, whom he deeply disliked.

At first, he tried to ingratiate with them, so they would like him and he, on the other hand, could manipulate them more easily. Nevertheless, he had kept playing his good-faced theatrical role only for about ten days. Then, Michael became the old Michael – the person, who always answered back his boss and made every effort to make him look stupid. Charlie sensed this a few times but his warnings came to no avail. Michael just continued to enter his boss's personal space.

His new apartment, rented by him with his first pay, was in much more prestigious neighborhood. There was less crime and it was absolutely suitable for a young specialist, who was employed in a medium level position in some company. Compared to the small bed-sit the apartment was a huge jump, like replacing a bicycle with a Mercedes. Despite the newly acquired social status, bought with most of his money, Michael's idea about how to do his work had remained unchanged. He believed that if he worked harder and applied himself more than anyone else, he would achieve much more than the rest and one day, he would become their boss. Aiming high in his work now, he did not make the effort back when he was still at university. He was an average student, who had to work during his course of studies, in order to support himself like most of his colleagues. Michael was convinced that his present job held every opportunity for him to replace Charlie and became the manager. Harry wanted the same with Poltic but his motive was pure hatred, where Michael's main motive was much more realistic. He believed that he was smarter and more capable than Charlie.

There was a gap in Michael's scheming plans – he was not aware in the slightest, of Poltic's existence and his ideas about things. Michael could never guess of the real reason why the person that had been placed to be in charge of them was clearly such an unsuitable guy. He could not even imagine how close he was to getting the sack. Teasing constantly Charlie and the arrogant behavior towards his colleagues might not be a very good reason to fire him. He was a capable worker, after all, and every company believed in keeping their qualified staff. However, the things Michael would get up to outside working hours were more than disturbing.

Michael had a very logical and reasonable explanation for this. His personal life was the time he could do whatever he wanted, with whoever he wanted and wherever he wanted. Even as a teenager, he was drinking alcohol without having any special occasion. With time, alcohol had become a fixed feature, a companion, in Michael's life but thanks to it he had managed to lose some of his best friends. Well, he had a simple explanation for this, too. These people had never been his friends, really. They just pretended because they wanted to be closer to the person, who could do everything twice as better than them. Alcohol was not a good reason to fall out with anyone, he believed. Actually, it brought people happiness and brought them closer together. That sort of firm belief could only exist in a sworn alcoholic's mind. Michael had a point to some extent. His personal life was his and he should not be held accounted for what he did in his spare time after work or at the weekends. Poltic had a different opinion – the right one. He paid Michael his salary, so the boss was always right.

He might be doing his job very well but his attitude after work could jeopardize Poltic's entire plan. What if Michael had a car crash or even hit someone on the road, then who was going to replace him? Deadlines would be missed, the work process would be disturbed and everything would just go to hell! Well, not entirely because the supermarket was not really of great importance, if not any, for fulfilling the end objective according to Poltic. It was more like a school project that Charlie and Young ones had go through and pass.

What was really curious in this case was how Michael could combine his professional responsibilities and his drunken outings to clubs and casinos every night! He deserved a medal for his efforts to keep up the two fronts.

More often than not, Michael would ask himself like any other reasonable person about who stood behind the incompetent Charlie. This question was not really eating him but came naturally to mind, taking into consideration what was kind of happening in the office when Charlie was about. As long as there was money for a drink and he had a company car, the world was panning out exactly how Michael wanted it, so who cared about anyone else? This, though, the start with alcohol and the finish of his world with that substance, led to some bad relationship with Lorrie, Kate and Tony. He not only regarded them as if they were below him, but he had to spend all day with them in the same room, and this, combined with his total non-drinking at work, would just tip him off the edge, quite often – in front of Charlie. Lorrie would take things too seriously, which resulted in her often crying after work for about an hour. It would be never to do with anything about her work but for Michael's obnoxious behavior.

"You ain't got the foggiest idea what you're doing here, do you? …just muddling through, eh?" This was one of the nastiest remarks Lorrie had ever heard about herself in her life. Tony told his uncouth colleague off for this but even he felt on edge when Michael was around, in the office. Kate, herself, was quite tough and she totally ignored her arrogant workmate. She got on quite well with Tony and this gave her the confidence to stand up to Michael a few times, recalling how he used to upset her at first.

So Charlie's employees worked in this tense environment for some months. Sooner or later, escalation of the tension was bound to happen – Lorrie would not be able to put up with Michael for another week. At the beginning, her decision to leave seemed like a vague and distant idea but now, it was very realistic. In a one-to-one conversation with Charlie, she let everything off her chest and again she burst into tears. He decisively promised her to solve the problem once and for all.

M. J. heard from Charlie about the dramatic events in the office. He had shared with him that the irritant for everyone was irreplaceable if fired and the building of the supermarket would get delayed. Michael was quite clever, really. He always offered to negotiate deliveries with the major suppliers and without him someone from the others would have to learn everything that

Michael was responsible for from the start. They never really initiated to join him on his important business meetings, for so much that they disliked him, so inadvertently, they had made him the key-factor of the group, more important even than Charlie.

Whatever he did, Poltic rarely hesitated. Also he believed that there are no irreplaceable people. He had to fire him as soon as possible, before Lorrie ended up in a psychiatric ward or his drinking and driving habit took his first victims. Poltic was finding the analogy with Harry very interesting. In both teams of four, there was a black sheep, who did not like the boss, neither did his colleagues. Michael, who was as young to be almost Harry's son, so much resembled him – like twins with a twenty years age difference. If Poltic fired Michael, he should really do the same with Harry, according to his principles. However, without both of them, this could lead to some unpredictable consequences for Poltic's plan. As a final decision, he believed he should spare Harry and get rid of Michael.

Poltic was about to break the bad news when he suddenly thought of something that really worried him. RA might be a bit stupid, they never asked any questions and just did their job to deserve their fat paycheck, but who was the black sheep in their group? In reality, they worked without supervision and Poltic could not know whether there was already a baddy amongst them. He only communicated with them indirectly and there was no way he could find out. What if the entire plan to form three teams of four people, who were so different in every way, had diverse qualifications, who felt united only by the heaps of money offered to them and were brought together to create and manage the biggest company for meat products in the country was wrong? Well, then, achieving the end objective could be impossible.

For the first time Poltic felt very doubtful about everything that he had been doing so far. For a moment, really just for a moment, he thought he might fail. Very quickly, though, he returned to his common sense and logical thinking. They pointed at the following: The Team was the most important and their constant surveillance was a must. Harry had calmed down a bit recently so real problems in this aspect were not expected in the near future. Receiving a report after report on what was going on in their homes, given by him, Poltic felt very pleased with his decision to have their lives at his disposal.

RA – this was where the unknown laid. Was it possible that their intellectual mediocrity could turn into their biggest weapon, which they could use against their super rich boss? Poltic was getting overwhelmed by paranoia for a short while. He decided that the time for the small detective to begin following four persons had come. Poltic realized that the circle would never end and soon he would have to get someone, who was going to watch the small detective and so on, and so on.

Before he made that phone call and assigned the surveillance of Johnny, Ted, Guillen and Emma, Poltic spurred his mind to find out who might be the bad guy amongst them. He had no information whatsoever about their relationships, hence, he plunged entirely into speculations, which he tried to make sound as realistic as possible. The most noticeable factor that disturbed the homogeny of RA was Emma. Her outstanding good looks were capable of jeopardizing the friendship of good pals like Johnny and Ted, or even distract Guillen away from his girlfriend. However, abstracting the female from RA was going to make the group feel like a man with one arm. Poltic just had to trust them that the men would treat her like a sister. He simply could not make her less attractive. He would have to remove her if she really got involved intimately with one of her workmates. So far, Poltic had not received any signs of it, so she was staying.

The next possible destructive element included, in fact, the two car mechanics. When Poltic employed them, he kept this at the back of his mind that they would outnumber Guillen and Emma and this could lead to a similar intolerance like Lorrie felt towards Michael. Of course, people were different and everyone had their own individuality, however, the good and bad features in each person were pretty much the same.

The third risk for undermining RA existed but it was rather unlikely. Guillen – the man, who had a family to support, was the most stable person in the group, but what if he was the delay fuse?

Poltic could not wait to find out whether he was right about any of this. He called the detective, who was going to give him the answer, and hired him to watch the four criminals. Poltic asked the surveillance to go on for no more than a week. He was interested to find out some information on only specific areas in their lives, like how often they met, where they did this or whether they argued and had any bad habits. If Michael could do his job perfectly well and in the evenings, to get almost paralytic from drinking, then, it might be feasible that the RA's good job so far, was also lined with some vices.

Alas, Poltic fell in his own trap, built of far too many logical conclusions, which impeded his common sense thinking. If he used it, he would have left RA alone to do their job. They could not be a threat because he really managed to bed some fear in them, when they first came to visit him in the fortress-house. Also, unlike Michael, they were totally replaceable, so there was nothing really to worry about because there was not much to lose. If they ever grassed on him and told the Police that he was making them destroy roads and beat people up, even then, he would never end up in a prison cell for there would be thousands of reasons that freed him from any guilt.

On the next morning, Charlie burst into Poltic's study with some terrible news, according to him. After hearing him out, M. J. smiled at the agitated visitor because he realized that all his yesterday's speculations had turned out to be wrong. Michael was going to be spared, at least for now. If Poltic had stick by his principles and dismissed him, then after he heard Charlie's news, he would have to leave him with just one employee. The mentally unstable Lorrie would have to work by herself and that, of course was impossible.

Two people of the Young ones had started their morning together, in one bed. That was the beginning of it all.

Tony and Kate

It was not the most pleasant experience for anyone to get up early in the morning to go to work. For Tony, this was not a problem. From his very first day, he had set his body clock to wake up at 6:30 am. The large workload guaranteed him a good night sleep, when his brain switched off completely. For the last couple of weeks, though, Tony could not sleep that well. He would wake up every few hours throughout the night, not for anything like to go to the bathroom, but to watch her. Kate, in contrast, would be fast asleep, totally unaware of the interesting pastime of her loved one. The hard work in the day time made her so tired for eight hours in the night as if she had transported herself to her own quiet sleeping planet.

Their story together evolved as usual – inadvertently. Their first month at work was sufficient enough for them to get to know each other and to both sense that something between them might happen. Tony was more confident of the two and he asked Kate one day out on a date. His invitation was politely declined with some made up excuses about being busy with her family. On the following day, Kate's colleague did not give up and asked her out again but to no avail. His aspiration was encumbered by the fact that he would see this beautiful woman for so many hours a day, would want to be with her but could not. Quite experienced in chatting up the girls, Tony knew that if he was turned down twice, he was wasting his time. He gave up but thought to try again in a month. Who knows, she might just give in then.

The work was going well, although, the progress and all the success was really down to Michael's efforts. Tony and Kate were also useful. Given that Tony had stepped back, this provoked Kate's interest in him, although, it was simply not appropriate for a real lady to openly show that she liked a certain guy. Knowing this timeless truth, she set upon thinking of a way how to make him ask her out again and then, to reenact the scenario of the surprised but flattered woman, who was more than happy to accept the invitation. A natural drawback not to ignore, of course, was how this potentially more special kind of relationship would affect their situation at work. What if Charlie got to know about them? Kate decided to give up on the idea and cross Tony out of her list with men that she could ever have anything to do with. Her desire to keep her financial stability overrode her emotional interests.

Their working time was until 5 pm, set out in the contracts, but very often three of the four had to stay on until later. The short time frames they were given to complete their tasks, especially at the beginning of the project, led to an hour or two – overtime per day. Michael believed he was above everyone else and almost never stayed. He would leave no later than 4:58. Charlie had tried to make him stay to help his colleagues but Michael never took on the request of his boss. It was 5 o'clock that said in his work agreement so he used this as the perfect opportunity to annoy Charlie by reminding him the facts.

One regular day at the office, Tony and Kate happened to stay at work until seven in the evening. Michael had left at his usual time and Lorrie had to go home and help her mother with dinner as some distant relatives were coming to visit them. Charlie was following the rule: "I'm the boss and can't stay long!" So he was off by 4 pm. The Tony's desk was next to Kate's and this helped the two young and attracted to each other people to constantly exchange some very unprofessional stares. They managed to finish their work almost at the same time and were ready to leave the office together. They were just going to walk the 150 meters to their parked vehicles side by side where from the car park, they were going to leave their separate ways and drive home.

Tony had already gone, when his work phone showed that it was her, who was calling him. He returned to her and after his unsuccessful attempt to start the diesel engine, he offered to drive her home. She could easily afford to call a taxi but Kate immediately abandoned this idea and accepted Tony's offer. He liked her so much and the worse was that she was so close to him all day every day. He had not forgotten about his previous two failures and now, when she was sitting right beside him, he felt he could not ask her out again. Three "no-s" would be like a smack in the face of the intelligent and good-looking Tony. They exchanged nervously a few words about work, just so there was no uncomfortable silence as if they were some teenagers. Then, they could only wait for this tormenting for both of them journey to end. Tony turned up the music to a level that a normal conversation could not take place and then he pressed on the gas, going twice over the speed limit, in attempt to suppress his anxiety.

He was fighting terribly with himself. Should he tell her that he liked her and ask her out to dinner or continue to behave like a complete idiot, showing as if he did not care about her anymore? Different emotions were also running through Kate's mind and body. She was only a step away from giving herself up to a romance with her colleague. Money won again and things remained as they were. Tony stopped outside the entrance, where Kate lived. He expected to hear a quick "thanks" and to find himself alone in the car. Ten seconds passed, when neither of them looked at each other, the radio was off, the engine, too.

Tony felt defeated and first let his feelings come out. He suggested he took her out to dinner – the long hours at work had made him hungry. He anticipated another gentle "no" on her part. Kate looked at him in the eye, in the same way they had looked at each other in the office, but this time the distance between them was just a few centimeters. Her reply made Tony incapable of driving for at least another couple of minutes:

"All right, where are you taking me?" From that moment onwards, they became inseparable in their free time and for the last two weeks, they had even moved in together. Until then, the former waitress lived with her parents like Tony did, too. Hence, living together was something they both looked forward to for a long time. They could not remember whose idea was that. It all happened as a bit of a laugh but the result was amazing. No arguments, quarrels or any acts of jealousy – they enjoyed only love and understanding, as if they had been together for years. Kate had let Tony very close to her but she had not changed her opinion that their relationship might jeopardize their work, so both of them made special efforts to keep their secret.

They rented an apartment in a residential district, where it was almost impossible for them to meet someone they knew. In this way, they eliminated any chance for the gossip to spread from mouth to mouth and somehow to get to Charlie. Of course, they never told him about their new place and he still thought that they lived at their old addresses. The members of their families had been instructed carefully on how to react and tell some made up stories to anyone, who came to look for them.

The main precaution was the way they went to work. Every morning, Tony would leave for work ten minutes before, taking a different route from Kate. And all this – in the name of love, which by the look of it, was serious and expected to last for a long time. Tony truly hoped that none of them would get fired if Charlie found out. Despite that there was no clause in their agreements, forbidding personal relationships with colleagues, it was noted that they were absolutely prohibited at the workplace. Charlie had pointed out a few times that they were there to work and not to look around as if they were hunting for a girlfriend. Well, recently he was doing it himself and hiding quite badly.

Tony believed that sooner or later, Charlie would find out about them. The way things were going, a possible marriage proposal or even the birth of a child, could not be concealed that easily. And why should they hide that someone had become a father or one had simply found the love of their life? So Tony decided to discuss with his dearest the idea of telling their boss about the relationship. He had a thought at back of his mind that if he brought up the subject, Kate might just leave and their fairy tale would end. It was her, really, that had placed the condition about the secrecy of it all. Tony knew that the money they received was a very good reason for neither of them to cause their dismissal from work. However, his point of view was slightly different: having money, lots of work, a car and an amazing flat but what for if he could not have Kate?

For the short time they had been together, Tony learned that Kate was not very good in the mornings until she had her cup of coffee at 7:30. That was why, he wanted only to provoke her interest on the subject that morning and leave her all day to think about his words. Then, in the evening, they would have a proper conversation about it. He was surprised, however, about the sudden change of his plan.

Every morning he would make breakfast for both of them, while Kate was still asleep in bed. That had always been the way until that day. A few days ago, when Tony really made the effort with some elaborate meal for breakfast, Kate felt obliged to get up before him at least one morning that week and prepare something.

Tony opened his eyes and stretched in attempt to wake up from his heavy sleep. Surprised by the fact that Kate was not next to him and the time indicated on the clock, he immediately got up. Usually, he would take a shower first and then smarten himself up in with a suit jacket, shirt and trousers, no tie, and then straight he would go in the kitchen. That day he wanted to find Kate before anything else, so he went and tried every possible room that she could have gone in. He found her in the kitchen, still in her nightdress, with a wide smile on her face that showed how happy one could be.

"Hey, you're up at last! Do you know how long I've been waiting for you?" She asked light-heartedly, while scrambling the eggs in the frying pan.

"I must have missed to hear the alarm."

"Actually, I turned it off and was going to wake you up with a kiss, when breakfast was ready. You got up before that, so now you owe me a kiss." Kate left the wooden spoon aside and turned around with her back towards the cooker. She was waiting for Tony to do his punishment for spoiling her conceived finale.

"If that's the case, then you owe me hundreds of kisses for all the times I've been making you something to eat!"

"You have ten seconds before the eggs burn." After this ultimatum, Tony stepped forward the woman he loved and kissed her more times than she asked for. He gently placed his hands on her hips. Getting her reward for her diligence, Kate returned back to her cooking and just a minute later she invited him:

"Have a seat, dear, breakfast is ready."

Tony had some difficulties with the first couple of bites, because the intention to discuss the situation and whether they should tell Charlie about them was blocking his throat. He left his fork on the table and looked at Kate very seriously, which was unusual for this early time in the day.

"What is it? Have I put too much salt, I only used little?"

"No, eggs are fine."

"Then what?"

"I think we should tell Charlie about us. I can't go on like this forever!"

"Tony, we've talked about this already!"

"Yes, we have but how long are going to hide for and live like this? Kate, I love you and I'd like to be able to show you this in our lunch break or when we are alone in the office. I just don't want to pretend as if I'm indifferent to you and you are only a colleague of mine. You are far more than that to me!" the words "I love you" were the key to her heart and Tony managed to predispose her.

"I love you, too, but we can get fired from work and you know it!"

"No one is going to fire us. We just have to announce it in the most appropriate time, say, this week. I'll speak to Charlie, if you feel nervous."

"Tony, are you crazy? This week? That's the most foolish thing I've ever heard! I don't want this. Imagine we both lose our jobs next week. Then, what are we going to do, where will we live – the rent of this place is far too much? Please, don't do it, Tony. We won't be able to cope; it will be very hard for us. Why do we have to do it to ourselves, now that we have everything we need! Yes, we have to hide about us but at least I know that the money in my bank account is going to increase next month, quite significantly! You can't get paid so high anywhere else. I've been a waitress and I don't want go back doing that again. To be honest, I doubt I can get something better than that." Her reasoning was irrefutable, indeed, and Tony totally agreed with her. Still, there was yet another point he brought up:

"You're right, Kate, but what if we get married? I just don't want the man, who pays my salary, to find out about us from the invitation to our wedding!"

"You want to marry me?" Kate suddenly broke into tears, melted at the prospect. No one had asked her to marry until that moment. In all her previous relationships, the men looked on her as just another girlfriend and they never got that serious with her to think of a possible marriage. Kate was so overwhelmed as if the wedding was going to be in a day or two. Tony himself did not realize, at first, about what he had said but when he was passing a tissue to his loved one, he recognized the seriousness of his words. The most curious thing about it was that they came out so naturally, which meant that he truly wanted to have a family with Kate.

"Yes, Kate, I love you and one day I'd like you to become my wife. But first, I believe we should tell Charlie we are in a relationship together." the potential future wife of his could not stop

204

crying but him going back to the main question made her force herself to calm down. She replied quite unexpectedly:

"All right, tell him."

Their struggle with themselves was too big and the stake was huge. They chatted for a bit longer on the matter, finished their breakfast and for the first time, they left together for work. Tony was driving in front of Kate's car. They both entered the office, still under the spell of this morning emotions. One could see that from the fact that they seemed a bit confused during the first ten minutes. They behaved as if they did not know what they were doing and had come to the wrong building. "When is Charlie coming?" This question was echoing in their heads and had no intention to go away.

The long waited person appeared just after 11 o'clock. He was in a visibly good mood, which gave Tony some extra confidence, where it made Kate feel the tension even more. The time for fulfilling the mission had come and both, Tony and Charlie, after the first made his request, found themselves on the landing outside the office, undisturbed by anyone.

"Just for a minute, Charlie, I want to ask you something!"

"Listen, you know you can tell me anything. Spit it out!" Charlie had really earned his trust, mostly from their Friday outings together, when he had proved that apart of being the boss, he was a friend, too. From the way that Tony asked him to talk in private, Charlie thought he was going to seek a friendly advice from him or something like this.

"Is it OK if I deal with the deliveries of the insulation materials today that Lorrie is supposed to do, and she gets on with the calculations that I'm responsible for? I think we'll do it quicker if we swap jobs, because I'm not that great with numbers."

"No problem, as long as the job gets done. Just ask her and if she doesn't mind, otherwise you'll have to continue with your present duties."

No more questions came from Tony, so Charlie decided that this was all and headed towards the restaurant nearby, where a portion of roast chicken and chips was waiting for him.

The initiator of this almost pointless conversation could not move for a few minutes. He felt as if his legs were made from lead, where his body was shaking uncontrollably. A sudden thought had come into his mind, the thought, which he had underestimated until that moment because he had given such significance to his love:

"Maybe, Kate's got a point and we should keep quiet about us and just continue as we are? What if we both get the sack? How are we going to get married? We won't have the money for the wedding reception and the expensive wedding dress. We'll not be able to afford the honey moon and all the rest that we need to get for the wedding." The prospect of a penniless life together just hit him and he felt thoroughly distraught. He could not understand why he was not afraid of getting fired just a moment ago and why he did not care so much about the money before. And as soon as he stood face to face with the man, who was going to decide their fate, Tony gave up. Were his motives not to tell Charlie buried so deep? At last, Tony came out of his daze and decided that he should discuss again in detail everything with Kate and then tell Charlie about whatever they had agreed on.

He returned in the office without showing the tiniest sign of emotion that could give out whether the conversation had gone well or it had been a total disaster. Kate constantly tried to meet Tony's eyes to see if she could find out something but he never looked at her, not even once. As late as 3 o'clock in the afternoon, he came to her desk with some documents in his hand. He passed them to her, although she was not supposed to receive them, and told her that he had postponed everything because the time was not right. Kate gave the papers back to him, nodded approvingly and carried on working, feeling a relief. Tony, however, had to think of something to tell her later that evening, something that sounded plausible. He did not want her to know that he actually worried about being in a situation in the future, where they had absolutely nothing but their great love. Well, love, as big as it could be, could not feed anyone.

On their return home, Kate straight away demanded an explanation about what had happened during the day and what did "the time was not right" meant.

"Maybe, you are right. How are going to live with no money if Charlie gets rid of us both?" dramatically pointed out Tony and looked down. Kate felt totally betrayed, and that was the person she the least expected it from.

"Oh, Tony, why are saying this now? You talked differently this morning! First, you tried to convince me that we shouldn't hide anymore and admit about our relationship, then you promised me the world and now – you want it all back as it was. I just don't know what you want anymore! I don't care about Charlie, I care about you and the money."

"I don't know, either, Kate! It seems money is more important than us, doesn't it? Would you carry on being with me if we lost our job?" He asked her, knowing the answer deep down. They had been together for only a few months and their feelings were far too strong for her to say "no". But what when time passed and they still loved each other but in a different way, then how would they live without sufficient financial resources. Their life would turn into a nightmare.

"Of course, I would."

"OK, this is what I wanted to know. I'll tell Charlie on Friday evening when we all go out again. Is this a deal?"

"It's a deal!" Kate replied, although her confusion was growing. She just said it, whatever happened. None of them talked about it in the next few days until Friday, otherwise they would seem like kids, who could not make their mind up. Tony managed to stop thinking about the money and only practiced his lines in his head. The hardest was how to start: "Kate and I are going out" or "We are seeing each other from time to time" They had decided not to mention that they were living together, everything – in good time.

Charlie really enjoyed the evenings when going out with his employees. He often felt like discussing something with them that was not related to work, like asking one of the girls whether they approved the way he was dressed or one of the guys whether they had watched the football match last night and what team they had supported. Poltic had prohibited all this but for Friday nights. Their meeting point was usually at the entrance of whatever club, they were going to, and getting there in their company cars was not allowed. Charlie insisted on everyone to have a drink, no matter how small. M. J. had advised him on this – a couple of beers would improve anyone's bad mood. Lorrie, who did not drink, would always order alcohol-free beer and no one, apart of Michael, would dare have a spirit drink. His contempt for his boss would disappear immediately after his second large one and they would become as if there were old friends. Charlie, who rarely drank, would sometimes end up having a horrendous headache on the next day, where Michael – he was an alcoholic, so had no problems.

Their next party evening was set for 10 o'clock. This time, Charlie had prepared a surprise for them – an amazing bar with ten pool tables. He hoped everyone was going to like his idea – a bit of food, a few drinks and to add – a few games of pool. He was not a great player. He had held a cue and a piece of chalk just three-four times over the years, when the cue was higher than he was. Despite his lack of skills in this game, his enthusiasm was great.

The few hours before the event, passed differently for each of the potential pool-players. Lorrie, who had long grown out of her teenage years had to listen to her mother's lecturing on the harmful effects of late nights and nightclubs and bars altogether. The hierarchy in her family did not allow the lower ranks that she was, to interrupt the higher. Her father was at the top, however, he hardly ever told her off, as she was his favorite daughter, whereas his wife would always act protective of her child. Lorrie's parents were very proud of her and more so – with her new job, which also helped the family budget, of course. After dinner the daughter went to her room, where she stayed until 9:30 and then called a taxi. At the door, she was inspected by her parents and after their approval of how she was dressed, they wished her a good time.

For Tony and Kate, the time until 10 was quite tense. Despite that they were watching television, a not bad film actually, neither of them was in the room in spirit. Kate was not really superstitious, did not have any lucky charms or anything like this, but something today, made her believe in fate. That morning, while Tony was reading the newspaper, he accidentally dropped the middle pages on the floor. His girlfriend picked them up and only by chance, her eyes noticed a job advertisement. It was for a waitress in the restaurant she used to work before a young man in a suit came to offer her a new job. The thought that she could end up back in her old workplace worried her all day, though; she managed to conceal well her superstitious fear. Tony was dealing with it all even better. Kate did not see a speck of concern in him. He skillfully tried to hide it as a strategic move, so Kate felt more relaxed about the whole thing. The truth was that behind his mask of cool, there was a man, who did not know even how to start that evening's conversation. The first sentence was still escaping him, somehow. This would have remained as it was, until the time came for him to actually say it. To get on time, they ordered a taxi for 9:10 pm.

Charlie had literarily banned everyone from arriving late and no one ever disobeyed his order, the idea of which again was given to him by Poltic. Michael would also turn up on time but he ignored the rule about driving their cars. He would always park his a few streets down from the club and then, after their drinking session, he would pretend that he was walking home but instead, he staggered to his vehicle. It was surprise even to Michael that he had never been stopped and checked by the Traffic Police. As there was no work on Saturdays, Michael believed he should drink as much as he could. He would start drinking well before he went out – everything that he would find at home – as if he wanted to improve his drinking record. He had all kind of alcohol in his mini-bar and when he ran out of something, he simply reached for another bottle. He was mixing his drinks, which led to him being drunk, inadequate and with sparkling eyes, and all that – by 7 pm. He sobered up a bit by 9:40, just so he could get drunk again, of course. He drove off towards the bar that he was supposed to get to within twenty minutes.

The tonight's choice had no alternative to anywhere else in town. It was the only bar, where one could try more than 70 types of beer and other spirits, order dozens of superb appetizers and dishes and at the same time, play pool on one of the ten pool tables. This was not some rocker's bar, full of smoke and idiots but a place, where middle-classed and good-mannered people enjoyed their evening.

At the arranged time, they all appeared, ready to storm the bar, in the name of the good time they were going to have that evening. Inside, there were already a couple of reserved tables, waiting for them – a dinner table and pool table. Charlie led his workers like a true leader and first went in. He had booked the tables over the phone and was quite surprised by the nice and comfortable interior. Instead of hard wooden chairs, there were soft leather sofas and many beautiful paintings on the walls, which gave the place a retro ambience – new and unusual for Charlie. His followers also showed their admiration for the décor of the bar. They were looking to the left, and to the right, slowly walking towards their table, which was shown to them kindly by the hostess. They settled down comfortably and ordered to the pretty waitress. From what she had just jotted down, was understood that Michael was having a double shot of whiskey as a start and Charlie – a pint of ale. The rest were true to their usual choice and ordered beer.

Only three meters away, there was the green baize-covered playing table, ready for the first game to begin. Charlie was not in any rush, although, he would look eagerly at the colorful balls every 30 seconds. He asked about what Lorrie, Tony, Kate and Michael thought of the bar. Lorrie was always the quietest, Tony and Kate were too anxious before the forthcoming conversation, so Michael was the only one to respond saying briefly that it is "super cool". He had dried up his glass and was just thinking of how to order another one. It was not so much an awkward situation – just the start was always slow. The food they ordered arrived, they also got another drink each and at background of the pleasant music, the two girls began to chat about women's stuff. Michael and Charlie had a little debate over the name of that guy on the sports channel, the best pool player, where Tony just butted in with the odd remark without really taking part in the argument. He was still missing his introductory sentence to Charlie, and it made him feel quite isolated in comparison to the others at the table. Another important part was when and where he was going to talk to him. Michael was sitting between them so the conversation could not take place, yet. Kate picked the end seat on purpose and it was not next to Tony. She had managed to move to a world of bags, shoes, clothes and what not, thanks to Lorrie, who was a very talkative expert on the subject. Kate learned about her enviable talent for making her own clothes and that some of her elegant suits were her own products. Lorrie's fascinating story about the different types of textile materials and where it was the cheapest to buy them from was interrupted by the boss, who asked Kate for a game of pool. She could not refuse – well, after all he was paying for this evening and he was calling the shots.

The former waitress knew a thing or two about pool, although, she had not played for a few years. She potted two balls with her break-off. Charlie was taken slightly aback by her skills and power and reached for his third beer on the table. His utter defeat he excused with the size of the table and the size of the cue, which apparently was a bit too short for him. Lorrie, Tony and Michael enthusiastically watched the development of the match and did not talk. Lorrie's personal psychologist, which she had to resort to after the numerous clashes she had with Michael, had advised her on ignoring him completely. That was if they could not improve their communication together. The cause of her mental unrest managed to order another beverage, while watching contentedly how his incompetent boss was losing from that silly girl, he worked with. Tony also followed the game and felt really happy that his dearest had won unconditionally. Her victory encouraged him to act after the game.

"She's good. Kate plays well. Did you see it? She could win against you all, I imagine." Charlie said defensively and sat down on his seat. "As soon as I get a bit more practice and get hold of a better cue, then you won't find it that easy playing with me."

"Sure, boss, it must be the cue!" Kate ironically pointed out and everyone burst into laughter. Charlie was quite excited and accidentally knocked his beer bottle.

"Oops! Sorry, it looks like my loss affects me in a funny way. Next time, I'll play with you, Tony. You don't seem that good at it like your girl by desk." Tony's mind somehow only grasped the words "your girl" in the whole sentence. "He knows …but where from? He's probably followed us! Life in fear is not a life!"

"Hey, Charlie would you come with me to the bar so we can order a more unusual brand of beer?"

"All right, Tony, but when we come back I'll have a game with you. Promise me, you won't run away! I need to win at least one game tonight." Charlie looked at Lorrie, Michael and Kate, who burst again into laughter. They did not laugh so much at the clumsy joke – Michael was simply totally drunk, Lorrie just could not easily stop, once she had started and Kate just tried to by in synchrony with the other two at the table. She wanted to suppress her growing anxiety, as she knew why Tony wanted to be accompanied by Charlie to the bar. It was not to get the beer only!

"Have a seat, Charlie. The barman is quite busy and we may have to wait a while."

"She cheated Tony, did you see?"

"Who? Oh, you mean Kate? I don't think she was cheating during the game. She's just slightly better than you."

"I just need to play a few more games and then she'll see!" This was not the case at all because he had five more balls left when Kate potted the black one. Tony, however, wanted to predispose Charlie for the forthcoming conversation and avoided the subject on how bad his boss was at playing pool. The barman almost jumped at their service. He was trying to please at least seven-eight of his customers at once. Very skillfully he refilled Charlie's and Tony's glasses with some Irish ale, holding them in one hand.

"Listen, Charlie, there's something very important I want to tell you. Let's stay here for a minute longer before we go back to the others."

"Sure, Tony, fire away. You know I'm your friend and you can tell me anything!" Charlie gave him a typical drunkard's hug, eager to hear about that thing. He was getting too close to Tony, who gently moved him about 10 cm away from him, leaving Charlie's arm still around his shoulders, and went straight to the point:

"Kate and I are seeing each other from time to time and we really like each other a lot. You are our boss and we think you should know it."

"What? That's unthinkable! Are you crazy? That's it! You two are out, Tony. You are finished." despite the quantity of alcohol he had consumed his words were produced in an adequate and confident manner so they just pierced Tony straight into his heart.

"Please, Charlie, not her! Sack me but leave her alone! Please, do it and you'll never see me again, I promise! Please, Charlie, leave Kate to stay at work…"

"I'm sorry Tony, I can't." Charlie was firm in his decision, although, he was aware that whatever happened, he had to first present the situation to Poltic. Tony looked down in defeat, on the verge of breaking down in tears. His pitiful expression in this moment did not reduce Charlie's anger but made him say a few optimistic words:

"One of you may stay but my boss doesn't tolerate any personal stuff at work. I'll try to put a good word for both of you but I doubt I could change anything."

Charlie's evening ended within ten minutes. His conversation with Tony was a killjoy and he did not feel like drinking or playing pool anymore. Michael was so drunk that he did not get it about what happened. Lorrie left a minute later after her boss. Kate and Tony remained at the table in silence. Aware of what happened, she only asked: "When?" in attempt to find out how long she had got to clear her desk in the office. "He'll call us tomorrow. He'll fire only me." answered Tony almost crying.

They did not say anything else to each other, despite the fact that they got back home together and went to sleep in the same bed. Tony had messed everything up. Kate did not console herself with the idea that at least she may was staying in the job because she knew she would have to support financially Tony from now on. She felt like hurting herself for such a non-loving thought, however, she was beginning to look on their relationship from a financial point of view. She had put all tender emotions at the back of her mind.

Neither of them managed to get any sleep. Tony could not think of saying a word to her, although he could see that Kate's eyes were open. He was feeling almost a physical pain from it all.

Charlie went home and his anger was growing by the second: "Now, M. J. will fire them and I'll have to stay in charge of just Michael and Lorrie, and everything will go to hell!" It seemed like this was the end of the world for him, the same like Tony but in a quite different way.

He got up in the morning, still thinking about last night's conversation he had with Tony. He dressed up quickly and without having a wash, unshaved, he ran out towards Poltic's house. He was in such a rush that even took the car for this short distance. At the entrance, he managed to fall out with one of the security guards for not opening the gate quickly enough and then he speeded in along the driveway. He behaved in the same angry way when the housekeeper opened the door for him and kindly greeted him with "Good morning!" Charlie went in as if she was not there and hurried up towards Poltic's study. This was the second time he entered without knocking at the door. He did not intend, however, to apologize for it this time. He did not even greet the owner of the house, who was calmly looking at some documents behind his desk. Charlie covered the distance between him and the desk in a couple of strides and out of breath he began with the news about the most outrageous thing that had happened. Poltic was sitting in silence, waiting for Charlie's emotional tirade to end. He could have taken him out in the garden, to calm him down but Charlie had started far too quick with his story.

"Everything's gone out of the window, M. J., these two fools have messed it all up! Tony and Kate, can you imagine? Last night, we went to a bar and everything was cool and then, Tony told me that he and Kate were together. M. J., how can I find such idiots, who managed to ruin everything in just a few months? I can't believe this is happening because when we sack them, the work on the supermarket will stop. By the time I find new people, we'll waste time, then, until they get to know their job – more time will pass, and basically, everything will go to hell! M. J., I'm getting fed up! I don't want this to happen! I'm just doing my job; everything's been going fine until last night and now – a total disaster! If I knew... if I only sensed that they had been together, I would have done something... I'm an idiot, aren't I? I noticed nothing!" Charlie's rage had turned into despair and Poltic decided it was time he joined in the conversation. He did not like to see when Charlie was letting his emotions to take over his judgment, instead of just looking at a situation from its positive and negative side and then make the right decision. Poltic had to wait a little longer before he spoke because the agitated young man had another important thing to share:

"I know, M. J., that you don't permit stuff like this at the workplace and that you're going to fire them but Tony asked me if I could leave at least Kate stay!"

"Firstly, sit down, Charlie! How do you know that I'm going to fire them and that I disallow that kind of personal relationships at work?"

"A few months ago, I think, you told me that this would jeopardize the work process and that would not be tolerated."

"Have I said this?" M. J. wondered. "Well, fine, maybe, I have. Things change all the time, Charlie – people's lives change, the way they want to spend it and the person they want to share it with." Poltic paused for a while to emphasize on the philosophical meaning of his words. "Tony and Kate are almost at the same age, both of them are quite attractive, they work together all day so it is very possible for them to develop some feelings for each other. They are predisposed for this by the circumstances."

"What about the work? Where do you put the work here?" Poltic leaned back in his comfortable chair before he answered. He felt slightly embarrassed that Charlie could not analyze the situation himself, taking into consideration that he was a part of it but required help from a person, who had never met Tony and Kate, and who had no idea what they were like as people. M. J. decided to forget about asking Charlie questions and instead, leave him to find the answers for himself. He was well aware that Charlie's mind was still blurred by the fixed idea that their relationship was something wrong. M. J. uttered straight to the point in the same way Tony did the previous night:

"They're staying, both of them!"

"They're staying…"

"Yes, they are. There will be a few conditions, though, which you are going to present to them next week."

"But why, M. J., I can't get it? Why are you not going to fire them? Common, M. J., just tell me because I'm going crazy! Am I the most stupid, here, that doesn't understand a thing?"

"Because, Charlie, love at the workplace can be destructive as much as it can be creative, sometimes. If one goes to work every day and there sees their loved one, this would give them the motivation to work harder, it would make them smile and make them feel happy. Both of them get a good salary, they belong to the same social class so there's a good prospect for something great and stable together, like having a family and, say, children." Charlie, who thought about everything from work's point of view, almost jumped in the air when children were mentioned. He did not have anything against them but just imagined Kate becoming pregnant and then she would not be coming to work for some time.

"That's the good side of the relationship, which we'll use now to our advantage. But do you want to hear the negative side or I'll move on to what you have to tell them on Monday?" Poltic was keen to see him off now because he had just received the small detective's report and could not wait to find out who was the black sheep amongst RA, if any.

"I do, M. J. Now I get you, where you coming from..."

"Good motivation, however, could be easily turned into a negative effect if they break off. It will be quite difficult for two people, who have been once close emotionally, to be good professionals, especially if they work in the same room. Hatred and spitefulness, thoughts will just become a routine for them and then we'll have to get rid of them. Remember, Charlie, hatred is as strong emotion as love – it's just a kind of love but in a reverse sense. The team principle will, then, suffer, which more or less is being, now, jeopardized by this Michael, so then the work will really go to hell!"

"You're right, M. J. You're right about everything. It's really better to leave them but I think we have to insure ourselves against them potentially falling out at some point in time." Poltic felt pleased that Charlie was finally beginning to apply some logical thinking about the problem and then, he moved on to clarify the conditions, which Kate and Tony had to comply with from Monday.

"It's very simple, Charlie! You'll just tell them that they should not exhibit any intimacy at work and if they even look at each other lovingly, or in some kind of personal way, they'll be sacked. Make it clear for them that work comes first!"

"M. J., I doubt that this will be enough. To tell them they can't look at each other sounds a bit, I don't know, a bit too much. Why don't we fine them or tell them that they'll work on a trial period?"

"Well done, Charlie, I never thought of this! We shall do it exactly how you've suggested. In this way, you'll scare them a bit, so they are on their guards in the future."

"I could even send them on unpaid leave indefinitely and then, on the second day, tell them they could come back to work!"

"Don't get carried away, now! We don't want one of them to end up in hospital from worrying or swallow some pills, do we?"

"All right, M.J., they won't do that anyway. But what are we gonna do if they try to hide it?"

"Hide what?"

"Hide that their relationship's finished and don't let me know? Then, what are going to do?"

"Charlie, haven't you ever fallen in love? If they split up, we'll learn about it on the next day, just watch them regularly. It will be written on their foreheads with capital letters: "We are not together anymore!" The sign will look bigger on Kate's face, so watch her more often."

"Oh, OK, then. I get it!"

"I doubt it, Charlie! Never mind, you, too, one day, will learn about these things. Is there anything else you are worried about? I can see you've calmed down now and can leave me alone to continue with my work, which is more than enough, as usual." Poltic tried to tell him in a roundabout way "Go, I'm busy" but Charlie did not get his message. He decided that there was time to raise another pressing question:

"What about Michael, M. J., what do I do with him?"

"You are nearly finished with the shop, right?"

"Yes, in about a month, maybe."

"As soon as Michael's contribution to the work on the entire project becomes unnecessary, i.e. you could carry on without him, I want you to let me know."

"I'm not sure if Lorrie's going to be able to stand him any longer... I constantly tell him off but she is so stressed out that one bad look from him and she's nearly ready to burst into tears."

"She'll be fine, Charlie, that's not a problem."

"How, M. J.? I can't put them to work separately, there's no way to do this."

"Well, there're 30 days, not 30 years left. We'll double her salary for this period and then after Michael's gone, she'll be back to her old wages. If she says a word to her colleagues about this, you'll fire her. Subject – over!" Poltic put an end to the conversation, but not Charlie:

"M. J., Lorrie doesn't care so much about the money, so this might not help!"

"Everyone cares about the money, Charlie, stop talking nonsense! Be assertive and when you're in the office, always stand up for her. During this month, Lorrie will be something like a sister for you and you'll have to look after her. And now, off you go and leave me to work."

"OK, M.J. Bye."

By the end of that day, Charlie managed to think over every detail of the forthcoming conversations with Tony, Kate and Lorrie. He missed to do one little thing, though. He forgot to call the couple in love and tell them the good news. This caused Kate and Tony to spend two days not speaking, looking or touching each other, as well as taking quite a few tranquillizers.

◆ ◆ ◆

Poltic reached for the report on the members of RA and buried himself in the lives of Johnny, Ted, Emma and Guillen. He had developed the gift for being able to look through documents very fast and in the same time, examine them in detail and understand the content. Instinctively, he would glean the most important information, without "wandering about" through the whole text. Thanks to his new talent he managed to find out, in less than an hour, the answers to the questions: who, where, what and most importantly – with whom!

The first thing he wanted to know about, was revealed straight away, because on the first page it was noted that no personal relationships had been formed between the persons that had been watched, to be precise – between Emma and any of the men. Poltic had explicitly stressed on the importance of this part of the surveillance and he did not doubt in the slightest that the small detective would approach his job very seriously. The document reported on every possible meeting that had taken place between any of the RA members. In the seven-day period of surveillance, RA had no assignment to complete, so everyone was going about their everyday life business. Ted and Johnny were hanging from dawn till dusk in their garage, even at weekends. Emma was training tirelessly in the boxing club. She did not go anywhere else, which made Poltic wonder why she could not find a nice fellow, who would take her out to dinner or to the movies. Instead, Emma hit the punch bag seven days a week, then she would fight in a few sparring matches, often with men, and then – straight back home. It seemed that her daily routine, she had forced on herself, was quite harsh. Poltic was pleased that the flow of big money had not made the two mechanics and Emma give up their old pastimes.

Guillen, the man, who lived a new life, in a new place with his family, had given himself up to spending his free time enjoying life in the company of his girlfriend and child.

Reading on, Poltic got to just two group meetings between the members of RA in that week, summarized in the report. The first one was at Guillen's place, which the detective described as a strangely quiet party. He, of course, was at that time still unaware of the presence of a two-year old girl, which prevented the adults from listening to any loud music or speaking from the top of their voices. The man, following RA, had most probably thought in that way because Ted and Johnny stopped in the off-license at 19:47, on their way to the so-called "party".

The second get-together happened in a place, where the "targets" could be watched throughout the evening and that allowed closer contact with them. This meeting was described in brief, too. Under "chatting about different subjects", the following was listed: education, work experience, cars, boxing and children. More or less, each of them had commented on the stuff, they knew about. It was also noted that only two people had moderately used alcohol that evening. "Emma and Johnny haven't had a drink, I imagine." Poltic thought, certain in their teetotalism, Emma – because of the boxing and Johnny – he was the driver for the group.

Poltic finished reading the report, skipping the last two pages. Everything was crystal-clear. Emma did not have a relationship with no one of the boys, they all did their own thing and on top of everything, when they were together – they had a great time. Poltic felt he should phone the detective but not to thank him – he had already been paid, but to ask him if he had noticed by any chance, any kind of tension between the members of RA. Then, he decided not to go ahead with the phone call. It would mean that he doubted the detective's professionalism and that was not the case.

Poltic was not an eccentric, nor did he do crazy things. Actually, his entire life was subjected to him doing everything in a rational and logical way, in order to achieve a maximum success. He was not a maximalist but rather something in between a perfectionist and a moderate maximalist, who understood that things should not be achieved at any price in this life.

However, this changed. He was possibly the only person in the world, who had been entrusted with such responsible task. Poltic knew how important his job was and he was prepared to do almost anything to complete it successfully. From the very beginning, he could have well started with setting up a regular company that was based on standard managerial principles and such of general validity. In the presence of unlimited financial resources, coming from THAT PLACE and the promise that he would be able to do anything he wanted, with no interference on their part, had encouraged him to develop a management strategy, which was out of the ordinary and did not have to be kept within certain budget, unlike others. If money was conditional, he would not have employed any of the Team. He would not have hired the Young ones, well, not at this high price every month, but instead, he would have resorted to the expertise of some experienced and qualified staff to work on this type of building project. And RA - the group was like the last nail in the coffin for the future company. Just one of them was enough to open their mouth and the media would turn up like a shot and tear apart anyone involved, no matter who was right and who was wrong!

Well, Poltic could afford to ignore all this, just because he had enough money to do it. His "machine" was going like clockwork and he was certain that any other company that could not afford to employ all from the Team or have people like RA at their disposal, would not have been able to achieve what he had managed. He was a step away from "swallowing" companies 1 and 2, along with number 6.

All Poltic's previous prognoses had proved to him that nothing could be predicted for sure. Nevertheless, the company was going steadily upwards and there was not any apparent reason for it to stop or slow down its progress. The worries around the three working groups were far too insignificant to affect the company in some adverse way or hinder its outlined future. Only time could tell if Poltic was going to achieve his goal. For the Team, that goal was the company to become number one in the market for meat products, where for Poltic, it was all about much more than that, about something that he had not told anyone, yet, and it looked like that he was not going to. The stake was far too great, greater than the price of a human's life, or even the lives of many people. If the model worked, if Poltic succeeded, then the entire idea could be "exported" and applied in other countries. After all, it was all politics; even people's personal relations involved some politics.

Could one call Poltic's objective humanistic? Alas, this was not the case and he knew it very well. Lately, he often felt conscience-stricken and could not find some peace. "A little longer, just a little longer and what will be – will be!" Poltic thought to himself in another moment of doubt, wishing to give up. Too many people were going to suffer.

Chocolate

Poltic had something of an obsession. He did not see it in that way but his desire to know everything that was there to know about his workers, to be precise – about the members of the Team, could be called more or less an obsession. Security was important, especially, when a lot of money was involved. Although, Poltic should have realized that the huge amount of money was precisely the reason why the four highly paid specialists were doing their job properly and there was not any real need for him to know where each of them went or what they talked about over the phone with a friend. They were still able to criticize him, hate him or mock him behind his back if they felt like it because he did not have the technology to stop them from thinking in a negative way about him.

Poltic had gone a short way since the beginning of his hard work. Not long way, but short, indeed. He laid the first brick in the new company by making the purchase of the house and now, he was a step away from getting hold of 1 and 2. The fact that his success was achieved in such a short period of time had made him forget about the other side of the coin. His mental stress was crushing at times that the big unshakable boss, who had an answer for everything, was nearly ready to give up quite a few times. Looking ahead, he knew that the conclusion of everything was near, he could sense it, and these positive thoughts really encouraged him a lot.

When a popular company changed owners, the media always represented the story straight away. Therefore, when the ownership of companies 3, 4 and 5 – some of the biggest manufacturers of meat products – changed, anyone who had a TV set at home, learned about these major deals, although, hardly any information on the buyers' names of was mentioned. The ordinary people could not care less about it. But the regular worker in one of these companies could be affected big time. A new boss was often associated with reducing the staff, which meant – immediate dismissals of workers, as well as some of the management personnel. Nothing personal! Poltic was against this type of ingrained models. He did not make anyone redundant, except a few managers of some departments, whose functions duplicated. The regular worker even got a pay-rise. That was such a relief for Greg.

Greg's family consisted of three people and the most important member was the seven-year old son of the worker, who had a job at the one of the meat factories of company 5. Its employees believed that they were of no value to the new owner and that he could easily decide to replace them. Greg also thought that and from the very first day he prayed for not losing his job. He was so used to it but his main reason was his boy, for whom he had to provide good education.

The kid would always wake up early in the morning, even at weekends. His father would get up just ten minutes earlier than him and had to get ready for 12-hour shift at the sausage factory. The long hours meant more money and better life for the rest of the family. His wife could not find a job. She had skills and qualifications but the location of their apartment made it difficult. It was only five minutes away from her husband's workplace but an hour's bus ride from the centre of town. The care for the child did not make it any easier. Greg's elderly parents could not look after him if needed as they lived a few hundred kilometers away. His wife was an orphan, which had not affected her in any adverse way or damage her mentally, but made her a very strong person, devoted to the welfare of her family through love, understanding and good care for their son.

Poltic, the person living in the fortress-house, who had unlimited financial resources and who had created a bit of a strange organization, did not suspect that he had the future of Greg's seven-year old son in his hands. Well, he was not just responsible for his, but for the future of hundreds of children, whose parents worked in his newly acquired companies. Poltic was not obliged, of course, to show any deep concern about his staff but he could at least show an interest, sometimes, in the lower level of his company. The Team members went regularly there and were quite well-known despite that they did not communicate with the ordinary workers. Poltic, on the other hand, had never visited in person any of the factories, apart of the old inherited company. He was not really afraid of meeting Greg or someone "replaceable" like him. He had just managed to completely forget the time when he lacked enough finances all those years ago, the days when he communicated with people, who were very different from those in his Team. All them and Poltic had somehow lost their humanity and kind-heartedness, refusing to relate to poor people, who were not so successful in life. The word "ordinary" they considered an insult, despite that the only thing that differentiated Poltic and the Team on one hand and the many regular people – on the other, was the money.

Greg was a bright and intelligent guy, who loved reading. He was clearly drawn to any technological gadgets. One of his childhood dreams was to make his own television set, because his mother never let him watch for long. She would always switch off his favorite electronic machine and would demonstratively send her little boy to bed. Well, dreams were far from real life. In order to become an electronic engineer and "play" with monitors, circuit-cards, main boards and what not, he needed an education. Greg could not achieve this. He had the capacity and potential but at the time, he fulfilled another of his dreams – he became a father. From then onwards, real life began, accompanied by constant lack of money.

Poltic had no family or children, except Charlie. What was really better – to be like the affluent Poltic or be in the shoes of poor but happy father – Greg? Probably, the truth was somewhere in the middle but who could say where this was? It was very unlikely that Greg and Poltic would ever meet. Was it fate or pure luck, but one day they did.

Poltic liked to do his shopping once a week. For that purpose, he used one of his bigger vehicles and not his black German limo. He already had five different cars in his garage and used each of them according to what he needed to do or where he was going. His convertible was for the nice, clear and not so sunny days. The others had different size boot he could drive them in any time of the year.

On his entry in the supermarket, Poltic fetch a large-sized shopping trolley, determined to fill it up with all kinds of food products. He could not get bored of walking down the alleys and looking for the goods he needed. Even after he spent two hours there, he did not mind to have another little wander. Finally, he queued at one of the cash-points. The cashier was very swift-handed and in a few minutes, the super rich but unknown customer began to load his products to be checked. He heard a kid's voice behind him, begging for some chocolate, which was firmly refused to him. Poltic turned around, mainly driven by curiosity, to see the bad dad and the hungry child. The father looked as if he had not had enough sleep and he was dressed in a way that indicated he had not been to a clothes shop in the last three-four years. Not to mention his shoes! The child was the complete opposite. The small boy was wearing perfectly stylish clothes, which together with his straight blond hair, made him look like a mini model. Poltic swiftly emptied the content of the trolley and the shop assistant packed everything in carrier bags. He was ready to get his wallet out and pay but before that, he reached to get a chocolate from the counter. It was the one the kid wanted, judging by his eyes still fixed on the sweet object. Greg did not see when the strange nice man gave his son a present. By the time poor worker figured out what was happening, the little boy had already stuffed more than half of the chocolate in his mouth. Poltic happily smiled at the sight of the child, munching on the dessert, denied to him a minute ago.

Why was the rich and the influential person feeling so happy by the small gesture, which cost him next to nothing? It was simple. For the first time in a long time, Poltic had a chance to peek in the other world, so different to his. It was where a bar of chocolate had become an expensive and unnecessary purchase. Greg saw his son eating the sweet black little squares and felt like a criminal. He immediately thought that the little one had stolen the product and just opened it.

"Thomas! Why did you take it? This damn chocolate!" The father was so tired that had not had the energy to get really angry.

"I gave it to him. It's not Thomas's fault. Don't worry, please! I just noticed that he wanted some and I bought it."

"Thomas, stop eating this chocolate and give it back to this man. I can buy him a chocolate, too! Who do you think you are?" Greg asked rhetorically and Thomas returned what was left. The permanent lack of money had forced Greg to erase any sense of pride he had but this time, the feeling had returned and he felt offended. Poltic realized that his kindness was being interpreted in the wrong way and decided that it was time to leave the store. Besides, the queue had been held up and some of the clients were beginning to get vexed.

"Hey!" Greg called out the stranger, who was just going through the exit of the shop. Thomas was told to go and wait near the car. "Wait a minute!" Poltic stopped, expecting to be reprimanded again.

"I want to thank you. My son loves chocolate but I can't afford to buy one every time he wants. Please, understand, that's quite an expense for me..."

"Oh, no problem, I just..."

"Yes, I know and I appreciate it!" Poltic regretted that he threw the rest of the chocolate and even thought to go back to the shop and get another one. Well, this would be truly insulting. Instead, he felt he should do something much greater for the stranger and his cute boy. He was a man of power, after all.

"May I ask what do you do?" Greg did not expect to be asked about his job and he did not answer straight away. So Poltic tried to find out more. "Tell me, please, where you live?"

"I live in the outskirts of town. Why are you asking?"

"I have, actually I work as... Do you want a new job?"

"Thank you but we have to go now. My wife's waiting for us and we are quite late. I've got a job and it's quite good, actually. I work in a meet factory, making sausages, at the..." and Greg mentioned the name of company 5. "The new owner even gave us a pay rise. We've heard rumors that he'll be paying us more in the future. Cheers, again, but now I really need to go." Poltic was gob-smacked. The man, he wanted to give a job and a good wage, was already working for him.

"What a small world!" he wondered, not giving much thought to which world he was talking about – his or that of Greg's. With his feet, firmly on the ground, he rarely showed any emotions. It was a sign of weakness but his encounter with Greg and Thomas made him feel weak. That night, he could not get a minute of sleep, thinking about the future of little Thomas. He bought him a chocolate; yet, his huge economic success would literally destroy the little boy. Poltic tried to diminish the adverse consequences of his task, he was about to complete, but it was not working out. In the morning, he jumped out of bed, feeling strong. He had overcome his hesitation, and had to go all the way to the end, though, the finale would have to be altered a little. The morning coffee increased his determination to win and he concentrated on the last major step.

The Young ones had completely taken up Charlie's mind. Following into Poltic's steps, he also had forgotten about his recent and not so affluent past, when he was at university and was living in a small and run down bed-sit. Poltic asked him to come by and reminded him to be on time. They often spoke on the phone but this time Charlie failed to notice the difference in his voice, due to Poltic's usual manner to give orders.

The loyal young associate knew the fortress-house very well, apart from one room that he had never been into. His attempt to find out, at the beginning, about what was in there, had failed. The door was kept locked. If Poltic wanted it this way, then, he really wanted people to keep their nose out of there. That explanation was good enough for Charlie, moreover, it wiped out his curiosity. He went in the house and instinctively headed towards the study of his host, where their meetings usually took place. Charlie knocked twice and pressed down the door handle. It was locked. Like a little kid, lost in a haunted house, he got confused about where to go. Clearly, there was no one in the kitchen and there were only bedrooms on the top floor. It was very unlikely that Poltic would see his guests there. Charlie explored all the options and finally, made his way to the mystery room.

He knocked again and pressed down the handle. He sensed that it would be open and yes, in a second, he was in. He frowned at the sight of long bare walls and just one big table and six chairs in the room, wondering why the owner had furnished such a huge room so scarcely. Poltic was sitting opposite opened door, with his elbows on the table, waiting for his important guest. One could not read any give away signs of emotions on his face, nor in his posture, about what he was going to talk in the next few minutes.

"Hello, M. J.! May I have a seat?" He asked as if he was a five-year old boy, asking for permission to go to the toilet. The unfamiliar surroundings made him behave a bit stiff. Poltic did not respond to the greeting but pointed at the chair, which the Team members would sit on, when making their presentation of a job well done.

"Hi, Charlie!" At last, Poltic spoke, a minute later than he should have responded. "How are our young builders doing?"

"They're doing fine, not long left now and we're done! The other day, I went to have a look and to be honest, we've built the best shop in town. Actually, there was just one other that is as good as ours, to be fair."

"And how are things within the group? Lorrie?"

"I always stand up for her and she completely ignores Michael. She is OK."

"That is fine."

Charlie did not say anything. He waited for another set of work related questions or some guidance and instructions about his behavior and ideas on the better ways of managing his workers. He noticed the set of three steps, as it was the most peculiar element in the room. Poltic made Charlie look up again, away from the architectural features and began with the explanatory talk.

"Charlie, I've always wanted to do something big, something great! Why did I return to this country after many years spending abroad? I did it, Charlie, because I was given the opportunity to become one of the most powerful men that has ever walked on Earth." Poltic started excitedly. "A lot of efforts, tireless work and a great deal of money are needed, if one aims at fulfilling their great and important goal. The last was given to me - money. I needed assistants, in order to apply my action plan and lay the foundations. I had plenty of money at my disposal." repeated Poltic and paused for a few seconds. An endearing image of little Thomas munching on the chocolate appeared before his eyes. Whether the word "money" distracted him with this recollection, he was not sure, but realized that he should concentrate on presenting the whole story to Charlie in the most truthful way.

"Money alone doesn't mean a great deal. It was impossible for me to manage it and invest it in the way I imagined it. I've just never been part of the big players' game. Yes, I know how turn seven-eight hundred thousand into a million in a couple of years. Everyone can do this. Say, we buy a villa in the outskirts of town. The property value steadily goes up, just because the town expands with time and the location of the house is not considered remote anymore. I can give you plenty of examples in the field of real estate but they're simply incomparable to the financial resources I had, when I accepted this job." Poltic felt like downplaying his professional duties by describing everything he had done and was going to do with the phrase "this job". "I had the opportunity to employ some of the best specialists in the country. Four of the top professionals agreed to work for me. If you remember, Charlie, I've told you that company I work for has different activities and its business in meat products is one of them."

"Yes, I do, M. J."

"Well, I've developed that side of the company, so in effect, I'm not an employee. I know, it sounds confusing and I hope you get most of what I'm saying. These four important professionals had to manage, organize and monitor the whole process and I had to direct them. Success in all ventures followed and everyone was pleased with the steady progress. All this is down to the unlimited finances of my company. The Team, as I called them, has managed to ensure we have the monopoly of the meat market in the country soon. Most probably, in a few months to one year, maybe two, all companies that manufacture meat products will be owned by me, and those that could not be mine, will be under my control, which is almost the same thing. I'll possess about 98% of that market, Charlie. It will be in my hands." Charlie listened to this extraordinary story and still could not figure out how it was related to his job and his staff, of course.

"The company's structure is straightforward. I am at the top, and then, it's the Team, whose members have the freedom to hire employees of their own, assistants and the likes. Another side of the company is managed by you, Charlie. The hierarchy there follows the same pattern – you are the boss and in charge of four people. And bellow are all the workers that you hire, which help you to complete your tasks. Am I right?" Poltic asked rhetorically and carried on.

"My people, Charlie, are professionals, who have the experience and plenty of connections and contacts, whereas, your guys are yet to become like them. I believe that it's good to rely on the old and highly efficient experts, as well as, give the chance to the promising new and ambitious generation. Do you understand, Charlie?"

"Not really, M. J., I did not get absolutely anything from what you've said so far. OK, you've built up a company, you have lots of money, you're about to become number one in the business with meat goods but I still can't figure out what's your point!"

"I would like you to become my business partner, Charlie, as you are my most trusted friend. I'll give you half of the factories I own. In that way, it won't look as if I have the monopoly of the sector before the authorities. I could find someone else to step in but I'd rather be you. Your positive answer will help me tremendously fulfill my task."

"OK, M. J. No problem, I'll help you but why did you need to say all this? Two words would've been enough, you know that."

"There's another thing, Charlie. I find it difficult to tell you."
Poltic had never looked so nervous in front of his young assistant.

"Don't worry, M. J., you can tell me anything."

"Once I've achieved my goal, I'll have to proceed to the final stage of the plan. It involves the disruption of the entire country, which will lead to a deep social and political crisis, Charlie, that will last for years, and which will change the country's political role and significance."

"Crisis, what crisis? Are you going to do something nasty, M. J.? But you're not that sort of person!"

"Listen carefully," Poltic raised his voice. "I have to go all the way to the end and show that my model is working, so we could implement it, later, in other countries that deserve to be destabilized…"

"But first, you'll damage ours, is that so?"

"Yes, Charlie, you could say this but this was how it was at the beginning. Now, I don't really want to cause such an adverse effect and I have probably never wanted this, really! It's my homeland, after all! I'm only thinking of applying the model to test its effectiveness, without anyone getting hurt. To do this, though, I desperately need your help. You have to help me and if anything happens to me, you'll be the one, who is going to avert any disastrous consequences. This is how it's going to be, Charlie. If one day I just disappear, wait for one week and then, inform the authorities that national security is under immediate threat. There is a small safe in my study; you've seen it. It's placed on the stand on the left side of my desk. In there are the documents that you need to take to the Police. It can be opened just once, so be careful! The code is formed by the numbers in the date of your father's death plus the numbers that are engraved in one of the steel spears of the gate. If it gets to this point, you'll have to find out which one it is. Do you understand, Charlie?"

"I got it, M. J., but why don't you just give up, especially if people might get hurt, you included? Just drop everything! You have money, so you can go and live anywhere in the world…"

"It's not that easy, Charlie! I've agreed to do this and I can't just go back on my word! Besides, if I try to leave the country and hide, I'll be dead in less than 24 hours. My only option is to go ahead with the initial plan but then simulate the end result and avoid causing the biggest social, political, economic or whatever else crisis in the country's history during peace-time."

"So there's no other way?"

"No, there isn't. Lately, I've been thinking a lot about this and I always come to the same conclusion."

"What about if you use the money for something that will prevent this from happening and make sure you or the country is not in danger? And then ..." Charlie tried to find a solution, unsure exactly how. "Or you could direct your efforts into a different sector of the economy, maybe! And, M. J., you, still haven't told me how your big investments, would plunge the country into a crisis?"

"I can't tell you that, Charlie, for now. If everything goes well, one day I shall reveal the secret to you. Subject's over. Thank you that you are willing to help. Very soon, I'll give you the documents that you need to sign, in order to transfer the ownership rights over some of the properties to you. Now, I've got more surprises for you! Your neighbors, the people, living in the four houses, which are exactly the same as yours, are actually the four my most important employees, I mentioned to you about. You may have seen them on the street, or when they are coming home after work – work that they have done for me."

"All my neighbors are working for you, even that annoying woman with the small toy-dog that doesn't look like anything?"

"Bob's wife? No, she is not."

"I think she is totally crazy, M. J."

"Yes, maybe you are right but let's leave this now. In a couple of days, I'm organizing a meeting with the Team, in this very room, and you'll be invited, too. The other thing that I have to tell you concerns your people. They have a different role in my plan than their present occupation. With the task to build a supermarket they're actually having a test to pass, you as well. I can say now that the results are very good and I'm fully satisfied with the work that's been done."

"Do you mean that your company doesn't need the store?"

"No, Charlie. It's not that at all. Building the supermarket is something like a mathematical problem, which you all have solved successfully. I never really needed it and even if I did, I could buy one already built or even, that was already working." Most people would have felt betrayed by Poltic's words. Charlie did, too. So Poltic quickly tried to change the effect of his statement by presenting to him the positive side of things.

"You and the whole team of young people are heroes!"

"Ah, what?" Charlie gaped at Poltic at the sudden change of things. Again, he could not understand anything. This feeling was becoming the norm for him every time Poltic sat opposite him, not to mention that it happened twice that evening.

"Forget about the shop, Charlie. You are young and ambitious; you've just graduated from university as promising specialists, who fulfilled successfully everything I asked from you. However, I'm about to entrust you all, Charlie, with something far more important, and you and your three employees will have to work by my methods."

"Four, M. J. I'm in charge of four people."

"Only three will take part in the new job and Michael will be dismissed one day before you bring the others to my house."

"Here? You'd like me to invite them to the house?"

"Yes, here. But let's get the meeting with the Team out of the way, first, and then, I'll inform you about the date and the time for the next one."

"M. J., what's going to happen to the supermarket? Are you just leaving it as it is?"

"No, of course not! You just pointed out that it's nearly ready, so it can be used for what it's for. Leave this to me."

"M. J., if you ruin the country so you achieve your goal, what are you getting out of this? What did they promise you?" That was the most meaningful question that had come out of Charlie's mouth.

"Nothing, that is of any real value to me, only money. Since I've thrown myself in the venture and until recently, I believed that the great idea itself is the most important thing, even than people. I wanted to become a great man, too, at the same time. This made me agree to do it. It was not for the money, really. I don't know how to describe it, Charlie, but most people would call it megalomania. Now that most of the idea has been realized, I understand the sense of superiority won't bring anything good to no one, but only me. People come first." firmly said Poltic, putting a stress on every word. Charlie looked at him inquiringly, and in expectation to hear about that great idea, at last. Alas, Poltic changed the subject back on to Michael.

"You should give Michael the sack very carefully and do it in the office, in front of everyone."

"Oh, I have no problem about this. I'll fire him with pleasure. He's been getting on my nerves for a long time, now. Moreover, he's just constantly upsetting Lorrie." Charlie said and inadvertently exhibited his fondness of the demure young accountant.

"No, Charlie, you really have to act very diplomatically and avoid letting your personal feelings to take over. Professional attitude comes first."

"That's not going to be easy, M. J.!"

"It will be easy. You're experienced enough, now!" almost told him off Poltic.

"Sure, M. J. OK. I'll do whatever you say!"

"Also, keep in mind that all of you will be working in different place, once he's gone, so Michael won't be coming to disturb you."

"Where?" Poltic did not respond, leaving all the details to be discussed at the forthcoming meeting. He went on to a personal confession:

"I'm proud of you, Charlie. You have come a long way and I'm very happy that you're going to be by my side until the end of my difficult task."

"Thank you, M. J.! Your high opinion of me means the most to me and I'm glad that you trust me." The host stood up and gave Charlie a big hug. Poltic, always very reserved, showed weakness in two days in a row. The image of Thomas also appeared in his mind for a few seconds.

"Now, go Charlie! I'll call you later to let you know about some details for the meeting with the Team, as well as about the way you should behave."

"See you soon, M. J.!"

Alone again, the question before Poltic was whether Charlie and he would succeed. He did not try to find the answer. His mind wandered to a very different place as if to forget about everything.

Poltic saw a nice and neat little house. It was the same one, where he had spent his very first years of his life. He found the old mosaic, the patio tiles that were not straight, and the overgrown garden, really charming. Poltic opened the gate and went into the garden. He looked around to see a neighbor on one of the nearby balconies. He could not see anyone and the silence was a sign that there were not any people around. He went across the garden to the entrance of the house and tried to get in. He really wanted to see his room, his bed, his toys, and his bicycle. The door was closed. He pressed on harder, but it would not open. Did his mind really lock that part or he had gone to the wrong house?

Poltic was feeling right in the middle between sanity and the place, where madness started. He went out to get some fresh air. As a man, who liked to analyze and criticize himself, he tried to understand how everything had changed so suddenly and acquired new form and new meaning. His environment remained the same, the people he was surrounded with – too. The new element was just Thomas. Poltic realized that his lack of contact with people from the lower social levels, together with the fact that he had not got a family and children, had invoked new feelings in him, which had been deeply suppressed by the huge workload, as well as, him pursuing his goal.

"Hmm, nonsense!" Poltic thought in disagreement with his own psychological profile that he had just made. "I've changed!" Back to reality, he thought about the meeting, where Charlie was going to be introduced to the Team. Charlie's introduction had never been planned because Poltic's initial idea was to keep all the branches in the management of his company separately. However, the task of the Young ones was going to get entangled with the Team's obligations, so it was better the person, who was going to look after them and protect them, to meet the Team in a controlled environment and not in one of the companies. Poltic believed that this was the right way. Well, he was quite wrong because the Young ones and the Team, even if they knew each other, their paths would never cross and neither side could get hurt. The paranoia about security and people relationships, in general, was taking its toll.

Simulation

Poltic was very surprised that he could not get in touch with one of the mechanics. He thought that it was impossible for them to ignore his call because, after all, he had instructed them to never part with the device. He did not try to think of probable reasons for this, but just rang Guillen and asked him to pass on the message about their new assignment. That evening, the best "military" unit in Poltic's scheme, which had never failed so far, got together in the flat of the former builder. All of them arrived on time, curious to find out about what their peculiar boss wanted from them this time.

"Mr. Poltic asked me to introduce you to our new mission. We need to follow his plan closely and not change a thing."

"What has he asked us to do?" Ted was getting impatient.

"Are we going to beat someone up again?" Emma joined in.

"Not exactly, the way I see it, we need to hurt someone, without meeting him. We're not allowed to touch him."

"And how is this going to happen? It's impossible! Hey, Guillen, you're not hiding anything from us, are you?"

"Shut up, Ted! Guillen will explain if you let him speak!"

"Thanks, Johnny. Listen all now! The boss told me... well, his words were, as far as I remember: "You have to fiddle with the brakes of a car. The registration plate is 4563, it's parked on 63rd Street." unquote. You all know where it is, don't you?" His audience nodded in agreement. "He also said that you Johnny, together with Ted, are going to do most of the job, whereas Emma and I will take care that nothing goes wrong. The only condition is that the brakes have to fail at no less than 70 mph, so the control of the car is definitely lost. A car can get to this speed only on Western Avenue, going towards the centre of town. If the motorway is very busy, this could lead to a chain crash and many casualties. To avoid this from happening, Mr. Poltic wants us to drive near the car until it just crashes somewhere and in that way, we protect the other vehicles on the road."

"Oh, yeh? As if…!"

"I've not finished, yet, Ted. Mr. Poltic wants the driver to end up in hospital and everything to look like an accident. Only we would know it's been intended."

"So we'll make a show, a little bloodied, though." Johnny sneered as if he was some butcher – not a mechanic. "Anything else he mentioned?"

"No, that's it, nothing else. He didn't go on about that much. Actually, the last thing he said was that we're getting double for this job!" Guillen concluded with the best news at the end. Johnny, Ted and Emma quickly calculated in their heads their huge payment, forgetting for a moment about the actual job they needed to do, which was in fact the hardest from the previous two. Johnny got back to reality first and uttered:

"We might have a problem. It's not easy to fiddle with the brakes, so they fail at such high speed. I don't really know how we gonna do this!"

"We could puncture the brake fluid reservoir." The only woman in the room suggested and everyone, apart of Guillen looked at her in a funny way. Due to their long experience, Johnny and Ted believed that women and cars just did not get along.

"That's a good idea, Emma, but do you know what speed the car will be driving at when the brakes are going to give in? No one could say this and it's very possible to happen when the vehicle is stationary." Johnny opposed the suggestion and continued. "We don't know the model of the car or anything about the brake's system and how we could damage it. I think we should go and try to have a look at it, first, and then, find out some information on the brakes' specifics. That will definitely help us. There's another problem, though, and one that's not to be underestimated. Say, we manage to do it and the poor guy is driving along at 70 mph, not being able to stop. We, on the other hand, are by his side, trying to protect others and at the same time, we are a step from crashing into him. Is that so?"

"I believe so. I know it sounds a bit scary but…"

"A bit? It's not just a bit, Guillen. Even Ted could explain to you why."

"The average weight of most cars is about two tons." Ted began as if he was a lecturer at university. "If a car stops at 70 mph, its braking distance will be about 38-40 m. With no brakes, it would only stop if it hits something hard and solid, like a concrete wall or a tree. Very rarely it would stop by itself, losing the momentum. The most common outcome is to hit another vehicle on the road, the result of which will be fatal for both drivers."

"How do you know? Every road accident happens differently. You can't predict what the car is going to hit and who's going to survive and who wouldn't."

"Ted's only speaking in general terms, so you can get the gist of what happens in a situation like this. Otherwise, Emma, you've got a point – no one could say how things will turn out. Go on, Ted!" Johnny encouraged him, seeing how the lady in the room had just knocked down his initial enthusiasm.

"In short, a car, driving at 70 mph can be very dangerous. If it crashes into another vehicle, a tree or just something solid, the driver will definitely die. So we have to watch it. If one of us gets caught in it, you know, we, too, will be driving at this speed, it could really get quite nasty."

"From what I got of Mr. Poltic, we are not supposed to get near but just keep the others at a distance."

"It sound easy, but I can assure you it won't be at all. Let's don't think about this right now. Before that we've got to figure it out how to set the brakes so they fail him as soon as he gets to 70 mph."

"By explosion, Johnny! We could set up a small explosive device behind the control panel that will block all systems in the car."

"No, Ted that's not an option. It has to be an accident, not a premeditated attempt." Guillen rejected the idea immediately. "Any other ideas?"

"How long have we got until the Big Day, Guillen?" asked Johnny in overexcited tone of voice.

"There are two days left, actually one and a half."

"Right, it means we don't have that much time and we have to hurry up. We'll all go and see what brand and model the car is. You two will look out if the Police turn up or some passers-by, while Ted and I try to open the vehicle."

"Why? We are not stealing it, are we?"

"We won't move the car, Emma. I just want to know certain stuff about the equipment and the model of the board computer. Then, we have to find from somewhere a car with the same board computer or even better – a car that is exactly the same model. That's not hard as long as the vehicle is older than 3 years. If it's a brand new car, it'll be too bad, but not impossible."

"And then, what?"

"We can do an experiment. If we succeed than, we'll have a good chance. Although, I wouldn't want you to hold out vain hope. I know the money's hell of a lot, but I can't promise anything."

"So what do we do if the experiment fails?"

"Then, Emma, we'll just have to phone Poltic and tell him that the guy won't be crashing his car anywhere but will be simply mugged on the street, instead, followed by a good beating. There's just no other way."

"Let's not come to rushed conclusions but try out the experiment, first. If no one has anything else to say, I suggest we head towards Street 63 and have a look at the car. Emma and I will be your cover."

Half an hour later, they stopped a few meters away from Harry's private SUV. Johnny double-checked the registration plate to make sure that this was the right vehicle. He was not very happy that it was less than a year old but on the other hand, he appreciated that it was brand new. He remembered something:

"Do you know that new cars are full of electronics and everything's controlled by sensors, gauges and all sorts of other gadgets?"

"What do you mean by that?" asked Guillen.

"I mean that we're not going to open it but tomorrow morning, we need to find one that's the same from somewhere. Then, we destroy its nice electronic brake system that, I'm sure, it's been integrated in this luxury and expensive car."

Johnny and Ted spent all night thinking about different solutions, which would bring them more money that they so much needed, so they could modernize their small and run down car repair business. On the following morning, Johnny phoned Guillen and Emma and asked them to pop by the garage.

The gate was wide open and one could see the cluttered interior. It was quite noisy outside and every car passing at high speed, managed to muffle partially people's voices inside the front of the garage. Emma heard a deafening sound, coming from a passing vehicle that probably had a wrecked exhaust pipe. She decided to wait for the roaring car to go away, so she did not have to shout over it, when saying something to Guillen. However, the vehicle did not go but stopped right outside the exit. It was a black expensive SUV, the same they looked at yesterday. There was Johnny, of course, behind the wheel, with a wide grin on his face. He was feeling over the moon that he could drive such an incredible car, while Ted was playing with the buttons of the powerful car-stereo. Their colleagues were taken aback by the predatory front of the jeep.

"Common, guys, jump in!" Johnny called out.

"Hey, we left the door open!" Emma shouted in his ear, in attempt to be heard over the 12 speakers in the car. Ted turned the sound down and replied instead of his friend:

"Who's going to bother with our garage? There's naught to steal from there!" Ted turned up the music again so it was bearable to listen. He was now anticipating getting to the place, he had suggested, where the crash was going to take place. Since they found a solution about the brakes, they called it "the crash" rather than – "the experiment".

They stopped outside an old factory at the gate, which strongly reminded them the one of the fortress-house. Despite the heavy weight and too much rust, Ted and Guillen, supervised by Emma, managed to open it enough for the SUV to pass through. Johnny drove in and parked a few meters away, on the other side.

"This car's not getting out of here in one piece!" Ted smiled wickedly.

"Common, Johnny, Ted, tell us what's going on here! What do you have in mind?"

"We are saying nothing, Guillen! Just watch! Are you ready, Johnny? Go on, show them all!"

The gas pedal was down to the floor, creating a surprisingly good acceleration, with the machine being so heavy. There was about 80 m from where the spectators were standing to the location of the nearest industrial buildings. The black vehicle was speeding up with no intention to divert and just crashed, head-on, into a wall, which almost entirely collapsed. A loud thunder was produced and the three bystanders instinctively plunged down as if expecting a bomb to fall over their heads. They just could not believe their eyes.

Aware of the scenario, Ted was running already about ten meters ahead of them, when Emma and Guillen rushed towards Johnny and the vehicle. Before they got to the smashed car, the door on the driver's side opened and Johnny came out slowly and triumphantly, without a single scratch on him. When he saw his workmates he raised his arms like a winner and bellowed from the top of his voice:

"Hurray! It was so cool! Did you all see this? This is the greatest thing I've ever done!"

"Are you all right?" Ted asked, more like, because of the adrenalin that rushed into his head, rather than from a sudden concern about his mate's wellbeing.

"I'm absolutely fine! Don't worry about me. Everything worked, well, it failed to work!"

"Why didn't you say something to us, Johnny? This was such a stupid thing to do! Imagine, you ended up getting hurt badly, then what? We don't have another car to drive you to hospital and an ambulance would get here no earlier than an hour. You jeopardized the entire mission. You're doing crazy, foolish things..." Guillen could have carried on with his criticism but got interrupted.

"You're very wrong. It was all under control." Ted stood up for his best friend. Emma could still not come round and crouched, feeling dizzy. Being into a fighting sport, she was not afraid of blood, but the scene with the car crashing into the wall, she just found it unreal. The stunt-driver noticed her, first, and the bad condition she was in.

"He's right, Ted, we should've told them. It was stupid. I'm sorry. Are you OK?" He whispered in her ear, thinking that any loud noise was going to hurt her even further. Emma took a few deep breaths in attempt to calm her pulse down, which was racing as if she was going to have a heart attack. Johnny stood up, leaving his beautiful colleague in piece, and addressed the accusations from his workmate:

"We've got a car, Guillen. It's just there, to the right of the entrance. We've parked it a bit further down. That's what we're going to use to get back, OK? I am really sorry! You should've been told."

Johnny went to see the smashed vehicle. He wanted to check what Harry was going in for on the next day: "Very bad injuries or immediate death! Mr. Poltic knows what he wants. Otherwise, he wouldn't explicitly choose the speed of 70 mph. He wants the driver dead, nothing less than dead! If he didn't want a fatal outcome, he would have picked a different speed."

RA male members helped Emma on the way to the car and drove off back to Guillen's place. They all avoided talking so they did not upset their "sister" any further. Johnny was dying to explain everything to them so he could clear his consciousness, especially after looking at Emma and the state she was in. They arrived at the grey residential block of flats and went up to number 21. The lift was not working, so they had to use the stairs, which proved to be a real challenge for Emma's shaking legs, even though, she was being supported on both sides by the men.

"Again, I'm really sorry! You'll see now, that although it all looked very scary, there was nothing to worry about!" Johnny began before his friends got into their seats. "I'm sorry, Emma!"

"You knew that nothing was going to happen to you? How could you be so sure?" Guillen asked.

"Before I come to this I want to go back from the start and tell you everything. Ted and I, we've had a few vehicles with the same type of electronic break system like this one, brought to us in the garage. Last night we called one of our regular customers. We heard that he had bought recently, exactly the same SUV like the one we're looking for. He came and we made the deal. He's a lawyer and it didn't take long to convince him by giving him 20 thousand over the real value. Mr. Poltic may be crossed with us but we had no other choice."

"How much did you pay?"

"Almost 100 thousand." Johnny produced a guilty smile.

"What? Why didn't you discuss this with us before you gave the money?" Guillen jumped up from his place. "If the boss doesn't approve, 100 grand is an awful lot of money. At the end, we'll all be paying for this!"

"We just had no choice. We had to make a decision fast, because it was very unlikely that we'd find someone else, willing to come over at 3 o'clock in the morning and sell his car to us that was exactly what we were looking for." Guillen saw the logic in this explanation and realized that there had not been any other way. He sat down on the sofa, less wound up, but far from calm. Johnny read this as implicit consent and continued.

"We've found out that the brakes work on the principle of electric impulse. You just press the pedal, which is connected to the four wheels electronically rather than mechanically. So a signal is sent to the brake system, which, then, activates and the vehicle stops. We could not cut off the signal sender from the outside, so we had to do it from the inside." he paused for a second and glanced over at Emma, who had got back the color in her cheeks and was listening carefully. "We damaged the device that was right next to the brakes and it stopped sending a signal to the wheels. What we had left to solve was the issue with the 70mph – speed. We set up one of the leads in the way when one presses on the brakes, it just gets displaced and they're out! The faster the car's going, the harder you press on the pedal. Well, yes but no!" Johnny quickly denied his own statement. "Because people press gently and slow down gradually, so the lead may not get disengaged. Here is our plan: We are waiting for the SUV at the crossroad; four vehicles will be involved. As soon as he gets on the motorway, I get right behind him. He accelerates to 70-80mph – a regular speed for a nice and straight road like this. One of us will be in front of him, Ted, driving faster to allow him keeping the velocity. If the front car slows down, the target will do the same, and inevitably – me, too. He may try to overtake but that won't be in our favor, either. The other two will be driving on each side of him, preventing any other car from joining in the same lane, cutting off my way or from getting in front of the SUV. I know it sounds complicated but I hope you get most of it. Now, here we come to the final and most dangerous part. Ted will suddenly press on the brakes, which will make the driver of the SUV do the same. He will be simply unaware that the brakes will fail to work from this."

"Are you sure that they'll fail right at this moment?"

"Yes, Guillen, I am sure, almost sure, not 100% sure but I am sure."

"But then the car will smash in to the car in front!"

"No, that's not gonna happen because Ted will just accelerate again to avoid being hit by the vehicle. He can do it!"

"Right, so that's it, is it?" Guillen uttered, thinking that there must be something else to hear.

"Well, yes, that's it!"

"We surround him from all sides, Ted steps on the brakes, he steps on the brakes, they fail and we just wait to see how he crashes into something. If that's your idea, really, what the hell did you do this today for?" Guillen's anger was coming back.

"I wanted to check something that I wasn't sure about. Now, I am. First, my crash was done at about 35mph. Keep in mind, with this modern car, there's hardly any risk for the driver's life. It becomes dangerous, when you drive over 50mph. I just wanted to get a feel of the brakes, when one steps on the pedal. In that way, I'll be able to set it up for the real target. I don't want to lie to you. I reckon we'll just need luck, too. It was quite easy today but I have to point out that I pressed on the brakes well before coming near that wall. So our target may do the same, before he joins the motorway, and figure out that something's not quite right. Yes, we'll need a lot of luck."

"Johnny, if the brakes don't fail the first time, we could force him to press on them a few times!"

"How do you mean, Guillen?"

"We'll just do the trick with braking and accelerating as many times as it is necessary!"

"Yes, but then, Ted won't know exactly when the enormous heavy vehicle is going to lose control and knock his back bumper off or even worse – it could hit him really bad."

"We could fit him with some special gear, like a helmet!"

"Oh, no, I couldn't wear a helmet, it's too claustrophobic!"

"You'll be fine. It's only for a short while!" Johnny scolded him.

"Which car am I going to drive?" Emma spoke for the first time, feeling a lot better. The three men looked at her and Guillen replied:

"Whichever you want, the one on the left side or the right, it makes no difference to me!"

"I don't mind either way. Whatever you say, guys."

"OK, it's all sorted, then! I believe, that's all to discuss and it's time to get down to it. Ted and I are going to prepare the car. We don't need a cover in that remote place, so there's no need for you, two, to come. Besides, it won't take us more than a couple of minutes."

"Where and when are we going to meet?"

"Get down to our garage, with Emma, at 5:00. I phoned here and there, today, and managed to find four vehicles that will be perfect for the job. See you tomorrow! Bye, Emma!"

Harry

It was the big day! Someone was going to lose their life in one of the many car accidents that happened every day on the roads. Who was going to be that time?

The ambush began at 6.00 o'clock. It was quite a chilly morning and anyone, who was out, had dressed as warm as possible. Only a couple of degrees below zero, the cold were not that bad, but it was the first time for the year, when the temperatures had plummeted – a clear sign that winter was coming. The fog made people feel it was colder. On a narrow street, just a short distance from junction that joined the main road to town, there were for vehicles, pick-ups, to be precise, that were waiting. Johnny had opted to use pick-ups for their steadiness and reliability, in contrast to a regular sedan. The size of the vehicles in length was important, too. The smaller cars on the road would be forced to keep their distance.

Emma was feeling quite nervous and fidgety in her seat, trying to get into the most comfortable position. The radio was turned off so it did not disturb her. She noticed Guillen in the car in front of hers, taking his winter jacket off. He was clearly getting quite hot in the small space. She also glanced at the other two vehicles, parked on the left side of the road, where Johnny and Ted were waiting in position. The quiet morning, together with the tension coming from the other three vehicles, made her look at her wrist watch every few seconds. She was not feeling that great. Things were going to get worse because their rich boss, Mr. Poltic, who lived in the vicinity, had missed to mention that most of the times Harry did not get up and go anywhere to work, but stayed in and worked from home. However, after a few hours in the house, often, Harry would drive to town in his private SUV. For the last two weeks, he could not use the company car and driver even if he wanted, because the vehicle needed fixing.

Harry left his home around lunchtime, oblivious to what was ahead of him. He had examined a few documents that morning, only to realize that he had to visit company 4 in person and sort out something important. He did not like spending hours on the phone, trying to explain issues that on the other side of the line, the person did not have the slightest idea what he was talking about.

Harry set off brazenly down the slight hill, ready to join the six-lane motorway in a couple of minutes. The four from RA were about to lose all interest in their difficult task and almost slept through the moment, when the black car whizzed by. Johnny was the first to react and start his engine. The rest followed immediately, all at the same time. On their way out of the narrow street, they spotted the target at about 50m ahead. The vehicle was indicating right. The five cars got onto the motorway, driving behind each other. The foot on the accelerator quickly changed their automatic gears all the way to the top. It was not time to stop, yet. Ted zoomed by and got in the front of the target. Guillen and Emma took side positions and prepared themselves. 50, 60, 70 - Emma anxiously watched the speed indicator, her hands – clutched around the steering wheel. Johnny was only a few inches away from the back bumper of the vehicle, forcing it to speed up even more. They had not arranged a code signal between them – it was all down to Ted.

The traffic was not heavy and there were hardly any cars on the road that could cause a possible problem and spoil the operation. Ted picked a good moment and stepped on the brakes, looking in his mirror for reverse vision. The black monster behind him was getting close fast, with no intention to stop. Johnny instinctively slowed down, when he saw what was happening in front of him. Guillen and Emma did the same. They resembled some kind of convoy of the man in the expensive SUV. Harry was aware of what his vehicle was capable of doing, so he felt calm when pressing indifferently on his brakes. If this idiot in the pick-up did not accelerate at once to a speed, appropriate for this type of road, then he would have to slow down even more. Harry's way of driving prevented the small lead, loosened by Johnny, from failing to send a signal to the hi-tech brakes. Ted realized that the plan would not work and besides, the speed was getting less than 60mph. The attempt had to be repeated, as many times as it was needed.

Ted accelerated again to 75mph. Harry followed at 74mph. Johnny, Emma and Guillen caught up with them. At that moment, out of the blue, Emma decided that an immediate change of plan was required. She overtook Harry, by cutting in between the SUV and Ted, at the front. Suddenly, there was a screeching noise from the wheels and a loud bang. Emma had stepped on her brakes, but unlike Ted, who left some good distance to avoid the crash at his first attempt, she did it as close as possible to Harry's car, so it would be inevitable, even for the most skilled driver, to escape smashing into her car. She did try to speed up but it was too late. The SUV's bumper had touched hers and the pick-up was hurled off the road. Harry jumped and pressed on the brakes but those were out and gone. Within seconds, he also ended up with 68mph in the ditch.

Guillen was shocked to see Emma's car flying off the road. Ted witnessed the horrific incident in his mirror for back vision. The three pick-ups immediately swerved towards Emma's smashed vehicle, completely ignoring the black SUV, which had crashed further down the road. Johnny knew that there was hardly any chance for her to have survived. Ted got out and ran towards the car, thinking about his failure. And Guillen, he could only curse their generous patron – Mr. Poltic.

In less than ten minutes, the Police, a fire engine and several ambulances appeared on the scene. The three men, worried sick for Emma, stood by her, while the medical emergency staff was trying to get her out and put her on a stretcher. The guys asked if they could go to the hospital with her, however, the Police had something else in mind. They were all taken to the station for a routine questioning.

There was the fear that sooner or later, it would be discovered that the four witnesses of this horrific road tragedy, had criminal records. Four offenders, driving the same vehicles, end up witnessing the death of a rich and famous lawyer, just 100m down, in his super modern car. It was a question of time for the detectives to sniff a rat and see their connection to the incident. That was of course, if the Police took the case seriously. One could say that intelligent detectives existed but most of them had lost part of their rational thinking, due to the hierarchy of the actual system. They all followed the rule that the boss was always right, even if that was not the case at all times.

On their way to the Police station, Johnny managed to warn Ted to be careful what is coming out of his big mouth. They were taken to three different rooms and the interrogation started. When three people were asked the same question, the answer could never be the same, similar – yes, but never absolutely identical.

Ted decided to make his story as short as possible but the interrogator kept going back, asking him new questions and making him repeat his statement a few times. Three hours later, he was led to go. Thanks to the detective and his never-ending questions, Ted was feeling exhausted. He was told that Johnny and Guillen had been let free two hours and a half earlier. Ted felt quite sick about it and thought: "Why was I held for so long and they've been gone for ages?" The answer laid in the fact that both his friends were very lucky to get a couple of reasonable cops but daft, at the same time, who had no interest to deal with some car crash and the muddled statements of the witnesses. It was just another road accident.

Ted found his friends in the hospital, sitting in the waiting room, looking like everyone in their situation – with eyes, staring at the floor and their arms crossed.

"How is she? Is she OK? Where is she?"

"She's undergoing a surgery at the moment. They don't tell us anything else." Said Johnny and looked down again. Ted sat down next to Guillen and as if instructed to do so, he got into the same position of despair. No one even thought of Harry. That day they killed a man, made everything possible so he died and succeeded. The mission had been achieved. Emma's life, however, could not be compromised. Time was running slow and no doctor came to tell them whether she was even still alive. Guillen decided to phone his family and get some support. He could not actually tell his girlfriend where he was and what had happened to his pretty colleague. He just needed to hear his partner's voice – so precious in a moment like that.

Johnny did everything he could possibly do not to think about death – not necessarily of Emma's or Harry's, but in general. As a child, he decided that people did not just die and truly believed, now, that Emma is alright and very soon she would join them and get out of this hospital.

The lack of information about her condition was affecting Ted quite badly. He stood up and started pacing backwards and forwards, like a beast in a cage. He would approach different doctors, who were passing through, but no one knew or had heard anything. He was about to hit the next person, dressed in white, who had refused to let him know about Emma's condition, when one of the many nurses, rushing about, approached Johnny and whispered something in his ear. Ted zoomed towards him and almost pushed the woman from the medical staff.

"We can see her tomorrow morning. The operation took a long time and she would need more time to recover."

"So she is OK, then, Johnny, isn't she?"

"I'm not sure what it all means but they've said she'll be fine. Common, let's go home now. We'll come back tomorrow."

None of them was able to get some sleep. Every attempt to close their eyes was accompanied by scenes of the crash: how the firefighters were trying to get the lifeless body out of the smashed pick-up or how Emma's arm hanged unnaturally from the stretcher and her face was covered in blood. In situation like this, the words somehow escaped. One would try to say something and realize that this was not going to help no one, neither Emma, nor – the person, on the opposite side, let along the speaker. Guillen could not remember anything from his half an hour phone conversation with his girlfriend. Johnny could not think of how they got to the hospital or even which hospital. The same applied to Ted, who realized that Emma was something far more than just a woman that he worked with. He felt he might lose his closest female friend.

On the next morning, RA went to visit their most precious member. There was still time until visiting hours, so they had to wait. Johnny went to the vending machine to get some coffee. Guillen strode off to the flower shop, opposite the hospital. Ted, alone, was just eager to see Emma, his Emma. Something had happened to him after the accident. There was this inexplicable transformation with him, screaming out a crystal clear message – Ted was in love. The personal life of the car mechanic was not that enviable, really. He found it quite difficult to speak to any pretty female customer, who had accidentally dented her easy to park small car. The beautiful stranger would make him speechless and thus, looking more stupid than he actually was. His good heart and friendly nature became invisible to the outside world for this short moment of wordlessness. Guillen got back to the third floor and placed his hand on Ted's shoulder, interrupting his dreaming about his bright future with Emma.

"Common, we can go in now!" he said, holding a bouquet of gorgeous red roses in his hand. Ted felt jealous and got the urge to just grab the flowers off his mate, so he could give them to his sweetheart. Well, even he was not that stupid to do such thing. Johnny quickly drank his small cup of coffee and followed the doctor, who was going to show them to Emma's room. On their way, the three men shivered at the unknown scene they were about to witness.

"You've got no more than 5 minutes. Speak quietly and do not touch anything, including her. If you have any questions, you are welcome to come and see me afterwards. I might be in the operational theatre but after I'll be at your disposal." They all realized that the doctor looked on his patients in a kind of cold and insensitive way – he witnessed death almost every single day. His words were very formal, which spoke for his total lack of interest in the person he might be asked about later. Johnny, Ted and Guillen took his impartial and dispassionate attitude the wrong way and they were ready to smack him one. The cold-blooded doctor left them to it and with a smile on his face headed towards the next patient that was in between life and death state.

"Hey!" Guillen whispered. "How are you feeling, Emma?" The three men were stand like statues by her bed, they could not move. A huge part of her head was in bandages and her right arm was in plaster. Otherwise, she looked good, much better than her dear visitors had expected. Her eyes were semi-open because the painkillers had not worn off, yet. She swallowed and uttered with much effort:

"I'm fine. And, you, are you all OK?"

"Yes, yes, we are alright, don't worry!" Ted quickly tried to assure her and leaned over just a few inches from her head.

"Look, what we got for you." Guillen said and showed the beautiful red roses from behind his back. Emma opened her mouth in a soundless "Ah!"

"Thank you, guys. I am so glad you are here. Was the mission a success?"

Johnny had not said a word, yet. He was feeling terrible, looking at his lovely and sweet friend, lying in the hospital bed. As soon as he entered the room, he was overwhelmed by the feeling of guilt, his enormous guilt. He had come up with the plan, he gave them the cars, he should have been at the front, instead of Ted, and could have done it right the first time. He was ashamed to even be in the same room with her. Emma's question, however, pulled him out of this state of self-pity:

"Yes, Emma, the mission's been achieved."

"The bastard is dead, we did it!"

"Keep your voice down Ted!" Guillen told him off. "Don't worry, Emma, everything is fine. You just concentrate on getting better as soon as possible because these two will be still hanging about in my place and there's no way I could watch boxing with them." Everyone got the joke and the white small room, full of life-supporting equipment, echoed with genuine laughter. Emma also laughed but the pain in her ribs turned her face into horrifying wince.

"Are you OK? I must call the doctor?"

"No, I am fine, Ted just don't make me laugh." Emma smiled again in a much more controlled way to prevent the sharp pain from re-occurring. The men felt a bit awkward because they thought of all sorts of jokes that the time was not right for. They stayed in the room for another minute as their time for visitation was up. A nurse came in and asked them to leave at once. Just before they fulfilled her impolite request, Guillen held encouragingly Emma's undamaged hand, Ted leaned to kiss her on the cheek, hardly touching her, where Johnny did not dare express such intimacy and just said:

"Bye, Emma, we'll come again tomorrow."

"To pick you up!" Ted added and the three guys left Emma, the main heroine in the yesterday's action.

From the start of their mission till that day, when they had their emotional meeting in the hospital, the three men had managed to learn an awful lot about themselves and life in general. One realized that he had found love. It had been right before his eyes all this time. Johnny learned that not everything that he had planned was going to happen exactly the way he wanted. He should always think about the safety of those involved, first. He did think that something might go wrong but did not imagine that Emma would end up fighting for her life. The accident made him realize how insignificant he was and that was impossible for one to have control over life. Johnny made a promise to himself that from this day onwards; no action or inaction of his was going to cause the death of another person. He was not going to kill anymore, no matter what kind of offer Mr. Poltic would come up with.

The person, who knew Emma best from all those night shifts they had spent in the small car, learned something very important –

family was what mattered most in one's life and family was the real meaning! Guillen could not wish even to his enemies to lead a worthless life.

The question was why one had to wait for something really bad to happen in their lives and then change and become better people?

Poltic had no answer to this question, either, but he was aware that extreme circumstances could make people change. For him, this was a simple encounter with an ordinary worker and his son. The positive outcome in this case was that otherwise, Poltic would have led to a huge crisis the country – in a spectacular, powerful and fascinating way, organized to the tiniest detail, without a single fire shot. His grandiose plan was a real work of art, which would remain unfinished. The finale of the picture would not be that important for the audience because it was simply not going to take place, after all.

Poltic had been living in the fortress-house for almost two years. Precisely 636 days had gone since he bought it. Every day for him was nothing but routine. He, basically, led a boring existence, had no friends and hardly ever did any sport. The quantity of information he had to process, as well as his constant thinking about what the next step should be, had given him a terrible migraine and had visibly aged his face. He needed some time off and not huge piles spy reports, documents and contracts. His work would usually get shared between dozens of people, some specialists in an averagely big company, not left in the hands of just one person. He had a chronic fatigue, which disappeared after the third or fourth cup of coffee, the only way to fool his body. His entire life was going around the big aim. He was probably the most obsessed and purposeful person in the country.

The enormous TV set was the final touch to the interior of the living room, so it looked completely perfect. Poltic settled down on the comfy sofa and turned on the black TV. He had no expectations about the news as he watched them every day. He just relaxed – it was one of the few occasions that he felt stress-free.

Road accidents happened all the time. Dozens of people would lose their lives but they were not all reported on the news, so it was not all dark and grim for the viewers. The demise of someone famous was regarded differently, especially in the newsroom, where death was saluted. It was good for the rating. Media staff resembled lawyers, although, the latter were much more insensitive. The leading news for that day was Harry. The short report right from the place of action, given by the reporter, made Poltic reach for the phone.

He was aware that their job was quite difficult and it was only natural for them make a mistake. A white woman was involved in a car crash, only meters away from the lawyer's black SUV. Emma was the weakling in RA. Poltic felt that she was too cherished to become a casualty if she died, but probably it was meant to be. Three men should not have left a woman to do their job. He saw how they were put into a police car and taken away. There was no information about anyone being arrested in connection with the accident. Therefore, Poltic had to just trust the female journalist, who reported that there had been several witnesses, who stopped immediately to help the injured. He was not sure how well RA would manage to hide their tracks. That was why he called his good old friend Daniel. The annoying detective, who interrogated Ted for three hours, was actually him. The policeman wanted to know exactly why Poltic was so interested in the witnesses of this horrific road accident. He could not find out anything of interest to him from Ted, so he decided to fulfill Poltic's request. No actions against Johnny, Ted and Guillen would be taken – there was not going to be an inquest, nor would they be prosecuted.

◆ ◆ ◆

Poltic had to think very carefully about his next step. The three subdivisions in the company had to be restructured. They needed to evolve and adapt to the new environment. Only Poltic could be in charge of their evolution. The meeting between him, Charlie and the Team had to be postponed for one very simple reason – Harry's funeral.

The harrowing event was going to distract Jane, Bob and Geri from their professional duties, at least for a day. On the other hand, Charlie was also going to lose a valuable employee, after dismissing Michael. Thus, the Team and the Young ones were getting down in number, which was going to affect the rest of their members. They would need some time before they got used to the idea that someone was missing from their working groups, until this event ceased to be the headline amongst them. Their new situation had created a sense of uncertainty. Poltic had two options for overcoming that problem – to find replacements for Harry and Michael or encourage the others to change their views about their way of working. He believed that this would be easier for the Team, as they were much more experienced. The lawyers, Harry used to work with, could also take his place. Well, whoever became responsible for the legal side of things from then on would have to do it separately and not be part of the Team. Poltic decided that a possible outside element, joining their group, would disturb the balance and the good functioning of their nucleus, composed of a stock broker, a sociologist and a consultant, would befall less effective. The situation with the Young ones was slightly more complicated. They all wanted Michael out of the company; yet, everyone knew that he was the motive force behind it. In order to cope with the new developments and overcome the absence of their most active member, the Young ones needed a change in their environment and acquire different methods of work.

RA required different type of restructuring. Emma was the only woman and this made her irreplaceable. Another female joining RA was out of question. Poltic could not even think in those terms, knowing about their closeness and friendship within the group. There was a problem, however, Emma would take several weeks to recover but she would be still psychologically vulnerable and traumatized, so it would be quite hard for her to do her job as expected. For a start, she was not going to fight ever again, no boxing till the rest of her life. Her right arm had been broken in such a way that it would not be very straight, once the plaster was taken off. If she attempted to do boxing again, there was the risk of breaking the same arm again, but this time irreversibly. Poltic expected her friends to empathize with her and support her but this, of course, would distract them from doing their job for him. Well, there was the option to let RA go, but he did not like the idea, especially now, so near to the end. He had to take some actions in person.

♦ ♦ ♦

"Hello, Emma!" the unexpected guest managed to get her out of deep sleep, under the influence of the painkillers. The drowsiness prevented her from showing any surprise when she saw Mr. Poltic. He began with yet another of his convincing monologues, starting with the facts:

"Emma, I'm not going to lie to you but your right arm has been damaged significantly. I want you to know that the best medical specialist will take care of you if necessary. However, it's doubted that you'll ever be able to box. I know how important this is for you and because of all this I've prepared a very special surprise for you. I hope it will compensate a little for your great loss. I'll come to pick you up on Friday and take you to a special place."

"Mr. Poltic," Emma said quietly. "what about the boxing?"

"I'm really sorry, dear, you won't be able to!" he expected floods of tears, on her part, but what she said next just shook him and proved that he really did not know her that well, as he had thought.

"Never mind, I can use my left one! Mr. Poltic, did we do the job? The guys told me that we managed to complete it."

"Yes, you managed your job quite alright. Now, I have to leave you to rest as the doctor gave me only a couple of minutes. See you soon, Emma!"

"See you, Mr. Poltic."

Poltic felt again that he got the wrong idea about her. Yes, boxing was important to her but people changed and their priorities in life changed, too. Her duties towards him, for which she received good income, came first.

Yet again, Poltic was wrong. Emma did not care so much about the money, nor did the job she had was that great. She was capable of forgetting about the boxing because she had friends now, friends that she had never had before. Sometimes a person needed very little, a nice word was worth much more to her than the huge and expensive gift she was going to get on Friday.

The day, when Bob, Jane and Geri learned about the tragic incident with Harry, the security guards did not allow them to enter Poltic's property. Their attempts to call him came to no avail, too. They were simply informed that the person they were looking for was absent from the fortress-house. They felt worried that their boss could not be reached in a time like this and decided to gather at Jane's place, so they could discuss the new situation. Poltic, of course, was going to learn everything they had discussed at their meeting from his next detailed spy report.

Poltic did not wish to listen to them. He knew what they were going to tell him. They were not little and they could cope on their own and live through it without his help. He wanted to concentrate on the next important meeting that required some careful preparations.

The ceremony for funeral started at 10 o'clock in the morning, without him. A few of his former colleagues, some friends, the Team and just three distant relatives had come to pay their last respects to Harry. Right at the end, Poltic appeared alone. He brought some flowers and laid them on the grave. All present, knew who he was. No one dared speaking to him. Bob was standing close to his wife. He did not look anywhere but at his boss. Jane and Geri, in their elegant black suits, were also staring at him, whereas he behaved as if he did not notice them.

Hidden behind sunglasses, Poltic's eyes met the members of the Team's looks, full of expectations. He approached each of them and asked if they could come to the fortress-house on the next day. He did not let a conversation to take place, because after each invitation, he moved on to the next person. Poltic felt quite uncomfortable at the funeral, taking into consideration that he was the murderer. The excuse that he was not directly involved in the crash and had only ordered it was discarded even by his own conscience. He was entirely responsible for it. He felt very strange, expressing his condolences to Harry's aunt. In his mind what he said sounded like: "I killed him and now I feel awkward to look you in the eye and say sorry!" He even remembered some good features of Harry's: his ingenuity, communicative skills, his persuasiveness and professionalism. Poltic could think of a lot more ways to describe him. And indeed, Harry was all that. For a second, he felt regretful for what he had done but he had no other options.

Poltic anticipated the forthcoming meeting with Bob, Jane, Geri and Charlie. To avoid their inevitable questions about Harry, he had to speak first and tell them everything they wanted to know. He felt a headache coming on, in response to the meticulous planning of his speech. Above all, he also had to provide Charlie with some answers. Poltic took only 5 minutes to instruct him over the phone and then as usual for that time of the day, he headed towards the kitchen. His strong caffeine drink, produced by his tireless coffee maker, only reminded him that he had still not talked to RA, since the completion of their task.

Guillen, Johnny and Ted had discussed in advance and rehearsed a few times what to say, so there were no discrepancies in their story. They all worried that they might get fired and lose their huge payment, or at least, it would be reduced because their "sister" had been let to get involved in an accident, in which she nearly lost her life. To their surprise, Poltic did not ask them about any details, nor did he take any interest in Emma's condition. They commented on this at their next visit to the hospital but when Emma told them about her unexpected visitor, Poltic's lack of concern made sense, then. So the members of RA were left alone to enjoy their lives, no questions asked and no changes made to their monthly income. They felt at ease and that was what Poltic wanted to achieve.

Three and Three

Bob, Jane and Geri were all dressed in black, showing their grief for Harry. They settled down, looking occasionally at the empty chair, where the lawyer was supposed to sit. Poltic went out of the room to meet Charlie – the last expected guest to come. The two of them joined the Team and Poltic opened the important meeting.

"Harry was a very valuable and, I would say, precious colleague to all of us. Without his professional support we wouldn't be here today. Our company is now only a step away from taking over the entire market for meat products in the country. And this is thanks to Harry!" Poltic made a dramatic pause, as rehearsed from the day before. "Two days ago, a terrible road accident took a dear friend and a colleague away from us. I know, it's just hard to believe that today Harry is not going to be present. Unfortunately, that's the truth."

Poltic did not intend his eulogy for Harry to turn into a killjoy but this was exactly what happened. Jane was about to burst into tears and Geri was probably going to follow her example. With so much sorrow around, three men and two crying women would make the meeting just pointless.

"We need to keep going!" Poltic stood up and raised his voice in a typical style of some medieval leader. "Harry would have wanted this, to see us how we carry on doing our job in the same way he did. He worked professionally, and was full of energy. He disliked anything that was mediocre and this made him even more effective in his quest to achieve the best. If I may describe him, I'd say he was a perfectionist. His interesting character did not fit with many people, even with me, at the beginning, I admit! After a few months working with Harry, I saw benefits from his excellent work, his desire for us to get to the top. He often wanted this even stronger than me. I can honestly tell you that I learned a lot of new things from our colleague." The audience had been won over, even Charlie, who did not know the main character. They all felt overwhelmed by Poltic's sincerity, especially, because they knew about Harry's resentment towards his boss. His words had managed to lift the spirits again. He sat down without any expectation to receive a well-deserved round of applause and changed the subject:

"Today it's a very big day for our company. This is Charlie, an Assistant Director, sent here by my patrons. He will work with his team on the new projects, about which I'm going to tell you today. Thank you for coming, Charlie. I hope next time you won't be that busy!"

"Mr. Poltic, doesn't this boy live in one of the houses on our street? I'm pretty sure!" Geri dared to speak just a second after the Assistant Director wished them "Have a good day" and left the room.

"Yes, he seems familiar to me, as well!"

"That's right, Jane, he is a neighbor of yours. Until now, he worked in a different field for the company. That's why I haven't introduced him to you so far. But in the coming months you'll be working partially together on the new projects."

"And they are?" Bob asked with the thought running through his mind that Harry would have asked this question if he was in the room in that moment.

"I can split them into three groups: new factories, transport and sub-suppliers. Before we start, however, who do you think should step in Harry's place and be in charge with the legal side of things? I think no one should. Harry was unique and I doubt there's anyone out there who could replace him in our working group."

"That's the best way, Mr. Poltic." Jane agreed with him. After her divorce, there was a sparkle between her and the deceased; hence she took things more personally than the others. Geri and Bob said nothing. Poltic noticed their face, showing that they were ready to get down to work. He did not waste any more time and began with another of his unusual ideas:

"Right, here's the situation at the moment. Our companies are in good shape. The same applies to our competition, in the face of 1, 2 and 6. We could say that the market has found its own equilibrium and no one is expecting some major shakes. We are not going to leave things as they are. Our objective is to become Number One, which means that we'll have to change the current status quo!" Jane raised her hand to add something.

"Yes, Jane?"

"I'm sorry to interrupt, Mr. Poltic, but things are not exactly how you've described them!"

"How do you mean, Jane?"

"Our companies have registered very small profit, hardly any, actually. And despite all the measures we've taken, in order to improve effectiveness that leads, respectively, to greater profitability, we haven't achieved any real progress. Our rivals, on the other hand, have. Slowly, but surely, they are going upwards. After our speculative actions, 1 and 2 are actually advancing without fail, not to mention number 6. Its revenue has doubled in this short period. "

"What are you saying, Jane?"

"I am saying that, if we compare the progress of our companies with that of the rest in the sector, we are definitely working at a loss, and if we don't do something about this soon, we'll go down to the level of when we got hold of them."

"So the situation is slightly worse than I've imagined it! In big business, there's success and there's failure! There are ups and downs in everyone's life. That kind of undulation is valid for our company, as well! As I said at the beginning, you're going to learn today how we'll shake the market a bit, all to our advantage, and how we're going to change the unfavorable tendency of getting marginal profits in comparison to our competition. We are going to build! Charlie and a few young specialists will be in charge of building three medium-sized meat factories. We'll rely on the latest technology in the field, which, as far as I am aware, has been introduced only by number 6." Poltic was getting excited and he was just going to talk about the interesting locations of the new factories, when Geri interjected:

"But...," she began hesitantly because no one had granted her the permission to speak. "we don't really need any more. This will lead to overproduction."

"Geri, that is correct, but I haven't finished!"

"Oh, I'm sorry, Mr. Poltic!"

"The three super modern units will be built right next to three technologically outworn factories that belong to 1 and 2. When they are finished, we'll let them work at the minimum of their capacity, so we don't end up with overproduction." Poltic stressed on the last word, in view of the comment Geri had just made. "Our aim is to make the Boards of Directors of the two companies see that we have the financial resources to progress and think that our business is more than profitable. That's not the case, but they won't know it. Money for the new projects has already been provided by my bosses. What do you think, Bob?"

"Mr. Poltic, the new modern factories will give us a better image and we'll probably get a slightly bigger share of the market, but I really doubt this is going to shake the position with the shares we are interested in. I can't really see how any of 'big fish' would want to sell."

"We shall see! What I want from you is a full cooperation and a free access for any of Charlie's employees to our companies. Don't worry about the building sites. They are not your business. Transport, however, is! You'll be in charge, from now on, of the new transport policy of the company." Poltic moved on to the next point of the agenda.

"I've done a quick investigation of our companies' transportation system. The conclusion is all the same: transport is a luxury. The numerous vehicles we use: trucks, cars and vans, are quite old, inefficient in fuel and constantly need repairs. I was surprised to learn that company number 3 has something like a scrap yard for trucks that are kept for some vital part that can be used for another truck when it breaks. That's out of question if we want to be the best in the sector. Apart of our old transport, we have significant problems with some of the routes. It's unknown to me why some drivers don't take the shortest one and save some distance, instead of driving 80 miles extra, sometimes. The engine becomes worn out and the fuel and oil consumption increases. We need new approach and new vehicles as soon as possible."

"Mr. Poltic, we are building three factories, aren't we? Where the money for new trucks is coming from? It will cost far too much to replace them all."

"Don't worry about the financial resources, Bob? It won't be that much, having in mind, the specificity of the new vehicles. We shall create our own means of transport that is unheard of until this moment in our country."

"It will be still quite expensive, Mr. Poltic. A truck is a truck and costs more than a car."

"Our trucks, Bob, will be different. Maybe, you've already heard that the big car companies are trying to find a solution to the problem with the oil and all fuels that derive from it. You know about the turbo-compressor that maintains the power but diminishes work capacity! What would you say about the hybrid type of cars, which have a petrol and electric engine, not to mention the different forms of bio-fuels!" Poltic only mentioned some of the methods, used for saving the energy. There were so many others that would have taken quite some time to be elaborated on. Besides, his audience was not car experts, nor did they specialize in the field of fuel systems! "We are going to scrap all of our trucks, irrelevant to what condition they are in, even if they're brand new."

"Why, Mr. Poltic?" Geri said indignantly, as if the trucks were her children, which she had personally raised from a small plastic toy to an enormous truck. "We dissipate more and more, instead of selling them on and with the money, invest in the new vehicles, and as such – cutting our losses."

"Moreover, the money we're going to lose or to be precise, the way we're going to do that, will make us look like some idiots."

"Jane, no one in this room is stupid. The building projects, the removal of all worn out vehicles and the integration of new technologies in our transport system, are the elements that will make us a leader in the market. I see you don't understand but I'm afraid, I can't comment any further. If there's anyone, who disagrees with our policy, although, even I find it somehow illogical and full of unnecessary expenditures, please feel free to resign."

Poltic resorted to the idea of them losing their far too lucrative jobs than they deserved, in the hope that they would stop constantly relying on their logical train of thought. The company followed its own strange logic that only Poltic was aware of. Everyone responded to his invitation for their resignation by looking down in grave silence.

"When we take over and have the monopoly on the market of meat products, you will understand the importance of all these unpopular measures. Now, I'm going to introduce to you, in brief, some of the technical specifications of the new trucks. They will have a special system, integrated in the roof of their trailer. It will be 20cm thick and about 3m long. The width will fit that of the trailer. This is a hydrogen system that will be connected to the engine, which is going to be in its standard place – in the front. This fuel system is at its final stage of development." The audience looked at him in disbelief. They were not experts in this field, but they were aware that no one had put hydrogen-fuelled cars into a mass production. They were just too expensive to make and quite dangerous, as well.

"Initially, the specialists have opposed to this idea, for being unsafe. The engine has been compared to a hydrogen bomb. Nevertheless, the safety indicators have been improved to acceptable level now. Well, there's another problem. If tens of thousands of hydrogen vehicles go on the market, which are environmentally friendly and to run them costs next to nothing, then, what's going to happen to all oil companies, or the standard fuels and all the petrol stations? Nobody believes the Association of the petrol manufacturers will allow mass integration of hydrogen fuel system, as long as there's still oil around. However, we are going ahead with our plan. Obviously, we can't hide the entire stock of 'black gold', so we'll have to change the situation in our favor. How are we going to do this? My patrons have already negotiated with one foreign company and have made a deal for 500 trucks. All of them, brand new, are going straight to another of our business partners, a leader in the scientific research field, related to hydrogen systems, where the trucks will be installed with the innovative fuel system. The trucks will have to stay put in the garages and wait, until we convince the authorities of their safety. All Green organizations in the country will need to learn about our noble objective. That is to replace every old vehicle that causes pollution and harms the environment with new and 100% clean motors. I imagine the possible argument is going to emphasize on the issue about safety and the danger of collision. That means we will have to apply an aggressive campaign and persuade the ordinary citizen that our trucks are safe and sound. Our argument lays in the fact that the fuel system will be inbuilt in a special cask, which is going to protect it against a possible explosion. Remember that, every step of this plan is scientifically substantiated. Safety is of up most priority to us. The petrol stations, or to be correct – the hydrogen stations, are going to be your task." Poltic looked at Jane, Geri and Bob.

"Mr. Poltic, you just explained to us that the oil companies will not allow hydrogen fueled vehicles on the road? How are they going to permit us build hydrogen stations?" asked Jane.

"We're going to pay for this pleasure, and we'll pay a lot! The advertising campaign and the proven safety of this technology will guarantee us the 'go-ahead', given to us by the authorities, however, the private sector, trading with conventional fuel, is a different story. We've made some calculations about the fuel consumption of all our vehicles for the next ten years. That figure will be the sum the companies, importing oil products, are going to receive from us. We can't deceive them in any way; thus, we'll have to pay up. These companies have power over the world; over governments and my patrons have decided to avoid any confrontation with them. We'll make them happy, also, by signing an agreement of confidentiality, which will guarantee that no one involved will ever disclose information about the new technology nor would we order more trucks than it has been agreed in the contract. This rule applies not just for us, but for the manufacturers of the hydrogen fuel systems and the actual vehicles which won't be able to sell their sophisticated products to anyone in the country."

"And how exactly all these things are going to make us the leader on the market? I just don't understand, Mr. Poltic – oil, hydrogen, trucks – this has nothing in common with the shares we need or the number 6, we want to buy."

"You just build the stations, Bob and the rest leave to me! You have the entire information that concerns the construction process in front of you. Examine it in detail. The locations have been worked out, according to the maximum distance that a vehicle could do before refilling with fuel, and that's 180 miles. This means that we need 38 stations, spread around in the country. The supplier of the eco-fuel is ready and waiting for you to do your job, first. You'll be also in charge with the PR-campaign and the publicity. I have no doubts that it will be much easier than the first time, when our advertising departments successfully disseminated the world report study about the insufficient meat consumption. Well, you weren't responsible for this, then, where now, it will be you. The second part of the documents contains some guidelines about the way you should conduct the campaign." Geri and Jane were already looking at them. "Please, concentrate on what's required from you and don't think about anything else. I'll take care of the rest. Do you understand?" A short 'yes', repeated three times, gave a 'green light' to moving on to point number 3.

"Before I continue with the subject of our new policy towards all our company's sub-suppliers, I want to remind you that you must behave towards Charlie as if it is me. If I learn that he's been mistreated in any way or there's been a bad cooperation between you, your employees and him, severe sanctions will follow. Now we got to the point, regarding the companies, which work for us or are connected to us in some way. All our companies get their meat material, 85-90% from their own live stock and the rest is bought from different farmers from all over the country. The ratio is pretty much the same in our rival companies. From now on, we cease depending on anyone. We will rely only on our potential and we shall terminate our contracts with all the current distributors of meat that we deal with. We will purchase all the slaughterhouses, which have been supplying us, at a double price. If they refuse to sell, we will immediately end our relationship with them. We may end up with a bit lower production capacity as there will be less material, although, I doubt it will get to this because we've been self-sufficient so far as a whole."

This point in the meeting agenda was totally in tune with the first two, supporting the policy of staggering expenditures. It seemed that the audience had resigned to this idea and no one made an attempt to comment. After all, the money was not coming from their pockets.

"We move on to the companies, which provide the technical support for our industrial units. We shall make to them the same generous offer, which they'll think twice before they refuse. Number 5 has hired an outside accountancy firm, which automatically makes it our objective to buy it. Again, they might decline our offer. If that's the case, you could take people from the administrative departments of the other two companies and deal with our books. Employ more people if you have to. Your job is very easy and it consists of just taking the contracts to the companies we want to purchase. I don't have all the written instructions, in terms of company names, prices and so on, yet, but I imagine, I'm going to receive them tomorrow. You will have them, too, a little bit later. Any questions?"

"You did not mention what we do if the technical support companies refuse our offer. We're not going to break up with them, are we?"

"Well, Geri we can't really do this. Who is going to take care of the expensive equipment that sometimes breaks down? If they decline, we'll just have to carry on working with them as before." By elaborating on their new responsibilities, Poltic had managed to erase the unpleasant incident with their colleague for a short while. He inadvertently, however, reminded them about Harry's demise.

"Mr. Poltic, who is going to draw up the contracts, we need to present to our partners? Harry is no longer here!"

"Who could do this better than him? Jane, I really doubt we can find a person like him. Still, let's not forget that there are plenty of good and capable lawyers out there. All legal matters could be passed onto some of Harry's former colleagues. I've already spoken unofficially to a couple of them and they have said 'yes'. As you know, the Law firm they work for and in which Harry began his career, is the most respectable legal company in this part of the country! If you find them unsuitable or the results of their work are unsatisfying, then you can find someone else."

"Mr. Poltic what is the time frame for our new projects?" asked Geri, who did not think much of or cared about Harry, while still alive. Nevertheless, she could not deny, like most people who knew him, his outstanding professionalism and his incredible efficiency at work. She could not say that black was white!

"Oh, yes, Mr. Poltic, how much time have we got? I believe, we'll need at least a year from now on!"

"That's the deadline for building the three new factories, Bob. You will be given no more than three months."

"How many... just three months?"

"It's not that soon and it is absolutely enough, Geri!"

"Please, explain, Mr. Poltic, because I believe that this is totally insufficient!"

"Look, you won't be wasting your time with the construction process. That's Charlie's job. The transport issue is almost resolved, in terms of fitting the trucks with the hydrogen fuel systems. So what's left to do, is building the stations, which you will be in charge of! The deadline in the project plan for this is exactly 45 days. The advertising campaign should take you about two months. I'm giving you 90 days, as I take into considerations the difficulties you may encounter, in terms of finding the right firms, which can build the hydrogen stations. There is an ill-grounded fear amongst some people in the sector, who would not undertake a project like this at any price. If there was not an issue with this, I would have given you even less time to complete your assignment." Poltic's argument was presented very well and the Team finally agreed to the three-month period for completion of their job.

"Thank you all for coming today, despite the tragic loss for our team. It's hard for all of us to overcome this tragedy but we need to try to move on. Have a good day today and good luck with your work!"

The guests felt free from the grip of their boss and gladly left the fortress-house, as if they were escaping from a prison. Bob remained put because he was kindly asked to do so. Poltic moved straight to the point. He was also becoming tired of talking about work:

"When would it be viable for you to get hold of more shares from companies 1 and 2, Bob?"

"Oh, it won't be very soon. About 2% are available to buy as soon as, but you asked us to leave them for now."

"Yes, that's right! We don't want to raise their suspicion and they realize that the increased interest comes from the same place."

"Wise move, Mr. Poltic, but the rest don't budge from their position. The price of the shares is going up and I imagine it will continue to do so until at least the end of this year."

"What is your opinion on the subject of the new factories, the hydrogen trucks or the idea we take over all our sub-suppliers and the companies, providing technical support for us?"

"Honestly, Mr. Poltic?"

"Yes, get to the point, Bob?"

"Like I said, building these factories is a pointless venture before it has even started! We could only improve the image of our company, with all the innovation technologies that we intend to introduce. This might slow down the progress of 1 and 2 but it won't stop it. I couldn't really comment on the transport issue, as I'm not an expert. Anyway, I believe that it won't affect the market. We are in competition, in terms of our produce, not the vehicles, which take the products to the stores." Bob watched carefully Poltic's stone face and was prepared to stop talking the second he saw a slight change in his look. Not even a tiny facial muscle moved, so the agent continued. "Mr. Poltic, there's no problem with the suppliers! We offer them enough and they are ours. But this has nothing to do with 1 and 2 and their shares. I'm sorry, Mr. Poltic, the shareholders that own what we need to go over the 50% just won't sell. There's no way and we don't stand a chance."

"There's always a way, always. Thank you, Bob, you are free to go now."

Poltic went to his study and devoted himself to his never-ending intellectual work. He had another meeting on the next day, with Charlie's team – the Young ones, and also realized that he had plenty of time to master his offensive towards the stubborn shareholders of 1 and 2. Soon, his numerous soldiers were going to join him in the battle to achieve his final aim, dangerous and short-tempered soldiers, who were ready to burst out any moment.

After leaving the big house, Charlie headed towards the office as he did every other working day. That day differed slightly from the rest because of one forthcoming event – Michael's dismissal. There was nothing unusual at the workplace, which was to give out any signs of what was about to happen. Charlie dropped the news, following M. J.'s instructions. He reasoned his actions with the words: "The Company no longer requires your services! Clear your desk and leave the car keys." Michael jumped from his chair and came just few centimeters away from the face of his 'incompetent' boss. His hands clenched into fists, ready to hit, but he changed his mind in the last second. Both young men were well built, so there was not going to be a clear winner, if they went for each other. Michael started to swear and pushed his boss, by applying moderate force. He left the building, throwing threats around and calling Charlie bad names.

Charlie's hatred for Lorrie's mental torturer had doubled and he was dying to crush him. However, he followed Poltic's instructions and just stood there quietly, without answering back to the nasty words, hiding his turbulent emotions. Tony, Kate and Lorrie were shocked by the ugly scene. They found themselves again alone in the office as soon as Charlie had told them about the next day's meeting with his patron. Deeply offended, he quickly left the building.

Half an hour before each of them appeared at the arranged meeting place, Charlie was already there, explaining to Poltic about what had happened on the previous day. M. J. listened to his story without interrupting him. Charlie was getting so fiery that when he finished, he looked ready to give a good hiding to anyone, who dared to cross his path.

"Calm down! Charlie, everything's fine because you behaved the way I've asked you to. I know it's hard for you to suppress your ego. Charlie, you are strong young man but you need to use your head before you resort to your physical strength."

"I would've wiped the floor with him…"

"What about the consequences? Let me draw you a picture! Say, you happen to read in the paper how a young manager fires his employee, first, and then, he beats him up – the poor, helpless and now jobless worker has been thrown out on the street!"

"But it wasn't like this, he just…" Charlie did not finish his sentence because the look on Poltic's face clearly said that it was not yet time for the youngster to speak.

"This thug is rich and owns several meat factories. He has a lot of money, which means that the victim can take advantage of this and make his nest with a good sum out of his pocket and have no worries for the rest of his life. Through the Courts, that's it, of course! The media will blow up the case and this stupid young boss will be all over the papers, on television and on the net. The sudden popularity, the court case and the reputation that he is a thug, Charlie, won't help us in any way. And what's the situation now? There was no beating and the Michael's dismissal was conducted in accordance with the clause in his working contract, which gives us the right to sack him without warning. Charlie, which scenario is better for us, for our objectives and for the company? Tell me, Charlie, which one is it?"

"The second scenario, M. J., is the better option for us, but…"

In that moment the security guards announced over the intercom that three identical cars had parked outside and their drivers insisted to come in with the explanation that they were expected. Poltic sent Charlie to meet them. He also left his study and went to change his clothes. The Big Boss could not show up in front of his staff, which was two levels below him in the hierarchy, in anything else but a suit. Well, his smart casual clothes, in which he was dressed at the time, were good enough, of course, but he had to play the game by the rules.

Charlie led the visibly hesitant young people into the room with the three steps. They, on the other hand, could not stop asking him questions, before the important man appeared on the scene.

"When is the he coming, Charlie?" Kate asked.

"Yes, yes, and aren't you going to tell us his name, at least?" Tony was curious, too.

"I can't tell you anything now. If you wait a little, you are going to find out!"

"What an amazing house! Is it all his, Charlie, common, tell us, please!"

"Yes, Lorrie, it's very nice, isn't it? I also lived here for a little while."

"Hey, Boss, yesterday, when you left us, Michael, then, came back to get his things. He didn't leave the car keys, though. I just thought you should know this."

"Thanks for telling me but don't worry, Kate! He'll give it back – the flaming bastard!" No one heard the last words as they were only produced in Charlie's mind. "Did he say anything about me?"

"And you're asking? Don't even wanna tell you about all the garbage he said! He was cursing and 'spitting out' all the swear words I know and more that I haven't even heard of, and at the end, he swore he'd find you one day and kill you, when alone." Tony did not think much of these threats, knowing that Michael was saying all this in anger. However, Charlie felt scared quite a bit.

"Who's going to replace him now? Would it be a guy, again?" Lorrie asked but he did not hear her question. Charlie was still deep in thought, worrying about the death threat. He tried to calm himself down and at the same time, the smartly dressed host entered the room.

"Good afternoon! How are you all? Charlie, would you sit over there, please, next to…."

"Lorrie, my name is Lorrie."

"Right, you must be Kate and Tony, then?"

"Yes, that's correct." they both replied in short.

"Good! We'll be talking about your case a little bit later, too. Now I know your names, it will be good if you learn mine. My name is M. J. Poltic and I represent a big foreign company." Poltic was looking around only at the Young ones, but not at Charlie. He wanted to study them well and examine the way they behaved, their gestures and posture, and last but not least, to find out about what their young eyes, which were staring at him, were saying at this moment. Over the years, Poltic had learned to consider a person's attitude as more significant and he attached less importance to what people said. Although, non-verbal communication could speak volumes, he knew that sometimes people's demeanor was deceiving and did not reflect their way of thinking.

"Under Charlie's guidance, you have all nearly completed your assignment. My patrons and I are satisfied with the results and we have decided to appoint a new task to you. The company has many business interests but its priority is to develop further its meat products manufacturing branch. In order our company becomes a leader in the field, we need to increase our production capacities, using the newest technology. Charlie's told me that you'll be finished with the supermarket soon and you'll be left without a job." Poltic made an attempt to joke but no one got it. He continued: "Three new factories will cover completely our needs, and the four of you will be the ones that are going to build them. To build one factory is an equivalent of the project you have just completed. However, you have to finish building three factories in one year. You have now the experience that will help you in this difficult venture. The locations have been selected and the land-sites have already become property of the company. What's left is for you to begin work. You have all the details and documentation, in terms of building plans, construction and machinery equipment, ready for you, at your new workplace. You will have unlimited access to the other factories we own, so you can get an idea how a fully operational industrial unit should look like. They are equipped with much older machinery, though, which reminds me to tell you that we'll have the manufacturer of the super modern technology at our hands within a month. What follows is that when you complete building the three industrial plants, the only company, which could install the equipment, will step in and do the job as a priority. This will take a certain length of time as all the machines and electronic devices are unique and complex to set up. In other words, if we were to do everything in the standard way and through the regular channels, the job will takes us at least a year, from our initial order to fitting the machinery. If we do it my way, applying my methods, it will take us 3-4 months." Poltic felt he was ranting on about things that had nothing to do with the meeting and decided to stop with the so much lengthy explanations.

"That's your job and Charlie will be in charge as before. You will be able to talk more on the subject with your boss, once you've got acquainted with the specifics of the project. You are completely free to hire as many people as you need to. I totally trust your competence to sign the construction process over to whatever building contractors you choose to. Charlie has assured me of your intelligent judgment. Moreover, let's not forget that you've got the experience now, from dealing with all sorts of building companies, while working on the supermarket project. The financial side of things is 100% secured. The budget's been approved, although, no figures will be disclosed to you, so you don't get distracted and influenced by it. Relax and just concentrate on your work, and don't worry about the money. I know it's absolutely sufficient. Any questions, before I move on to your new living arrangements?" Poltic thought it was a good idea if he changed the format of the meeting, where he spoke and his guests listened in some kind of trance.

"I'd like to ask you something, Sir!" Lorrie first responded to his invitation. "You want from us to manage the construction of three meat factories, if I understand correctly?"

"That's right, they will manufacture different meat products."

"But how could we possibly do this? It is totally out of our league! We had so many problems with the supermarket... All these companies, they wasted our time about simple things. I think, I'm talking on behalf of my colleagues and I firmly believe that we can't do this."

"Mr. Poltic, none of us knows how to build such a specialized industrial plant. We just can't." Tony shrugged his shoulder helplessly and gave a good example. "It's like asking us to go and explore Space without a spaceship."

"Hey, what's the matter with you?" Charlie scolded them, looking at the never-going-to-be astronaut. "Don't you hear what the sketch is? The building plans are ready, the location, everything's arranged, in terms of equipment, the money is not an issue, and you are scared, having doubts! That's not the way to react!"

"But, Charlie, even if we knew how to do this, we couldn't possibly finish in one year..."

"Tony is right, the time frame is very short!" Kate joined in and tried to prove her argument. "Do you remember, Charlie, when we all started with the supermarket and we couldn't sign an agreement with an interior design firm for two weeks? And then, the delivery of the lighting features got delayed... The flaming lamps cost us nearly 20 days! No, it's impossible to do it in one year!"

"We did it at the end! What's the matter with you all?"

"Be quiet, please!" Poltic felt slightly out of place, when he was supposed to lead the show. "The uncertainty of the new project clearly makes you hesitant and doubtful. And you are right to be so!"

"M. J., they can do it, we'll manage!"

"Charlie, you will manage or you won't, there's no other way in between." Poltic pointed out philosophically. "Ladies and Gentlemen the complexity of your new task requires a lot of effort. I clearly understand that. Each of us has their limits, mentally and physically. If there's more work that needs doing, then, it means that we will hire more people. In that way, your workload will be totally manageable, and you will find that it's within your professional capabilities. You will be the managing body, where Charlie and I – the controlling element. The entire work and responsibilities that you had to deal with so far, now is going to be passed over to the personnel you are going to employ. By delegating, you will manage to complete what's been required from you. I hope you understand what I'm talking about! You are going a step up the ladder! You will become the managers." Poltic resorted to such detailed explanations, when he noticed the bewildered look on their faces. They appeared as if trying to estimate how much water there is in the World Ocean without the use of a calculator. None of them gave him a sign, whether they had grasped his point, so he carried on:

"You need to show your management skills, as much as you can, because your staff will have to be responsible for the project details, not you, like it's been so far. Find the best specialists and leave them do the job, under your close monitoring, of course."

"It won't be easy, Mr. Poltic, it's just the three of us. We'll need a lot of people and it will take quite a while to find the right ones. Time seems again to be a problem!" said Lorrie.

"Charlie's going to help you. He will be working equally hard, along with you, so the absence of whatever his name was, will not reflect your work in any way. I'll need you to think carefully before you give me your answer. To make it easier for you to decide, I'll explain the new working methods or to be precise, I'll tell you about your new workplace, which Charlie is going to show you tomorrow."

"Do we get a new office? Great! The old one was on the small side a bit."

"It's not exactly an office, Lorrie, you'll be given new apartments, where you can live."

"Apartments? Where are going to work, then?"

"New methods of work will be applied from now on and you will do almost everything from home. There will be no need to go to an office or some other special working place! Here are the details. All the job interviews will take place in an apartment, designated for that purpose, which will be situated in the same building you'll be living from now on. Your working day should go like this: You'll be free to get up whenever you wish, but if we keep in mind the numerous things you will have to do, I doubt that this will be later than 8. Then you go down a floor below and together, you work out the priorities for the day."

"This is what we did, anyway, Mr. Poltic!" Lorrie just noted.

"After you hire more people, you just leave them to do their job. From time to time, you will monitor their work. You only take the initiative, when something important needs to be resolved and you don't feel you could delegate it to any of your employees."

"So we'll be something like Charlie."

"Exactly, Kate! I need you to understand the structure of our hierarchy correctly, so you don't find yourselves up to the eyebrows with paperwork and thus, feel disheartened about achieving your goals. The donkey work should be done by your people. Again, if we imagine a ladder, you're going a step up, where your personal assistant picks up the phone, not you, and where you decide which company to negotiate with but it's not you, who do the talking. Do you get me?"

"Yes, Mr. Poltic, totally," Tony said. "and it's very different from the way I've imagined it."

"It is all clear to me, too, Mr. Poltic, but why do we have to live and work in the same building? Can't we just go there to work and not change the place we live at the moment?"

"That's a requirement, Kate that I cannot change, so relocation is your only option. The other alternative, of course, is to leave our company." Poltic did not really want to threaten them with getting the sack. However, the Young ones took his words literally.

"Oh, no, no, Mr. Poltic, we just wondered, that's all. If the job requires this, then, we don't have a problem with it. We'll move. Is that right, girls?"

"That's right, we don't have a problem." Lorrie was heard to say. Kate also confirmed her consent.

"I'm very pleased to hear it. The apartments are quite spacious and luxuriously furnished. A company with our resources would never offer unsuitable accommodation to you. I'm positive that you will like them."

Charlie was looking at the shiny varnish on the top of the table with his arms crossed in front of his chest. He was thinking about the words of his former colleague. His fear of the death threat, he never actually heard, was growing by the minute, so it was his desire to share this with M. J.

"The actual beginning of your new project won't happen for at least a month, until you find and hire your personnel. I don't want you to rush into this and offer the job to first candidate, turning up. Select people with the right qualities and multi-task skills. Charlie will have the last word, so you'll be persuading him about the choices you make."

"How many people do we need to employ and where are they going to work? If they are taking over the main work from us, then, they'll need an office like the one we have, well, we've had up to now!"

"Everything is going to take place in the same building you are going to live, Lorrie. But don't worry, no one will have access to the floor, where your two apartments are located."

"But it's three of us, Mr. Poltic!" she noted and wondered how he could get it wrong. Charlie's boss was not a simple man.

"Well, I imagine that you guys," he nodded at Kate and Tony. "would want to live together as you have been so far! Or am I wrong?"

"You know? But how? He doesn't know about it!" and Tony quickly glanced at Charlie.

"What do I have to know?"

"Tony and Kate will be living together in the same apartment. The other one is for Lorrie." Charlie felt awkward, as he had been seeing them every day, but had no idea that they had been living together. When they had told him that they were an item, they had obviously missed to share this detail with him. And what was the most curious about all this was that Poltic had never seen these people before.

"How did you know?"

"Right now this is not that important, Charlie! Let's move on. Your valuable workers will be coming to work every day to the offices, located on the entire floor, two levels below your living quarters. They have already been furnished with the most modern office equipment that's available. So there are ten small offices but if you think that you need more people than that, we shall make some interior changes on the lower floor. We own that building, so we could make any alterations we want, as long as that helps your work and improves your efficiency."

"I think we'll be fine with eight to ten people, the most, Mr. Poltic!" Lorrie thought out loud.

"It depends, actually, at least three people will have to be responsible for the technical side of things. We're talking about a factory here, with all this machinery and so on. It's not just some shop." Tony joined in.

"Tony, Kate, Lorrie, I'd like to draw your attention to an issue that you haven't had to think about before. Your new position in the company hierarchy determines some specific requirements, regarding your attitude from now on. I'll be plain and short. Your social status will improve by receiving a double salary and replacing your current vehicles with limousines of the highest class. The problem is that when one has that much of material goods and benefits at your age, this may result in you forgetting where you've started from, as well as there's a danger for this to reflect on the way you treat people around you. Your future employees will receive a good, even high income, I would say, however, it will be much less than yours. So you will have the upper hand of them but under no circumstances should you treat them differently. Demonstrating your superiority over them, in any way, will not be tolerated whatsoever! Charlie will be watching for any display of haughtiness, arrogance and indirect or obvious derision, on your part, towards the people below you. That's very important to me! If I only hear that about you behaving even in the slightest like this, you're going to lose a lot more than just your job. You will lose everything!" His authority over them was very big in that moment and the Young ones felt as if the Prime Minister or the President was addressing them in person. "I believe that this is the general framework of everything, which is concerning your job. If you don't have any questions, I will have to ask you for your final decision!"

"May I summarize what you've said, Mr. Poltic, and you could tell me if we've understood everything right?" Poltic nodded in agreement and gave the floor to Lorrie. "All of us – my colleagues, Charlie and I – will live in the same place where we'll be working together with our, e-r-r, our…"

"…our personnel." Kate came to her aid.

"Yes, our personnel… And we'll tell them what to do and make sure they do it. And in a year, we'll have three new factories."

"Charlie won't be living there. He has his own place to live. He will come to work with you every day as before. The rest, as brief as it was, is correct!"

"What if we miss the deadline, despite all our efforts and those of our workforce?"

"There will be penalties and fines, Lorrie." Poltic replied but quickly tried to put their minds to rest. "Don't think about the time frame now. When you get into the work process at your maximum speed and things start to fall into place, I may decide to postpone the deadline, but only if there are very good reasons for the delays and your failure to complete the target within the year is well justified. And now, I'm waiting for your answer. Is it a 'yes' or a 'no'?"

"Mr. Poltic, would it be alright if you leave us for a minute before we give you our answer?" Good old Poltic would have never allowed that type of free discussion any other time, let along – someone like Lorrie telling him to leave a room in his own house. He would have just made a statement after statement, not letting anyone else to speak, and then, he would have simply asked for their decision. This time, however, was different and Poltic gave to them 10 minutes – a good time for him to have a cup of coffee.

"You as well, Charlie!" Lorrie, who was totally love-struck, looked at her boss. He on the other hand, believed that his presence was welcome and felt slightly offended from the fact that it was her, who asked him to leave the room.

Charlie, the outcast, found M. J. in the kitchen, so he decided to mention about Michael's threat.

"Hey, M. J., do you think my people are going to accept? What I mean is, when they accept, do you reckon they'll manage the job?" he started in a roundabout way. At the same time, a trickle of the refreshing hot drink came out of the coffee maker.

"I hope so. They have the skills but seem a bit diffident. I'm going outside to get some fresh air." Poltic looked at his wristwatch. "I'll be back in eight minutes if you could wait for me. I want us to go back in there together. And another thing, I need to talk to you after the meeting."

"OK., M. J.!" Charlie was looking forward to this chat, although, he did not know what they were going to talk about. Whatever it was, he doubted that it could erase the image in his mind, picturing raging Michael, who was determined to kill him.

Lorrie, Tony and Kate did not take long to make their choice. Lorrie's fear that the time frame for completion was not enough had almost disappeared. Poltic had explained to them the whole scheme of things, with regards to their work, and the fact that they did not have to worry about the budget, swayed her decision towards a 'yes'. Her colleagues had slightly different motives for giving a positive answer. Although, they had some reservations about the one-year period, Kate and Tony could only think about their future together. And to have one, they needed a good income. They gave their consent very quickly with the clear thought about the piles of money that would go into their joint kitty.

"Hello, again, guys!" Poltic greeted. Charlie also entered the room and went to sit in his place.

"Mr. Poltic," the spokeswoman of the group began. "we accept the new assignment and despite that we've had some second thoughts about the deadline, we will do our best to keep it."

"Wonderful! You made a wise decision."

"They sound more like my people now, M. J."

"There is something else Mr. Poltic. I have a personal request!"

"I'm all ears, Lorrie, fire away!"

"I'd like it if Charlie lives with me in my apartment."

"Lorrie?" the man next to her jumped from his chair. "Are you crazy? I thought we've agreed…!"

"Shut up, Charlie! Don't pretend you are surprised by her request. You've been together, how long now? …for two, three months?"

"But how do you know, M. J…?"

"Not now, Charlie! If he wants the same, Lorrie, I don't have a problem with it! You should keep your personal life away from the workplace, like Tony and Kate. I know a lot more about you all than you think. If your professional life is affected by any squabbles at home, I'll have to take some immediate measures, which you are not going to appreciate."

"Thank you, Mr. Poltic. I hope Charlie and I won't have any problems. Although, we got together only recently, our relationship has been very good so far and we'll make everything that is possible it continues to be so." Charlie did not say anything. His girlfriend had made herself clear and his comment was unnecessary.

"Anything else anyone wants to add. Lorrie, any questions?"

"No, Mr. Poltic, there isn't. We're ready to get on with the project."

"If that's the case, I can only wish you good luck! I hope whenever Charlie comes to give me a report on how you're doing, I only get some good news."

The host stood up and shook hands with each of them, after which the visitors left the house. In the room with the three steps, there were just Charlie and Poltic now. Lorrie's boyfriend was not in the mood for any small talk and asked straight to the point:

"Be honest, M. J., are you watching me and my people? Have you ever followed us?"

"I beg your pardon? I've never had! Charlie, where did you get this idea from?"

"How do you know about me and Lorrie, then?"

"I'll tell you, though, you're really wasting my time! You're clearly head over heels in love with her that you can't think straight! The security guy at the business centre, who you show your pass to every day on your entry, gives me a report in person. He writes down the exact time everyone comes to work and respectively, when they leave. This is how I know how many hours each of you does and whether you've been to the office at all! The most recent information I've been getting, you idiot," Poltic gave him a friendly smile. "is that you arrive at work together with Lorrie and leave for home, again, with her. Also sometimes her car has been sitting parked outside your house, a few hundred meters away from here. I can see with my eyes, as anyone else can should they decide to look in that direction!"

"Hey, I'm sorry, M. J. I'm such an idiot!" Charlie mumbled and looked down.

"Relax, Charlie, and stop worrying! Everyone, who's in love, gets a bit stupid sometimes. By the way, Lorrie is a wonderful woman."

"Do you really think that? She is very smart, even more than me, I think!"

"Without a doubt, Charlie, she is. Now, though, I need to tell you something very important."

"So you like her, then?" Charlie asked but Poltic had already changed the subject.

"Our progress is being hindered. The company cannot take over the competition, in the face of 1, 2 and number 6. The measures I envisage to undertake, including the new factories, will change the current situation to our advantage but I really doubt that they will help us acquire the companies we've marked."

"How do you mean, M. J.? Are you saying that building the factories serves no purpose to anyone? Is that the case with the shop, too?"

"No, Charlie, that's not what I mean! We do need them and they have a special place in my plan. What I want you to do is if you could meet someone very important. If you convince him to sell us his share, then, only two percent will keep us away from the controlling stake of number 1. This will be a real break-through for us. It will turn things around and it will make my job much easier! I'll be in a position to approach one of the other shareholders and get hold of this percentage we need. At least one of them will say 'yes', once I make my lucrative offer. Before I can do this, I need the shares of the person I want you to negotiate with. I trust you Charlie because I believe that you're the only person, who will do the job right! Let's not forget that our chances are not that great. The person, you are going to meet, has no particular reason to sell and he's definitely not stuck for money."

"I'll work on him, M. J., so he'll want to sell us his own mother!" the future negotiator rubbed his hands excited at the prospect.

"I doubt it, Charlie, but who knows, you may succeed if we make sure you're prepared well enough! I want you here every day from tomorrow, when I'm going to give you all the instructions you need. Also, you'll be able to tell me all about Lorrie, Tony and Kate, in relation to how they find their new situation."

"About what time should I take them to have a look at their flats and the offices?"

"That's up to you. Well, that's it for now, Charlie. You can go now as I've still got work to do."

"M. J., can I ask you something? Hmm, I need your advice!"

"Go on, but be quick, Charlie."

"Michael, the guy I sacked yesterday, has threatened to kill me. I'm not scared but think you should know…"

"Is that it? Don't worry about him I'll take care of this." Poltic stood up and left without saying 'good bye'. Charlie did not take any notice of his strange and rather rude behavior. "Maybe, I should buy a gun!" was the last thought he had before he left the fortress-house and went back to his own, where Lorrie was already waiting for him. Naked.

The Hall

Friday was a day of keeping some promises.

Poltic did not particularly like hospitals. He found the visits disturbing for the patients there, as much as it was for their relatives and friends. One could quickly get used to the smell, but dealing with the uncertainty, was different story. The time in there stood still, and it was always hard to fight back all those dark thoughts, whether one was going to live or if they would ever walk again.

Poltic had made a special arrangement with her doctor for the patient to be discharged at twelve o'clock lunchtime. The surgeon had insisted she stayed until Monday but Poltic convinced him with assurance that Emma would be taken care of, in the following few days, by trained medical staff. The doctor's concerns were related to her head injury and a possible brain damage if she falls accidentally.

Emma's boss knocked a couple of times and entered the room. Like Guillen, he was a real gentleman, who brought to her a beautiful bouquet of flowers.

"Hello!"

"Hi, Mr. Poltic, I did not expect you that early!" Emma replied, looking a bit sleepy. She had lost sense about the days and nights because she slept most of the time.

"It's noon, now, Emma. It's such lovely day outside and it's time for you to leave this hospital. Or you want to stay a bit longer?"

"Oh, not at all, but I think, the guys are coming to see me around 5…"

"Don't worry. I'll let them know about the change of plan."

"Thank you, Mr. Poltic! Thank you for the flowers, too. They are beautiful!"

"I'm glad you like them, Emma. I can see you are not dressed, yet, so I'll go and wait for you. When you're ready, just come down to the entry. You only need to sign some paperwork at the Registration Desk."

"Mr. Poltic," her official form of address was slightly out of place in this situation.

"Leave out the "Mr. Poltic" part. Just "Poltic" is fine, Emma! It will be much better for both of us."

"Poltic, I haven't got any clothes. The boys are bringing me some but I don't have anything to change into now! The clothes I had during the crash have been thrown away and this nightdress is definitely inappropriate to wear outside!"

"Well, you won't have to go on the street in your nightdress. I've parked the car right outside, so it won't be a problem to just get in like this. But if you really insist, I'll try to sort something out."

"Don't worry Mr." She paused and then corrected herself. "Don't worry, Poltic. There's no need. I'm going home, after all, and can change my clothes there!"

"Emma, I'm not taking you home straight away. First, I'd like to show you my present for you. Right then, I'll wait for you outside, so you can gather you things."

A minute later, Emma got out with a small handbag on her, the only item that had survived after the accident.

On their way, Poltic phoned one of the famous lady's boutiques in town which name he had heard several times from Jane. Being a very well-mannered affluent client, he wanted to make sure he was met by the manager at the entrance of the boutique. He deliberately mentioned the name of the VIP customer, Jane, who always got special treatment there.

The very special clients needed less than an hour to finish with the shopping. Poltic quite liked Emma's male style of buying things who was now dressed in a nice green top and some denims. She did not make use of the smart leather jacket, as that day was unusually warm. Poltic paid the bill and thanked the kind manager in person. He rewarded the two helpful shop assistants with a tip that was equal to their wages for two months.

"Emma, would you like to go to another shop?"

"That's more than enough, Poltic. I don't actually have money right now but when I go back home I can pay you back."

"No, Emma, you don't owe me anything." she did not know what to say to this, so she remained quiet, not willing to argue with him. Emma was finding Poltic's personality very interesting. He only spoke when he had to and the strangest thing for her was that he always found the right words. He never hesitated, looking at the ceiling, for instance, before he had to express himself. The young woman sensed that Poltic would not say a word about where they were going until they actually got there. They slowly got into a traffic jam, which did not look that it will clear soon. Emma felt that it was the right moment to ask a question.

"Poltic, where are we going exactly? Are we near?"

"Yes, we're not far but at this speed, it will probably take us another half an hour."

"But where?"

"You'll see very soon." Poltic said in short and became silent again.

At last they arrived. Poltic turned off the engine and got out of the car, so he could open the door for the lady. He thought for a second about giving her a kind of present, which was like offering a bicycle to a disabled person. The doctors had explained in great detail, using a lot of terminology, about her inability to box from then on. There was no sign of psychological trauma, at least, at first sight. If there was any, it was the right time Poltic learned about it.

The new sport centre in town was designed to accommodate for 12 types of sport. Its modern equipment attracted anyone, who had the urge to stretch and do some activity in their free time. There were lots of children, too, doing their daily training, in the hope to fulfill their dream and become great sport stars one day. Emma was walking along the long corridor and her strange boss gently held her undamaged arm. They stopped, where Poltic wanted to prepare her about what was behind the closed doors. Naturally, he could have revealed the secret straight away but he feared he would then, has to run after her and console her.

"What's this exactly?"

"It's a sport centre, Emma. I know you're done with the boxing and I imagine, it's very hard for you to accept the facts. As it is my entire fault, I really want to compensate you for your loss somehow."

"There's no need, Poltic! I was never going to make anything out of it, anyway. My arms are not long enough, I'm quite slow with the legs and no matter how much I put into training, I never got any better! I was just not born with the talent. Boxing taught me a lot and made me a disciplined person. It gave me everything that I've ever wanted. Now what's left for me is to enjoy watching others, live or on television, people who can really box. It was a great pastime for me, and I believe, I'll find something else to do, although, I doubt it will be that interesting."

Poltic listened to her carefully and he could not understand her logic. Her total obsession with the sport and even the way she pronounced the word "boxing", proved to him how much she loved it. It was hard to believe how she had accepted parting with the love of her life so lightly. Moreover, there was no display of tears, a weakness or a sign of depression. Well, obviously Emma had made the right choice – to move on. The entire image he had created in his mind about her from the rare occasions they met just went into pieces.

"I'm glad that you take things into your stride." Poltic opened the door of the Hall. "It's all yours. You are the owner and the manager of Boxing Club 'Emma'. I've hired a few people that know about the sport, but if you don't approve of them, you can employee anyone you want."

Emma had a long look at the empty big hall, the two rings that had never had a drop of sweat spilled on them, the punch bags, hanging from the ceiling.

"Do you like it?"

"Yes, Poltic, I do. It's awesome! I don't know what to say. I've never even dreamed of having my own boxing club. Thank you, Mr. Poltic, now I can be close to my sport again, though, outside the ring." Emma had mixed feelings. She had given up the idea that she could ever fight again but at the same time, she really felt like going in for a quick sparring. Poltic could be the one in the opposite corner and they could have just a 10-minute training session. Her hand was not up for it, though.

"Let's get out of here, Poltic. Thank you for my present again. I promise to make it the best boxing club in the country." her eyes were filling up with tears.

He drove her back home without to mention about the new task he had set up for RA. It was not the right time. Poltic thought he would just call Guillen, who could pass the message on to the rest of the group. The instructions were as simple. If the man went less than 20 meter nearer that person, Poltic had sent a picture of Charlie via one of the security guards, this should result into a heavy beating. If the offence was repeated, even stronger physical force should be applied again.

Poltic inadvertently missed to mention that Emma had been discharged from hospital and the guys were unpleasantly surprised, when they went to visit her again. The sudden panic about the missing patient was short-lived, after a simple phone call. Flooded in tears, she quickly told them where she was. She did not know why she was crying but she knew that she should, because after the last tear had dried up for good, hard work at Boxing Club 'Emma' waited to be done.

The nurse, Poltic hired, was sent away on the second day. Emma's condition was improving fast, so she did not need her services anymore.

That day Charlie was playing the role of an estate agent. He showed Tony, Lorrie and Kate their apartments, the office floor, the terrace, basically everything. The modern and luxurious interior could not ever possibly evoke a negative emotion in anyone. Moreover, the technical equipment was a good level above anything they had ever been in contact with. Kate's remark about the place she was going to share with Tony was about its size, apparently far too big for two people. However, no one could take this as a serious complaint. After the lengthy tour around the entire building, the foursome settled in a spacious hall, situated a floor below their apartments, which they called the Conference Hall. The entire afternoon, the Young ones discussed all sorts of topics. Interestingly, they did not talk much about their future work but chatted mostly about Poltic's personality.

Standstill

The company was functioning as normal, with the only difference that it was costing triple to make it work than if Poltic had set it up like any other standard business. The Team was successfully buying the small firms, they needed, by making their offers to them so lucrative and out of their imagination. At the regular meetings with Poltic, the members never once raised again the subject about the big expenses. They managed to keep the deadline of three months, right to the last day. On the 90th day, the last transfer of the trucks was completed and all hydrogen stations were completed.

The "safe" technology was well publicized through an intensive advertising campaign. The public had mixed feelings about it all. The majority approved of the idea about the eco-friendly transport, used for delivering the meat produce of three companies. Well, there were the radical activists on the scene, too. People, who always fought against everything and everyone, whose only motivation was, fight itself, rather than the idea to achieve a real effect. The authorities approved of the new technology, after an elite number of scientists defined it as a step towards the future, completely harmless and safe.

The Team's job turned out to be much easier than they had expected. They did not come across a single problem that could delay them or made them change their way of working. The lack of troubles amongst them had naturally passed onto their boss as a feeling of security. Every time they had a meeting, he waited to hear for some bad news, just for a change. There was one obstacle they had to overcome, in the whole period. The manufacturer of the sophisticated machines played the 'hard-to-get' game, at first, although, he was offered far too much than the standard price. Moreover, Poltic's order for his three new factories was going to inject even more money in the company, making the owner incredibly rich. As often people did, he wanted more than he deserved. The reason was obvious, he lacked the skill of knowing when to stop, due to his inability to realize objectively and understand about what he was really worth. The stubborn fellow gave in at the end after going into some heavy negotiations for a whole week, which helped him get 20% more of the offered price. Poltic could afford this, of course.

Bob had the obligation to keep his boss informed about the situation on the stock market. For the last three months the detailed analyses well written by the broker agent had nothing new to report. Companies 1 and 2 were untouchable. Their shareholders, who had power over the percentage, he needed, were not selling under any circumstances. They had no reason to. Poltic expected this but he secretly hoped that Bob was going to give him some optimistic news soon.

The progress of the Young ones had not changed the situation, either. The foundations of the three new factories were ready. The huge investment and the modern technologies were broadly publicized. However, the completion of building the factories in time was not going to have any effect on the market, as Poltic hoped. The only positive result was the improved public image of the company, according to one of Geri's recent sociological surveys.

And Charlie? The idea that, if well prepared, he could persuade one of the big shareholders to sell his 8% share of number 1 just fell through. It was not really Charlie's fault, who did everything to the tiniest detail, and in the way that Poltic had asked him to. The marked businessman was known for taking a risk. He had made a lot of money in a very short space of time. He was very adventurous in every financial deal he did, often risking to fail and lose enormous amounts of money. So far, though, he had more successful financial operations than not. Charlie offered him a slightly higher price for his shares. He explained the reasons he wanted to buy them and the reasons that they should be sold to him. His arguments were solid and just when he was about to receive the famous "yes, I do", his opponent asked to postpone the deal for a week, so he had time to think about it. The same happened at their second meeting. The man was just too greedy rather than resorting to his common sense. He simply knew that time was on his side, he had money and besides, he was a member of the Board of Directors of company number 1. After this explanation, Poltic did not send Charlie to go to, yet, another meeting with the shareholder.

There was no plan 'B' and although, plan 'A' was closely followed, it just led to nothing. The standstill made Poltic much calmer. He stopped looking for non-existing solution. This did not mean that he had stopped thinking of at least dozens of crazy and unrealistic ideas. Anyway, he completely accepted the reality and he knew that he had no other alternative but to acknowledge it and wait. Until then, the Team and the Young ones had to simply do their job as usual.

A week after week, a month after month, there was no change in the situation and everything remained as before. The new eco-trucks crossed around the country, filling up with fuel at the hydrogen stations, built especially and only for their benefit. The construction of the three factories was completed – a clear sign that they would be ready to welcome their highly sophisticated equipment very soon, which was going to help them produce a lot with very little effort. Poltic managed to buy almost all the small subsidiary companies, all his contributory, but very important business partners and almost all the suppliers – from those, which provided the packaging to the ones that made the uniforms for his workers.

During all these successful but monotonous days, Poltic often thought of Thomas and Emma. He considered them very much as people from the same category, despite the fact that they had nothing in common. The father of the little fan of chocolates got promoted and received a pay rise. Now, he could take a better care of his family. Poltic could not think of any other way to help him.

Club 'Emma' was doing very well. There were plenty of people, who wanted to enroll and do boxing. Poltic visited the Hall to see the owner twice in the first month. After that, he would come once a week, not to do boxing, but to move to a world, which was far different from the one he lived in. He would meet there the guys from RA, who were coming to keep a good shape. The club was also the place, where they came to update him on how was the new assignment going. Apparently, Michael had got himself a new job and had not been even near Charlie. The good news did not make Poltic end his surveillance because he could not think of anything else to give them to do.

His relationship with the Team remained unchanged. It was true that they got together to discuss only work but Poltic believed that they could find other topics and interests in common to talk about, such as he freely chatted about with his close friends from RA. The disparity in their status was soon forgotten and the guys, together with the former boxer-girl, had welcomed another 'family' member of RA. Every time Poltic met up with Guillen, Emma, Johnny and Ted, he felt that he wanted to be someone, who went fishing with his friends at the weekend and had an ordinary job from Monday to Friday that never paid enough. And despite that, this imaginary man was far happier than the real Poltic, who was only striving for his greatness. When one had little but enough, they wanted everything. This statement fitted best the motives Poltic had to throw himself into the venture of destroying an entire country. The fact that one person was capable of achieving this, made that person great. However, his obsession, his mania and desire to discover something new, had actually made his life miserable. And amidst all this, companies 1 and 2 did something much unexpected, as if they wanted to help him win and put an end to everything. Who was the strongest of its day now?

Merging

Mr. Robinson guided his biggest enemy into his second 'home'. The cold handshake made it more than clear that these two were far from friends and that it was unlikely they would ever become ones. They knew of each other but they had never met in person. They hated each other but never spoke. One could sense an attraction between them, a business attraction that often occurred between rivals. Ben had initially requested for the meeting to take place on neutral grounds but subsequently, he agreed to play the role of the guest. After all, not every day a person like him had the opportunity to be invited to a place, where normally he could not ever set foot, unless he was heavily armed. Until then, the two rival companies had not communicated before at such a high level. The meeting was a precedent in their mutual history. In the past, both leaders had made an attempt to meet but it never happened, due to their stubbornness to show who was greater and more powerful than the other. This sort of childish competition made every opportunity for a mutual business endeavor fail.

"Thank you, again, for coming!" The good manners and sleazy smile made Ben alert, in case his host tried to put a fast one on him.

"Give it a rest, Eric! Get to the point. I agreed to come because you are talking about some serious stuff in your invitation letter that our company cannot afford to ignore. I'm here now, so don't try to mess me about!"

"OK, Ben, let be it. Let's do it the easy way. We're going under, 'mate'! I wrote that our company is having serious difficulties, with regards to our future, only because I know how much you all want to see our demise and this will make you come over. Interestingly enough, you're exactly in the same position and by the look of your smug face, it seems you haven't even realized."

"Wait a minute! What the hell are you talking about? We're doing absolutely fine! I don't care about your problems, we haven't got any!" Ben was beginning to regret about coming here, only to listen to some nonsense. The conversation was getting out of hand. Their next sentence was about to turn into an accusation or a slander. Eric was also dying to teach the idiot about good manners, however, he decided to mellow things out like a civilized host.

"Let's stop with offensive language, Ben! Please, hear me out."

"Well, as you're asking me so nicely... Go on."

"For the last several years, an unknown foreign investor has been taking over the smaller meat manufacturers, our competition. The foreigner, as my colleagues and I called him before we learned his real name, was the one, who did this nuisance with that World report study that stated people should eat more meat. You remember that we all lost, even though for only a month, some of our markets and a significant amount of money."

"If you're going to bore me with stuff that's long passed and that I very well know about, I might as well go now!"

"They are buying us out, Ben! That's why I've invited you today. The company that now owns the three others below us is buying our shares out, available on the stock market. And do you know what the worse bit is?" Eric got fed up with his moron of a guest, who was showing disrespect towards him. He really felt like beating him but decided to defeat him with words. "Few months ago, a figurehead had tried to buy out one of our biggest shareholders and thus, ensure that the foreigner crossed over the 50% benchmark. You know very well that if he gets hold of our company, his next step, logically, is to crush your pitiful company, considering that he owns the rest big ones in the sector. One against all sounds daunting and not at all very nice, doesn't it?"

"But how?" asked Ben still not convinced any of this could be true.

"We learned about it in the last minute and managed to stop the deal, so we are out of danger for now. I've invited you so I can warn you! Poltic – have you heard of this person, Ben? He did not succeed with us. I'm positive, though, that he'll try the same thing with you. I'm not sure exactly how many percents he's out before he could get hold of your controlling state but I doubt it's that many. He puts his hands on your company and that's the end of us, too. No matter how difficult we find this but we really have to watch each others' backs."

"Eric, I think I understand your game! You're in this together with Poltic, playing against my company! Your secret is out!" Ben stood up from his chair. "I've wasted enough of my time. And Eric, you can't fool me around! Not me! Don't bother seeing me off." His arrogance only showed how full of himself he was in that moment. Eric, however, could not let him go and make this meeting prove to be absolutely pointless. He stood in Ben's way, right in front of the door:

"You're going nowhere, Ben! Not before I tell you everything. Please, go back in your seat! Try to forget for just 5 minutes that we are in competition and just see if you could think like a regular guy. If Poltic and I were in any sort of business partnership, your company would have been erased from the face of the Earth by now. Please, sit down, I'm asking you for the last time! There are other problems that obviously your company doesn't know about." Ben would have really enjoyed hitting him once, no matter that his opponent was much bigger than him. He calmly fulfilled his host's request.

"If you're not with Poltic does it mean that you're against him?"

"It's a firm 'yes'. I think we could do something together against our rival but we'll talk about this later. Until then, Ben, I'd like to draw your attention to something very interesting that I believe you are aware of, no less than me. He's building three brand new factories, right at our doorstep. To be precise, two of them are near my units, and one is next yours. My research shows that the market doesn't need any more in that region. But he is building, either way!"

"Do you know why?"

"I've got no idea and I haven't received a good enough answer by no one, so far. As far as I know, they are going to be equipped with super modern machinery and this of course, doesn't come cheap!"

"So what? He's got money to waste! We haven't been really bothered by this and you also confirmed that this part of the country is totally provided for, by our own factories. Poltic's new ones will serve no purpose to anyone!"

"Don't you get it, Ben? He's got so much money that he has never stopped throwing it around even for a second, since he's set foot in this country. He is paying his staff almost double. He'll need more workers for his new units. Where do you think he is getting them from? He'll get them from our factories!"

"Eric, you're getting now paranoid! I'm very well aware of the market situation and that of this particular region. You'll see! His new factories will soon turn into empty and abandoned buildings."

"That's not the point! I know he can't do much to us in this part. I just wanted to give you an example about his financial power. Ben, he obviously has an awful lot of money and it's only a question of time, when one of us feels pushed into accepting yet another of his generous offers."

"It won't be us!"

"I hope so, but the game is getting heavy now! The bastard won't just give up from his good will. Have you been watching any television recently? I'm constantly seeing commercials, advertising his products on the screen! And what are the headlines these days that are getting on nerves?"

"It's about the eco-trucks!" Ben replied without hesitation.

"That's right, his eco-trucks! He is becoming very popular and we, now, look like the bad old factories, which used to pollute the environment." The two men had calmed down and, now, talked like adults. Ben was beginning to see, though a bit late, the truth in Eric's words. The situation was looking less rosy to him than before he came into this building.

"What are going to do?"

"I don't know! If I knew, I wouldn't be here now, telling you all this stuff. Together with the Board, we discussed different measures we could apply; in order to suppress the growing popularity of our competition but the truth is that our budget for advertising has been almost depleted. We couldn't afford investing in any new technologies, either. So we thought that, maybe, together we could find a way! Have you got any ideas, Ben?"

"Well, I can't say anything before I speak to the members of our Board, Eric. To be honest, we are not in good shape with our advertising but at least our profits are not that bad! Maybe, that's one of the reasons we haven't paid much attention to what's going on with Poltic's new projects. Listen, Eric, we are not really friends and if business was going alright, we'd never need to become ones. I would like to invite you to our central office next week, where I can tell you our decision. Besides, I'll have the chance to find out what percentage this guy Poltic has taken away from us by then!"

"I believe, it's around 38%, but still do your checks to be sure."

"Hmm, how do you...?

"You and your how...!" both of them burst into laughter, knowing very well that every company made sure that they've got an informer integrated amongst their rival's personnel. That was, yet, another public secret.

Eric confirmed that he would come to his guest's headquarters next week and saw him off. Despite the temporary warm-up, his hatred for Ben had not really disappeared, quite the opposite.

Alone in his office, Eric called his secretary and asked to appoint a meeting with the Board for later that day. He intended to tell the members all about his conversation with Ben and hoped they would all try to think of the best strategy for when he went to meet him again.

After a three-hour pointless discussion, Eric and the most significant people in the company had come to a decision that it was best if they offered to Ben an agreement between the two companies that was only binding for the shareholders, who owned the majority of shares of both of them. The idea was to make them sign it and declare that they would not sell up to Poltic under any circumstances. The contract was not going to give any opportunity to neither of the two firms, for any interference in each others' policies. The older members of the Board were finding even the proposal itself of being downgrading enough, not mention the actual forthcoming agreement. However, as there was the danger for them to lose much more than their dignity, they all agreed and thus, achieved one of the strangest absolute majority in the vote that had been registered in the company's history.

On the third day, considering the newly developed situation, there was the question that circulated around – Who was Poltic? What did he look like? No one could give an answer. Their 'nightmare' had never stood in front of a camera, his picture had never been taken, and his voice was also unfamiliar. Eric knew roughly where Poltic lived but he did not have his exact address. He decided that if no one had ever seen him, he should find out himself that the guy really existed. He did not doubt there was such a person as this was confirmed to him at first hand.

The idea about meeting the manager of number 2, the information on the market situation and the facts about all their shares being purchased, all this was kindly presented to Eric by, yet, another greedy for power and money person, only a day, before that person found his death in a car crash, on the motorway.

In reality, Harry had only grassed about Poltic's intention of becoming a monopolist in the sector, as well as, he gave information on Bob's maneuvers on the stock market. He could not possibly know about the eco-trucks and the new factories because he left this world too early. His hatred for Poltic had reached its peak and the lawyer felt that he just needed to do something. No matter how hard he had tried, he never managed to find out who were Poltic's mysterious patrons. Harry was a real professional and when he realized that he was making no progress in this, he stopped wasting his time. He decided to change his tactics. He could dethrone Poltic by different means.

His scenario was very simple: if 1 and 2 united, they could win over Poltic. And Harry, the informer, who worked for the interests of the newly formed company, was going to be the sole reason for his defeat. When he met up with Eric, he had described to him the entire plan in the greatest of detail and emphasized on their certain victory over Poltic. Naturally, at the time, Eric found the idea of any partnership between him and his rival ludicrous. The current invasion, represented by new factories, new transport and huge salaries, had made Eric remember Harry's words, who had tried to convince him that there was no other way of stopping Poltic. Eric felt a bit sorry about the way he threw the lawyer out, especially now, when it looked that Harry had been right all along. Well, his greed for power was too great! In return for his services, he had wanted to become a lifelong member of the new business formation Board of Directors and receive 10% of the company's market value.

Eric was completely prepared for the big day. He climbed up the stairs to Ben's office, holding the agreement under his arm. On his way, he thought about how easier everything would be, if the two companies really merged. Merging, yet, was probably the best option. Ben, on the other hand, had some very interesting seven days, when he discovered a number of new facts. He was impressed learning about the eco-trucks and their eco-characteristics – they were even 'cleaner' to drive than a kid's bicycle. Ben felt shocked at the fact that the investments made for Poltic's new factories were so huge that he had to double-check that it was not a print mistake. The secretary looked at the data over and over again, only to give him the same answer.

Eric took the seat offered in Ben's far tackier office, which displayed a grand library, paintings, worth hundreds of thousands, on the walls and even flowerpots with two huge ficus plants. Near the entrance, there was a metal sculpture of a doe. The thick carpet was well impressive with its rich colored patterns.

"It's Persian! I paid a lot for it and I see it was worth it if it drew your attention."

"Yes, it did, but I haven't come here to indulge in looking at your carpet. Common, Ben, it's your turn!"

"All right, Eric, so we'll talk like we did last time. This suits me to the ground! That means we won't waste time trying to lie to each other."

"I never lie!"

"Of course, neither do I!" Ben produced a sly grin. "Do you know, Eric, I've been trying to find out for a whole week…? What exactly is your plan? I confess, you were very convincing last time but there's something that's bugging me. Well, that was until the day before yesterday, when I got a lot of info on our friend Poltic and his dubious activities."

"Ben, do you still think I'm trying to deceive you in any way?"

"Deception's not the right word, actually, because that's practically impossible! However, there are a few inconsistencies between our research and what I've heard from you last time."

"And what's that? The percentage is 39 instead of 38? If that's what it is, I admit that I've misled you!"

"Oh, no, you were very precise there, but your gloomy analysis lightened up in my hands, somehow!"

"Stop with your metaphors! What didn't you like about it?"

"Imagine, Poltic had about 40% of each of our companies…"

"There's nothing for me to imagine, this is how it is!"

"Fine! The shares we own are distributed amongst the members of our Board in such a way that none of them has more than 8%. Poltic, though, needs to get at least ten."

"Yes and…?"

"Don't you remember how scared you were last week, when you told me that you managed to prevent him from buying your company out? I've checked and what I've found is that if either of the old 'dogs' in the company sold their shares, Poltic would still remain with less than 50%. It's exactly the same situation with us. The threat, Eric, becomes possible, only if two or more people sell their shares. Knowing my people very well, I can modestly declare that it's just not going to happen. One could fall for Poltic's generosity and make a mistake, but two people? Never!"

"Is that it? It took you a whole week to reach this obvious conclusion?"

"It's enough, I'd say, unless you've got something to add, which you've been hiding from me!"

"Ben, I'm not hiding anything, not now, neither before! It seems that you still haven't grasped what I'm talking about! I fear Poltic's power, his inexhaustible resources, his new technological advances and equipment that we haven't even seen, yet. He does things slowly but surely. I'm aware of the fact that he needs two shareholders from both companies. I fear that his intensive advertising campaign will make him even more popular and that in 5-10 years, his company will win in the race for attracting more clients and then he will destroy us! If we don't want to be his slaves or become his victims, not now, nor in ten years, then we need to take some measures and prevent us from what's happening."

"Hmm, I don't really want to say this but you are right, Eric! I admit I didn't look at things that deep until now and certainly, I couldn't see the problem that far into the future."

"Things are not that bad now, Ben. We are getting some good profits and we still have control over the market, but for how long? Do you want me to tell you something interesting? I saw Poltic."

"You what...? Did you meet him?"

"No, of course, I didn't. I know where he lives. So I sent some people to watch him and take pictures of everyone, who goes in and goes out of his house. I got his photo on the second day."

"So he exists?"

"Oh, yes, he does. I've never had any doubts about it but simply wanted to know who we are going against!"

"What does he look like?"

"I don't know really. On the picture, he's sitting in his car, which has tinted windows, and he's wearing sunglasses. You can't see much, just a silhouette. But that's not the point, Ben, even if he's been wearing a skirt in his free time! The question is: what are we going to do? I'm here today so we could find a way of counteracting his endeavors!"

"But how can we do this? I couldn't think of a solution and the Board of Directors needs further detailed information on the activity of our rival companies. To be honest, they are not that bothered, as long as people like us take care of their company."

"I know. It's the same with me."

"I've thought about what you've been saying, about the money. Poltic invests a lot in the factories, which are destined to fail. Where does he get it from, all this money?"

"Somewhere from abroad, I imagine! Poltic has no relationship with any of the banks in the country. I've checked."

"Where from, then? Who is his sponsor? If we find out, we could draw him on our side!"

"I really don't know but let's leave the source of his money alone. It's none of our business. I brought a draft agreement between our companies!" Eric outlined, in brief, the eventual commitment of the main shareholders in both companies to the idea of not selling their shares to Poltic. Ben was about to take the documents, when Eric threw them theatrically in the bin.

"This is absolutely useless, Ben! We need something far better and much more secure!"

"Like what?"

"Let's merge! I think we've got no other option. You and I, we'll be at the top of the biggest and strongest company in the sector. Poltic could never win against us."

"Eric, are you crazy? No one would let us do this!"

"Don't you understand?" he raised his voice in the way they both did at the first meeting. "There's no other way!"

Ben had never imagined that the two companies could merge, even hypothetically. The initiator of this idea, the person, who had made the first move towards them getting close, wanted far too much from him. However, Eric's enthusiasm was rather contagious and Ben felt that he kind of wanted to be part of the future super-company.

"Eric, let's say, for a minute, that this was possible. How would you convince the Board of Directors of your company to agree?"

"It's very simple, they don't have any choice. The rich bastards will take the bait about anything I tell them."

"No, it's not going to happen! Mine won't agree to this. Moreover, the public won't understand why companies of the rank of Mercedes and BMW have decided to merge. It's just ridiculous!"

"It's all in the advertising! Can't you see? Poltic has managed to persuade the entire population that his new hydrogen bombs – the trucks, are absolutely safe!"

"Well, aren't they?

"Look, I can't say for sure. I'm not an expert but from what I've heard, if one explodes it will destroy everything to the ground for 30m in diameter."

"Eric, let's forget about merging. It's absurd! Why don't we meet up with Poltic for some negotiations? This will give us a chance to find out about what he's planning. We could tell him that we'll never sell the shares he needs and he will just give up on the idea."

"That's not possible. We simply can't get to him and he would never agree to see us."

"We could try. You can't be sure until we try."

"Listen, Ben, we either merge or go our separate ways in the fight against Poltic, until one of us falls into his hands. It might happen in ten years but it will happen. It's inevitable!"

The time for getting a respond was up, so the guest decided to end the meeting. He had no business there if he was unable to force the right solution onto his opponent. Ben was visibly engaged in deep thought.

"All right, Eric, just give me a few days and the Board will approve of the merging."

"Thank you, Ben. We simply don't have another way out! My people will be ready, too, in about a week. Then we'll just work out the details of the merging. See you soon, partner!" these were Eric's final words. The company car drove him straight to the shareholders, who were waiting for him, stressed out, in the enormous Conference Hall. None of them was prepared to hear the news. They were ready for anything but not this. The fear, set firmly amongst the shareholders, made them easier to manipulate. They felt that the question for them was to have everything or nothing!

After one week, the mutual agreement to merge was followed by very hard work on the lengthy and complicated procedures. Careful precautions were taken so the Enemy didn't find out. Ben and Eric wanted to surprise Poltic by announcing the facts rather than declare some future intentions.

At the same time, Poltic just carried on living his uneventful and rather boring life, waiting for the end to come. He was hiding in his shell and had even stopped looking for the key, so he could get out of there. This key, he hoped to find, in some non-existent economic move, which could lay the desired monopoly on his plate. Although, all branches of his company had registered success, his pessimism was prevailing. He left everything to fate, in which Poltic, naturally, did not believe. So the days were just passing.

The existence of the new mega company was announced for real at a special press conference. The media filled the screens with information about one of the most significant economic events of the decade. Poltic learned the depressing news from the newspaper headlines. Well, a person like him regarded it as a reason to celebrate. At last, after more than a year of standstill, there was the change. He managed to produce a smile, feeling pleased with the current developments. His loyal personnel immediately tried to get in touch with him, all very worried, but he had abruptly told them to mind their business. Charlie, however, burst into the fortress-house, stressed out from the news. He believed that it doomed the entire cause of his friend and employer.

Everyone was wrong because they could not understand Poltic's view of things and the way he interpreted the situation. He firmly believed that the merging was to his benefit and that it was time to repeat his most successful strategy, he had applied up that moment, the strategy that had helped him achieve his outstanding progress since setting up the company. It was going to be so much easier, now that he had to deal with one enemy. Contrary to all common sense, where bigger meant stronger, Poltic regarded that as something easier to destroy.

The overexcited visitor reacted every time in the same way, when his ideal world was shaken by some perfectly normal natural disasters. Charlie was about to start a lengthy monologue about the scale of the storm, which was going to affect all good people on this planet. Aware of this, Poltic decided to avoid it and did not let his guest, who was still out of breath, to speak.

"Listen, you'll ask questions later. I know you are excited."

"Excited? This is the end, M. J.!"

"Yes, their end, not ours. Sit down and listen, as I'm not going to repeat it over and over again, until your agitated brain starts processing the information. Firstly, I want you to forget your opinion on the new company for several minutes, at least, until you leave this room. You'll make my job easier if you stop being so prejudiced and put all negative emotions on one side."

"OK, I'll try, M. J."

Poltic looked calm and even happy. He had an important question for Charlie before he resigned to, yet, another of his long monologues:

"How are the Young ones doing? Do you think they can keep to the deadline?"

"We are running late by about a month, M. J. As I told you last time, we're doing our best but it can't happen any earlier."

"A month is fine! But tell them, please, that this is the maximum delay I can allow. If they need more time, they'll have to work without getting paid, until the projects are completed. This measure might not be that motivating for them, but it's my wish and they will just have to comply with it." the way Poltic had put it, could only receive a respond like: "They are not some wizards, are they?" However, Charlie decided to bite his tongue.

"I imagine, you want to know about our next move, now that our rivals have merged in their fight against us? I'll tell you, Charlie. Some time has passed since we did our most winning move. The report study about the insufficient meat consumption brought us a significant success but it was not enough for us, in order to acquire companies 1 and 2. It was soon forgotten and things went back to normal."

Charlie knew nothing about the real dealings of the company at the time, when the report study was made public and Poltic put the prices down. It was not until a few months ago, when M. J. told him all about his speculative move, for no apparent reason.

"Until today, I believed that we could not make a significant progress. I thought that our actions and new projects did not really affect the first two companies in the sector. Well, I was wrong. They merged! Without even knowing, our sworn enemies have just signed their own death sentence." for a thousandth time, Charlie could still not grasp what Poltic was talking about. Sometimes, the young man thought that M. J. was mentally ill, hence the crazy stuff he was going on about. However, after the end of every meeting they had, Charlie realized what Poltic's deep idea was and he understood the way of thinking of the man, who was intellectually, at least, two levels above him.

"I'd really like to know what made them agree to follow this course of action! I doubt, I'll ever know. Besides, it seems the newly formed company will be very short-lived. Charlie, you all need to carry on working as if nothing's happened. After you manage to calm your people down, please, keep an eye on them, so they don't get distracted with what's going on with our competition. The Team is also under pressure but they, as well, will continue working as before. We should not display any interest in the merging of 1 and 2. I'll tell you why, Charlie! Everyone is less cautious these days, due to the high emotions, caused by the recent events. No one would ever think that we're going on a quest for the monopoly right now, when the market leader is so strong! Their confidence is our weapon. They will have some huge problems to deal with in the forthcoming future, created by the expanded slow administration. Also the human factor of their joint company is not to be ignored. To increase their efficiency, they'll have to optimize the structure, which will result in a number of redundancies. Well, this might only be a hypothetical prediction of mine, but I'm actually certain that it will come true. In the meantime, while they are trying to optimize their company, we will have our three new factories fully operational. Charlie, I have to admit that when I heard the news, I felt a little worried. The first thing I wanted to do was to look back and look into our short history as a company, then, to analyze the reasons for our rise at the beginning and how this could help us now. And I realized, Charlie, that instead of trying to find some new ways of fighting against the new company, I should simply resort to something that is well tested and that we've used before. The answer is in, again, very well conducted advertising campaign that is combined with a definite decrease of our prices. I really don't know why I haven't thought of it earlier but waited for something to happen, first, to show me the solution! The report study, Charlie, saved us at least five years of development and thanks to it; we managed to acquire a significant share of the market, in a very short space of time. We'll do the same, Charlie, and this time, it will be much easier because we have to look in only one direction." Poltic had excluded completely number 6 from his plans, in the last year. He just knew that there was not much he could do about it.

"Speculation has made a lot of people rich, but at the same time, it has made more people live in misery. The State, which is the most sophisticated historical concept, in terms of governance and authority, has developed some good mechanisms to prevent anyone from selling their stock and products under the market value. We, however, can justify our prices and we'll make everyone respect that. Of course, this time, we won't be that drastic in our actions – we'll cut the prices by 20-30%. This will make our rivals work at a loss and soon, the Big Fish will start selling their shares. Technology will prevail and ensure our victory!"

"How? M. J., I just don't..."

"I know, you don't understand! I'll make it simple for you, Charlie, and explain the most important, in a few sentences. The produce, coming from our new factories seems to be unnecessary in the region, they are being built but there's a demand for our products in other parts of the country. We shall transport the overproduction to the places that there is a market for, using our eco-trucks. As you know, our transport costs us almost nothing and the hydrogen stations will make it possible for us to reach to any point in the country. That's not that important, though, because it will make our share of the market increase only little. Our main move is to announce a three-year permanent price low of all our products, manufactured in the new technological factories. Of course, our excuse is going to be Science! The rest of our factories will support our offensive by cutting their prices, too, but only for a few months. They are still using older machinery and they wouldn't be able to sustain themselves if they do it for three years. In this way, will inundate the country with our cheap quality produce and thus, we'll manage to bite into a significant share of the market, well before the new company gets back on its feet, if I could describe it like this. The price of their shares will plummet because it will be impossible for their products to compete, with regards to price. At first, no one's going to sell, until they realize that they couldn't operate their business at a loss for three whole years. And then, they'll start coming to us of their own accord. The shareholders will be begging me to buy their shares before they lose their value completely." Poltic had become so excited by the image of his future triumph that his body was slightly shaking as if electricity had passed through him.

"What if they get really stubborn and refuse to sell, despite their losses?"

"Yes, there is a chance for that, but I really doubt it! Charlie, I may be someone, who doesn't follow the standard economic logic of things, but don't forget that the people, running the new company, are not like me. Within 2-3 months, someone will come to me, pleading. I'll be able to take control over them, then, and soon after, I shall cause the biggest crisis in the modern history of this country."

"M. J., you are not going to do this, are you?" Charlie asked quickly. He could notice the evil sparkle in Poltic's eyes.

"No, I'm not going to, but I could!"

"But if they still don't want to sell their share, no matter how much you offer them, then, what are you going to do, M. J.?"

"If this happened, Charlie, I'd think of another way to do it. But let's not think about possibilities like this!"

"M. J., is this going to be the end? When we take over the monopoly, there'll be nothing left for you to try to achieve! Am I right?"

"A man, Charlie, always has to have dreams and goals to pursue, until his last breath. I will find another aim that is important to me and which I truly hope, it would make me far happier than I was in the last few years. Actually, I could really achieve my initial idea only if I devastate the country. Many times in the past, I felt ready for this. Now I believe that innocent people should never suffer just because of me. Some time ago, Charlie, I met a child in the shop. The little boy loved chocolate very much but his father, who just happened to work in one of my factories, could not afford this enormous and unforeseen expense. I bought the kid a chocolate."

"What are you trying to tell me? Why do you tell me this story, M. J.?"

"This story changed me as a person. A small kid and the whole situation, made me think about all these people and their children. They would have never had a chance if I decided to go all the way to the end. I'll give them that chance, Charlie, so all these people could live their life the way, they wished. My final serious problem is whether my employers are going to approve of the theoretical explanation of the model, created by me! I have to point out that they are still waiting to see the development of a very deep crisis, caused by me, put into practice. That was my promise to them. I will not allow this crisis to happen. And I could only elaborate on the ways and methods of how one could cause it to happen." Charlie had never seen Poltic so emotional and truthful before. He had removed the mask of an authoritarian leader.

"They'll, like it, M. J.!"

"I hope so. This was what I wanted to tell you, Charlie. Now I need a rest, so you are free to go."

"Yes, it's time for me to go, anyway, M. J. I need to see my busy bees, who are probably a bit confused about the news. I'm really glad that we're getting so near the end, M. J., and soon, all this will finish. I believe in your success!"

"Me, too, Charlie, me too!"

"See you soon, M. J.!"

Theory and Practice

The most significant person in the country was not a nervous man by any means. However, when he was going to be confronted with such a huge hazard and the stakes were very high, Poltic felt that he was getting quite nervous. A polite administrator kindly asked him to wait, until he was called.

Poltic had achieved everything he fought in the last several years. His monopoly was a fact and now, he owned more than half of his rival company's shares. The advertising campaign and the new factories managed to crush his opponents. After Poltic announced the three-year cut in prices, by 25%, most of the main shareholders started to leave the sinking ship and redirected their interest towards new ventures. Poltic had paid them so much that they could easily start up a new business, all over again. The two 'brains' behind the merging, Eric and Ben, were far too good professionals, so they were deservedly left to manage the company. Just out of precautions, Poltic had appointed the Team as their boss.

The pyramid structure had two points, in terms of ownership, and it was one-pointed, with regards to the company management. This meant that Poltic and Charlie had shared the ownership of the numerous factories between them, so M. J. did not get accused of total monopoly. The single-handed management of this corporation was totally within the Law and the Team very openly managed all the companies that were owned by two people. It was a free market economy, so Poltic and Charlie just happened to choose the same people as their managers.

Poltic's extraordinary company had also raised and trained three young specialists. After they managed to build the supermarket and the three factories, the Young ones were going to carry on working different construction projects. Poltic had an idea to go into the hotel business, but a man like him would not even bother to build hotels, unless they were unique in some way. M. J. wanted to construct huge underground tourist sites, where the holidaymakers were going to be guided to the surface, via a complex network of tunnels, so in no time, one could get to anywhere they wished. It sounded incredible and on the verge of fantasy to many people, but Poltic knew that his out of the ordinary ideas will bring again success to him.

He looked at his wrist watch and realized that he had been waiting for 18 minutes.

Poltic had sent a detailed report about what it could have happened if he had completed his mission. He had not missed a thing in his written statement and he hoped that his mysterious patron would not get angry by his refusal to press the button for real. Strangely enough, Poltic's report was so well written that his presence today could prove to be unnecessary. Any averagely intelligent person, who had read his account, could easily jump on the first plane, going to the country and pull the trigger, if only everything was followed step by step.

Poltic had not hidden anything, like a secret plan 'B' or some loophole, from the organization that had given him a total freedom in his work, as well as some 3 billion. It had never requested a single receipt from him, not even once. Honesty and trust were above everything and this was exactly what Poltic expected in return, as soon as they called him in. He did not think he was going to be met at 'gun point' but who knew what was going in the other person's head, the one that was having the last word.

On his way for here, Poltic thought about the different periods he had been through. He remembered all the people, who had helped him achieve his success. He recalled the small, but very capable detective, as well as little Thomas, the child that loved chocolate. The image of Daniel also appeared in his mind. The inspector had contributed a lot, especially because he had initiated RA.

Ted, Johnny, Guillen and Emma had enriched his life far more than the Team could have ever done. Their life was unfair and hard but it had made them loyal and decent people. They really appreciated their huge salary and they were prepared to deserve it, where the members of the Team believed that they deserved their huge payment well before they started their hard working day. The Young ones had evolved in a very interesting way. At the beginning, their attitude towards money was not dissimilar of that, RA had, where now the young specialists were getting closer to the Team, in that aspect. Despite all, Poltic was feeling proud of everyone, though, regarded Charlie and RA as the closest to him.

His regular visits to Emma's club were purely unforgettable for him. It was a great experience, full of jokes that no other employee of his could ever provide him with. Emma treated him like a stepfather. Ted and Johnny were great to be round for any car fan. Guillen was the most intelligent and often surprised Poltic with this characteristic of his. Their differences had helped RA to become good friends and incredible working team. Poltic really wished he was one of them, although, this was not very likely to happen, considering his current position. After this trip abroad, he had promised the boys that he would buy them a modern service-garage, where they could do everything that they most enjoy doing in life. Emma had convinced him to throw his suit, at least once a week and go to the club to do some boxing, whereas Guillen had been insisting for ages that the boss came over to meet his family. Poltic had so much to do, when he got back that he did not know where to start. Actually, he knew what he wanted. He needed a woman.

Charlie had become a new man, since he started living with Lorrie. He even had a different look on his face and seemed much more balanced and calm than before. Well, he had not become suddenly the sharpest knife in the drawer, but at least he had found his own work pace. Aware of this change in his young friend and the reasons for it, Poltic felt slightly jealous of Charlie. He was over forty now, and there was no one waiting for him in the evenings, in his big empty bed. Every time he went to Emma's club, Poltic witnessed some sparkles being exchanged between Ted and Emma, where Johnny was successfully chatting up one of the girls there. The conversations he had with Guillen, however, had affected Poltic the most. He was often saying from the bottom of his heart that he would do anything for his wife and child. They were simply the centre of his universe. This made Poltic, with the help of his friends from RA, to secretly arrange for Guillen's wedding, as he had not legally tied the knot with the mother of his kid. The wedding reception was taking place in just two days. In order to turn all these plans into a reality, Poltic had to make sure that no one else executed his plan and no one caused the biggest crisis in the country.

At last, he was led to come in. He left everyone outside: the Team, RA, the Young ones, Daniel, Thomas, and completely alone, he stepped inside the office of his boss. He sat down and waited, this time, to be permitted to speak. This moment was one of the few, in which someone else had got into Poltic's shoes. The man in his sixties, who had a moustache and was dressed in a suit, glanced at the folder that contained Poltic's report.

"We've expected you to fail, M. J., but obviously, we were wrong. You have really managed to develop a successful model. Our analyzers confirmed that it could be put into practice. Congratulations!"

"Thank you, Sir!"

"We found your final request quite interesting: "I refuse to complete my task till the end because of the huge and thoroughly undeserved impact this would cause to my country and its people!" the man quoted Poltic's statement, he had memorized to the last letter. "In this respect, I believe I owe you an explanation, M. J. What you ask is what we want and have always wanted."

"I don't understand!" Poltic said and realized that these words had not come out of his mouth for some years now.

"When we asked you to do what you had to do, we exaggerated things a little bit, in our instructions that you needed to bring the State to a halt. The truth is that we have never intended to harm your country. What we've really had in mind is to find out whether one could develop a strategy to destabilize a certain country, a strategy, as you very well know that does not involve any use of weapons but purely - a lot of financial resources. And our condition was all this to be done by one man."

"What if I did do it? What if I really kept my promise and made everything I've described in my report a reality?"

"You must remember that we've asked you to inform us before you decide to take any actions. Basically, we would have stopped you! We misled you consciously because by aiming too high, we knew that you would do your best to achieve your mission. And besides, forgive me if I'm wrong, but you seemed rather attracted to the idea?"

"Yes, you're right, but I've felt like this only at the beginning. Now I think, you are saying this simply because you know that this is what I want to hear."

"I'm not lying to you, M. J. We are not monsters! The purpose of this entire project was to find a way how to deal with future enemy countries, which could put the world peace under a threat. Again, the condition was to use only money and no arms, and everything to be done by one person. You showed us that this is totally possible and we're very grateful. You will get everything that we've promised to give you. Do you have anything else to add before my personnel escorts you to the airport?"

"Actually, there is one thing! Don't do it. Do not apply the model in my country. These are my people and I would feel terrible if anything bad happens to my fellow countrymen. When I agreed to this job, I didn't realize that the fate of so many people, women and children, was going to be in my hands. Yes, at the beginning, I was mesmerized by the idea and its greatness. Isn't it fascinating to be able to damage the system of an entire country to such horrible degree and thus make it become politically insignificant, and destine the majority of its people to a life of misery?" M. J. felt how his adrenalin was rushing through his veins. "Later," he carried on with regret. "I realized I didn't want anyone, who didn't deserve it to suffer. I believe, you should try the model out, where politics could not work anymore and the only alternative is the use of arms. Instead of annihilating the enemy with bombs, in a few months, you simply need to find someone like me, who can apply the model."

"You're contradicting yourself, M. J., from what you've been saying in this very same room."

"I know but people change. Different events change them. The bigger the events are, the bigger the changes! It looks like that I'm no exception of this rule and I've changed, too."

"Hmm, and all this just for the idea itself!" the man, who Poltic did not know the name of, said skeptically. "That's fine, M. J.! That will be all! Thank you very much again."

"I have one more question to ask before I leave."

"I'm listening."

"I was given this opportunity but why did you choose me? I'm no more different from any averagely intelligent person. I don't have any special gifts or skills that make me exceptional in any way."

"Ha, is that it? I don't know, M. J., I guess it was just luck, exactly the same luck that had brought you here today! You've mentioned it a couple of times in the text yourself. You say that you've achieved your mission through pure luck. Well, that will be all, M. J. You can go now and if we need your services again, we'll call you. Until then, you've got a few hundred millions, which you can spend on anything you wish."

Poltic's expectations about the meeting to last for at least two-three hours, where he would be cross-interrogated by a few people, proved wrong. He left the headquarters of his employer and got on the first flight home, where he was going to bring the good news to the only person in the know - Charlie. The country was not going to suffer. The Team, the Young ones, RA, Thomas and Poltic's thousands of workers could continue their work as before. They could carry on living their lives, which, as it occurred, had not been that much under a threat, after all. The future was possible again!

The evil had been avoided. For now! Poltic was convinced that somewhere, sooner or later, his model would be put into practice; a model, which was based on three general principles: financial power, aggressive advertising and most important of all, new technologies.

How?

The key to this was a monopoly. If one owned a whole sector of the economy that would make them as powerful as they could be. Poltic's idea was to overtake the meat production industry, where many people had taken an employment. This would have guaranteed the social aspect of the future crisis. Having achieved the sole ownership of all major meat factories, excluding number 6 which was going to inevitable bankruptcy very soon, Poltic believed that, then, the easy part would follow. The transfer of all their financial resources to some overseas banks, was an operation that could be done overnight. However, the factories would remain intact. Poltic's solution was to destroy all production capacities in the country and there was a very simple way how to do that. The highly sophisticated machinery in all factories would suddenly break down and the companies that had produced them would prove unable to fix them. It would be just impossible. Science was the key aspect in Poltic's idea and he knew very well that technology was not always perfect. By the way, a month after the final invasive step, Poltic bought absolutely every manufacturer of special equipment related to the former companies 1 and 2.

He believed that even the non-active industrial units should not be left intact. Hence, he had planned numerous incidents to take place in all his factories and make sure that they would never work again as before. The plot also involved poisoning all the livestock, accidentally or deliberately, and then, to be incinerated, so there was no chance for any of the meat to go for consumption.

Poltic was aware that this would hardly cause the huge crisis he really intended to happen. Only about 35 000 of his workers would have ended up on the street, jobless, the number of which could rise to some 100 000 affected people, if one included their immediate families. The social shake-up would not be serious enough that the authorities could have not coped with, using all the country's reserves. The number of 100 000 people was far too little to be that significant and the total absence of meat in the shops could have been easily overcome and dealt with through intensive imports, and this - in no more than a year. In that time, at least several new factories would have got built and equipped with machines, imported from other countries.

The trucks comprised another facet of Poltic's idea. He had planned his innovative transport to become the final straw of this really impressive crisis, a crisis, which was going to make the country politically insignificant and doom thousands of people to a life of misery. With regards to creating a political crisis, Poltic was aware that the bigger the social crisis was - the bigger the one on the political scene.

During all this time that he was planning his plot, he had often wondered about what the most important element was for the right functioning of a country? What was the key factor that if eliminated, any country in the world could be easily led to a crisis and drawn to a halt? Poltic considered his idea about the meat products as a very good move not because the vegetarians were a minority but because meat was a product of paramount importance. Yet, this would have not been enough. The idea about the trucks had appeared in his mind, as if out of the blue. He had never driven a truck and had no interest in them but suddenly; they had become his favorite means of transport. After several months of research, Poltic found out what one of the most significant elements was for any country. He had come to the conclusion that there was nothing new in this world, and that all genius ideas had been thought of, spoken out or written down somewhere, and one simply had to discover them again. Poltic knew that infrastructure was the blood circulation system of a country. If it failed, the body had no chance of survival. Clearly, many people could easily come up with a similar anatomical analogy - from road construction workers to plenty of medical students.

One would need some destructive resources to really be able to damage a road system that comprised of thousands of miles of motorways, A-roads, B-roads and so on. Poltic resorted to developing his own "army" for that purpose. The trucks had been installed with safe fuel systems, which had been also proved to be environmentally friendly. Thanks to some good advertising of these characteristics, Poltic managed to implement such an original commercial means of transport in his own country. He got the idea for the hydrogen systems from a documentary about eco-alternatives to petrol fuelled engines, he accidentally happened to watch on television. Poltic had made a lot of effort to track down the leading company, which specialized in developing such units. Strangely enough, the manufacturer had financial difficulties at the time because the competition, in the face of the petrol companies, had made a stand against its activity.

There was a slight problem with his plan. Considering that the engines had been installed in special safeguard units then how could the trucks damage the road network? Well, this could have been achieved quite easily. Poltic was not that good at Physics but he had some knowledge about few of the general principles. He was aware that the enormous pressure, which characterized the hydrogen systems, was protected against impact, however, high temperature, applied to a specific point in the cask would surely cause the inevitable explosion. He had examined very carefully the plans of the devices, which were kindly presented to him by the manufacturer and came to the conclusion that anyone could make the trucks explode, if they only knew where and how to direct the flame from an ordinary lighter, close enough to the container. Poltic had decided to make the trucks to explode and then, blame it on some technical fault. His plan envisaged many drivers dying but there was no other way - he could not do this without any casualties.

The hardest part of the preparation was about the right locations of the explosions. Poltic did his research on all major roads in the country and came to the conclusion that the aspect of their destruction was as important as the effort to prevent the road services from repairing the damage, soon after. He wanted to be sure that once a huge crater had appeared on the motorway, it would not be patched and filled in, on the following day. Therefore, he carefully chose the locations, so it would take the authorities at least a week for the major roads and a month - for the less significant ones, for them to get back to normal.

Poltic's malicious plan was very realistic and feasible and it was not just some fantasy of his. It represented how the power of the human mind, together with a very large sum of money, invested in advertising and new technologies, could achieve some really horrific results. His newly developed strategy had changed the essence of global warfare. Without the deployment of a single foreign soldier, almost every country could fall into a deep crisis, caused entirely from the inside, if the model was applied and adjusted to its national specific characteristics. Yet, Poltic had concluded at the end of his report that money was at the heart of everything, because without it, it would have been impossible for him to acquire the new explosive technologies, to apply the right advertising methods and last but not least, to afford to hire the Team, the Young ones and RA. Besides, Poltic would have not agreed to do this, either, if he was not getting paid. He was very proud with his model but he was more proud that he was able to prevent the crisis in his own country. It was time for him to start living like a normal citizen with the small difference that he had so much money that he could not even spend.

And where did all the billions come from? Which was this organization that sponsored M. J. Poltic all this time and now had his report in their hands? The answer was so apparent that no one would have ever guessed. There was one and only structure that could provide so many resources, in order for such an expansionistic aim to be achieved. And this was…